The Trials of TRASS KATHRA

"What is that – rain?" Brother Incera said, dumbfounded. "How can it be raining inside the dome?"

Kali looked up, biting her lip at the impossibility of it. If there was any advantage to this unexpected development, it was that the guards had stopped and were doing the same.

"It *hurts*," Incera said.

He groaned as the flesh of his palm seemed almost to liquefy, spiralling slowly about itself as if a corkscrew had been stuck into the flesh and turned. Kali grabbed his hand and stared as the skin and the bone beneath it melded together in a moving circle of white and red scar tissue, forcing out blood, that then slowly progressed through his flesh until it had burrowed a hole right through to the back of his hand. Incera groaned again, more loudly, as the ends of lost sections of cartilage and sinew snapped or contracted, twisting his hand into a grotesque parody of itself, like the misshapen claw of some old crone.

What the hells was this stuff? Kali thought.

WWW.ABADDONBOOKS.COM

An Abaddon Books™ Publication
www.abaddonbooks.com
abaddon@rebellion.co.uk

First published in 2011 by Abaddon Books™, Rebellion Intellectual
Property Limited, Riverside House, Osney Mead, Oxford, OX2 0ES, UK.

10 9 8 7 6 5 4 3 2 1

Editor: Jonathan Oliver
Cover: Greg Staples
Design: Simon Parr & Luke Preece
Creative Director and CEO: Jason Kingsley
Chief Technical Officer: Chris Kingsley
Twilight of Kerberos™ created by Matthew Sprange
and Jonathan Oliver

UK ISBN: 978-1-907519-64-2
US ISBN: 978-1-907519-65-9

Printed in the US

TWILIGHT of KERBEROS

The Trials of TRASS KATHRA

MIKE WILD

Abaddon
Books

WWW.ABADDONBOOKS.COM

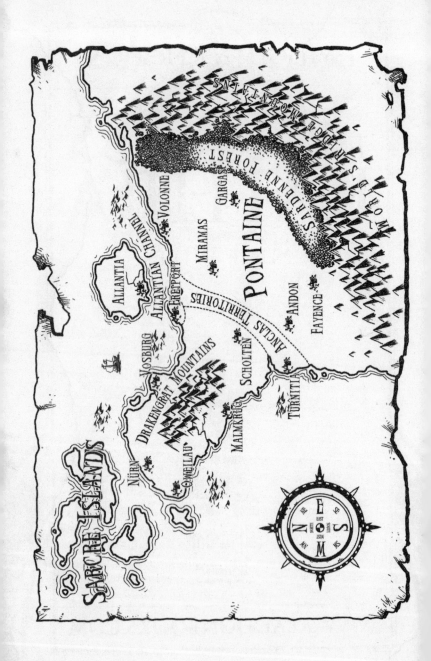

CHAPTER ONE

ONE YEAR AFTER Kali Hooper last laid eyes on Killiam Slowhand she came face to face with her lover once more. The reunion, if such it could be called, was brief; he a sketch on a stray handbill plastered to a storm-lashed steeple high above Scholten Cathedral, she a flailing, cursing figure sliding hopelessly down its slates in the direction of thin air and certain death.

Despite this, Kali couldn't help but snatch up the sodden parchment and gaze on it curiously. The bill advertised a travelling carney and its main attraction, Slowhand. Except Slowhand was now 'Thongar the Golden Archer!' with the emphasis very much on the 'thong'. The tiny posing pouch in which he was pictured hid little – which, okay, was quite a lot, she'd grant – but she'd seen those bits before. It was the burgeoning beer belly, sparkling body paint and peaked feathered cap that were new to her.

So it was that when she plunged off the steeple, her cry was a mix of bemusement, hilarity and desperation.

"Waha? Wahahaha! Wahaaarrrggghhh..."

The wind snatched away the handbill and Kali shut up. It wouldn't do to alert the Faith with her noise – especially if that noise was a splat. She concentrated instead on finding a way to halt her fall, perhaps to make the violent night that had caused her to lose her footing in the first place work *for* rather than against her.

She was high enough, fortunately, to allow herself to simply drop and look for a second, and this she did, though unfortunately there seemed to be nothing more substantial nearby than the curtain of water pouring from the steeple, acting as a backdrop to her descent.

Then, lit by a sudden and powerful sheet of lightning, she made out a ramshackle trellis-work of iron behind the filthy liquid curtain, guttering meant to carry the ocean unleashed by the heavens which, like herself, had been overwhelmed by volume and unremitting strength. What rain the guttering did carry filled it beyond capacity and bubbled, foamed and spurted from every joint, threatening to break the protesting labyrinth of pipes and send a tangle of iron crashing into the courtyard far below.

Kali spotted one pipe ready to go and, twisting with a grunt in mid-air, snatched through the waterfall at the column of over-stressed iron. Already loose in its mooring, pulled further by her weight, its top half broke from the wall, a jet of filthy grey water erupting in her face. Another jet came from its disjoined gutter above, plastering her hair flat, and Kali flubbed her lips, spitting away the clinging strands. Dammit, she'd just had her hair done, too.

Jerking to manoeuvre the pipe, Kali clung to the roughly wrought metal as, with a groan, it bent further away from the steeple until it projected at the diagonal, then swung her weight around, forcing the metal to the side and rotating it back in against the wall. The stress on its lower half was now so much that it was starting to snap but that didn't matter – if it did crash to the ground the Faith would think it a victim of the storm, and it had served its purpose anyway. Even as she had manoeuvred the pipe, Kali had already spotted where to leap next, and she threw herself through the air to grab a horizontal section some feet away.

Water splashing and beading coldly on her already chilled hands, Kali dangled there for a second, gasping, and watched the piping she had abandoned break away to tumble down the vertiginous side of the steeple tower. It turned end over end until it almost disappeared from sight and then bounced across the courtyard below with a series of barely audible clangs. It gone, she looked around her, regaining the orientation she had lost in her fall. Her sudden departure from her well-planned route across the rooftops had caused her to lose sight of her destination – the reason she had come to Scholten tonight – and it was a few seconds before she found it again. Then there, between annexes of the sprawling cathedral complex, she once more pinpointed her goal.

Perched high above her, atop a sheer wall dotted with maybe a hundred or more yellowed, candlelit windows beyond which berobed shadows roamed, the dark dome that was the domain of Brother Incera sat.

It remained a long climb away, but Kali knew she had to reach it during the azure night hours. Not only was this the only time she could guarantee Brother Incera would be present, but she would simply never make it through the complex during full daylight. There were too many Faith around for that. Far more than there had ever been before.

Kali was about to move again when, far below, she heard the solid slamming of a heavy door and looked down to see a small group of Faith scurrying across the courtyard cobbles to investigate the noise of the fallen pipe. For a second they paused in the rain, staring up at the cascade of water and shaking their heads in dismay, and as another flash of sheet lightning lit the wall Kali pulled her legs up towards her middle, making herself as small as she could to avoid detection. Luckily the downpour left the Faith in no mood to tarry, and they returned whence they came. The door, caught by the wind, slammed shut behind them.

Kali breathed a sigh of relief and lowered her legs. Her feet found purchase on another piece of guttering running parallel and below that to which she clung, and she used the two in tandem to inch her way to the corner of the steeple tower and onto its east facing. There, sheltered some from the storm, she transferred to another vertical stretch of pipe and, testing its solidity, began to ascend to a position where she could again work her way to the dome.

She climbed haltingly, moving from shadow to shadow, because the wall of windows was right behind her now, and she was acutely aware that all it would take was one casual glance out into the darkness for her game to be up.

It was an unusual feeling, being so wary of the Faith. But then, as with her own life, things with Makennon's church were not what they had been. The Anointed Lord's self-proclaimed 'Only Faith' had begun to change not long after the encounter with Bastian Redigor in the Sardenne, transforming over the year from the despotic though superficially benign church it had been, to the simply despotic. Many of its flock now lived as much in fear of its torch-wielding priests as they had once lived in awe of them, and as if the Eyes of the Lord, the Overseers and the Order of the Swords of Dawn hadn't been enough of a handful, there were some new kids on the block. Recruited from mercenary factions, the Red Chapter had swollen the Faith's paramilitary forces until they had begun to rival the Vossian army itself and, working alongside their more pious comrades, their presence across the peninsula was total. So total that most people had become afraid to even think.

What was more disturbing, those brave souls who did dare speak out against the apparent hardening in attitude of Katherine Makennon had started vanishing. It wasn't, of course, unusual for dissenters of the Faith to vanish but, where previously they might have expected to meet their end in the naphtha chambers beneath Scholten, there had been no sign of the smoke that meant the burners were in use. No, these people were simply gone, and the words on the lips of those who had lost loved ones was that it was to 'a fate worse than death.'

She herself had narrowly avoided being one of them. The day of the memorial service to the victims of the Sardenne a year ago had, of course, ended with her verbal attack on Makennon and, while she was willing to concede that her comment about the tassels on her tits might have been a little inappropriate, she *had* been unusually shit-faced and so would have expected little more than a prompt ejection from the speakers' platform. That, though, hadn't been what happened. In the absence of Slowhand, the one other person she'd have thought she could rely on had instead ordered her arrest. Jakub Freel. Dammit, how could she have been so wrong about him? How could she *and* Slowhand have been so wrong? The bonds of friendship they both thought they had forged with the undercover Allantian prince were clearly not as strong to him, and the fact that Freel had subsequently ordered her to be incarcerated in the Deep Cells pending what he called 'relocation' severed them completely. It was only the fact that after a month her cell had been unlocked by some unknown ally – to this day she didn't know who, though from the peculiarly misshapen handprint on the lock she was certain it wasn't Freel – that she hadn't found out first-hand what it meant to become one of the 'disappeared'.

Ironically, thereafter, she'd been forced to make herself disappear. Declared an outlaw by Freel, she'd been hunted wherever she went by Overseers and Eyes of the Lord, by every priest in every town, and by the mercenary-bolstered Order of the Swords of Dawn, some of whose ranks had scant regard for the vows taken by their brothers. They were, in short, a bunch of psychopaths fit to rival Konstantin Munch or even the Ur'Raney, and their constant snapping at her heels made an already difficult task even more so. This past year she'd been forced to skulk in the shadows and rely on the shelter of friends during her investigations, and there had been a few close shaves during it. One particular group who'd had the temerity to get *too* close were now entombed for all eternity inside Black Johnson's Crypts, and if they had any hopes she was going to return and release the seals, they had another think coming.

Fark 'em. She had a world to save.

But the question remained, from what? Or, more accurately, from what *exactly*? Kali heaved herself onto the roof and took a breather, crouching at its edge like a gargoyle, silhouetted by the body that dominated the azure night sky. The gas giant hung there like a giant, malevolent eye and was the reason she had come here in search of Brother Incera.

The gas giant was not Kerberos, however.

It was the Hel'ss.

Kali bit her lip as she stared at the object she had first seen from the deck of the *Tharnak*, when it had been nothing more than a smudge on the side of Twilight's distant sun. It was a smudge no longer, but a fully fledged part of the heavens in its own right. And while it shared many characteristics with Kerberos, though was of a more violent, redder colour, it differed from its counterpart in one very important respect.

It was drawing closer to Twilight every day.

Kali recalled what she had managed to piece together about this cosmic entity since she had first learned of its existence, and whichever way the facts were interpreted, things did not look good. From the vastly expanded and darkened sphere of Kerberos that she and Pim had experienced during their visit to the past in Domdruggle's Expanse, to the countdown that marked its approach at the Crucible of the Dragon God, to Bastian Redigor's revelation that the last time the Hel'ss appeared his race died, and that this time it was the turn of the humans, there was only one inescapable conclusion.

It wasn't just the Hel'ss that was drawing near, it was the End Time.

"This world is called Twilight for a reason," the dwelf at the Crucible had told her. "Once in an age, to every civilisation, a great darkness comes."

And it seemed to have fallen to her to help stop it.

Whatever 'it' was.

Her destiny as one of 'the Four'.

The Four. Gods, she was coming to hate the phrase. Because despite having learned what she had about the Hel'ss, her knowledge of who and what the Four were was almost as scant as it had been the day she'd first heard the phrase beneath the floodwaters of Martak. The strange undersea creature she'd encountered there had spoken cryptically of 'Four Known To Us,

Four Unknown To Each Other, Four Who Will Be Known To All',
but the fact was its comments remained as annoying a riddle
now as they had then – more so considering she had met two
of the Four and they were as much in the dark about things as
she was.

Oh sure, she knew who her brothers-in-arms were: Lucius
Kane, Shadowmage; Silus Morlader, Mariner; and Gabriella
DeZantez, Sister of the Order of the Swords of Dawn, now
deceased and ascended to Kerberos, but what was the connection
between them other than the physical and mental gifts they each
possessed? What the hells were they, was *she*, meant to do? To
make matters worse, the only one to whom she had not spoken,
who just might know something, Silus Morlader, hadn't been
seen for months, and the rumour was that both he and his ship
had been lost at sea.

That was the problem. It seemed she was being stymied at every
turn. Even what had been such a promising lead – the so-called
'Halo Files' that Querilous Fitch was meant to possess – had,
after months of effort, ultimately proved fruitless. A seemingly
endless amount of cajoling, bribery and tracking of Querilous
Fitch's past movements had led her eventually to a priest to
whom Fitch had given the files for safekeeping, but on going
there she had found the priest's house razed to the ground by
forces unknown. The only lead she'd gained was from a remnant
of parchment that mentioned the island of Trass Kathra, but that
wasn't much of a lead at all, because Trass Kathra – the Island
of the Lost – was exactly that: lost. The place was a myth, a
rock in the middle of nowhere that had vanished long, long ago,
pummelled under the waves supposedly by the gods themselves.

Banging her farking head against the wall. That was what she
had been doing. Then it had occurred to her – if doors were
slamming in her face every time she tried to find out more about
'the Four' then maybe, instead, it was time to find out more
about the threat they faced.

To take a closer look at the Hel'ss.

Literally.

And with Merrit Moon's elven telescope having been destroyed in the k'nid invasion, there was only one other place on the peninsula she could do that.

Kali moved on, working her way across the storm struck rooftops towards her destination. The route was complex and treacherous, and for anyone with normal abilities it would have been suicidal, an impossible challenge. But Kali's preternatural prowess got her where she needed to go in a little over an hour. Not that her passage was without incident – at one point she was forced to negotiate a precipitous wall of old but barely rooted ivy, flinging herself from one section to the next as each ripped away, at another to shimmy above a rumbling portcullis as the crunching boots of a Faith battalion marched through it into the night, and at yet another – somehow the most nerve-racking of all – having to inch her way past the apartment windows of her old sparring partner, Katherine Makennon herself. The Anointed Lord was home and awake, silhouetted with her back to her before a large, roaring fire, staring motionlessly into it, but her presence made Kali feel strangely uneasy and she felt it best not to disturb her reverie by knocking and saying 'hi'.

The most dangerous section saved itself for last. The 'bridge' between the wing she was on and the wing she needed to reach was a stretch of flat rooftop filled with lightning rods that caught the raw power of the heavens and transmitted it to the sub-levels of the complex and the Old Race technology in use there. The violent night meant that bolts of lightning were striking one or more of the rods every few seconds and, threatening to overload, the rods were subsequently discharging the strikes to other rods, causing arcs of bright blue energy to flit between them randomly. There was no way Kali could predict a safe route and a single touch would burn her to a crisp, and so the only thing she could do was trust in her reactions, pray to the gods, and run like the hells.

Her brain buzzed heavily, feeling like lead, as she rolled, somersaulted and flung herself through the deadly and ever moving web but she made it, the only sign of her running the gauntlet a scorched and smoking bodysuit with a few slashes across the arms and one particularly revealing one on her arse that was going to give Dolorosa a dicky-fit the next time she snook home.

Gasping, she came at last to the dome within which she hoped to find Brother Incera. The structure was much larger close to than it had appeared during her approach, as one might expect considering it housed the Faith's so-called cosmoscope. The immense arrangement of lenses and mirrors that magnified the skies above Twilight had been considered by many within the Church to be a blasphemous, sacrilegious object but somehow it had survived the Faith's puritanical purges over the years, as had its keeper, Incera himself. The aging Brother probably knew more about the vagaries and mechanisms of the heavens than anyone else on Twilight, and for that reason Kali hoped that he, amongst a Faith who, troublingly, seemed to have accepted the Hel'ss as a part of their religion, might be able to enlighten her as to what the entity was and what the hells was going on.

A sheet of lightning illuminated Kali as she paused at the base of the dome, frowning. She might have reached it but getting inside was another matter. The actual entrance to the dome was one floor down, inside the cathedral, and other than risking further close encounters with the Faith the only other way in was the gap in its curved surface out of which the cosmoscope viewed the heavens. And that was currently positioned almost at the apex of the dome, trained, it seemed, on Kerberos.

Kali jumped back at a sudden grating in the rooftop beneath her feet, and realised that the dome was turning. She looked down at its base, where thick greased wheels revolved along a circular track, and then upwards, where she could just make out the nose of the cosmoscope being realigned to a different viewpoint. The angle and degree of rotation left little doubt in Kali's mind that it was turning to face the Hel'ss, and Kali guessed – hoped – that Incera was doing what she'd hoped he would be doing – comparing the two celestial bodies like the man of science he was. Because if Incera's curiosity was piqued sufficiently for him to do that, then she just might not have to force the information she needed out of him.

Kali dug into a pocket of her slashed silk bodysuit and

withdrew a small tube, the base of which she rotated. The tube was one of a number of Old Race devices she'd scrounged from Merrit Moon some months before, reasoning that if she'd become Public Enemy Number One she needed all the assistance she could get. From the top of the tube a magnetic wire shot upwards to wrap itself around the cosmoscope, and Kali pulled the wire taut and climbed, grabbing onto the broad cylinder of metal. She heaved herself upwards with a grunt, her chest pressing against the cosmoscope's outer lens, and then she flipped herself onto its top from where she was able to work her way inside the dome.

It was a tight squeeze but at last she made it through. She dropped to the floor of Brother Incera's observatory; a wet, smouldering and bedraggled figure looking like something that had dragged itself from the depths of the Strannian Sulphur Swamps.

Three acolytes stopped what they were doing and stared. One of them made a move for a bell suspended in a niche in the wall, but as the young woman was about to raise its accompanying hammer to sound the alarm a voice from the operative end of the cosmoscope said, "No."

Kali turned, water sloughing from her to form a puddle at her feet. The man who had spoken continued to stare into the eyepiece of the cosmoscope but waved a hand behind him, shooing the acolyte away from the alarm. Though she couldn't see his face, Kali guessed that the older, more hunched looking form beneath the Faith robes was who she had struggled here to see.

Brother Incera turned a moment later, a look of curiosity on his face. There was also an intrigued twinkle in his eyes and superficial resemblance to the old man that reminded Kali very much of Merrit Moon.

"Leave us," Incera said to the acolytes. "And say nothing to the guards."

The acolytes did, though casting vaguely suspicious glances behind them.

"Thank you," Kali said after they'd gone. "For not raising the alarm."

Incera shrugged. "It isn't every day an old man has the chance to gaze upon two new and, may I say, impressive celestial bodies."

"I'm sorry?"

The astronomer coughed, glancing with some embarrassment at her chest, then up at the cosmoscope itself.

Kali blushed. What she had wasn't much but she guessed if they were magnified a few hundred times...

"Oh. Right. Look, I'm sorry about that but it was the only way I could get to see you. Brother Incera, my name is Kali Hoo –"

"I know who you are, Miss Hooper. Among the Faith, your exploits have become a matter of some... consternation over time. I know also why you are here."

"You do?"

"Take a look," Incera said without preamble. He gestured at the cosmoscope's eyepiece and Kali moved hesitantly towards it.

"Kerberos and its new companion," Incera said as she did so. "To the naked eye, so very similar, aren't they? On closer inspection, not so at all."

Kali placed her eye against the eyepiece and pulled back slightly, blinking. For a second she was puzzled as to why a device so advanced should produce such blurred results, but then she realised that the lenses would have been set to Brother Incera's eyesight, which was likely not so acute as her own.

Her hand moved to the side of the cosmoscope and her fingers found and manipulated dials there, adjusting the instrument's focus until the Hel'ss was outlined clearly and starkly against the background of the cosmos.

She gasped.

Brother Incera had been correct in his observations that while the Hel'ss superficially resembled Kerberos, in close up the difference between the two was marked.

Where the azure surface of Kerberos was scudded with the layer of clouds Kali now knew to be the souls of Twilight's dead that were drawn there, the surface of the Hel'ss was, in comparison, almost bare, resembling less a gas giant as some impossibly large, translucent brain. The more Kali studied it, the more she began to discern gaseous filaments reaching out from its surface across space and almost stroking the atmosphere of Kerberos, and the more uncomfortably aware of some sentient presence up there she became.

It could just have been her imagination, of course, but it wasn't, as what happened a moment later proved beyond doubt.

For a second, just a second as Kali watched, the entire surface of the Hel'ss suddenly and unexpectedly reorganised itself into a reasonable semblance of a face. Her face.

Kali pulled back with a gasp.

"Are you all right, Miss Hooper?"

What the hells *was* that? Kali thought. Was it even *possible*? But she had seen it with her own eyes – whether the Hel'ss was trying to scare her off or else imprinting itself with a knowledge of who she was, it had just demonstrated that it was a living thing.

It was telling her it *knew* her.

"Miss Hooper?"

Kali shook her head to clear it of the image. "Yes... yes, I'm all right. Sorry."

"My brethren have come to believe," Incera continued, "that the entity is some form of herald of Kerberos itself. That it is the first sign of the beginning of the cycle of their becoming one with their God."

That would explain a lot, and not for the first time in her dealings with organised religions Kali wondered where they got this shit. "You, I take it, are not of the same mind?"

"I am a man of science, Miss Hooper, not so easily persuaded."

"You also said *their* God. Hardly the kind of scepticism I'd expect from such a long-standing member of the Faith."

Again, Incera shrugged. "When we began, the Faith were not quite so fanatical as they are now. There was room within their ranks for people with open minds. Free thinking souls. Our acceptance was tolerated for the tactical advantages our pursuit of knowledge might bring to them. But, one by one over the years, our numbers became depleted, until only I remained." Incera smiled. "Somehow up here, in my little nest, I managed to evade the fundamentalist brooms that swept away the unworthy."

Kali realised at last that, in coming to see Brother Incera, she had made the right choice.

"The Hel'ss," she said. "What do you think it is?"

Incera sighed, moving to the walls of the observatory where a number of large parchments were strung one atop the other. The astronomer flipped them, revealing his sketched impressions of objects the cosmoscope had revealed to him over the years.

"There are many strange things in the heavens, Miss Hooper. I have seen worlds of flame and worlds of ice, worlds verdant and worlds long dead, and worlds that seem nought but smoke or shifting shadow. I have seen the stars by which they are lit and, on occasion, I have seen the children of worlds flit between them in tiny ships. I have seen great coloured clouds seemingly of no substance that take the shapes of everything imaginable by man. I have seen flares and streaks of fire that would incinerate Twilight would we be unlucky enough to feel their touch. But nowhere, Miss Hooper – *nowhere* – have I seen anything like the body that grows nearer to our world every day."

"You're saying that it isn't just some kind of... wandering star?"

"I would stake my reputation on it."

Kali thought about the filaments. "It seems, somehow, to be connected to Kerberos."

"Indeed it does. But what form, what purpose, that connection takes, I cannot say."

Kali decided it was time to let Incera in on everything, and the astronomer listened with growing horror as he learned about the fate of the Old races and its cause, and how the same threat was now returning to Twilight.

"It has to be stopped," Kali concluded. "But I have no idea how to do that."

Incera swallowed. "Miss Hooper, I'm sorry – neither do I."

He hesitated for a second, as if remembering something, but whatever it was remained unspoken as there was a hammering at the door to the observatory.

"One of my acolytes must have reported you to the guards," he said. "You have to go."

"In a minute," Kali said. She was used to the hammering of

guards on doors and had become quite adept at calculating exactly how long it would take them to break through. She had time yet. "I want one more look at this thing before I go," she said, moving back to the eyepiece of the cosmoscope.

Incera glanced nervously between her and the door. "You must hurry."

"Don't worry," Kali muttered, and then, "Oh gods."

"Miss Hooper, is something wrong?"

"I've a feeling the guards are the least of our problems," Kali said. "It's the Hel'ss. Something's happening on the surface."

"Let me see."

Incera shoved Kali aside and stared into the eyepiece for a second. Kali knew he was looking at the same sudden and strange disturbance on the surface of the body that she had – a kind of broiling – and then the eyepiece flared with a light so bright it left a burned circle on Kali's retina. She didn't want to know what it had done to Incera's eyes.

"Oh," the astronomer said, staggering back from the cosmoscope. "Oh, Lord of All."

Whatever had caused the light, for it to be so intense through that tiny an aperture could only mean it had been blindingly so on the surface of the Hel'ss. And, what was more, the reason for it no longer needed to be viewed through the cosmoscope.

Through the break in the dome, Kali could see the entire night sky above Scholten filling with scintillating drops of light, intermingled with the rain and falling towards them.

"I think we should leave."

"Is something happening?" the astronomer said, blinking to restore vision. "What is it. Tell me!"

"I don't know. But trust me, it doesn't look good."

"What do you see?" Incera demanded.

But before Kali was able to give him an answer two things happened.

The first was that the guards at the door managed to break through and moved towards them, and the second was the first of the drops falling from the Hel'ss arrived, punching right through the metal of the dome.

Most hit the floor in short, sizzling spurts but one hit the palm of Incera's right hand.

"What is that – rain?" he said, dumbfounded. "How can it be raining inside the dome?"

Kali looked up, biting her lip at the impossibility of it. If there was any advantage to this unexpected development, it was that the guards had stopped at the sight of the strange downpour.

"It *hurts*," Incera said.

He groaned as the flesh of his palm seemed almost to liquefy, spiralling slowly about itself as if a corkscrew had been stuck into the flesh and turned. Kali grabbed his hand and stared as the skin and the bone beneath it melded together in a moving circle of white and red scar tissue, forcing out blood, that then slowly progressed through his flesh until it had burrowed a hole right through to the back of his hand. Incera groaned again, more loudly, as the ends of lost sections of cartilage and sinew snapped or contracted, twisting his hand into a grotesque parody of itself, like the misshapen claw of some old crone.

What the hells was this stuff? Kali thought. Some kind of acid? It was certainly acting like acid on the dome and the apparatus beneath it but she had never seen acid act the way this was doing on flesh. The liquefaction, the strange warping of Incera's hand, the lack of actual burning, it was as if the flesh were somehow being undone and *remade*.

Gods, if the stuff should hit something vital...

Kali wanted to shout *get out, get out now!*, not just to Incera but to the guards as well, but knew it was already too late.

The first tentative drops of the glowing rain were but a vanguard of what the Hel'ss had released on them, and the true downpour hit the dome with a vengeance.

Hundreds of drops punched through the dome and impacted with the observatory floor, creating a sea of sizzling holes. They were followed in rapid succession by more, many splashing and burning into the wall of the round chamber, incinerating Incera's charts, others punching into the cosmoscope itself, shattering the lenses mounted at both ends.

His eyes only now focusing, Incera stared at the ruined device and its cracked, smoking glass half quizzically, half in horror, but then found himself being bundled away from where he stood, thrust to safety by Kali. Her sudden manoeuvre sent the two of them crashing to floor where Kali rolled them over and over, their bodies narrowly avoiding the impacts of more of the potentially deadly projectiles.

The guards possessed much slower reactions and were not so lucky, and the first of them were felled instantly; one clutching at his heart through a widening hole as he collapsed with a gasp to the floor, the other simply toppling forward with a stunned expression in his eyes and a hole the size of a gold tenth in his head that was spiralling into his brain. This sent their brothers in arms into panic, stumbling over their fallen comrades in a dash for the door, but the rain was heavier still now and they had barely made a move before each of them was struck multiple times.

Kali caught fleeting glimpses of the same strange spiralling of flesh as the rain did its work, and within seconds they were writhing in agony on the dome's floor, their limbs and joints twisting and bending until they were grossly malformed, in some cases reduced to vestigial flaps of skin, until the guards resembled a twitching, spasming collection of involuntary circus freaks. Even the two who had been killed instantly were not spared the horror, their bodies shrinking and morphing before her eyes, spreading patches of flesh now just exposed veins and arteries seeping dark puddles of blood onto the floor.

Kali wanted very much to close her eyes – wished she could do the same with her ears, too, against the agonised screams – but she couldn't. She had managed to roll Incera under the cosmoscope but he was struggling against her, unable to cope with what he was seeing, trying to get away. That wasn't her only problem.

Above them the cosmoscope was buckling beneath the rain, its own integrity compromised, and it was only a matter of seconds before it fell onto them, crushing them beneath its riddled mass. Then, suddenly, a chunk of it did drop a foot, and as Kali struggled to hold it off them, Incera fled her grip, making a dash for the door.

Kali had no choice but to leave Incera and the guards to whatever fates might befall them and just do her best to stay alive. There was nowhere to run, nowhere to hide, and survival would be purely a matter of luck.

Dodging beneath chunks of metal she hoped were thick enough to absorb the lethal impacts, she darted from one to the other until, in turn, they began to collapse above her. Increasingly desperate screams sounded from all about her but all she caught were fleeting glimpses of bodies between metal – legs stumbling, torsos falling, heads slamming fatally to the floor – as she kept moving and the rain continued to fall.

Trembling, Kali moved and huddled, moved and huddled, and thought that the downpour was never going to end. When, suddenly, it did, she was left with a slight ringing in her ears and an inability to accept, for a second, that she had, in fact, survived. Then the groans of the deformed and dying, audible now that the rains were gone, coupled with an ever growing pool of blood that was seeping almost languidly into her last hiding place told her that she was, indeed, experiencing the aftermath.

Slowly, cautiously, Kali emerged from beneath the buckled metal, and gasped at what she saw.

The observatory dome was all but gone and most of the guards dead but, miraculously, Incera lay propped against the remains of the far wall of the observatory still, though barely, alive. Kali quickly moved to him, noting he was in a very bad way, his legs all but useless, part of his torso appearing to have been turned inside out, revealing glistening organs, head slumped to the side, blood trickling slowly from a mouth that gaped now almost to his ear.

"I'll get you some help," Kali said.

Incera held her back.

Through his deformed mouth, he spoke in a kind of half gurgle, half drawl. "Nohh. Theh'el khill yooo."

"I can't leave you here like this!"

Incera gave a weak laugh. "Mhaybee is worshe than it lhooks. Yooo harve to gho. Shtop... whatever ish happenink."

"I wish it were that easy. Without the Halo files, I don't have the faintest idea where to start."

Incera's eyes widened. "Haylo Fihles? Thart what I wash goin to tehll yoo. The enforsher, Freel, has the Haylo Fihles."

"*Freel has them? How do you know that?*"

Incera pointed weakly at the shredded remains of his research. "Brought me something to anahlyze frohm them – a stahrchahrt."

"He wanted to know about the stars?"

"Yesh. Nho. Nhot the stahrs themselves but what they would lhook lhike from a location here ohn Twilight. Whanted me to calchulate where iht wars."

"And did you?"

Incera nodded. "Aht sea. Fhar beyond the Storhmwall. Ttharn any ship has ehver sailed."

"At sea? But that doesn't make sense."

"If there were an ihsland there. Freel mentioned ah name. Trahss Kathra."

Kali felt as if she had been hit with a sledgehammer.

"Freel's found Trass Kathra? It exists?"

"Having ship built right now. At Gransk."

Gransk, Kali thought. The Faith shipyards. She couldn't believe that she had a lead after all this time, and it had to be her next destination.

Beneath her, Incera convulsed suddenly with pain, and she moved to lift him, to find him help, despite the danger. But then the sound of bootfalls on the stone stairs leading to the observatory signalled the approach of more guards, and Incera once more shoved her away.

"The uhniverse should be constant," he said, staring up at the exposed sky and the Hel'ss in particular. "Bhalance, counterbalance, everything in plhace." His face darkened. "But that... *thing* doesn't belong. You are the only one who can shtop it. Gho..."

Kali stared at Incera for a second, then nodded. She moved to the edge of the observatory and then, with a last, concerned glance back, disappeared beyond the remains of the dome.

Incera stiffened as the sound of bootfalls reached the broken door and a fresh group of guards flooded in, recoiling from what lay before their eyes. Then the guards parted and Jakub Freel himself strode into the remains of the dome. Ignoring the gasps for help from Brother Incera, the studded leather clad man ran the links of his chain whip through his hands as he slowly and thoughtfully gazed at the carnage before him.

"Sir!"

Freel turned in response to the cry from one of the guards, who had moved to the edge of the newly created parapet and was pointing out across the rooftops of the cathedral. In the distance, a small, body-suited figure leapt from one building to another, gradually working its way towards the edge of the complex.

"It's the Hooper woman, sir!"

Freel sighed heavily. "Why does that *child* always leave such destruction in her wake?"

"Sir?"

"Never mind."

"Do we go after her, sir?"

"Don't be a fool. You would not have a chance of catching her."

"But, sir –"

Freel glared at the man, who staggered back as if physically struck.

"Th-then your orders, sir?"

"Have this mess cleared away," Freel said, his gaze deliberately taking in Incera along with the other bodies. Then he paused, deep in thought, his jaw twitching. A whole year and the combined efforts of the Final Faith had not delivered Kali Hooper into his grasp, and now the little minx had reappeared at what he considered to be a pivotal moment. Maybe it was time to adopt a different tactic – to, as it were, take out some insurance against any further interference. Even if it did not prove necessary, it would at least bolster the numbers for his plans for the near future.

"Alert the Red Chapter," he said, "Have them mobilise the Eyes of the Lord and the best men they have, and find everyone Kali Hooper has contacted in the last year. If I can't lay my hands on Miss Hooper herself, then I think it's time that her little network of helpers started to disappear..."

CHAPTER TWO

THE PALE LORD pushed the problem of Kali Hooper to the back of his mind and strode the shadowed halls of Scholten Cathedral as if born to them. The delicious irony in the fact that he, the Final Faith's First Enemy, was now as accepted a part of these rarefied environs as the Anointed Lord herself was not lost on him, and frequent flashes of lightning so strong as to wash away all colour from the hall's stained glass windows – mirroring his own, true pallor – illuminated a self satisfied smile. Neophytes, Enlightened Ones and Cardinals alike mistook the smile for a sign of his blessing and nodded reverently, bowed in supplication or scurried aside, dependent on rank, as he proceeded with single-minded determination to his apartments.

These humans' attitude amused Bastian Redigor. But why shouldn't they treat him so? Since he had taken possession of Jakub Freel's form in the Chapel of Screams, they had come to owe him much. The changes he'd instigated in the Faith had both strengthened and buoyed their Church, hardened it in its resolve and redefined it in the face of its flock, all of these things ostensibly preparing it for what both its ministers and ever-growing number of worshippers believed was soon to come.

The Ascension.

Yes, the Ascension. The central tenet of their Church. The long-awaited and much sought moment of rapture when they would, each and every one of them, become one with their God.

What utter nonsense.

The poor, deluded fools really did have as little idea of what was happening as the Hooper girl had when she'd faced him at Bel'A'Gon'Shri. Less so. At least the bloody and battered little tomb thief had known some kind of threat was nearing her world, if not its actual nature; whereas these zealots, blinkered by their own teachings, believed it harmless, even benign.

It was not wholly their fault, this ignorance. The fact was, he could control many things, but the one thing he could not control was the appearance in the skies of the Hel'ss. Visible in Twilight's azure haze for months now, its presence lessened little even during the day. There was no avoiding it, no escaping it, and, if only to prevent the inconvenience to his plans that a mass panic might cause, it had needed to be explained. In such a way that suited his purposes. The glamour he had therefore insinuated into the minds of key members of the Faith's elite had ensured they interpreted the approach of 'the other' as part of the process that would, as they wished, deliver them from their mortal coil into the embrace of their Lord of All.

He had given much thought as to what form this glamour should take, considered many scenarios, but in the end it was a corruption of the actual truth that served him best.

The 'other', he said, was a herald of the coming Ascension, which appeared in the heavens to facilitate the rapture itself. While it was true that the Hel'ss *was* linked to Kerberos, it was, of course, nothing of the kind, but he saw no reason to share this part of the entity's sordid history with the humans. They would, after all, all be gone before they found this out.

Oh, how simple it had been. While initially worried about the degree of will it would take to weave such a deception in the minds of so many, it had not taken long for the part truth to take on a life of its own. Such was the pliability of true believers that they were willing to accept anything that bolstered their own beliefs, and while it was true that he had been forced to 'tweak' the minds of a few who began to express doubts, the slavering vegetables they had become were no longer a problem. Otherwise the elite of the Final Faith had delivered his wondrous news to their underlings who had, in turn and through means subtle and otherwise, dutifully instilled that belief in the minds of the masses.

So it was that the thing that was about to annihilate them all was perceived to be an object not of death but of life. Glorious, everlasting afterlife.

Yes, they were fools. But they were happy fools.

Even Makennon – although it was true to say she was less happy than most.

Ah, Katherine, Redigor thought. He missed the feel of her, her *inner fire*, as it were, but in his new guise it would not have been appropriate for him to take advantage of the Anointed Lord in that way. If he had been capable of feeling sorry for anyone, he would have felt sorry for Katherine. The woman – strong, proud, but fallibly human – had barely been released from servitude to him when her mind had once more become no longer her own. She, of all of them, had required the most delicate manipulation because she had felt his touch before, and with one slip he could have revealed his true self to her. He could not remove her faculties in the way he had with the others, she was too prominent for that, so instead it had been necessary for him to... *deaden* certain parts of her mind. On the surface, she continued to perform her role as Anointed Lord as she always had but, when her official duties ended for the day, Makennon could now be found locked in her apartments, staring into her fire, in whose flames she sought but failed to find that part of her mind she sensed was awry.

It was almost a pity. He had promised Makennon at the moment of his 'death' that he would crush her church, but now, through his own manipulations, she was likely to miss it.

Bastian Redigor sighed and reflected on events of the past year. A year – it was nothing to an elf, not even the blink of an eye and, yet, saddled as he was with this human form, it had seemed eternal. Probably no less so for Jakub Freel who, in unguarded moments, he could hear screaming in fury from somewhere deep within. Redigor admired the Allantian for his strength – even after all this time, when he should have become nothing more than a whimpering echo of his former self, Freel protested with the same strength as he had when first been lost. He was not, however, quite strong enough, and it took only a few moment's concentration on his part to quell the internal rebellion. Yet still, when his energies could have been engaged in other matters, it was bothersome.

But not for much longer, he hoped. Because in doing what he was going to do for the Hel'ss, he very much hoped that the Hel'ss would do something for him in return.

Guards stiffened to attention and then moved aside as he reached his apartments. The Pale Lord barely acknowledged their presence as he swept inside. As the door was closed behind him, he allowed himself a moment of weariness, and leant against the wall with a sigh.

As always, when he entered this so-called sanctuary, the first thing that struck him was how painfully *human* it was, and he rued the pretence that made it necessary to keep his private space in the style of Jakub Freel. Long as he might for things elven, he instead had to surround himself with the trappings of the sometime prince of Allantia, and these *creature comforts* sickened him. No less so, in fact, than the sound of that damnable Eternal Choir, whose caterwauling voices and specious songs penetrated even these thick walls. It had been beyond his – or rather Freel's authority – to have them silenced, and so, instead, he had ensured that they suffered for their art by living up to their name. A small conjuration had bound each and every one of the singers to their positions, where they had been forced to remain since he had taken up office that seeming eternity ago. A secondary, smaller conjuration ensured that observers saw and heard nothing beyond the norm, and only he knew how they stood there now, their emaciated, undying forms with their desperate eyes struggling for release but finding all they could do was continue to sing.

It wasn't much but it was poetic. And it would have to do.

Thankfully, there was one part of his apartments where he could escape both Freel's trappings and the Eternal Choir. The inner sanctum – or prayer room – that was common to the quarters of all the Faith elite was sound-proofed and sacrosanct, and no one bar the occupant would dare set foot inside its walls. Safe in this knowledge, Redigor had removed the small altar and kneeling stone that had sat in the centre of the round, windowless chamber and replaced it with a circle of power drawn upon the stone flags of the floor. It was inert as he entered the chamber but, with a small wave of the hand, the runes that made up its pattern pulsed with a bright blue light and, a second later, an equally bright blue and slightly sparkling fog swirled dreamily in the centre of the sanctum.

Not even slowing his pace, Redigor walked into it. Through it.

And was somewhere else.

The cramped, circular confines of the prayer room gave way to a much larger space, one that not only looked different but felt and smelled different, too. Here there was a chillier aspect to the air, and a tang of brine about it, and if you listened very, very carefully, the sound of waves and gulls could be heard from somewhere in the distance.

Away from the cathedral, in this quiet place, Redigor succumbed to a greater tedium than mere weariness, and for a second actually staggered then steadied himself against a wall, his lips pulling back in pain. Only here, far from the stage on which his act needed to be maintained every day, could he acknowledge that it was far more than weariness affecting him.

The fact was, his possession of Jakub Freel required little effort on his part, but what *did* require effort, and sometimes a great deal of it, was ensuring the body did not succumb to the rigours of the dark magic he would have it employ. The channelling of such forces through an elven form exacted some small price on the physiology, but channelled through a human it was the cause of a biological rot that had to be monitored and addressed almost constantly.

Redigor pulled up the sleeves of his tunic and examined the black weals that writhed on the skin of his forearms like living tattoos, leaving necrotised patches of flesh, and knew this pattern was reflected on other parts of his body as well. He knew this because he could feel the burning the writhing brought with it.

A year in human form was, indeed, a long time, and he was unsure for how much longer he could stem the tide of the rot. Already he could feel it manifesting itself in his internal organs, feel them throb and twinge as they threatened to collapse. If that happened there was every chance he would not survive to see the arrival of the Hel'ss. What he needed was a way to rid himself of it. The problem was that though he possessed the capability to take another host, that act would be self-defeating, not only because it would remove him from this position of power but also because he was running out of time. There was no chance he would be able to reestablish himself before the Hel'ss arrived. The only solution, therefore, was not to run from the rot but to eliminate it completely, and it was with this, that if the legends were right, he believed the Hel'ss could help.

Redigor took a deep breath. In the centre of the chamber was a large tank-like structure, wrought of iron and studded with thick rivets strong enough to contain the weight of water that one or two portholes on its side revealed to be contained within. The water was the colour of algae and had clearly come from the sea. There was a dark shape barely discernible at its heart, the size of a tall and stocky man.

Redigor waved a hand and wheels on the side of the tank began to turn. From within, the sound of sloshing and draining water was heard. It was not the first time Redigor had drained the tank but, each time, it had been refilled in order to preserve the items he'd contained within. Different items. This time as the water drained away, foot by foot, what was revealed was not the figure of a man but a woman – a woman carved of wood.

The water gone, Redigor proceeded to a hatch between the two wheels and heaved it open with a metallic groan. Water continued to stream down its inside and pooled at his feet, but Redigor paid it no attention, his eyes fixed on the ship's figurehead.

Half rotten, encrusted with barnacles and with its joints accentuated by embedded layers of seaweed, the figure was twice his height. It thrust forward, staring over and beyond him, and looked almost desperate, as if seeking a wave it knew it would never ride again. Its features were smoothed by the erosion of years at sea, yet still distinguishable: the half-gown that had once connected it to its ships prow, the curve of its torso and breasts, its arms pressed to its sides, and its head, once crowned with flowing locks of hair, reduced now to a layering of rotten, jagged and jutting wood. What stood out the most, though, were its eyes, larger than those of a real human; blank orbs veined not with blood vessels but the grain exposed by their carving, that stared straight ahead and yet saw nothing at all.

But he would make them see.

It was time to awaken this lady.

Redigor closed his own eyes, falling into a deep concentration in the silence of the chamber. After a second, a sibilant whisper could be heard drifting from him, although his lips appeared not to move at all. The words he spoke were strange, short and clipped at first, though became longer and louder, and each began to overlap the other until eventually it sounded as if a crowd of people were whispering in unison with Redigor. Still, though, his lips did not move.

But as the volume increased yet more, others did.

With a sudden, almost horrified inhalation of air, the mouth of the figurehead opened, and at the same time, its eyes. What had previously been dead wood was suddenly transformed into the semblance of human eyes, though they were grotesquely distorted, bulging, matching the size and shape of the carved orbs themselves. Cartoon eyes, fishmen's eyes – or perhaps the eyes of a suffocating and drowning man.

Which was exactly what they were.

The eyes' grotesque appearance was made even more so by the fact that their gaze flicked about the chamber in panic, settling on Redigor, their surroundings, even trying to look down, presumably in search of the form that should hold them. They saw nothing, of course, for the body they had once inhabited wasn't there, and the eyes widened in terror.

Water vomited from the figurehead's mouth.

"Who were you?" Redigor asked.

The eyes shot to him, though still flickered wildly, trying but unable to tear themselves away, to make sense of what was happening.

"*I don't know.*"

Redigor sighed, wearily. The human race's hold on their existence was stupefyingly weak, hardly worth the effort of their drawing their first pathetic breaths at all.

"Answer me," he demanded.

"*My... my name was William... William West, sir.*"

"And *what* were you, William?"

"I... I was second mate on the *Fulsome Wench*, sir."

Redigor nodded. This at least confirmed he had summoned what he wished – necromancy was so prone to strays and intruders, chancers from the fringes of the planes. It confirmed also that West was on the crew manifest of one of the ships he had despatched beyond the Stormwall. The translocation rituals that Makennon's people had perfected recently had come in very handy in that regard: one moment these ships had been sailing safe waters, the next unknown and lethal seas thousands of leagues away. The magical cost of such translocations – and of retrieving their almost universally doomed remains – had left him exhausted physically, but, as the Eyes of the Lord he had earlier attempted to send beyond the Stormwall had been brought down by its preternatural energies, he'd had little choice.

"You know, do you not, William, that you are quite dead?"

"Yes, Sir. I'm sorry, Sir."

"There is no need to apologise, William."

"I... I wasn't, Sir. What I mean is, I'm sorry for my Meg, my wife, and Rob, my boy. They're all alone now."

The smallest of smiles curled Redigor's lip. West could not know that it was he who had sent him to his death. "Do not worry yourself, William... the three of you will be together again soon enough."

"Can you promise me that, Sir?"

Redigor's smile widened. "Oh, yes. I can."

William was silent for a moment and his eyes stared beyond Redigor, as if picturing that time. Then he spoke again.

"Is there something you wish of me, Sir?"

"Yes, William," Redigor said. "I want you to show me what you saw."

"Sir?"

"Before you died."

The dead sailor's eyes started to flicker. "I... I'm not sure I want to do that."

"And why is that? Because it would cause you pain?"

"Yes. The memory."

Redigor's eyes, and his tone, darkened. "Is this the kind of pain you would like instead, William?"

Something carried with Redigor's words and suddenly the mouth of the figurehead began to wheeze and gurgle. Its eyes, in turn, became even more grotesquely deformed than before, flecked with veins that bulged with blood, threatening to burst despite the fact their owner was already dead. William's voice became a series of strangled, bubbling gasps, the sound of a man desperate to breathe but finding only water where air should have been. Where a few seconds of these gasps would normally have ended with the silence of liquid filled lungs, and of dimming eyes, however, here they simply continued, a frantic and agonising and wild-eyed struggle for relief that the Pale Lord let continue for two minutes or more. When at last Redigor released his hold on his summoning, William West's eyes stared forward glazed.

"That's better," Redigor said. "Now... show me."

Before him, the vitreous of West's eyes began to cloud over, as if beset by cataracts, and then began to swirl. At first it was like looking at a reflection of something indistinguishable in a mottled and tarnished mirror, but then the swirls began to coalesce into the view of a storm-tossed seascape at night. Redigor leaned forward and allowed himself to be drawn into the scene – in, and very far away. He found himself travelling out from the peninsula, through the Stormwall and over an endless expanse of ocean. Land disappeared far behind him until there was nothing but water. After what seemed like an eternity an object became discernible on the horizon, and after a few seconds it resolved itself into the shape of a vessel. Then he was sweeping up to the hull of the ship, and then aboard, where at last he came to rest, or at least as at rest as the vision of a man who was trapped on a sinking ship could be.

This was what West had seen moments before he died, and as his gaze shifted across the panorama before him, his fellow, doomed crewmen could be seen, too, frantically working the sails and ropes on the deck of their ship. The *Fulsome Wench* was already breaking apart, and there was nothing they could do to save themselves, but that didn't matter to Redigor. He didn't care about their deaths and it was not their deaths that he had summoned West to see.

Redigor waited patiently, disappointed too many times. The seascape of the other side of the world was by now a familiar vista to him – as familiar, that was, as an endless expanse of maelstrom could be – but he needed to see more. And to see more, the location had to be right, the conditions had to be right, the *stars* had to be right. The chances of a translocation bringing him close enough for these conditions to be met were, of course, infinitesimal, and he was already prepared to be disappointed once more. Then, suddenly, his eyes widened.

Something...

Redigor's eyes narrowed as he studied the last moments of William West's mortal existence for the finest detail, and at last drew in a sharp breath. There, a glimpse between masts and rigging, of a star pattern that seemed similar to that on the chart from the Halo files. Then as Redigor watched – or rather as West's perspective shifted – a clearer view, the heavens revealed in all their glory.

Not just similar to the star chart. A perfect match.

This was the place. He had found his destination at last.

All he needed to do now was confirm what he believed.

Redigor's attention shifted from the night sky to West's

immediate surroundings. The *Fulsome Wench* was sinking, its hull already half beneath the waves, and as a result what the second mate saw was wildly skewed, disorientating, obscured at times by the flailing bodies and screaming faces of his shipmates. Redigor was annoyed that they were stopping him seeing what he wanted to see in the few moments of their lives that remained.

West sank beneath the surface and suddenly all was a maelstrom of air bubbles and darkness, but then, for the briefest of times, he came up and Redigor smiled.

There. No more than snatches and glimpses, but enough. Outlined against the night sky, in the distance, a darkened island of sharp and jagged rocks whose desolation was palpable even through this vision. And before it – washing the island again and again from view – a swirling, unnatural body of water that was responsible for the sinking of the *Fulsome Wench*.

It was fitting that William West should choose that moment to breathe his last and drown. Fitting that the eyes of the figurehead dimmed and reverted to wood once more.

Because their job was done.

He had seen something *in* the water. *Part* of the water.

The legends, it seemed, were true. There was hope for him yet.

The Hel'ss wasn't just approaching Twilight.

It was already here.

CHAPTER THREE

"EXCUSE ME," A voice said, loud and demanding enough to be heard above the general hubbub in the tavern, "but I think there's something wrong with this stew."

Everything in the *Here There Be Flagons* stopped. Red Deadnettle half way down a jug of thwack; Fester Grimlock and Jurgen Pike about to slam down winning hands of Quagmire; Pete Two-Ties and Ronin Larson arguing, as they always did at this time of day, about the true depth of Bottomless Pit and how many times one of them would have to throw the other idiot in to fill it up. Even Hetty Scrubb, gigglingly high on one of her many 'combustible herbs' lapsed into silence with an uncharacteristic look of horror on her face.

Behind the bar, Aldrededor stopped towelling down the bowls of those regulars who had seen nothing fit to complain about and mouthed, "Oh, Gods, no..."

All eyes turned towards the kitchen door.

It was a delayed reaction, but the sound came soon enough from within. Hoarse yet high pitched, and, to those who didn't know otherwise, somehow strangely... reptilian.

"*Heeeeeeeeeeeeeeeeee...*"

The man who had complained, some kind of city fop by the look of him, couldn't help but look at the door, too. And though he couldn't say why, he started to swallow rapidly and involuntarily.

"Did I say something wrong?" he said, glancing around in exasperation.

A hand slapped down on his right shoulder. "If I were you, friend, I'd get out of here now. Get out while you can still father a child."

Another slapped down on his left. "But run fast, for her knives, not to mention her tongue, can sever your manhood half a league away."

"Knives? Tongue? What? Who?" the man gasped. "You're joking, right?"

Both regulars burst into raucous laughter, and the man looked relieved. But the laughter stopped abruptly, leaving only shaking heads and deadly serious expressions.

"No."

A dagger thudded into the wooden beam right next to the man's head, quivering so fast that a few seconds passed before it ceased to be a blur. The fact that bits of moist, sliced onion slithered down and then dropped off its blade did not make it appear any more homely or less lethal.

The frame of the kitchen door outlined something long and thin and oddly disturbing that appeared there and began to make its way towards the table where the man sat. He tried to run, as advised, but suddenly, almost preternaturally, the something was there, looming over him, and despite all his survival instincts he couldn't help but sit and stare in mesmerised astonishment at its long, hawk-like nose.

"*Oh, please, don't stare at the nose,*" someone whispered urgently from nearby.

Dolorosa shot them a look, and then, with an intake of breath, drew herself up to her full height, folded her arms and smiled. With the lipstick she was wearing, the smile looked something like a spray of blood at a murder scene.

"You havva the complaint?" she said.

"No, n-no. L-lord of All, no," the man stuttered quickly, but then realised there was no denying what he'd said. "Well, all right, yes, it's your Surprise Stew..."

"And wotta seems to be the problem?"

"Urm, for one thing, look," the man said, pointing, "there's something moving in it."

"Yes?"

"Well, something moving in it wasn't quite the 'surprise' I was expecting."

Dolorosa's eyebrow rose. "The leetle redda thing? It issa macalorum. It infussa your dish with flavour. Itta loves to do so."

"Macalorum?"

"It issa local 'erb. It ees a bastardo to catch."

"Catch? Excuse me but herbs don't run away."

"Nor do they 'ave bladders." Dolorosa watched as the small red herb squirted something into the stew, and shrugged. "Whatta can I say?"

The man swallowed. "Are you saying that this macalorum is *peeing* in my stew?"

"It issa full of vitamins."

"Okay, right," the man said doubtfully, poking in the stew with his fork. What looked like a couple of white eyeballs bobbed to the surface. "But what about these?"

Dolorosa peered intently into the bowl. "Ah. You avva me there."

"What? You don't know what they are?"

The question prompted a slap about the head. "Of coursa I know whatta they are. Eet wassa the joke, you stupeed man."

Dolorosa emitted what for her passed as a laugh – *hahahahaharrrr!* All of the regulars in the Flagons echoed it. *Hahahahaharrrr.*

"Then," the man asked hesitantly, "what are they?"

"They are, owwa you say, the love spheres ovva the purple skoonk."

The man paled. "You mean its –"

"Delicioso, yes?" Dolorosa interrupted proudly. "A rare delicacy and," she cast a glance at Red Deadnettle, the ruddy-faced poacher raising his tankard and nodding back, "locally sourced."

The man picked up his napkin and wiped the edges of his mouth slowly and solidly, as if trying to erase even the memory of what he had so far consumed.

"Let me get this straight. Am I to understand I've been eating vermin's gonads and the waste products of an over-excitable, incontinent weed?"

"You havva the problem with that?"

The man stood abruptly, his chair making a loud scraping sound on the wooden floor. He tossed his napkin angrily down onto the table.

"Madam, do you know who I am?" he declared.

"You'd be wiser asking who *she* is," Aldrededor muttered behind the bar. He shook his head. "Be merciful, my wife."

"Have you ever heard," the man continued, "of the *Miramas Times*?"

Dolorosa had, of course. It was the oldest news-sheet on the peninsula and, back in the day, had often reported her and Aldy's maritime exploits. Out of the many headlines the two of them had engendered, her favourite remained *Perilous Pirates Pillage Pontaine – Again!*

"I see that you have," the man said, smiling. "Have you heard, then, of its respected food critic, H. Borton Jeckle?"

"Yes!" Dolorosa blurted. "Wait, no."

"*I*, Madam, am H. Borton Jeckle."

"You *never* are."

"Indeed I am. And I came to your establishment today to consider bestowing it one of my coveted Jeckle Moons."

Dolorosa's lips curled back. "You feelthy purravert..."

"Madam?"

"No one flashes their bottom inna my taverno!"

"It is an *award*, Madam. A mark of distinction that is highly regarded by anyone of taste. A Jeckle Moon means that the food in an establishment is of an exceptional quality."

Dolorosa's smile suddenly reappeared, twitching, and this time on the other side of her mouth. She swept her hand back through her hair.

"Anda you say I am to be considered for one of these Moons?"

Jeckle considered his stew one more. "I regret, Madam, only if it is indeed provided by my arse. And only then while it is leaving your establishment. The fare you have served me today was the most disgusting and repellant concoction it has ever been my displeasure to con – "

The last syllable disappeared down Jeckle's throat along with two of his teeth, and with surprising sprightliness for a man of his age Aldrededor leapt the bar to support the critic as he staggered against a wall.

"You must forgive my wife," he said, glancing towards the far end of the tavern where, up a small flight of skewed steps, sat an empty Captain's Table. He grabbed Dolorosa's arm as it tried to go for the knife still embedded in the wooden beam. "She is... missing a friend."

"She is missing her marbles," Jeckle protested through bloodied lips. "I demand an apology, Sir!"

Aldrededor sighed as he and his wife struggled. "Dolorosa, apologise to the nice man."

"I willa not."

"Perhaps," Aldrededor gasped, "it might be better if you leave. Your meal is, of course, on the house."

"Correction, sir. The meal belongs in a horse."

"*Heeeeeeee...*"

"Oh, now you have reminded her of her friend again. Please, for your own safety, leave now."

"Sir," H. Borton Jeckle said, "you do not have to ask me twice."

The much respected food critic of the Miramas Times exited the *Flagons* with an harumph and the swish of a tailor-made cloak. Outside, his carriage awaited, his driver slumped in a doze at the reins. As H. Borton Jeckle mounted the rig and deposited himself into his upholstered seat, he reflected that while the county of Tarn was indeed a delightful place, and the *Flagons* itself ideally situated for the sort of weekend sojourn his readers might appreciate, there was no way on Twilight he could recommend it to them. Just the opposite, in fact. On reflection, he supposed he should have expected little more from a tavern that was reputedly owned by a female outlaw.

He prodded his driver in the back, demanding they begin the long journey home.

The driver tipped forward onto the reins, causing a disquieted stirring from the horses. It seemed he was not dozing but dead.

"Broggle, Lord of All, man," Jeckle said, slithering back out of the carriage. Maybe the sun had got to the poor fellow, or maybe his heart had seized, but whatever the cause it was damned inconvenient. If he couldn't find another driver he might have to spend the night in this hellshole while he sent a runner for a replacement.

"Broggle, you're fired," Jeckle declared.

The body of his driver twisted as he prodded it, falling onto its back on the seat. He stared, glassy-eyed, up at Jeckle and the critic's mouth opened and closed like a fish as he saw the blood red slash across the driver's throat. The man's livery was sodden and stained through.

Grabcoins, he thought, with a thudding heart. Probably in league with that Hooper woman. Well, that settled it. Another reason to warn his readers to stay away. Actively discourage them from coming anywhere near here, in fact.

A hand clamped tightly over his mouth while the point of a blade pressed into his spine.

"Who are you?" a voice breathed into his ear. The hand was released briefly so that he could provide an answer.

"Jeckle. H. Borton Jeckle," he answered quickly. He swallowed as some kind of flying sphere hovered in front of his face, as if examining him.

There was a moment's hesitation from his assailant. "The food critic for the *Times*?"

Jeckle's eyebrows rose but, his mouth covered once more, he could only nod. A half sob escaped him, muffled by the hand.

"Then this is unfortunate, Mister Jeckle, for I find your column edifying. But you are not who we hunt and we cannot alert those inside to our presence. Do you understand this?"

Of all things, H. Borton Jeckle thought, what, don't be ridiculous, man! What could a grabcoin know of my column? He never vocalised the thought, though, as a moment later he felt something so sharp it didn't even hurt slash across his throat, and the only sound he could make was a gurgle.

His wide-eyed, spasming body was lowered quietly to the ground, where it subsequently produced a large red puddle, and died. His assailant stared down, thinking how Jeckle's job would have benefited had he lived. In his profession it would be a distinct advantage to have two mouths.

He signalled his men, who emerged from the bushes in which he himself had hidden, and in absolute silence they moved towards the *Flagons*. The shadows that they, and at least six Eyes of the Lord flitting about the tavern like angry flies, cast fleetingly at the windows went unnoticed as, inside, there was a communal burst of laughter.

"LOVE SPHERES!" PETE Two-Ties bawled, his voice cracking into a hoarse wheeze as he used a dirty handkerchief to wipe tears from his eyes. "The man was a buffoon!"

"Flashing his arse!" Fester Grimlock cried.

"He didn't realise you knew who he was!" Red Deadnettle joined in. He took a deep slug from his jug. "The bit about the macalorum!"

"No, Red, that bit was true," Aldrededor said, eyeing him steadily across the bar.

"It was?" Red said, shrugging. "Well, it's never done me any harm."

"Whatta makes a man like heem think we would like to be in his stupeed guide," Dolorosa said. "'Madam, do you know who I am?'" she mimicked. "Pah!"

"Perhaps you should have keeled him," Jurgen Pike mimed, "lika thees." His hand stabbed down repeatedly, as if holding a knife.

Dolorosa suddenly loomed over him as she had over Jeckle, arms folded tightly across her chest, fingers drumming. "What issa thees stupeed accent in whicha you speak?"

Hetty Scrubb splurted out the cocktail from which she had been attempting a quivering sip, and once more giggled uncontrollably. But the giggle faded a moment later as the surface of her drink was unexpectedly covered by a fall of dust from between the skewed wooden beams of the ceiling. The Flagons being so old it was normal practice to cover drinks against the possibility of such falls, but only on the occasions there was someone upstairs.

Hetty's eyes moved suspiciously upwards, one slightly slower than the other, and just as the two levelled out the fall of dust was followed by a low creak of the timbers. From behind the bar, Aldrededor looked over at Dolorosa and shook his head at the slight look of hope in her eyes. They were all aware of the circumstances that dogged Kali and neither of them had seen her for over two months, and when she did return to say hello and dump her washing, their adopted offspring always used a different means of entering the *Flagons*, in case she had been compromised.

The last time she had come, she had come from upstairs.

"My 'usband," Dolorosa hissed. "I theenk we havva the uninvited guests."

"Then, my darling wife," Aldrededor responded, with a twinkle. "I suggest we prepare to repel boarders..."

Aldrededor moved to the chest by the Captain's Table, heaved it open and drew out a crackstaff – one of the few still working that had been left behind by one of Jengo Pim's men – and flicked it on. It crackled softly, like hand-held lightning. Dolorosa, meanwhile, plucked her kitchen knife from where it remained embedded in the wooden beam, and from her garter produced another, far more deadly looking blade, which she proceeded to toss full circle in her palm. The two of them looked towards the base of the stairs.

"Stay where you are," Dolorosa whispered to Hetty Scrubb and Pete Two-Ties. "Red and Ronin will look after you."

"Give 'em one for me," the diminutive herbalist requested. She rose and hopped from leg to leg, punching the air before her. "In the nuts. Yes, yes, in the nuts."

"The only place she can reach," Pete Two-Ties sighed.

As Dolorosa and Aldrededor approached the first two risers, Red Deadnettle slid from his stool, far more gently and quietly than might be expected from such a giant of a man, and, from beneath, withdrew a large wooden club. Ronin Larson, the blacksmith, joined him in standing guard, his weapon a molding hammer he kept perpetually slung on his broad leather toolbelt and which he now pounded into his open palm. From his grin, it seemed he was looking forward to molding a few Final Faith faces rather than metal for a change.

Unfortunately, neither he nor the others were prepared for the type of attack that was to come. The ground floor of the *Flagons* was thrown into chaos as three of the whorled glass windows were smashed in a series of determined blows from sword hilts, and through them came three canisters that spewed a green fog across the bar area.

"Swamp gas!" Dolorosa hissed, and began to cough uncontrollably. As did the others. A few seconds later they were all on their knees, weapons dropped. The gas began to dissipate and, as it did, the door to the tavern was kicked open. Swords of Dawn flooded the room, each placing a weapon at the throats of those who were incapacitated.

But other than stand guard, they made no further move.

They were waiting for something.

And that something was the creaking of the tavern's stairs as they signalled the arrival of a figure descending them. Their uninvited guest, it seemed, knew how to make an entrance.

"My name," he said, "is Gregory Morg."

Dolorosa squinted at him through stinging eyes, a man dressed in robes and armour that identified him as neither Swords of Dawn or Faith, but somewhere in between. He was likely one of those damned mercenaries Jakub Freel had conscripted. "This tavern is now commandeered, and you are in the custody of the Final Faith."

From their prone positions on the floor, Dolorosa and Aldrededor cast worried glances at each other, knowing full well what this was about. The bastards were finally coming after those near and dear to Kali, presumably in an attempt to flush her out. It wasn't for themselves they looked worried, however, but for the innocents in the bar – Peter, Hetty and the rest – whose only connection to Kali was to provide her with a cheery welcome home after one of her adventures. They didn't deserve to be treated this way.

"The old man and woman, these others," Aldrededor pointed out, "know nothing. Let them go."

Morg smiled coldly and stepped off the stairs so that he towered over the Sarcrean.

"If I let one old man go, then I would have to let another go, too," he said, clearly referring to Aldrededor. He sneered. "Along with his ancient crone of a wife."

Dolorosa spat on his feet.

"Calm, my darling," Aldrededor soothed. He stared up at their captor, touching the sword held at his throat. "Do you intend to execute us, is that it? Send a message to Kali Hooper?"

"Then you do not deny your association with the outlaw?"

"Would there be much point?"

"Not really."

Two other Swords of Dawn entered the tavern. "The perimeter of the property is secure, sir. No sign of further insurgents."

"You have checked all of the outbuildings?"

"All apart from the stables, sir. They seem to be locked."

"Then *unlock* them, man!"

"We tried, sir, but the lock is strange. Inscribed with patterns."

Morg's eyes narrowed and he grabbed Aldrededor's chin and forced it up. "Runes. What do you keep in the stables?"

"What do you normally keep in stables, Gregory Morg?"

"Behind a rune-inscribed lock?"

Aldrededor grinned widely. "We stable some rare breeds."

"The bamfcat. If it's here, the girl may be close by. Shatter that lock and slay anything within."

"Horse isn't here," Aldrededor said. "Neither is Kali Hooper."

"We shall see. As for our captives," Morg said, "bring the wagons."

"Wagons?" Aldrededor repeated.

Morg smiled. "You'll all be taking a little trip. Relocated, as it were."

"Interesting," Aldrededor commented. "I hope somewhere sunny."

"My 'usband," Dolorosa whispered urgently in his ear, "we cannot allow ourselves to be taken, and we cannot allow them into the stables."

"I know this, my lovepeach," Aldrededor responded through still grinning teeth. "Be patient."

Dolorosa looked about herself, confused. What was her husband on about, patient? They all of them had swords at their throats and as far as she could see there was no immediate way out of this predicament. Then her eyes caught sight of what Aldrededor had obviously been referring to. While the rest of them had simply dropped their weapons her husband had managed to conceal his. The crackstaff was perched at an angle between the flaps of the bar and, what was more, remained charged, crackling softly to itself, out of sight. Dolorosa did not fully understand these strange devices but one thing she did know was that, if left idle like this, the crackstaff would eventually purge itself of pent-up energy.

There was going to be a bang.

"Everybody," she said, meaning her own people, "I suggest you sticka your heads between your knees."

Regulars and Swords alike looked at Dolorosa questioningly, but it was already too late.

From the tip of the crackstaff erupted a bolt of darting, twisting blue energy that blew the flaps off the bar and struck a Sword who had the bad luck to be standing in its way. The energy bolt tore through his body armour into his chest, exposing the white bone of his sternum. He was punched into the air, slamming into and smashing another of the tavern's windows. The flaps, meanwhile, both solid chunks of wood the size of sewer grates, blew to the left and the right in an explosion of splinters, hitting two more of the Swords, decapitating one and shattering the sword arm of another. These men, or what remained of them, flailed into their own, and in the chaos that ensued Aldrededor and the others made their moves.

The swarthy Sarcrean pushed his captor from him, leapt and rolled back over the bar, then snatched the crackstaff from where it now lay on the floor. He discharged it into the face of a Sword who tried to follow. Dolorosa used far more primitive but no less effective weapons, snatching her twin blades from beneath her and simultaneously thrusting them back and up, hissing in satisfaction as she felt them puncture flesh. As she rolled from beneath the Sword's collapsing body, she booted Red's club over to where the giant poacher could grab it. As he bent to do so, a

Sword who tried to stop him found himself with a new and unique perspective on life as Red's club swung round solidly, knocking his head permanently sideways.

Dolorosa snatched a glance at Morg, whom she noticed had retreated a few risers back up the stairs from where he watched the battle with narrowed eyes, and then at her husband, who was sweating and grinning as much as she.

"Justa like the old days on the sheep!" she declared and, though it showed her skull and crossbone bloomers for all to see, couldn't resist bounding onto and from a table, using a curtain as she might a sail to swing out across the room and boot two more of their captors in the face and off their feet. She landed on the bar and from there urged on Red and Ronin. The giant first swung his nailed club up between the legs of another Sword, and then grabbed the poor unfortunate by the neck, racing him across the tavern to ram his head into the bragging box, where he collapsed twitching and screaming, stung by whatever was inside. Ronin, for his part, moved through the Swords with his hammer swinging in a blur, forcing all before him to dodge or duck the momentum of the heavy blacksmithing tool. Even Hetty Scrubb and Pete Two-Ties helped out, the former reducing one Sword to a spasming heap by blowing him a faceful of her latest herbal concoction, while Pete confounded another by more intellectual means.

"Stop!" he shouted, as the Sword was about to bring the hilt of his weapon down on him. The Sword was surprised enough to do so. "I half faint, sorting out these idiots!"

"What?" the Sword said, bemused.

"Anagram!" Pete emphasised, punching a finger at the cryptosquare in the newssheet he held. "Five, five..."

"What the fark are you talking about, old man?"

Pete rammed the rolled up newssheet into the Sword's eye, causing a cry of pain. "The answer's 'Final Faith' you moron," he announced.

It wasn't the deadliest of attacks but it served its purpose. Pete slipped by him while the Sword stumbled against the wall clutching his face.

Slowly, he and the others fought their way to the exit,

Aldrededor providing covering fire with the crackstaff as they moved. Furniture, glassware and ornaments were shattered or sent flying from the blasts, and Aldrededor comforted Dolorosa as she watched the inside of her beloved tavern blown apart. Both knew there was no choice in the matter, however, as their first priority was to protect what was within the stables, to say nothing of their friends. But as they, the last to back out, emerged from the door of the *Flagons*, they noticed an unexpected quiet in the courtyard behind them.

Both ex-pirates turned slowly. Their friends were lined up before more Swords, weapons once more at their throats. Behind the line of prisoners two barred prison carriages stood waiting.

The regulars of the *Flagons* stared at them apologetically.

"Sheet," Dolorosa said.

A slow crunching from the doorway of the tavern heralded the reappearance of Gregory Morg as he walked slowly out to them. He took the knives and crackstaff from their hands.

"What do you think this is?" he said. "*A game?*"

For the first time, Morg hefted his own weapon, a cruel looking battleaxe that had been slung on his back. He walked to the line of prisoners, considering each but then choosing one seemingly at random. He nodded to the Sword holding Fester Grimlock and, as he moved away, span with a roar and sliced the battleaxe up through Fester's torso. The merchant was thrown off his feet, twisting in the air with the force of the impact, and when his already dead body landed with a thud, his innards were forcefully spewed from his body in a glistening, steaming heap.

Hetty gagged, while the rest of the regulars railed ineffectually against their captors.

"Bastardo," Dolorosa said slowly.

"Any further resistance and I kill another of you," Morg said, reslinging his weapon. The murder of Fester Grimlock had meant nothing to him.

Dolorosa studied the mercenary, and Aldrededor smiled as she spoke. His beloved had always possessed a keen tactical mind. "It is my guess that we are being taken as some kind offa insurance, yes?" she said, nodding at the wagons. "A deterrent against our

Kali acting against Jakuba Freel. If that issa the case, I doubt he woulda be very pleased if he discovered you had keeled *any* of us, hmm? Or arra you going to prove me wrong?"

Morg's eyes narrowed and he sighed.

"Put them in the wagons," he said to his men. "I'm going to take a look at this mysterious locked stable of theirs."

Again, Aldrededor and Dolorosa shot each other a glance, trying, and failing, to work out a way of stopping him. It was obvious that what they needed was some kind of diversion but what was not so obvious was who provided it.

Hetty Scrubb nodded at them, then mouthed for them to be ready to get the hells out of there. The ex-pirates' eyebrows rose – neither had been aware that the perpetually high herbalist even knew they had something to protect.

Puzzled, they watched as Ronin, Red, Jurgen, Pete and finally Hetty were bundled into one of the wagons, its barred door slammed shut behind them. They shot a glance at Morg, who was fiddling with the rune lock on the stable door, and then were themselves ushered to a wagon. Whatever it was Hetty had in mind, they hoped she would do it quickly.

She did.

Just as Aldrededor and Dolorosa were about to be bundled into darkness, the rear of Hetty's wagon began to pour smoke, a cloud so thick and cloying it immediately threw the Swords surrounding it into confusion.

"Fire!" one yelled, but Dolorosa knew better than that. This was Hetty's *special* pipe in action, the one she'd been forced to ban from the *Flagons*, and if anything was going to take the Swords' minds off things, this was it.

Aldrededor and Dolorosa took their cue, racing through the black hallucinogenic cloud of while the Swords battled to re-open the wagon and extinguish the pipe. They met Morg half way. The mercenary made an immediate angry dash for the two of them and, while Aldrededor steeled himself for a confrontation, Dolorosa shoved him on, rolling up her own sleeves instead.

"I will 'andle thees. You do what you 'ave to do."

"My wife," Aldrededor protested, "this is not some errant

customer you are dealing with, Morg is a dangerous man."

"And it is a long time since I have had the pleasure of keeling one. Now, do as I say, 'usband!'"

The Sarcrean was about to protest further but it was too late, battle joined.

Before Morg could make a move on him, Dolorosa pivoted on her right leg, skirt flying, and delivered a roundhouse kick that sent the mercenary staggering back, snarling at a bloodied lip. It took Morg only a moment to recover and come at her, but Dolorosa was ready once more, meeting him with a flying kick that again sent the man staggering, this time flat on his back. As his wife roared and raced in with the intention of keeping Morg down, Aldrededor made the sign of the Gods and left her to it, heading for the locked stable door. Where it had proven problematic for Morg and his men, however, it was nothing for the ex-pirate. As the sounds of confrontation continued behind him the lock fell away before a series of rapid and deft gestures. The stable door creaked open and Aldrededor span back to face Dolorosa.

"Hurry, my darling. We have –"

The Sarcrean's words dwindled into silence as he saw Morg had proven himself the better after all. He held Dolorosa in a neck lock, her back pressed against his front. The love of his life no longer looked furious or determined, only ashamed and defeated – and somehow old. Older than she had ever looked to him before.

Time, he reflected, was indeed catching up with them.

"Dolorosa..." he breathed, and then, to Morg, hoping that his wife had been right. "You will not kill her."

Morg smiled coldy. "Perhaps not, Sarcrean. But if you do not surrender, I can and I will do almost as much..."

"Aldrededor," Dolorosa hissed. "You must go."

"Not without you, my wife."

"My 'usband," Dolorosa insisted, eyeing the shadows beyond the stable door. "You know what is at stake – *go*."

Morg's eyes narrowed suspiciously.

"What exactly is at stake, old man? I warn you, don't make a move."

Aldrededor's eyes flicked from Morg to Dolorosa, lingering long and hard over his wife's distressed face. But as their eyes met and he held her gaze he knew she was right. What he *should* have known, after Fester's death, what that Morg would not hesitate to act.

Morg made good on his threat. Without any further warning, he shoved Dolorosa out in front of him and, as she stood there looking confused, two sharp blades – her own sharp blades – were thrust suddenly through her. Dolorosa stiffened, her eyes widened and, as the projecting lengths of the blades glistened with blood in the light of the sun, she made a sound that was not unfamiliar to Aldrededor but was nevertheless horribly strange.

"*Heeeeeeeeeee...*"

"DOLOROSA!"

"A crone as scrawny as this," Morg said, "she's lucky I missed the vital organs. She will, though, bleed to death unless I grant her medical attention. Now, old man, why don't you show me exactly what's in that stable?"

Aldrededor was about to do exactly that, caring about nothing other than getting help for his wife, when Dolorosa vigorously shook her head. The act clearly caused her great pain.

"Aldy," she said, in a guttural voice, "do what I said. 'E will not let me die."

Aldrededor swallowed rapidly. "*I cannot take that chance.*"

"You *must*. They cannot get their 'ands on the sheep."

It would have been funny, had it not been so true, and Aldrededor knew it.

"If my wife dies," he growled at Morg, "there will be no place you will be safe, no sanctuary you can hide in or shield you can cower behind. I will hunt you down, I will find you, and then and I will kill you."

"Lika thees," Dolorosa muttered weakly.

Aldrededor stared at her wavering smile, swallowed again, and immediately turned. He was inside the stables and slamming the door shut behind him before Morg could make another move. The rune-inscribed lock re-configured itself.

"You and you, get this woman in the wagon," Morg snarled to his men, who had just relieved Hetty of her pipe and were working their way through what remained of the smoke. "The rest of you," he added, releasing Dolorosa's body and slamming his fist on the doors of the stables, "raze this thing to the ground."

Morg's men responded, and within a minute they had gathered torches and surrounded the stable. The soft thrumming of the flames of their torches was, however, drowned out from a growing sound from within the stable's walls – a thrumming again, but this time one which made their heads ache and was quite clearly caused by something other than fire.

"What in the name of the Lord of All?" one of the Swords muttered.

The roof of the stables suddenly began to rise upwards, not from any mechanism designed to make it do so but from the sheer force and pressure of something rising inside. As the roof broke apart in broad splinters, the walls, too, began to press outward as if the something inside were turning slowly as it rose. The walls began to fall away like discarded cards.

Bowing to these pressures, the entire stable exploded outward and something rose from its ruin, a sleek flying shape the length of three carts, that then hovered in the sky. An uncountable number of black vents flapped on its side, shiny and looking like the shifting of reptilian skin, and on the underside of its hull, orange orbs pulsed.

The Swords, even Morg, staggered back. But Dolorosa, being dragged to captivity, caught a glimpse of her husband at the flying thing's helm and smiled. Seeing the repaired *Tharnak* airborne once more, she watched as it hung there for a second, acknowledging her, before banking gracefully and disappearing above the rooftop of the *Flagons*.

Morg stared after it, his lip curling in anger. He stared at the *Flagons* and then at his men.

"Burn it. Burn it all."

CHAPTER FOUR

THE RED CHAPTER'S cull of Kali's friends was swift and simultaneous. Their targets tracked by Eyes of the Lord, squads of Freel's mercenaries struck across the peninsula at the same time Gregory Morg raided the *Here There Be Flagons*.

Exiting the Three Towers in Andon, on his way to a certain club in the Skeleton Quays for an engagement he hoped he couldn't get out of, Poul Sonpear spotted a number of spherical shadows scudding about his own as he progressed down the alley he used as a short cut. He immediately dropped into phase, thinking himself safe in the half realm accessible only to members of the League of Prestidigitation and Prestige, and was somewhat surprised to be joined there by four black-clad figures – shadowmages, by the look of them. Sonpear began to muster defensive spells – skull shield, ball of immunity, flash – but his assailants were ready for him. One countercasted with slow, another with silence, while the final two physically wrestled him against a wall, restraining him while a scrambling collar was clamped around his neck.

Sonpear recognised the collar as proscribed technology, Old Race, and as he felt its effects numbing his faculties, his mind raced. Why was he being targeted? Who were these men? What did they want? There was only one possible answer, and he tried, but failed, to send a telepathic warning to the one person with whom he maintained a permanent link. The message that would never be sent was, *Kali, they're coming for us...*

ELSEWHERE IN ANDON, Jengo Pim lay on his bed in the Underlook Hotel, clutching his greasy knife as he imagined the Hells Bellies writhing before him. The hideaway of the Grey Brigade was unusually quiet, most of his boys out on jobs for the night, leaving only twelve or so snoring in nearby rooms. As Pim gnawed on the leg of meat his knife skewered, swilling it down with a chunky Allantian red, there was an unexpected creak from the floor below. The thief frowned, then shrugged – the Underlook was an old building, prone to shifting. He rejoined his fantasy, wiping juice from his mouth with a satisfied sigh, when a second creak – this time the drawn out, pressured creak of foot on floorboard – impelled him to extract his knife and slip off the bed, eyes narrowing suspiciously.

He moved onto the landing and stared down the main staircase. As he did, a candle was snuffed below, then another and another, until all was black. A shape – possibly more than one – flitted through the darkness. Visitors, Pim thought, but no problem – the old hotel didn't take kindly to *unexpected* guests.

Pim tapped gently on bedroom doors, rousing sleepers, and then flipped a lever on the wall. A dull clank and ratchet sound signified that all of the traps on the ground floor were now active, and as his men slipped silently down the stairs with garrots tensing and daggers gleaming, he was confident that caught between a rock and a hard place, whoever had checked into the Underlook this night had no chance.

A series of screams met him from below, and protesting cries as traps were tripped, but a chill went through Pim as he realised the voices in both cases were those of his own men.

He called out – no reply. How could a dozen of the best thieves in the business be taken out so easily? His mind raced, trying to identify who might possess a strong enough grudge against the Grey Brigade to launch such an offensive. It was only at the last moment, after he had slowly taken the stairs himself and swift, shadowed figures came at him, driving him to the floor with a yell, did he realise what this was all about. Her name, as blackness descended, was the last thing that passed his lips.

"Hooper!"

As PIM'S ROAR echoed through the Underlook, Martha DeZantez knelt by her daughter's graveside in Solnos. There was no body in the grave, but that didn't matter, because it was here that Gabriella was remembered in spirit, next to the grave of the man she had loved, and it had become a place of peace and remembrance. She would find no peace today, however, as for a second her heart seized as she heard Gabriella's voice, as clear as day, warning her against something, and then shadows loomed suddenly over her. A second later all that remained of her presence was a flower with a broken petal lying on the ground.

In FAYENCE, ABRA Sarkesian had just wheeled his Abra-Kebab-Bar into its lock-up for the night, woeing the takings of the day, when a shadow at the rear of the storage area caught his eye. The lock-up had provided an emergency bolt-hole for Kali Hooper on more than one occasion, he dropping awnings to hide its existence the moment she rode into it, and his heart lifted to see she had sought his shelter once more. But the face that emerged from the shadows was not Kali's – not even close.

So IT WENT. Peninsula wide from Oweilau to Malmkrug to Turnitia, Vosburg to Freiport to Volonne, anyone with recent contact with Kali Hooper, however minor, simply disappeared. But not everything went according to plan. At that moment in Gargas...

* * *

A GLOVED HAND prevented the bell on the door of *Wonders of The World* from tinkling as it opened. Yan DeFrys motioned his heavily armed men into the shop in silence. He'd been told his target was a strange one, rumoured to possess a faculty for bodily transformation, and had decided his best tactic for capture would be to simply overwhelm him. He'd hoped to have all of his men inside before he was alerted but it seemed that was not to be. Though the shop had appeared empty through its windows, the old man was suddenly there, appearing as if by magic.

Yan DeFrys sneered. With a shock of white hair and beard, and what looked like a pink horse blanket over his shoulders, the old man shuffled about the shop waving a feather duster over piles of stock. *This* was his target?

"I'm closed," Merrit Moon said.

"Then you should lock your door, Mister Moon."

"Why? Others respect the sign hanging there. You see what it says, hmm? 'Go Away' is what it says, and I'd be obliged if you did so."

"We're not here to shop, old man."

"No? Some pongbegon for you, I think. Wooh-hoo, yes. And you, sir – in you I sense a man with a frustrated wife. Knickerknocker Glory's what you need. Direct from the Sardenne and very good for the old early *oooh*, if you know what I mean."

The mercenary to whom Moon had spoken moved forward, but DeFrys held him back.

"We have no interest in your trinkets, trivia or fetishes, old man. We're here for you."

Moon continued to shuffle about, apparently not listening. It was odd but for a second DeFrys got the impression he seemed to blur between locations rather than physically move. DeFrys nodded to two of his men, who moved to apprehend him. Moon looked up as they began to weave their way through piles of stock, and manoeuvred himself behind others when they drew close. This happened twice more and the mercenaries cursed in exasperation finding direct pursuit impossible. The stock had been arranged in such a way that it formed a miniature maze seemingly designed to frustrate their every attempt to reach their quarry.

"That's right, that's right," Moon said. "Have a good look around."

"I already told you, old man," DeFrys barked. "We have no interest in your goods."

"Today's special is a boozelhorn made by the Yassan of the Drakengrats. It's said if you blow a boozelhorn your enemies comprehensively fill their trousers. Would you like a demonstration?"

DeFrys growled; game over. He bashed away a pile of stock, hurling pots and jars to the floor. Some clattered through an open trapdoor which Moon moved towards.

"I expect there'll be quite a mess," he said. "Now where did I put that shovel?"

"Stay where you are, old man!" DeFrys ordered as Moon began to descend. His men crashed after him, reaching the opening just as the old man's head vanished below. It was odd but just for a second he thought he saw the old man disappear *before* he disappeared – that was, before passing out of view beneath the floorboards. It had to have been a trick of the light. It was difficult to tell with his men crowding around.

"What are you waiting for?" he shouted. "Follow him!"

DeFrys expected to hear the sounds of a scuffle before the old man was dragged back to the ground floor. But there was only a puzzled cry from one of his men.

"Sir, he's gone, sir!"

"What?"

"The old man, he just seemed to disapp... no, no, wait, he's here. I think."

"Make up your mind, man!"

"I could have sworn..."

DeFrys bit his lip. This whole thing was damned peculiar.

"Don't let him out of your sight," he said. "I'm coming down."

DeFrys descended the ladder. Half way down he paused, running his hand over a light tube that illuminated the lower level – the kind of light tube, Old Race technology, that he had only ever seen in archaeological sites or the sublevels of Scholten Cathedral. What were they doing in a primitive market town in Pontaine?

What, for that matter, were all the other objects down here?

The old man stood on the other side of the cellar, smiling. In the artificial light he looked somehow strange, almost flat and two dimensional.

"An impressive collection, isn't it?" he said. "Reserve stock which I normally only make available to special customers. Those I trust to use it properly." His expression darkened. "Some of it I don't make available at all."

DeFrys looked to where the old man was pointing. Beside him was another small chamber beyond the cellar, one that appeared to normally be hidden behind a display cabinet that was, for the time being, swung open on concealed hinges. His eyebrows rose at what he saw in there – even if he didn't necessarily know what it was he was seeing.

"Do you realise how many years it has taken me to collect these items?" Merrit Moon said. "How many sites I have risked my life to explore to bring them here, to safety?"

"Proscribed technology," DeFrys said.

"What has come to be known as proscribed technology," Moon said. A needless repetition that brought a momentary frown to DeFrys' face. "Proscribed by a Church which has neither the wit or wisdom to use it properly." He turned towards the chamber, staring wistfully at each object in turn. "Here there are devices that can change the nature of a man or his surroundings. Devices which can control the weather, bringing rain or sunshine depending on which is your desire. Devices which can turn the tide of a war..."

DeFrys stepped off the bottom rung of the ladder and took a step towards the old man.

"Why are you telling us these things, old man?"

"I once told a protégé of mine – perhaps you've heard of her – Kali Hooper?" Moon went on. Again it struck DeFrys as a non-sequitur, "that she had to take great care in what she released into the world. I have to tell you the same now."

"These objects will be confiscated, old man," DeFrys said. "Examined by experts within our ranks..."

"I doubt, however," Merrit Moon continued, "that you will pay much notice to what I say."

"What?"

"I couldn't take them with me, you see. Had to leave them behind. But I cannot let them fall into your hands. Simply cannot. It would not be right."

"What?" DeFrys said again.

He stared hard at the old man, his face questioning, but Moon simply stared impassively back. A sudden tug of fear gripped the mercenary, for now that the old man was so close the sense of unreality about him that had been so nagging seemed more pronounced. He took a step forward so he was standing nose to nose with the man he was to arrest. His target had no body heat, no body odour, no substance at all.

"For that, I am genuinely sorry," Merrit Moon said.

DeFrys swallowed and put out his hand. It passed right through Merrit Moon.

"Genuinely sorry..." Merrit Moon repeated.

Suddenly everything made sense to DeFrys. Moon's seeming to blur as he moved. His momentary disappearance at the trapdoor. But most of all his inability to answer a direct question. The old man wasn't being obstructive or evasive – he simply wasn't answering questions because he hadn't heard them!

These last few minutes this... projection had been delivering a pre-recorded lecture.

And class had just been dismissed.

"It's a trap, get out, get out!" he shouted to his men, but too late.

As the walls around DeFrys began to throb and glow with strange green veins, he found himself scrabbling for the rungs of the ladder alongside his men. Forcing them off it, in fact.

His breach in officerial responsibility was academic, for his men would never report him. The cellar of *Wonders of the World* exploded with a force no human bomb could have achieved, and a second later the rest of the shop – ground and upper floors –

followed suit. DeFrys was running for his life from the building when it was wiped from the map, and the concussion hit him like a giant sledgehammer in the back. He was thrown forward to land crookedly and heavily on his front, the impact forcing out an explosive grunt.

As Gargassians began to run towards the site, pointing and gasping, it took a few seconds for the mercenary to cease moving forward, his twisted body ploughing a furrow in the ground where he'd landed, his jaw carving a rut.

HUNDREDS OF LEAGUES away, Merrit Moon was eating a sandwich when he felt his old life vanish forever, the event transmitted to him by the elven sensory sphere he had left behind with the holographers in the shop. The One Faith, the Only Faith, the Fewer Faith, he thought philosophically. And continued to chew.

The knowledge that he no longer had a home did not come as the wrench he thought it might, surprisingly. The old place had never been the same since being all but demolished by the k'nid, and even as he had been packing the cracks they had left with the elven compound he had named detonite, in readiness for the Faith forces he knew would inevitably come for him, he hadn't felt particularly sad. There were some things the k'nid attack had destroyed that could never be replaced – his elven telescope, ironically the first thing that had seen them coming, among them – and he was far too old to seek out and gather such treasures again. To surround himself with such seemed folly in these changing times, in fact.

There was, of course, also his health. He wasn't ailing – in fact, for a man of his age he was in quite superior shape – but that was wholly due to the ogur corruption that continued to taint his body. The solutions and elixirs he had perfected to keep his transformative affliction in check continued to do their job, and while he still possessed the thread-engineered antidote that Kali had brought from the Crucible, he resolutely refused to use it. It wasn't that he didn't trust it – because of its provenance its efficacy was beyond question – but that, as he'd told Kali that night in the *Flagons*, to use it just didn't feel *right*. If he were honest, he had never been able to shake a conviction that what had happened to him had happened for a reason, and in the light of recent developments he was becoming more convinced still.

He had not told Kali this but the fact was, since the Hel'ss appeared, he was changing more than he had been. Not changing more frequently – although the bouts did seem to have their own accelerating timetable – but more dramatically. He sighed and raised a trembling hand, watching as the sinew and tendons beneath his skin pulsed and throbbed. These painful phenomena were not just linked to his hands, either, the same effect manifested itself at different times throughout his body, and he could not stare at himself in a mirror for more than a few minutes before one such tic or another materialised. All of these felt different to the Thrutt transformations – for one thing they occurred spontaneously, without the raised adrenalin that normally acted as a trigger – and the only conclusion he could draw was that his body was responding in some way to the presence of the Hel'ss. The question was, why?

This, he had no answer to – yet. What he did know was that these occasions were something to which he could not risk exposing his friends. The feeling of unfettered power that accompanied them both terrified and awed him, and if it were to be unleashed, beyond his control, when anyone was nearby... he didn't like to think what would happen.

So, in the end, he'd decided to leave. What choice did he have? The interesting thing was that it hadn't been at all difficult to choose where to go. And for one simple reason.

He could not stop dreaming of the World's Ridge Mountains.

They were calling to him.

And he had answered – or at least relocated to their vicinity in the hope he would there find out what the dreams meant. The lower to middle heights of the World's Ridge still hid Old Race sites he had been too inexperienced to challenge as a young man, and too incapable of challenging when old, but now he had, if needed, the physical means to survive, what better time to explore them? He had not, after all, lost his interest in *learning* of the past, far from it – the ever growing presence of the Hel'ss in the skies was surely an indication that the fate of the Old Races was more relevant than ever.

Moon picked himself up, biting into an apple to finish the lunch he'd eaten, and strolled to the mouth of the cave he was using as a bivouac. It actually wasn't so much a cave as a recess halfway up the side of a sheer and precipitous wall of a much, much larger cavern, and what Moon's dwarfed figure saw as he looked out made him crunch deeply and appreciatively on his fruit. The bite and subsequent self-satisfied sigh seemed unnaturally loud in the vast expanse. Every archaeologist on Twilight – what few true ones there were – dreamed of the ultimate find, but most had to content themselves with second best. But not he. Not any more. The sense of wonder and magnificence he had felt when he had first set eyes upon this site was not misplaced, and he once more revelled in the name he had given it.

The Gallery.

Most caverns had galleries somewhere within them, of course, but few in an artistic sense, and none on the scale of what he'd found here.

As soon as Moon stepped into the bosun's cradle he had strung beneath his makeshift living area, he came face to face with a small section of ancient cave painting, covering the entirety of the vast wall in which his bivouac was set. So close to, it was impossible to discern what the painting depicted and, even from the other side of the cavern, it was difficult, the primitive art obscured by growths of vines, creepers and other vegetation. Moon had spent the last few weeks negotiating the wall in the cradle, laboriously clearing the growths away, but had even now completed only perhaps a quarter of the work needed to fully reveal the painting. Further clearance was not on his agenda today, however, and had not been for the past two days, ever since he had discovered what appeared to be the entrance to a chamber hidden *within* the complexity of the painting itself.

It was all really rather exciting, and Moon hummed to himself as he used the complex system of rope pulleys and fulcrums it had taken him a week to assemble to pull himself along the wall.

Stone projections at certain points required that he moved down and then across again, and then down, up and across once more, but the old man was patient, in no hurry to get where he wanted to go. The cradle at last ended up suspended before a small ledge.

Moon stepped from the cradle onto the ledge to face a cryptoblock. What lay before him was not quite so daunting as it seemed, however, he having worked on it full-time since its discovery. Though cryptoblocks had become something of Kali's speciality, he'd retired the previous evening having only one last element to arrange, and though its proper positioning had confounded him through the night, the solution had at last popped into his head over lunch.

It was all very simple, really.

Moon pushed a block of the puzzle inwards and then immediately pulled it out again. A second later the ratchet that had been triggered by the pressure sprang into place. The cryptoblock collapsed before him.

"Well, well, old man," Moon whispered to himself, "I guess you haven't lost it, after all."

He took a breath and stepped into the unsealed chamber. He cracked an elven lightstick that he took from a satchel and moved it slowly about. A flare of light bounced back from something reflective in the centre of the room.

Just one object in the whole of the chamber.

My, my. That *had* to be important.

The old man cracked more lightsticks and scattered them about the floor of the chamber. He found himself staring at an object perched on a podium that appeared to be some kind of metal dodecahedron. It was difficult to tell because its material was so polished that it shone like a tiny sun.

Moon circled it slowly, his hands almost but not quite touching, as if the object were his partner in a slow waltz. Then he dropped to his haunches, licked his lips, examining it only with his eyes.

"What have we here?"

Tentatively, he reached out a hand, intending no more than the gentlest caress of the object's side, but a sudden spasm – the kind of spasm he was by now all too familiar with – made his arm jerk violently, and instead of caressing the object his hand knocked it fully from the podium to bounce across the opposite side of the chamber.

Not *now*, Merrit Moon demanded of himself.

But it was too late.

There was a grinding noise from the surrounding walls.

Protective failsafes. Preventative measures. Proof that the mysterious object was as important as he'd suspected it to be.

Or, to put it another way, a trap. And very likely a deadly one.

Moon wasted no time. Despite the pain and the throbbing in his arms and legs, not to mention the agonised flaring at the back of his head that made him feel as though someone was scooping out his brainstem with a spoon, he loped around the edge of the podium and grabbed the object, jamming it into his satchel. Then he turned towards the entrance, noting that a thick stone slab was already descending where the cryptoblock had been. His days of rolling beneath such things were beyond him and he knew he didn't have much time, and so the last thing he needed as he made a dash for the shrinking exit was for another spasm to hit him, this time harder than ever before.

He belly-flopped onto the floor, lay there gasping and groaning. The same hand that had triggered the podium's weight sensors stretched out quaveringly towards the closing gap but the slab was already two thirds of the way down. He knew there was no way he could make it.

Too slow. Too old. Despite thinking that his... *condition* could help him be young again.

Merrit Moon's head slumped to the floor of the chamber, and he sighed. But despite the fact that he was clearly doomed to die, he smiled to himself. Perhaps better this way – doing what he loved – than facing the unknown future that his physical instability offered him. It was, he reflected, the way Kali would have preferred him to die.

Kali. He swore he could almost hear her now. Though, admittedly, sounding less articulate than imagined.

"Gahh! Uuung. Get in there, you farking... "

He looked up and saw the silhouette of a figure outlined in

what remained of the exit. A figure which rammed something into the dwindling space between slab and floor. The length of wood, if that's what it was, was already splintering and cracking beneath the weight of the stone.

"Kali?" Moon queried.

"That's me," the figure said. A head appeared in the gap. "Look, old man, I'm sorry to be a pain and I know this is all a bit last minute but I need someone to look after my bamfcat."

"What?"

"Well, y'know, putting him in kennels is just *so* expensive..."

"What? What are you talking ab –"

He broke off, just as something else did the same. "Look out!"

"Shit!" Kali yelled, seeing the wooden support give way. She at least proved herself capable of rolling out of danger, even if it was in the wrong direction. As she bumped into Moon, the stone slab slammed shut behind her.

Kali stared at the old man, saw how the entire surface of his body seemed to be... rippling.

"Hi," Kali said breathlessly. And then, "Old man... are you all right?"

Moon felt his spasms start to subside, struggled into a sitting position and dusted himself down.

"Am I all right? Do you realise what you have just done?"

Kali gave a cursory glance around. "So we're trapped. Not the first time for either of us, right? And for once we have two minds to figure a way out."

The walls surrounding them rumbled again. And with an expulsion of dust juddered an inch closer to them.

"Quickly?" Kali added, with a sheepish grin.

"Oh, there's no rush," the old man said wearily, all too aware that their predicament was his fault. "You're inside a Bevvel's Conundrum."

"I am?"

"Otherwise known as Bevvel's Chamber of Unending Torment. Think yourself lucky you've never come across one. In the time it takes to contract – about a week, I believe – they say that in your mind you die a thousand times. Each time imagining the final, slow constriction of the walls, the pressure as your internal organs are squeezed, and the cracking and splintering of your bones as they're crushed beyond recog –"

"Do you *mind*? Fark me, have you always been this blunt or is it an age thing?"

"There is no need for foul language, young lady."

"Well, I'm sorry, old man but... don't you think we'd be better employed trying to determine a way out?"

"There is none, believe me. Bevvel's construction is based on cryptoblock dimensional dynamics."

"No trap is foolproof, old man."

"You are welcome to try to prove that."

Kali did. During the time it took her to exhaust possibilities, the trap contracted once more.

"Shit," she said softly. "Shit, shit, shit."

"I told you..."

"I had to try."

"... about the language."

Kali glared, and slumped in a corner, hitting the stone petulantly as it rudely juddered forward once more. Then it occurred to her.

"Hang on," she said. "Wasn't that a bit... quick?"

Moon's eyes widened and he stuck his ear to the floor. "There is something wrong," he said. "The gears sound misaligned."

"Cryptoblock dimensional dynamics have *gears*?"

"It's... complicated. It took me a lifetime to work out how much so."

"Well, I'm not going to have a lifetime to catch up unless we do something."

At Kali's feet the elven lightstick that Moon had activated fizzled out. In the resultant darkness there was another crunch of gears.

"Don't suppose you have any more of those?" Kali asked.

Moon held up one more, lit it and laid it at their feet.

"Dark soon, then."

"Quite so."

The two of them sat there in silence for a while – or at least silence punctuated by the juddering of stone. Kali reckoned she'd got about two hundred and forty seventh into imagining her thousand deaths when it proved too much. She started to hum.

"What are you *doing* here, Kali," Moon asked.

"I came to say goodbye. Found your note at the shop. Just before they came and... you know."

"Goodbye?" Merrit Moon repeated, ignoring the reference to the fate of his shop. "Kali, I wouldn't have stayed out here without seeing you once more. I would have found a way."

Kali shook her head. "I'm not talking about you, old man. I'm talking about me."

Moon hesitated. "You're imagining you're going somewhere you might not come back from? That isn't like you."

"No. Yes. I don't know. I... just have a feeling about this one."

The old man placed his hand on hers. "Where?"

"The Island of the Lost."

"Trass Kathra?"

"Trass Kathra," Kali repeated. "It exists."

Moon turned away. His mind raced, weaving and reweaving a thousand separate strands of knowledge he had accumulated over the years with an equal number of theories. He shared none of them with Kali because she was involved in every permutation and every permutation ended the same way – he would lose her from his life in the same mysterious fashion she had arrived. It had been so convenient to forget this child had been found as a newborn in some kind of Old Race 'pod' that hadn't been seen since. He had pretended to himself that she had been normal but, of course, she wasn't – with such an origin how could she be? – and, now, maybe, if Trass Kathra was involved, was the time her past came home to roost. The fact was, all the old legends associated Trass Kathra with the End Time, so maybe Kali had found her ultimate destination at last.

One thing seemed undeniable. If that was the case, he had to be certain she got there. And to do that, he had to get her out of the deathtrap that his own curse had stuck her in.

Moon broke suddenly from his introspection, and began to slam his fist on the stone floor of the chamber, making Kali start at the unexpected violence of it. As he continued and the skin of his fists split, leaking blood, she tried to stop him, but he shrugged her off, intent on achieving what could be their only salvation.

"What the hells are you doing?" Kali asked.

"Leaving," the old man said, simply.

His blows became more powerful because he became more powerful, his head snapping back and the irises of his eyes changing as he purposefully unleashed his inner ogur – and what he had found lay *beyond* the inner ogur. Sitting in the corner of the shrinking chamber, Kali swallowed, because although she had witnessed his transformation into Thrutt a number of times, what was happening now went far beyond anything she had ever seen.

Every muscle in the old man's body was expanding, he himself becoming taller, broader, bigger, and with the extra strength this granted him he was able to shatter the stone of the floor and expose the gears beneath. These, too, he pounded, though not mindlessly, and suddenly the contractions of the Bevvel's Conundrum became more pronounced and more frequent, reducing the area of their confinement by half in a matter of seconds.

"Old man...?" Kali said.

The chamber jerked inward once more, and Merrit Moon stood.

"Get beneath me," he said. There was a timbre in his voice deeper than any previously heard. Kali looked at him, saw his expression, and obeyed, huddling in the old man's shadow, though the truth was he appeared hardly old, in fact hardly a man, any more.

The chamber shuddered again, and Kali felt the cold touch of stone nudging at her heels.

It was at that moment that the light went out. The old man's explosion of anger had subsided but, instead, she heard a low growl. An inhuman and even un ogur-like growl. The growl of something *incredibly* powerful. And then the growl turned into a roar and she heard the sound of massive fists punching outward, fists which shattered the stone around them, reducing the walls of the Bevvel's Conundrum to dust.

As the dust settled, she looked up. Something massive and incapable of speech loomed over her. But its message, as it offered her a hand, was clear.

Time to go.

Kali followed the beast like creature to the exit from the cavern, watching its form dwindle as they progressed upward. By the time they reached the surface, Merrit Moon was almost himself again, though Kali couldn't shake the image of the old man's transformation from her mind, far more violent, far more dramatic than it had ever been. She waited until his breathing steadied before asking the question that had to be asked.

"Merrit, what happened to you down there?"

Moon raised his eyes to meet hers. "I'm sorry if I frightened you."

Kali smiled, touched the old man's arm with its enlarged cartilage, tendons and muscle that even now throbbed and pulsed beneath the skin.

"You could never frighten me, old man. I'm just concerned. I don't understand what's going on..."

"Then that makes two of us."

"It's unlike you not to have some kind of theory."

"Oh, I have a theory, all right. But you're not going to like it."

"*Tell me.*"

"I'm staring to believe..." Merrit began, then paused.

"What, old man?"

"I'm starting to believe that I was never meant to leave the World's Ridge Mountains. I mean after what happened, after I died. That it happened, how and where it did, for a reason."

"The ogur cave?"

"The ogur cave," Moon repeated. "I think it's.... calling to me."

"What?"

"Don't ask me to explain it – I can't. But I think there was far more to my transformation than corruption by the soul scythe. A purpose."

"Some kind of destiny? Gods, old man, you know how I feel about destinies."

Moon sighed.

"We may not be talking about destinies, young lady, but a single destiny. That somehow you, me, Slowhand, Aldrededor and Dolorosa, *everyone*... we're all caught up in something beyond our control. Something that, in different ways and perhaps with different participants, has happened before."

"There's a hole blown in your theory, right there," Kali said. "Slowhand's gone, right?" Her voice changed in a way Moon couldn't quite fathom. "Doing his own thing."

Moon sighed again, more heavily.

"I wouldn't be too sure of that."

Kali span on the spot, trying to take in a hundred different possibilities at once. But the only thing that made sense saddened her deeply. It was that there was something she had to do, and there was something Merrit had to do, and that their paths were going to take them to opposite ends of their known world, perhaps never to return.

"Merrit," she said, "is this goodbye?"

"I don't know."

Kali pulled in a breath, huffed. The sun was rising over the peaks of the World's Ridge, far above. "Well, I know one thing," she said perhaps a little too quickly, moving towards Horse, "and that's if you're going, you're taking Horse with you. If anyone can look after you, he can."

"Kali, I don't even know what my ultimate destination will be."

"Then," Kali said, stroking Horse's snout and refusing to turn around and face the old man, "when you no longer need him, let him go. It may not be the Drakengrats but it is the mountains, and he'll feel at home there." She stroked the bamfcat's snout again. "One thing's for certain – he can't come with me."

Moon didn't move for a second but simply stared at Kali's back, understanding that she didn't want to prolong this any more than he did. The bamfcat snorted softly, plaintively, and it was clear that he, too, knew what was going on.

The old man rose, kicked out the remains of the campfire, and slung his bags across Horse's back. But he kept one small bag back, handing it to Kali.

"A few toys I salvaged from the shop's cellar that might help to keep you safe," he said. "Also something I found in that trap. And my notebook, incomplete but –" Moon shrugged.

Kali nodded, took the saddlebag. Again, she did not look at Moon as the old man heaved himself up into the saddle, seemingly trying to close off the world. She did, however, start involuntarily as the bamfcat began to move off.

"Old man," she said after a second, staring after him. The physically altered Moon looked so *natural* on Horse's back, and Horse beneath him, as if somehow they had always belonged together. "Take care of yourself."

Moon smiled and then aimed his gaze at the rising slopes ahead.

"You, too, my daughter. You, too."

But what he thought was, *Please let there be someone out there, so you don't have to go through this alone.*

CHAPTER FIVE

THE ROAR OF the crowd, the smell of greasepaint and everything covered in shit. All the fun of the fair. While the towering, brightly-lit wine-glass that was Miramas's famous Theatre of Heaven dominated the stormy horizon, the Big Top drooping in a sodden field a couple of leagues outside the city was another class of venue entirely. Rain hammered down here as it had for hours, battering the already unstable looking canvas and threatening a blow-down, while the muddy footprints of those who had risked life and limb by venturing inside the tent for the night's performance splashed and popped incessantly, flooded to overfilling.

Among the sideshow stalls, freak cages and calliope music machines of the abandoned midway, pigrats – the usual inhabitants of the field – snuffled up half-eaten mool kebabs and sugarfloss, which they chewed greedily before adding to the mire. Attending to their toilet, they had no interest in the occasional cheers from inside the tent but looked up briefly when, from the other side of a candle-lit stretch of canvas, came the sharp snap of a thong followed by a pained hiss and a word that sounded like "*nyyyyyynnnhg.*" A moment later they scattered, farting and honking, as a shadowy mass stumbled into the canvas, making it bulge out like an oversized balloon animal gone wrong.

The strange shape emitted a rumbling burp and attempted to right itself, stumbling again not once but twice. The pigrats were not to know it but the player in this unusual piece of shadow theatre went by the name of Killiam Slowhand.

And Killiam Slowhand was shit-faced.

The archer was taking another slug from his bottle of twattle when it was snatched from his hand, pouring beer down his bare torso and washing away the glitter he had half-heartedly rubbed on only minutes before. He blinked, and then the sound of the bottle being slammed onto his dressing table made him start.

"Started early again, I see?" Shay Redwood said. The petite, dark-haired Oweilaun woman kept her voice low but it was no less cutting for it. "Or is it that you just haven't stopped?"

The archer regarded his interrogator with half-focused eyes, wobbling backward slightly. Hands planted firmly on her hips, Shay stared solidly back up at him, though her expression was not so much accusing as concerned.

"The second one," Slowhand burped after a second. In all their time together he still hadn't worked out why he couldn't help but be honest with the woman. "The 'not having stopped' bit, I guess."

"Fark, Slowhand. You know this can't go on."

"Can't see any reason why not."

"No?" Shay said. She plucked the archer's quiver from the dressing table and extracted one of the arrows. She used the tip of one to prick the soft flesh of her thumb, which took no pressure at all. "These things aren't toys."

Something flared in Slowhand's head, an old memory, but he kept control of it. "I know that," he said steadily.

"I'm no toy, either," Shay responded, unphased. "Slowhand, it's me out there, in front of your arrows, and the only thing that stops me dying at the hands of a drunk is that what you do comes naturally to you, like breathing. You're just too good an archer to ever miss."

"So what's the problem?"

"*You.* You're the problem, can't you see that? Look at you! You're stagnating here. You jump through the same old hoops every day, not because you enjoy it but because it stops you thinking of anything else."

"The only thing I'm thinking of is paying my keep."

"Yeah? That's not what I hear when you talk in your sleep. Talk of traps and treasure, of long lost secrets. And night after night, without fail... Kali Hooper."

Slowhand hesitated. "Sorry. It... she... doesn't mean anything. It was a long time ago."

"It was a *year* ago, Liam. Only a year. And I think you have unfinished business."

"Shay, I promise you, I'm not –"

Shay placed a hand on his cheek. "I know you're not, lover. But clearly you were involved in *something* back then that just isn't letting you go. Think about it, eh? Maybe it's time for you – for both of us, if you'd like the company – to find out what."

"I'd have no idea where to go."

"Maybe you'll know when you get there." She cocked an ear as there was an announcement from the ring. "But for now, Mister Thongar, what say we get this show on the road?"

She went on before him, disappearing through the vorgang with a smile and a flourish that was greeted with rapturous applause. A few moments later, the chanting began. And then the drums. And then the screaming.

The screaming was his cue and – glancing at the bottle but forsaking it – Slowhand pulled in his stomach, put on his best heroic grin and followed his partner into the ring.

There, Shay was already in the grip of the orcs. They weren't real orcs, of course, but Griffin, Mosk, Thane and the rest of the crew in moth-eaten and less than convincing orc costumes, but that didn't matter as neither he nor, he was willing to bet, anyone in the audience had ever encountered a real orc in their lives. It was a matter of debate whether the creatures existed on Twilight at all.

The whole act was the grand finale to the show and presented as a set piece in which he, Thongar, had to rescue Shay from a sacrificial ritual orc-estrated, as it were, by the supposed beasts of the mountains. To his surprise, it had become a runaway success. Maybe with that thing – the Hel'ss – hanging in the sky people, despite what the Filth told them, needed to believe they could still cope with the unknown and, in however small a way, he was satisfying that need. Despite the scenario's pure fiction, it had, ironically, been only a few performances in when he'd realised he'd gladly sacrifice himself in order to rescue Shay for real. Ever since they'd met in that tavern in Scholten – she persuading him to run away to the circus, just for fun and just like kids, that very night – the pair had grown closer and closer, their relationship blossoming until he had begun to think of them as soulmates. He would have been more than happy to forget that he had even *had* a previous life, if it hadn't been for the dreams.

The dreams.

As he'd had to night after night for months, Slowhand quashed the lingering images of the dreams by throwing himself into his act with gusto. As the crowd cheered him on, he leapt from papier-mâché rock to papier-mâché rock, despatching the monsters who threatened Shay with a dazzling display of bowmanship. As Shay struggled against the bonds on the sacrificial frame built on the highest rock, his arrows thudded into the orcs from all directions, and Griffin and the others made their pratfalls on cue, roaring as they clutched the shafts embedded in the thick padding of their costumes, tumbling to their deaths. That they, as much as Shay, trusted him to deliver his arrows with unwavering accuracy said a lot about the bond he had developed with them all and, as usual as the climax of the act approached, Slowhand was concentrating so much as to not let them down that he had forgotten his dreams completely.

The last of the marauding orcs fell and the climax of the performance arrived. It was the most difficult shot of the evening, one that required him to be static, and he struck a suitably heroic but steadied pose on a rock halfway up the fake mountainside.

In his sights was an orc shaman dancing directly behind Shay, and the arrow he was about to fire was firstly to sever the chain holding Shay's arms aloft, and then continue to strike the taller shaman in the chest, punching him off the rocks and 'killing' him triumphantly.

Slowhand tensed. Despite the gap of only inches between Shay, chain and shaman, it wasn't the aiming of the arrow that presented problems but the power with which it was delivered. Too little and the chain would not shatter; too much and it would puncture the padding of Thane, his friend. Slowhand's grip on his bowstring tightened. His eyes narrowed. On the summit of the fake mountainside, Shay winked and smiled.

Her eyes were filled with the same absolute trust when they jerked wide in shock, and then almost instantly glazed over. As Shay slumped on her chains, she did not react at all to the pulse of dark blood that ran down from the centre of her forehead and over the bridge of her nose to drip onto the papier mache rock.

A rumble of unease ran through the audience, and then came deafening silence. All eyes stared at the projectile embedded firmly in the centre of Shay's forehead, registering part disbelief and part expectation, benumbed by the fact that the shot had been so perfect, so unwavering, so exact, that it couldn't be a mistake. In other words, it had to be part of the act, and the great Thongar had amazed them again, if only they could work out how.

Slowhand himself simply stood there, Suresight hanging at his legs. The sights and sounds of the ring – that place of smoke and mirrors, of unreality – seemed suddenly painfully loud and vivid. He saw crew and fellow performers move to him from backstage and through the crowd, their movements slowed as if in a dream, cries of shock coming as drawn out drawls. Bent Dez Fagin, Little Jack The Giant, Five Ropes Lucy, none of them could believe what had happened.

Slowhand didn't know what to think. All he knew was that Shay had trusted him, and had died at his hand. He raised that same appendage, his arrow hand, palm up, before his eyes, and stared at its shaking form as if it were nothing to do with him at all. It took him a second to realise that in his other hand, hanging as limply as Suresight, the arrow remained.

Did it matter? Shay wasn't to know that, was she? She would have had no time to realise that the projectile that had instantly snuffed her life and thoughts had not been unleashed by him, for there was no reason why she would think there should be another. In one stunned moment his love would have gone to her grave believing, however infinitesimally fleetingly, that he'd failed her and the drink within him had let them both down.

But it hadn't. *He* hadn't. The arrow was still in his hand.

Slowly, with a rush of pressure in the ears, the world about him returned to normal. The first thing he heard were the screams from the audience – screaming not because of what had just happened but because they, like his friends, were being manhandled out of their seats and propelled towards the exits. The people doing the manhandling were strangers, but there were a lot of them, and all dressed in black. It wasn't difficult to guess who they were but, if further proof were needed, the black spheres that moved through the air between them provided it.

Filth, Slowhand thought. Then, feeling the slightest disturbance in the air, he instinctively span as a projectile identical to the one that had killed Shay – a crossbow bolt, not an arrow – sheared by him to thud into the fake rock on which Shay slumped. His archer's expertise immediately calculated the arrow had not been fired to take him out, too, but only to incapacitate by hitting him in his drawing arm.

Slowhand's eyes narrowed as he stared at a figure clad in black standing on the opposite side of the circus ring to him. Unlike the others – males – the black she wore hugged a lithe and supple figure with flowing red hair, and her crossbow was raised and primed once more, and she smiled as she fired.

The smile faded as Slowhand instantly brought up Suresight, re-notching his arrow as he did, and released it without a moment's hesitation or calculation. It split its opposite number in two as it came.

As the broken halves of the bolt and Slowhand's arrow dropped to the sawdust of the ring, Suresight was already primed to fire again. But across the ring his attacker had jettisoned her crossbow in favour of twin swords that she drew from sheathes on her back, and even as Slowhand's arrow sped through the air towards her, the swords moved, reducing the arrow to slivers.

A trick reciprocated, the smile returned.

"Who are you?" Slowhand hissed.

"Someone employed to do a job. A *real* job, that is, not this posturing and preening that passes for your excuse of a life."

That sounded *personal*, Slowhand thought, but now was not the time to explore why. "What kind of job?"

"Shepherding. If you weren't so out of the loop, you'd know that most of your heretic friends are now guests of the Final Faith. You took a while to track down. I volunteered for the job."

"Is that so? So what happens now?"

"I deliver you. I get paid."

"Confident. But you just killed my girlfriend, so I think I'll have to spoil your plans."

"I don't think so."

"You really don't have a lot of choice."

The girl nodded and, out of the corners of his eyes, Slowhand was aware of Faith moving down the aisles between the now empty seats, closing on the circus ring. A second later, he was surrounded by a solid wall of crossbow wielding robes. The message to him was clear – you're outnumbered, archer. You might take down some of us but you'll never stop us all.

No? Slowhand thought. And in that instant heard Shay's voice in his head.

It comes naturally to you. Like breathing.

Maybe Slowhand didn't need telling, but he might have needed reminding, and he moved in a blur, plucking arrow after arrow from his quiver and unleashing them before his newly found circle of friends had chance to react. Six of them went down with arrows embedded in their throats or through their hearts, three more with tips positioned as exactly as had been the bolt that had killed Shay. Slowhand moved as he fired, allowing none of the figures to draw a bead on him while at the same time circling the ring so that the girl and her swords could not draw close. Despite this, his accuracy was undiminished, and the eyes of those who were not felled by arrows widened as much in shock as those who were.

But Slowhand was not quite as invincible as he appeared. Though his archery prowess was indeed undiminished, the physical effort it took to maintain was already starting to take its toll, and Slowhand found himself uncharacteristically breathless. There wasn't really the problem, though, because while he could nevertheless maintain the pace needed to eventually finish off every single one of his attackers, he carried a quiver stocked not for battle but entertainment.

In short, he didn't have enough arrows to go around.

Slowhand felt the contents of the quiver as he plucked the next arrow from it, confirming, as he'd calculated, there were only four arrows left. Three of these he used to drop twice as many Filth, each arrow shot with such force that it passed through two men at a time. The last arrow he withheld. The smile returned to the girl's lips and was echoed on the faces of the survivors as they saw the archer's predicament, and as one they began to move in.

Slowhand turned in a slow circle, bowstring creaking, the arrow pointing at each Faith in turn but not released, until it was aiming directly at the girl's heart. Still, he did not release it, holding her gaze as she sensed victory and her smile grew. Then, as she raised her swords, he swung Suresight directly upward and released the tension that had kept the arrow from play.

The arrow shot high above the ring, tearing through canvas and anchoring itself, and Slowhand rose on the whizzline attached to it. He leapt from it into the web of rope rigging that filled the hemisphere, that part of the Big Top where the aerialists performed, and sat like a spider in its nest. His attackers now far beneath him, Slowhand saw there were nine of them left, ten with the girl. She was already angrily despatching her men towards various ladders and poles that accessed the upper tent, but Slowhand was ready for them, clambering swiftly along the ropes to the centre of the hemisphere, where lay the riser ring through which most of the Big Top's rigging was tied off. The band that encircled the king pole – the central support of the whole tent – was a confusing snake's nest of thick and intertwining guy lines but, as everyone mucked in together on the road, he was no stranger to them and knew precisely which to loosen or untie to create the utmost havoc beneath him.

His new friends were about to discover just how dangerous a place a Big Top could be.

Two ropes brought down the gantry from which handlers controlled the trapeze lunge ropes, and another one of the wheels from which hung the cloud swings, the ropes on which support performers swung out over the audience to hold their attention while the next aerialist 'trick' was readied. Both structures first collapsed sideways, dropping to forty five degree angles as their guy lines whizzed through their pullies, then, as they whipped free, both fell to the big top's floor, those Filth who were using them as a means to reach him falling with them, screaming. Slowhand's satisfaction on hearing the crunching impacts of his attackers' bodies was, however, short-lived, as three crossbow bolts thudded into the king pole next to his head, and he immediately dropped down through the rope spiderweb, grabbing onto one of its strands and swinging rapidly, hand-to-hand, down it towards its connecting quarter pole.

The quarter pole – and the seven others that ringed the arena – were the medium supports of the Big Top, positioned where they were to prevent sagging, and each rose to a point where the Big Top's triangular roof flaps were lashed together, separable in case of an emergency. This, Slowhand reckoned, qualified as an emergency and, dangling by one hand, he quickly undid the lashings on one side, then rapidly shimmied, crossbow bolts thudding about him, along the skirt of the tent to the other. He undid the lashings there, too, and the entire section of canvas roofing flopped inwards, dropping down like an exhausted dog's tongue. From the expressions on the faces of the Filth it headed towards, climbing the tower to the high-wire, it was clear they thought it an inconsequential threat, but they had seriously underestimated the weight of such a section of canvassing – wet or not – and were slapped from their positions with another bone-crunching thud and appropriate screams as the flap hit them, almost overbalancing the tower itself.

Slowhand needed to gain height once more, and he flipped himself from the guy rope into the air, grabbing onto the lip of the flap adjacent to the one he had dropped, then heaving himself onto the roof of the Big Top. Dressed as he was, he hissed against the cold and hammering rain, and his bare soles slithered frustratingly on the buoyant canvas as he pounded determinedly up, but eventually he reached the Big Top's cupola, and, through the gap in the roofing, out of which projected the king pole, flipped himself back inside once more.

The last of the Filth – the girl aside – had now managed to reach the spiderweb of guy lines some twenty feet below him and, spotting his return, were aiming crossbows, but Slowhand had already worked out what he needed to do. He dropped from the cupola onto one of the guy ropes that made up the spiderweb, the impact of his landing sending a tremor throughout the lines, and the Filth staggered, one of them involuntarily loosing a bolt he'd primed into the chest of a comrade-in-arms on the line next to him. The skewered Filth fell, clutching the line desperately for a moment before dropping away, and the resultant second tremor gave Slowhand all the time he needed to work his way across the web and boot his unsteady opponents from their perch.

Far below, the girl side-stepped the falling bodies as they exploded beside her, and raised her gaze slowly upwards. Eyes locking with Slowhand's, she smiled and then made her way to the ladders that would eventually bring her to him. Slowhand's jaw tensed, knowing his final opponent was in a different class entirely to the rest, and his eyes darted around the hemisphere, working out the moves he would need to counter those she would doubtless bring. Unarmed, dressed in nothing but his thong, the possibilities seemed limited, but then, almost unwillingly, he remembered a phrase that had many times been used by Kali Hooper.

Make it up as you go along.

Slowhand calculated the girl's route and made his way to one of the surviving lunge gantries, drawing in a trapeze on a guide rope. As he'd guessed, she was already doing the same, stepping onto the horizontal swing, intending to use it to reach him. She didn't get the chance, Slowhand bringing the fight to her by kicking off at the same time she did.

The two of them clashed in the heart of the hemisphere but, neither practiced on the acrobatics tool, did so clumsily, and the wind knocked from the pair of them, they were sent spinning wildly in opposite directions. Slowhand struggled to bring the trapeze under control, the Big Top and, more threateningly, the girl looming in his vision in a series of skewed, disorientating and vertiginous flashes, and then the two of them impacted again with a thud and an explosion of air and spittle. The collision was slower this time, accidental, but that didn't stop the girl taking a swing at him with one of her swords, and Slowhand only just escaped decapitation by dropping from his standing position to grab the trapeze bar with his hands.

He swung away from the girl, knifing his legs to gain momentum to cross the hemisphere, and gained a moment of precarious rest on the edge of the trapeze platform from which his opponent had kicked off. Twisting, he saw that she was doing the same on his, using the time to position herself with her lower legs wrapped about the trapeze ropes, freeing both hands for her swords, and then he was swinging once more, as she was swinging towards him.

Heading inexorably towards her, Slowhand had nothing with which to block the coming blades but the trapeze itself, and with a grunt he flipped himself back into a standing position. As the girl rushed towards him, he violently jerked his body sideways and downwards so that the hand rail of the trapeze rose up to parry the blows. Swords met wood, one deflected harmlessly but the other cleaving the trapeze in two, and the archer immediately grabbed the guy line of its left half, swinging out with it as it broke from the right.

The manoeuvre caught the girl by surprise, and Slowhand already had another one coming as, with a further twist of his body, he swung his now singular support around in a sweeping circle, heading directly back towards her. The girl gasped as Slowhand's feet smashed into her side and her trapeze was again sent spinning, this time so violently that its guy lines wrapped

themselves about each other like plaiting hair. As she struggled
to bring it under control, Slowhand swung in again, wrapping
his legs about her entangled form and twisting an arm so that
she released one of her swords into his grip. The girl roared in
fury and swung at him with her other weapon, but Slowhand
had already released his legs and was swinging away. It was
only after a second that he realised she had nevertheless cut
cleanly through his thong, and he was now completely naked.
Once upon a time he might have reflected that the combination
of nakedness, girl in black leather and lots of ropes would have
held much promise but what had happened since – who was he
kidding? What had happened *today* – quashed any such thoughts.
Make no mistake, this girl might have been hired to capture him
but this was rapidly turning into a battle of life and death.

But here was not the place to fight it. If he was going to take
the girl on on even terms, now that he had one of her swords,
he needed space, and needed it quickly. The girl already freeing
herself from her entrapment, Slowhand swung away, flinging
himself from the trapeze rope onto one of the surviving cloud
swings, and from there shimmying up the rope to the wheel that
suspended it. From there, another couple of leaps took him back
to the section of roofing he had released, and then back onto the
exposed upper surface of the Big Top.

The girl was right behind him, and Slowhand backed up as
she pulled herself up onto the outer canvas. For a second the
two of them stood there bent and gasping in the hammering
rain, weapons poised, and then the girl came at him, yelling like
something possessed. Slowhand did his best to defend himself
under her furious barrage of blows, blocking and feinting, but he
was being constantly forced back and barely managed one thrust
himself, and it didn't take him long to realise that, despite the
weapon, they were not on even terms at all. The girl was good.
Very good.

She swung again, and Slowhand jack-knifed at the waist,
avoiding her blade. The move threw his balance and he fell onto
his back, slithering into one of the valleys of the undulating
canvas, and cold water rushed to pool about him in the depression

he had made. The girl launched herself at him, blade destined for his throat, but a moment before she struck Slowhand raised his legs, caught her, and sent her tumbling over him. He scrabbled around as she scrambled up, and the two of them circled each other, struggling to regain their footing.

"Who are you?" Slowhand gasped.

"You asked me that."

"No. I mean who are you, *really*?"

"I'd have thought you'd have known that. After all, we don't look that different, he and I. And after what you did, I'd have thought his face would have been etched in your mind forever."

"Who?" Slowhand asked, confused, but then her brow, her nose, her mouth started to transform into another face, one that, as she'd said, didn't look that different at all. He was suddenly back on the battlefield outside Andon during the Great War – *the Killing Ground* – lining up his shot to take out the general of the enemy forces as his brothers-in-arms breathed expectantly, desperately about him.

"My gods," he said, "you're John Garrison's daughter."

"John Garrison's daughter," she replied, her face hardening. "And Ben Garrison's *sister*."

The boy, Slowhand thought. He had never told anyone, not Shay, not Hooper, about the boy. The reason why he had laid down Suresight and left the military after the events of that battle. Pits of Kerberos, what the hells had he been doing there, on that worst of days? A *child*, no more than eight years of age. No one had ever quite been able to work it out but later, when casualties had been identified and someone had told him who it was that had died, speculation was that he had been running to help his father in the face of defeat, help him in the way only an eight year old boy would have thought he could.

And he, Slowhand, had killed him. Because the fact was there had *never* been a perfect shot that day. But there had been *a* shot. A shot through the heart of a figure who had looked bigger than he was, clad in the battered helmet and chain of a dead soldier. A shot that had punctured his body and continued on to impact with Garrison's forehead. A shot that, in a spray of arterial blood, had killed the child instantly.

"What's your name?" he asked.

"Beth."

"Beth, I'm sorry. I didn't know."

"You took the shot."

"*I didn't know.*"

"You murdered my family that day. All I had."

"Yeah? Well, you just murdered mine."

Garrison's daughter laughed. "You think that makes us even?"

Slowhand studied her eyes. It was clear the girl had only used the Final Faith's resources to help track him down, and it was equally clear that there was going to be no reasoning with her. As much as he'd like otherwise, there was no way Beth was ever going to understand or accept his remorse, and there was no way that, because of what she'd done to Shay, he was just going to lie down and die. The Killing Ground, it seemed, was never going to let him rest.

"No. But it means one of us has to die here."

"Yes, it does."

Both paused as, through the opening in the canvas from which they had emerged, three Eyes of the Lord appeared, hovering.

"So what about your contract?" Slowhand said, indicating them.

"Fark it."

Beth roared and flung herself at him again, sword cleaving the air. Slowhand blocked and his blade locked with hers, and for a second they strained against each other, but then, with a deft flick from her wrist, the archer found himself disarmed, his weapon flipping away to land, tip down and quivering, piercing the canvas some feet away. He leapt for it but Beth was there before him, throwing herself forward to skid on her stomach along the wet surface, snatching it back into her grip as she went. She stood, possessing both swords once more, and, grinning manically, sliced the air in a complex pattern before her. All Slowhand could do as she came again was retreat, sometimes tumbling, sometimes skidding and sometimes somersaulting, until the two of them had completed a full circuit of the roof of the Big Top.

Momentarily, he found himself teetering on its edge, wondering if he would survive a slide down its outer surface, but the cages and calliopes were far below, and without clothing or padding of any sort – unless, he reflected bitterly, you counted his slight beer gut – it was unlikely he'd emerge unbroken. He finally had to admit to himself that, despite his challenge, he'd been bested, and his best chance of survival was to return from whence he'd come.

Slowhand began to scramble back up the sloping canvas, to the cupola, intending to flip himself back inside the Big Top. He was aware with every step that Beth was right behind him, swords slashing, but while he half expected to feel one or the other or both of them slicing into his flesh, he didn't at all expect to hear the tearing of canvas beneath him. He span, saw that the girl had clearly changed tactics, and the multiple rents in the canvas that she had sliced with her swords were lengthening towards him, their pace exacerbated by his own weight.

A gap appeared beneath him and he plummeted. Desperate grabs at the rigging in the hemisphere failed, and there was nothing between him and the floor of the circus ring far below.

Slowhand hit hard and at an awkward angle, having twisted himself to avoid being impaled on rigging beams, the wreckage of his own making, which projected up on his either side. Landing on these might have been more merciful. He roared as his bad arm snapped under him, emitting cracks as loud as gunfire he heard again and again, reverberating in his other bones. His leg, almost rigid as it impacted, thrust its bone up into his pelvis, creating further waves of agony as the pelvis shattered and the sheared bones of his leg punched out through the flesh of his upper thigh. He felt his ribs snap, puncturing his insides so that he felt as if he'd been flooded with hot soup, and as the shockwaves from the impact travelled up his spine, he felt vertebrae mash together until something sharp and pointed rammed up into the base of his skull, filling him with a dizzying disorientation that made his consciousness swoop in and out of a black pit.

He barely heard his own loud, long groan as his body at last settled into a shattered heap.

From somewhere, however, he retained enough awareness to realise that though the fall hadn't killed him, he had far from escaped death. He forced himself to turn over, tears flowing involuntarily with the effort and pain it brought, and through pulsing waves of shadow stared upwards and saw the wavering shape of Beth descending on a guy rope. She would take a few seconds to reach him and he knew he had to get away. All he could do, however, was roll sideways, the pain causing him, despite himself, to mewl like a baby, and find a hiding place under the crumpled sheets of canvas he had earlier released and which had now fallen completely to the ground. It offered little to no protection – would only prolong the inevitable by a matter of moments – but still he was possessed by the urge to swathe himself in the darkness, like a wounded animal returning to the depths of a cave.

His breath was loud beneath it, but in the darkness he shuffled himself further and further in. But then, when he could move no further, he simply lay there, his heart pounding.

An eternity seemed to pass but he could *sense* his opponent drawing closer. Then, as the canvas tightened about him, he knew Beth was standing right over him, trapping him.

What would it be? Slowhand thought. A swift blade thrust through the cloth. Or would she simply wait there as he suffocated beneath a shroud of his own making?

All Slowhand could see in the darkness was Shay's face. For a second it transformed itself into that of Kali Hooper, but then, as quickly as she had appeared, Hooper was gone and Shay was back again, smiling her unjudgemental, caring smile. He chuckled softly. Too late, it seemed, he'd found where he belonged. With *whom* he belonged. Too damned late for both of them.

Slowhand blinked as the canvas was torn from him and Beth loomed over his broken body. Surrounded by the hovering spheres of the Eyes of the Lord, she seemed like the centre of some dark universe. But then something else appeared in the universe, a hazy, blurred shape that trundled into existence behind her, and he was dimly aware of her turning in shock, gasping a name that he surely misheard. He hadn't imagined that Beth would be afraid of anything, but she was afraid of the owner of that name.

"You are disobeying orders child," a voice said. It was a strange voice, breathless and high. "The Faith want him alive."

"I... I'm sorry, sir," Beth responded. "But this man is a murderer."

"No. He's a soldier. A mindless, regimented drone."

No, Slowhand wanted to respond. *That's not right.* But the sudden sound of a larynx being crushed silenced him. It wasn't his own. He tried to focus, work out what was going on, then saw. Beth was a foot above the ground, legs kicking, hands struggling to free herself of an invisible grip.

"You can't do this," she gasped.

"Why is that?"

"Because we're on the same side!"

"I think not."

Beth Garrison stared imploringly at the hovering Eyes of the Lord.

"But they'll see! At the cathedral, they'll see!"

"I don't think so," the shape said. Slowhand saw the outline of a hand being raised and, simultaneously, the Eyes of the Lord detonated, the resultant shrapnel tearing holes into Beth's shocked face. But she didn't suffer. Instead, her head snapped abruptly to the right, neck broken by the same invisible force that had held her aloft, and she dropped to the floor like a stone. Slowhand could feel her body heat already fading beside him.

The shape trundled closer, revealing itself to be some kind of wheelchair. But a wheelchair built by a madman. Looking like a mobile torture device, tubes with needles wove slowly about its surface, occasionally injecting its occupant with coloured fluids, while bladder like things inflated and deflated, hissing and gurgling with air and water that seemed somehow to sustain him. It was an impossible, nightmare thing, but nowhere near as impossible or nightmarish as the shrivelled figure that was the centre of its attentions. Despite the state of its occupant Slowhand recognised him immediately.

He hadn't misheard the name, after all

It was Fitch.

Querilous Fitch.

The psychic manipulator stared down at him, smiled.

Not long after, Slowhand felt what was left of his bones begin to crack, and he began to scream.

CHAPTER SIX

KALI REACHED GRANSK lying on her stomach sandwiched between slices of creev. The thick, blubbery material used to line the hulls of ships for buoyancy did not feel very buoyant, pressing down on her and holding her immobile like the blankets of a tightly made bed. It was damp, hot and stifling between them, and the creev stank so badly she was constantly on the verge of throwing up. It was an urge she'd quelled by snatching swift lungfuls of air through a raised flap of the stuff whenever it had been safe to do so.

She was denied that luxury now. Her last glimpse of the outside world had been of the cart which carried the creev itself becoming sandwiched between Final Faith wagons, part of a convoy which was forming to snake down the cliff road into Gransk. Just before she'd closed the flap, she'd studied the wagons pulling into line behind her, wondering what the large, cigar-shaped, canvas covered objects they carried were. The only thing she did know was that they were not the only wagons out there. Far from it. Whatever kind of ship Jakub Freel was building here, he seemed to be throwing at it every resource the Final Faith had.

Kali felt the cart dip beneath her, beginning its descent into the town, and she pictured the scene outside her hiding place.

Once a small and tranquil fishing community, Gransk had grown into something quite different since the Filth had adopted it as the location for their shipyards. Adding both docks and dry docks for the construction of their coastal clippers and patrol boats, most of the original fisherfolk had over the years been driven away, replaced by a coarser breed of peninsulan labourer who'd stamped their own identity on the town. She'd visited the place on a couple of occasions before now, and while the Filth had found it necessary to garrison a few Swords of Dawn to ensure that the work they commissioned was actually carried out, they had for the most part left the inhabitants to run the town for themselves. Now, though, it seemed to be a different story. From the number of delays, shouts and barked orders Kali heard from beyond the slices of creev, security had been upped considerably. It didn't take much to figure out by whom, or why.

The cart came to a stop and Kali was aware of the presence of soldiers gathering about it. She felt a slight lurch as the cart's driver climbed down, presumably in response to a signal from one of them.

"Your goods?" a deep but muffled voice enquired.

"Creev, sir," the driver responded. Kali was relieved to hear his voice remained calm. He was aware of her presence but there was not a hint of betrayal in his weary tones.

"Creev? That's all?"

"Yes, sir."

There was the sharp scrape of a weapon being withdrawn from a scabbard, and then another, and Kali sucked in breath, knowing what was coming. What kind of lunatic they imagined would secrete themselves in this pile of shite she couldn't imagine, but the guards had clearly been ordered to be thorough.

She froze as swords thrust into the slices of creev. The blubbery substance deflated and released puffs of noxious gas. She was grateful that the odour was so rank that they were reluctant to make the inspection *too* thorough. Nonetheless, one or two of the thrusts came too close for comfort and Kali quietly contorted herself each time, like a magician's assistant inside a sword trap.

"You're clear. Papers?"

A shuffling, and a cough.

"These seem to be in order. Pondeen's Maritime is on the western harbourside. Proceed directly there, unload your shipment and then turn your cart around."

"Around?" the driver said. "But I intended to stay at the tavern. It's been a long haul."

"Turn it *around*, old man. Trust me, you don't want to be in town tonight."

Kali frowned, wondering why. The old man questioned the soldiers no further, however, and the cart sank once more as he resumed his position. A clicking of his mouth spurred the horses on.

Kali remained still, listening to more muffled voices and sounds, not of soldiers this time but the activity of Gransk. The cries of men at work, the shifting of cargo, the screeching of razorgulls as they circled overhead hoping for pickings from the goods being loaded. She did not listen without reason – if she were to slip from her hiding place unnoticed, she'd have to time her move carefully. After a few more minutes of the cart negotiating the narrow streets of the town, the sounds became more mooted and Kali knew that the cart's driver had steered her to a place of relative inactivity, as requested. Listening again to be certain no one was around, she slithered from between the slices of creev, placed a bag of full gold in his hand, and then vanished into a side alley, from where she intended to get her bearings.

The other end of the alley opened onto a main thoroughfare. Kali took her squallcoat from her backpack and slipped it on. A sailor's cap she had procured elsewhere she jammed on her head, the peak lowered to obscure her features. Then she took a breath and, with hands in her pockets and head down, slipped from the alley and joined the throng of people heading towards the dockside.

The port came alive around her, voices amplified among the packed and overhanging buildings of the streets.

"Ragfish and jumpo, guv'nor? Two tenths a bag."

"Ropes, hawsings, nets!"

"Hey, sailor, fancy yer chances with Mair behind the crates, do yer? Goworn, you'll never get the chance out there now, will yer?"

"Hand over yer purse, lad or... ow! Fark! Pits o' Kerberos, what d'ya do *that* for?"

Kali smiled and lowered her elbow as the grabcoin raced off into the crowd nursing a bloody nose. She ignored all further solicitations, weaving slowly through the crowd. It had been her intention to spend some time listening to gossip, trying to glean information, but where she'd expected the locals to be quite forthcoming considering the amount of work Freel had brought to town, there were surprisingly few mentions of the ship, and these only in hushed tones. Instead, she began to work her way directly to the dockside where she had at least gleaned Freel's ship was berthed.

And then stopped.

The ship had come into view far before she expected it to, a consequence of its size. She could see little detail of it from where she stood but that made it none the less awesome. Made of materials that were almost entirely black, including its sails, it appeared in view like some gigantic wall, towering over the dockside, blotting out the horizon completely, casting a shadow over the lower half of the town. It left no doubt in her mind that this was the place where she would find all the answers she needed.

"Don't you go near that ship, young lad," a voice said suddenly from beside her. "Arsk me, she's cursed."

Kali turned to see a grizzled old seadog. "Cursed?"

"Aye, cursed. I've seen men carried out o' the bowels o' that thing with their flesh rottin' off 'em, as if they got the worst case o' the hic there ever was. An' before I did I heard their screams from inside its hull."

"Screams?"

"Agonised screams. As if their souls had been touched by the devils themselves. An' that ain't all..."

"It isn't?"

"Oh, no. I swear to ye, the very instant they rolled that monster outta dry dock an' into the waters, the ocean *boiled*. Stay away from 'er, I tell ya. Stay away!"

Boiled, eh? Kali thought. That was certainly enough to get a girl's attention.

She nodded, flipped the seadog a coin, and began to move with renewed determination towards her destination. But she had not got far before her progress was rudely interrupted.

Her gaze fixed on the looming wall of the ship, she did not notice the sudden kerfuffle in the crowd about her, and the first thing she knew of its cause – something moving at speed out of a side alley – was when that same something barrelled into her so hard she was winded and knocked off her feet. As she thudded unceremoniously onto her backside, Kali cursed her assailant for not even having the good grace to apologise for the collision. Then she realised there was good reason for the omission.

Three Eyes of the Lord darted out of the alley, spinning about while they re-orientated, and then tore through the air after the figure, which was now half way across the street.

Kali double-taked on the spheres and the fleeing figure. The first thing she noticed was the Eyes of the Lord's prey wasn't so much running as rolling along, the reason for this being that he appeared to have no legs. Instead, he was perched on a small, wheeled platform which he was thrusting along with sweeps of thick and powerfully muscled arms. Kali wondered if he was perhaps a veteran of the Vos-Pontaine war and, like so many, had lost his limbs in one of its horrifying battles. He didn't look like one, though, when, for a fleeting second, she caught a glimpse of a solid, gnarled face almost wholly obscured by a thick beard which had, of all things, a number of small, tin bells woven into it.

Her first instinct was to spring upward and help him, but before she could she realised she had problems of her own. Unnoticed until now, her tumble had dislodged her cap from her head and, with it lying a few feet away, her true appearance was revealed to all.

One of the three spheres stopped dead in its pursuit of its prey, backtracked a few feet, and then darted towards her until it hovered directly in front of her face, staring her, as it were, in the eyes. Kali realised she had only a few seconds before the information it was gathering was processed by the Overseers back at Scholten Cathedral, and then she would have been tracked by the Faith. She leapt up and rid herself of the problem with the only thing that came to hand. Plucking a large fish from where it lay, dull-eyed, on an adjacent stall, Kali held it tightly by the tail, swung it round in an arc and batted the Eye of the Lord hard enough to send it careering through the air. As bits of fish splattered the crowd, the sphere ricocheted off one wall and then another and yet a third before it plummeted, smoking and sparking, through the cloth awning of a stall further up the street, bringing the whole lot down around it.

"Fore!" Kali shouted.

Her unique solution to the problem couldn't help but attract the attention of the other two spheres, and also, for a second, the figure on the wheeled platform, who paused and regarded her curiously. There was no time for introductions, however, as one of the two remaining spheres veered off towards Kali while its partner resumed its pursuit of its original prey.

Kali cursed – an ancient Drakengrattian powerword that made even the hardened inhabitants of Gransk gasp and step back in shock – reflecting how her plan to clandestinely go about her business had so rapidly turned to shit.

The Eye of the Lord now in hot pursuit, Kali fled into a side alley running parallel to that taken by the bearded stranger, and as the alley jinked to the right, his must have jinked to the left, because the pair found themselves meeting again, though heading swiftly in opposite directions. A few seconds later, when Kali jinked once more, they were again heading directly towards each other. They nodded as they passed. By the time they encountered each other for a third time, Kali had had enough, but thankfully another plan had popped into mind.

While she considered it a little unnecessary to shout "duck!" to her fellow escapee, she did so anyway, and then ran right at him, seemingly playing chicken. At the very last instant before their two forms collided, she flung herself to the side, bouncing off the alley wall with an *oof!* before continuing her flight. As she'd hoped, the pursuing Eyes of the Lord were not so nimble in their reactions and the two spheres impacted with each other directly above the bearded stranger's platform, knocking each other askew, taking a few seconds to regain their equilibrium. It was enough time for both parties to lose them in the backstreet maze. The last thing Kali saw of the maybe veteran was his platform throwing up dust as it disappeared into yet another alley, and then she, too, veered left, right, right, left and left again in what she hoped was a dizzying enough series of manoeuvres to ride herself of her sphere for good.

Breathless now, Kali turned at last into a long, featureless alley – and stopped dead in her tracks.

One of the Eyes of the Lord hovered at the other end, blocking her escape route. Kali turned and found the second hovering where she had come in. She span on the spot, studying the alley for an alternative means of escape but seeing none, and even if she took to the rooftops – a favourite ploy guaranteed to confound any normal pursuer – it would do little to help her against the omnipresent spheres.

Both Eyes of the Lord began to move towards her, closing the gap between them, but just as they drew near a staggering, singing figure suddenly emerged from a plain and hard to spot doorway just a few feet away. Though she would clearly be observed going in, it would have to do for now, and Kali grabbed at the door before it closed, spinning herself inside.

Fug and the smell of her favourite thing greeted her, because on the other side of the door was a bar. The fact that it had been unsigned hinted that it was likely frequented only by those who knew it was there, clearly the kind of back street watering hole visited by sailors who traded in exotic and illicit goods. Consequently, the face of every customer within snapped towards Kali with expressions ranging from curiosity to startled guilt to snarling, outright belligerence, and more than one hand dropped to a blade sheath concealed under clothing. Even a game of arrows taking place in the far corner stopped – literally, with the tiny projectile frozen in mid air – the ship's first mage whose throw it had been pausing time to weigh up the unexpected arrival.

Kali had no time to weigh up anything, knowing the spheres were only one or two seconds behind her, and she darted for a booth in the most shadowed area of the bar, vanishing into the dark. This action alone seemed to mollify the regulars – if the girl was hiding, and in this town she could only be hiding from the law, then she was all right by them – and they turned back to their business.

"This booth is occupied," a voice growled in the darkness beside her. "Fark off."

Kali jumped. The ill-mannered request had come from right next to her. But, dark as it was, the booth was clearly empty. Kali shook her head. Must have been a trick of the acoustics in the place.

Something prodded her sharply in her ribs, near her breast, prompting an indignant "Ow!"

"Go on, ar said. Fark off."

"What the hells?"

Another prod.

"Are ya deaf, smoothskin? Or is yer just plain stupid?"

"Now wait one pitsing min – " Kali began. She turned with the intention of snapping off whatever it was doing the prodding but at that moment the door to the bar was booted wide open and sunlight flooded in. The regulars, who were used to the door never being open for longer than it took someone to duck quickly and furtively inside, squinted and shielded their eyes against the brightness.

Silhouetted shapes appeared in the light. Two spherical shapes that floated slowly inside, followed by two armoured human shapes, Swords by the look of them. The Eyes of the Lord had brought reinforcements.

"Aw, me mother's bollocks, now ya've gone and done it," the

voice next to Kali cursed. "Come on, then, smoothskin, ya'd better get under here."

Kali felt something thrown over her, the weight and texture of one of Merrit Moon's horse blankets. She became immediately aware of two things: that the blanket stank worse than possibly anything else she'd smelled in her life, and that its stink originated with the hunched figure she was sharing it with. He was so bad he seemed to have to transfer his excess stink through some form of osmosis. What Kali didn't expect, therefore, was his next comment.

"Great Gods, smoothskin, ya stink like a mool's arse after a bad case o' the trots."

"*I* stink?" Kali gasped. But then realised the creev had likely left her with a body odour problem of her own.

"Keep ya bloody voice down, or ya might bring more attention than me cloak can stand."

"Cloak?" Kali blurted. "You plan to hide from the patrol under a pitsing *cloak*?"

"It fooled you, didn't it?"

"It was dark, then!"

"Trust me, smoothskin."

"Oh, sure. Better idea. I'll go stand in that corner with a lampshade on my head!"

The figure sighed. "For a small 'un ya've got quite the gob on ya. Do me a favour and shut it for a second, eh?"

"*You* are asking for –" Kali began, but stopped as the spheres and Swords, so far having concentrated their activity on the patrons near the bar, turned their attention to the booths. Kali froze as the Eyes of the Lord floated before her, and could almost feel the Overseers in Scholten peering at her intently.

"You, Allantian," one of the Swords barked. "We're looking for two fugitives – a girl and a short, thick-set man." He hesitated. "On a trolley."

Allantian? Kali thought. Not only did she – and, as far as she could tell, the Great Pongo – not look remotely Allantian, but the numbers were wrong. The Sword also paid no heed to the fact that the two of them were hiding under a blanket, which if she'd been him she might have found just a tad suspicious. She supposed you got what you paid for.

"Seen no one," the figure next to her said. "Just enjoyin' a drink."

The soldier's eyes narrowed, as if suspecting something but unable to put a finger on what.

"Your trade?" he demanded. "What business have you in Gransk?"

"I grease knobs. Luggleknobs."

"What?"

"They assign ya to a docks an' ya don't know what luggleknobs are?"

"Well, no..."

"Then ar suggest ya watch your footing around town, greenhorn. Now why don't ya leave an old lag to his drink, eh?"

The soldier hesitated, but the bluff – if that's what it was – seemed to work, and he turned away from them with a grunt.

Kali gave it a moment before she spoke.

"What are luggleknobs?"

"Haven't a clue."

"Thought so. What just happened? Why did he think *we* were an Allantian?"

"Ah, that. Cloak o' Many Contours. Handy bit o' kit."

Kali felt a stirring of excitement, despite the stench. "This is an artefact?"

"Artefact?" the stranger repeated. "No, just me old cloak."

"And what does this cloak do?"

"Fools the eyes, mainly. You thought this booth was empty when you sat here, right?"

"Right. But the Sword clearly didn't."

"That's why it's called a cloak o' *many* contours. It adapts to what it's covering. You were a bit too bulky ta simply hide."

"*Bulky?*"

"Don't get your knickers in a twist, smoothskin. Yer can't help yer size."

"Are you talking about glamour?"

"Aye. Portable glamour."

"Then it *is* an artefact!"

"I told yer –"

"It's just your cloak," Kali finished. She sighed, getting nowhere. She looked at the bar, saw the Swords and the spheres were leaving, and then pulled the cloak off their heads, sucking in fresh air. She, too, made to leave.

"An' where is it yer think you're goin'?"

"They've gone so I'm going. I wish I could say it's been a pleasure."

A hand clamped about her forearm, solid as iron, and Kali turned to look at her companion for the first time. Wreathed once more in shadow, his face was gnarled and grizzled, hairy and a little pug-like, and comprehensively covered in scars. Even the scars had scars. None of these features were how Kali recognised him. It was the bells in the beard that were the giveaway.

"*You.*"

"Aye, me."

"Okay, that's it. I'm definitely off."

"Ar wouldn't. The Swords'll be on full alert after our little runaround. Probably take 'em til nightfall to calm down. Whatever business ya have in Gransk'll have to wait."

Kali slumped back in her seat, supposing he was right.

"Okay," she acceded. "So what do you suggest we do for the next few hours?"

A guffaw. "What else do ya do in a bar, smoothskin? We DRINK!"

He shouted to the bartender and, a second later, two pitchers of frothing ale were slammed down on the table. They were followed in rapid succession by two more. And two more. And two more. Kali matched her companion drink for drink, wetting her whistle with the local brew – clanger – then suggesting they moved on to something stronger. She ordered the guest beer – wobblehead – and not pitchers this time but the full barrel. The bartender eyed her suspiciously as he rolled it over, but Kali simply wiped her mouth, burped and tossed him a pouch of full bronze. The weight of it erased all worries from his face.

Kali drank and thought about her companion's odd appearance, the artefact that was 'just' an old cloak, the way he had of speaking. "You're not from around here, are you?"

"Depends on what ya mean by 'here'. I haven't fallen from that thing that's appeared in the sky, if that's what yer suggestin'."

"I'm not. I've a lot of theories about what's up there but one of them isn't that it's filled with rude little men."

"Bugger off."

Kali thought carefully about what she said next, but was pretty certain of her suspicions before she spoke. "What happened to your legs?"

"That's somethin' of a personal question, don't ya think? Why don't you tell me why yer tits are so small?"

"Hey! I know they're small, all right? So, come on, answer the question – were they blown off? Amputated? Eaten by a ravenous shnarl? Or did they just rot away holding all that beer?"

"Mind yer own business."

Without warning, Kali pulled away the remainder of the cloak covering her companion. As she'd suspected, the trolley on which he'd ridden had been discarded under the table and he was sitting there with a pair of legs that were fully formed – small, but fully formed.

Her companion sighed and struck a match, lighting a huge pipe he had produced from a pocket. He blew smoke from his nose. Three distinct plumes of smoke at the same time.

Kali nodded. There was only one kind of nose that could do that, and the last one like it she'd seen had been on a desiccated and mummified face sealed inside the Old Race machine she had purloined to reach the Crucible, the machine she'd named 'the mole'.

Three nostrils.

"Fark me," Kali said. "You're a dwarf."

The figure snapped his gaze further towards her, so much so that the tin bells woven into his beard jangled. Then he took a deep, thoughtful draught of his ale and a pull on his pipe, inhaling hard before replying.

"Ya seem to be quite unphased about that fact. Most people

might find it surprising that they were sitting having a beer with one o' the Old Races. Particularly as most of 'em think we're a myth."

"I'm not most people. I've met some of your kind before. Sort of."

"Pah! Bollocks."

"It's true. Okay, one of them had only a bit of dwarf blood running through his veins and the other, well, he was half dwarf, half elf – a dwelf called Tharnak."

The dwarf's eyes widened and without so much as a by-your-leave he planted both his palms on Kali's chest.

"Hey! What the hells do you think you're doing?!"

"Just checkin' summat," the dwarf said, apparently satisfied.

"Yeah, there are two, all right!" Kali snapped. "Pits of farking Kerberos, are you some kind of pervert?"

"What do you know about the dwelf?" the dwarf asked, ignoring her protest.

Kali, despite her indignation, was intrigued.

"Long story. The question is, what do *you* know?"

The dwarf stroked his beard, regarding her with great care.

"You haven't told me. What brings you to Gransk, smoothskin?"

"I intend to take passage on the Black Ship."

"Is that so? Well, now, that might present a bit of a problem."

"How so?"

"Because I intend to sink it."

"What the hells are you talking about?"

The dwarf began to chuckle heavily into his beer, as if she had asked the question of all questions. "That, smoothskin, is also a long story. A long, long, long story. Longer than you can imagine. And it begins where that ship is goin'."

"You're talking about Trass Kathra."

"That I be."

Kali's eyes narrowed. "Is that where you're from?"

The dwarf didn't answer for a second. And when he did, it wasn't an answer at all.

"Jerragrim Brundle," he said, sticking out his hand.

"Kali Hooper."

"Well, now, Miss Hooper. You and I have a lot to talk about."

"We do?"

"Not least that I think I've been expecting you."

"What?"

"As I said, it's a long, long story. But here is not the place for it's tellin' –"

"Where, then?"

Brundle studied her. "That rather depends on what happens later."

She got little more out of him, there and then, other than small talk over their continuing drinks. So many continuing drinks that even she began to feel their effects. But no more so than Brundle. After a few hours she was rocked back in her seat as the dwarf slammed his tankard into hers, sending ale flying everywhere.

"Ya know, for a smoothskin, you can down yer drink as well as a dwarf!"

Kali flushed. Despite the circumstances, she suddenly felt immensely proud, as if holding her own with one of the Old Races was vindication of everything she had tried to discover over the years. Maybe, she thought, that all she'd ever wanted – all she'd ever *really* wanted – was to get shit-faced with the people she admired the most.

"Yer not so bad yerself!" she responded, slamming her tankard into his.

Ale foaming and dripping off their heads, she turned to one of the bar's tiny windows.

"It's dark. Time to go?"

"Time to go," Brundle agreed.

As Kali and Brundle exited the tavern, a figure sitting hunched at the bar turned slightly to watch them go, the light from the doorway illuminating a hard face framed with greasy black hair, and a strange 'x' shaped scar on his upper left cheek. He didn't know who the shortarse was or why he was here – didn't, in fact, even recall him coming in – but the presence of Kali Hooper came as no surprise at all. He expected he'd be seeing her again quite soon.

First, of course, he, too, had to get aboard the boat. The security he'd checked out earlier that day was comprehensive, and while he could have got aboard by taking down a couple of guards where they stood, they would eventually be missed, and that would spoil everything. No, if he wanted to get aboard he'd have them *take* him aboard, and for that the fact that even some veteran sailors in town refused to sail on the vessel worked in his favour. It was already short of crewmembers and he had significantly increased the odds that they would need to find more by arranging a little accident by the dockside some hours before. The cargo crates that had inexplicably sheared from their crane had crushed at least six of the pre-assigned crew and injured a good few more. Enough for Freel to have to resort to emergency measures to find replacements.

Gransk was not that big a port and so it was only a matter of time.

The stranger stared into his drink and waited for the crack on the head that signalled the arrival of the press-gang.

CHAPTER SEVEN

THE FAITH HAD indeed stepped down from alert as Kali and Brundle emerged into the darkness, and though patrols were still present in the streets, their regular circuits of the shadowy alleyways were easy to predict and avoid. The pair of them made their way down to the waterfront, but from the shouts and hammering and clanging of tools it was clear before they got there that the coming of night had not quietened their destination as it had the rest of Gransk.

The dockside remained a hubbub of activity, all of it centered around the Black Ship Kali had until now seen only from a distance. She and the dwarf hid behind crates – Kali the only one needing to duck to do so – and watched as Faith came and went on the gangplank, labourers carried supplies aboard, and workmen dangled on ropes at various points along the hull, securing rivets and otherwise effecting preparations for the ship's seaworthiness. One of the strange, cigar shaped objects she had seen in the convoy was being loaded by crane, joining seven others which had already been secured to the deck near the ship's stern.

All in all, It looked to Kali as if the ship was going to sail that very night.

And what a ship. Kali couldn't take her eyes off it. As huge as it had seemed from the street, it seemed huger still here. Constructed of rune-inscribed metal plating rather than timber, its prow curved threateningly downwards like some great insectoid proboscis, and sweeping back from it, overshadowing its decks, were a series of static sails made not of cloth but metal again. The shape of half shells, eight of them, they appeared to be currently at rest, receding one atop the other, as squat almost as the ship itself, like some armoured carapace. The effect was so streamlined and organic, the vessel looked less ship than predatorial beast.

What struck Kali more than anything was that it also had two hulls. Each resting in the water some twenty yards apart, the vessel straddled them as a bridge might straddle pontoons in a river, and this made the ship seem even more solid, seemingly unstoppable in all of her dimensions.

Kali whistled softly.

"Never seen a cat before, eh?" Brundle said.

"Cat?"

"Catamaran. Two hulls make the vessel much more stable in the water. Standard design for a dwarven warship."

"This is a *dwarven* warship?"

"Based on one, anyway. Though ya can tell not built with *passion.*"

"Why in hells would they build a dwarven warship?"

"Seein' as there's no one to go to war with anymore, survival'd be my guess. They have to get through the Stormwall first, don't forget. And then there's uppards o' two months' sailin' ahead o' them, in some o' the wildest seas there is. Then there's the things that live out there. Chadassa Raiders, untershraks, the Great Weed. And, o' course, there's the weather – the sunderstorms can rip an ill-clad ship apart wi' one strike."

"I'm beginning to get the picture," Kali said.

"Oh, that's not all, smoothskin," Brundle cautioned. "'Cos if they survive that lot, they're gonna need somethin' as immovable as me tenth wife's arse when they face the swirlies..."

"Swirlies?"

"The swirlpools, smoothskin," Brundle said, as if it were obvious.

"What are swirlpools?"

"They're the barrier between the island an' the rest o' the world." Brundle tilted his head upwards, at the looming shape of the Hel'ss. "A little legacy of our friend up there. Quite the *lasting* legacy, I might add."

"Hold on again. There's a relationship between the Hel'ss and Trass Kathra?"

Brundle laughed. "I wouldn't call it a relationship as such. Unless o' course yer thinkin' o' me and me thirteenth wife, may the bulbous bitch rot in Zlathoon. Nah, smoothskin, last time around that thing up there did its best to obliterate the island, an' what it left behind makes what's left o' the Stormwall look like a squirt o' piss from a babby's knob."

Kali shook her head, struggling with the surfeit of information. "Wait a minute? Last time around? Are you trying to tell me that the Hel'ss has been here *before*? And what do you mean – what's *left* of the Stormwall?

"Like I said, it's a long –"

"Enough! Who the hells are you, Brundle? Where do you come from?"

The dwarf shot her a glance, raised an eyebrow. "Didn't ah tell ya, smoothskin? Trass Kathra's me home. I'm what yer might call its caretaker."

"What?" Kali said. "*What?*"

But her befuddlement fell on deaf ears. Brundle was already moving, taking advantage of a quiet moment on that part of the dock to shift position. With a growl of exasperation, Kali followed him to another hiding place nearer to the ship, behind a stack of barrels.

"Will you *please* tell me what's going on?"

"Right now ah think we'd be better concentrating on what's

going on with the ship." The dwarf pointed. "Take a look."

Kali turned her gaze in the direction Brundle indicated. There was fresh activity on the gangplank – or for the moment, to be more accurate, before it. A number of wagons were arriving on the dock, and from the first of them Jakub Freel alighted, followed by a number of mercenaries. Kali was hardly surprised to see Freel here, but what did surprise her was what was forcefully disembarked from the wagons that lined up behind his.

Civilian prisoners. Hundreds of them.

"Well, now," Brundle muttered. "This is interestin'."

Kali ignored him and looked on as Freel and his men took up position at the head of the gangplank, inspecting the prisoners as they were ushered aboard the ship. Led by them in wrist and ankle chains, like slaves, Kali saw men, women and children who, by their varying modes of dress, seemed to have been taken from all across the peninsula. She knew instantly that she was looking at the 'vanished', those who had spoken out against the Faith and been imprisoned for their beliefs, and she gasped as she began to recognise some familiar faces amongst them. *Too many* familiar faces.

There were some of Jengo Pim's men – among them, Pim himself – and there... oh, gods. Red. Hetty. Pete Two-Ties and others from the *Flagons*. There, too, were people who had become friends after helping her with supplies and information in the last year: Martha DeZantez, Gabriella's mother; Abra, and Poul Sonpear, the mage from the Three Towers, his powers clearly constrained by what appeared to be a scrambling collar about his neck.

And there...

Dolorosa.

Dolorosa but not Aldrededor.

Alone.

The woman was injured – badly. Being carried aboard the ship on a stretcher. But despite her condition, still scowling. Spitting in the faces of the Faith gathered around her. Had she been able to wield a knife, she would have been slitting their throats.

Good girl, Kali thought. Yet still cringed as the woman was

taken below decks with those who had preceded her.

Kali wasn't having this. She made to move from behind the barrels but Brundle's iron grip held her back.

"Easy, easy," he said.

"Those people are *friends* of mine. Family."

"All the more reason we get aboard that tub secretly," Brundle countered. "You'll not be able to help with one o' the Sword's namesakes stickin' in yer belly, now, will ye?"

"Oh, so now *we're* going aboard, are we? I thought you were going to sink her?"

"Ah may still have to. But for the time bein', things have changed."

"You're right, there," Kali responded angrily. She tried to struggle from his grip but Brundle reasserted his strength, pulling her back.

"Listen to me, smoothskin," he growled, more serious than she had ever seen him. "It is imperative that you stay alive. *Imperative*, do you understand me?"

Kali swallowed, shocked by the outburst. "Why?"

Brundle smiled. "Ah think yer know that, lass. Ah think you know that."

Kali pulled her arm away, and Brundle let her, knowing she was going nowhere. At least for the moment. Because then events took an unexpected turn.

Prisoners continuing to be ushered aboard, Jakub Freel took up position at the head of the gangplank and shouted across the harbour.

"Miss Hooper, I know you are out there And I would suggest you surrender yourself to me now!"

Dammit, Kali thought. The Eyes of the Lord must have got a good enough look at her after all. Or maybe Freel just *expected* her to be there – let's face it, if she were in his shoes, she would. The question was, what was he up to? What happened if she didn't surrender herself?

"Kali," Freel went on. "We know each other well enough for me to call you Kali, don't we? As you can see I am amassing a good number of your friends aboard this ship. A sufficient number that I am able to spare a few. Therefore if you do not reveal yourself within one hour, I shall kill one of them. If you do not reveal yourself thereafter, I shall kill another every ten minutes. Do I make myself clear?"

As crystal, you bastard, Kali thought. In fact the message was so clear that Freel didn't dwell on it. His ultimatum delivered, he stepped down once more, going about his business as if a threat to commit mass murder was nothing to him. Nothing at all.

Beside Kali, Brundle blew out a breath.

"Ah don't think ah like this man," he said.

"I thought he was a friend, once," Kali replied. She made to rise again and Brundle once more held her down.

"I thought we'd been through this?" he said.

"What choice do I have?"

Freel had her in a stalemate and the only way to break it was to take the initiative. But if she was going to give herself to Freel, she was going to do it her way. The *only* way she could.

And as the ship showed every sign of sailing soon, the time to act was now.

"You'll get yourself killed," Brundle warned.

Kali winked. "That's never stopped me before. You sticking around?"

"Oh, aye, I'll be sticking around," Brundle replied. He seemed to find his answer amusing somehow.

Kali sighed. "And let me guess – you'll tell me about it some other time?"

"That's about the long and the short of it, smoothskin."

Kali narrowed her eyes. "Was that a joke?"

"No," Brundle said warily. "Why?"

"Well, you know..." Kali said. She flattened her palm and moved it up and down, comparing their heights. But all she received in response was a blank expression. "Oh, never mind."

Kali continued on, darting from crate to crate along the dockside, until she reached a spot behind where the prisoners' wagons had arrived. Most of them had been embarked now and, as she'd hoped, those remaining were being manhandled by only a couple of Faith, confident their charges in chains would present them with little resistance. They were also just out of sight of the main part of the dockside, which served her purposes perfectly.

Kali waited while one of the two was occupied dragging a particularly recalcitrant prisoner from the wagon's rear and then stepped up behind the other and tapped him on the shoulder. Clamping one hand over his mouth, she swiftly delivered four nerve-numbing blows to spectacles, testicles, wallet and watch, – and then caught his boggle-eyed, paralysed form as it fell, dragging it out of sight. There she delivered a knockout punch to the man's face, just because she felt like it, and no more than a couple of seconds later, dressed in the Faith robes she stripped from her victim, stood beside his brother, who had only now managed to extract his charge.

Kali apologised mentally and jabbed the prisoner in his side, forcing him into line with his fellows. Their passage to the ship coincided with that of more Faith who, between them, dragged the semi-conscious forms of men who appeared to have been press-ganged, and, for the sake of camaraderie, she jabbed one of them in the side, too, quite harshly. The man, with a mane of long, black hair and a strange, 'x' shaped scar on his left cheekbone, bucked and, clearly not as out of it as he seemed to be, raised his head and glowered at her. The glower turned into an unfathomable expression as he caught sight of her face under her hood.

Kali frowned, though had no time to ponder the look as she and her companion, the last of the prisoners shuffling in their midst, reached the gangplank. A few yards above Jakub Freel stood momentarily studying each prisoner and, though this was the first time Kali had managed to get this close to him since the Sardenne – longed to find out what had *happened* to him – she knew she dared do nothing. If what she had planned was going to work convincingly, she had to walk a fine line between success and failure.

She kept her head low as she and the prisoners passed beneath Freel's gaze but, despite herself, couldn't help but pause as they almost touched. Though she and Freel hadn't known each other long, the experiences they'd shared had been intense, and such experiences tended to stamp the aura of a person indelibly in one's mind. And the thing was, the aura felt wrong. Everything about the man beside her rang alarm bells – his stance, his attitude, even his body odour, and Kali felt a shiver run through her, as if someone had walked over her grave.

Or as if someone had crawled out of a grave.

Kali shook herself, and began to push the prisoners forward once more. But it took all the willpower she had not to freeze when a voice behind her spoke two words.

"Kali Hooper."

Though Freel had apparently recognised her, there was still a chance he'd think himself mistaken – that her stance, attitude or perfume had triggered some erroneous mental connection. What she had to do was continue bluffing her way through by giving no sign of recognition at all.

It was a reasonable plan, spoiled only by the fact that two Swords of Dawn immediately blocked her path. As they did, she felt Freel move up close behind her, and then her hood was pulled quickly back.

Okay, Kali thought. It was a fair cop.

She turned. A face she had not seen in a year filled her vision, staring down at her. The sight was strangely disconcerting. The same rugged, unshaven features were there, the same intelligent, piercing and curious eyes, even the slight smile which, though rarely seen, had betrayed the humanity of the man she thought she had come to know. This *was* Prince Jakub Tremayne Freel of the Allantian Royal Family. And yet. And yet his humanity seemed missing, somehow, as if some unknown events since she had last seen him had erased that aspect of him. Now, despite the smile, a cold cruelty seemed to seep from every pore.

"Jakub Freel," Kali said.

The strange, cold smile curled slightly at one side, and Freel bent almost melodramatically to whisper in Kali's ear. He was making it clear that this was just between the two of them.

"Sorry. No."

Kali's heart missed a beat. Her gaze snapped back to Freel's eyes and what she saw there made all of her confusion of the last year make sense. Though she had struggled to reconcile the actions of the man she had come to know in the Sardenne with those of the man who had returned with Makennon to Scholten Cathedral, changing the nature of the Church completely, it had simply never occurred to her that the two men were not necessarily one and the same. And if this wasn't Freel she was confronting, there was only one other man – though, of course, man was not the word – who had the power to take his place. Someone who had considerable experience in the exchanging of souls...

"Redigor," Kali said. "You farking piece of –"

Freel motioned to the Swords who'd blocked Kali's path and they each grabbed her by an arm, holding her firmly. Then Freel cocked his head to one side, his smile broadening, and when he spoke once more, it was to all.

"I have no idea what you're talking about."

"Listen to me!" Kali struggled in the grip of her captors. "This man is not who he seems to be!"

There was a murmuring from the ranks.

"This woman," Freel countered, "is Kali Hooper, the outlaw."

The murmuring intensified. Kali would have been flattered were this not all so *wrong*.

"I'm no outlaw!" Kali shouted, piecing together why it was that the Faith had such a price on her head. "This man, this *imposter*, made me so – the same as he has done with all these prisoners – so that I, they, couldn't interfere with his plans!"

"My *plans*?" Freel roared. He regarded the massed ranks and then pointed up at the evening sky, where the strangely nebulous shape of the Hel'ss loomed on the opposite side of the horizon from Kerberos. "All of the Faithful here know my plans, and they are to do all we can to welcome the Herald of the Lord of All. The Herald of our Ascension!"

"The Hel'ss is no herald!" Kali argued. "And the man standing before you knows this! He knows because he is the Pale Lord. Your First Enemy!"

Kali's revelation didn't quite have the effect she desired. While some townspeople did draw in a breath and make the sign of the crossed circle of the Faith, the ranks of Swords and brethren began, disturbingly, to laugh.

"The Pale Lord is dead!" one shouted. "The Anointed Lord did smite him."

"He wasn't smited... smoted... pits, he wasn't smitten!" Kali protested, cursing herself for her lack of religious vocabulary. "He's here! Before you! Now!"

"No! His plans crumbled before the might of the Final Faith!"

"Heretic!"

"Outlaw!"

"I was there!" Kali shouted. "I was there, saw what happened. I understand your believing what you do but he still lives and –" Kali indicated the ship " – this, *this* is his plan..."

The ranks roared. Jakub Freel raised his hands to quieten them.

"If this outlaw is correct," he told them, "then perhaps she can explain this plan." He turned to Kali questioningly, the smile still playing on his face.

Kali looked as though she was about to speak, but growled in frustration. "You know I can't do that. I don't know what the fark you're up to."

Redigor leaned in. Another little confidence. "Maybe it's something to do with the fact that as you denied me the return of my race, I intend to deny you yours."

"Bullshit. There's something more to it than that. With you, there always is."

"Do you hear?" Freel shouted to his people. "She doesn't know!"

"But I'll find out," Kali added with determination. "I promise you that."

Freel sighed and ordered all men, but those who held her, back to their duties. It was clear that Kali had lost any advantage, even if she had one to begin with. Their attention away from the pair, Freel leaned into her once more.

"I doubt it," he said. "Only one of us can come back from the dead."

Freel withdrew a glinting dagger from his tunic and raised it. Kali's eyes widened and in that moment she knew that if there were any vestige of Jakub Freel left inside his own form, Redigor must have snuffed it like a candle flame.

"You'll regret doing this to my friend, elf," she said.

"No," Freel answered. "But you will regret coming here."

Kali stiffened as he ordered his men to hold her more firmly, and then grasped the back of her neck with one hand. She gasped in shock and pain as, slowly and deliberately, he carved two intersecting lines into the skin of her forehead, following these with a carefully drawn circle, enclosing them. Kali didn't need to see the pattern being cut into her flesh to know that she had just been branded with the mark of the Final Faith.

Blood began to seep into her eyes.

"The best place on the human body to guarantee a healthy blood flow," Freel said. "And one of the longest to heal. Even with your powers of recuperation these cuts will take time to recover... more than enough time for our purposes."

Kali shook her head and blinked to try to rid her vision of blood, but it was flowing too freely and she stared at Freel through a veil of red.

"Lash her to the figurehead," Freel ordered. "Once we pass beyond the Stormwall, the untershraks can have her..."

Kali struggled in the Swords' grips as they attempted to turn her away from the gangplank, but their gauntlets were clasped tightly about her, impossible to shift. This coupled with the fact that she was all but blinded made it difficult to gain any advantage against them and she knew it was only a matter of moments before her plan – of which being lashed to the figurehead was not part – was ruined. The one thing she couldn't have anticipated was that it wasn't Freel she'd be dealing with but Redigor, and his method of despatching people was far too final for her liking.

Thankfully, though, a sudden commotion from the gangplank provided her with just the distraction she needed.

At first, Kali wasn't sure what was going on, but soon saw that one of the Faith's press-ganged sailors had fully regained consciousness and wasn't at all keen on what was happening or where he was being led. Kali saw it was the same man who had glowered at her earlier. Not emerging from unconsciousness, then, but merely choosing this moment to make a pain of himself.

Whether he was doing it deliberately to help her, she didn't know.

Unexpected ally or not, the sudden flurry of activity surrounding his protestations gave her the chance she needed, and she threw her weight forward, making her captors stagger onto the gangplank with her. She immediately felt a lessening of their grip as their minds were filled with more overriding concerns, namely that on either side of them was now a drop into the waters of the harbour, and heavily armoured as they were, this was a place they'd prefer not to be. Armour and water did not mix. Their potential fate was illustrated quite graphically as, in the midst of the chaos her lurch had caused, one of the Swords near to the base of the gangplank suddenly found himself colliding with the protesting prisoner and his centre of gravity was thrown. With a cry of alarm the Sword tipped over the rope that edged the gangplank and plunged into the dark waters of the harbourside, sinking instantly beneath the surface.

Kali reminded her captors of the precariousness of their situation by swinging herself around as much as she could, and as their own momentum threatened to tip them after their friend, both released their grips. Freel, caught in the middle of the turmoil, spotted Kali's sudden freedom and his hand dropped to the chain whip at his belt, but by then it was too late. Kali blundered back up the gangplank and fled along the deck.

Freel ordered his men to follow, and they did so eagerly, welcoming the renewed solidity of the deck beneath their feet. Kali, meanwhile, ran, tearing away part of her bodysuit to wrap as a makeshift bandana around her forehead. The cloth did not stop all of the blood, but helped some.

As she heard the thudding of the Sword's boots after her, she made her way to the rear of the deck, finding herself amidst the cigar-shaped cargo she'd seen earlier. This close to them, she realised just how big each canvas shrouded object was – much taller than herself, and broad, too – and she dodged between them, hiding. A second later the Swords arrived and Kali waited until they had passed her hiding place to burst forth and head down the other side of the ship's superstructure. Between her and the bow, however, more Swords appeared, and Kali had no alternative but to go either into the superstructure, or up. She tried one door and another but all were locked, and so, with a grunt of exertion, grabbed onto a rail and heaving herself upwards and upwards again. She was standing now on the forward sloping, ridged carapace formed by the ship's folded sails.

Kali looked down. The Swords climbed after her but she'd bought the time she needed.

"Just where is it that you expect to go, Miss Hooper?" a voice asked.

Kali span. Jakub Freel stood at the opposite side of the carapace. He held his chain whip coiled before him.

"I was looking for the bar," Kali answered calmly. "The ship doesn't do room service."

"No. Only doom service."

Kali paused. "Did you just say that? Did you just say 'doom service'? Gods, man, did you really used to speak like that? No wonder the elves died out..."

Freel – Redigor – didn't answer. Only moved towards her over the rise of the carapace, allowing his whip to uncoil and trail full length behind him.

Kali readied herself for what was to come, knowing full well how proficient Jakub Freel had been with his singular weapon. She saw no reason why Bastian Redigor wouldn't have inherited this particular prowess, too. This was quickly confirmed as, with a flick of his forearm, Freel brought the whip to life and the single strand of chain separated into nine tails, each cracking down and sparking on the metal sail beneath them.

As sparks shot towards her face, Kali flipped backwards, increasing the distance between herself and Freel's deadly lashing. Freel was just as fast, however, and even as Kali landed on her feet, the multiple strands were sweeping out, each trying to trip her before she fully regained her balance. Kali's instincts were quick enough that she was able to dodge the majority of the sweeping chains, leaping above or cartwheeling over each as it passed beneath her, but a subtle flick of Freel's wrist brought the last one in faster than it was appearing to come, and with a bone-cracking impact she felt her ankle struck and then give beneath her.

Kali rolled with the blow, turning a tumble into a shoulder roll, but the slight miscalculation had given Freel momentary advantage. Her ankle didn't feel broken but it did throb like the hells and couldn't take much weight, and as Freel's whip came at her once more, Kali was forced to throw herself backwards rather than hobble out of the way.

She landed awkwardly on her behind, winded, near the edge of the sails, and cried in pain as a second dart of the metallic snake caught her on the forehead, tearing away her bandana, lashing the wound there and allowing the blood it was producing to flow freely once more.

Kali shook her dizzied head in an attempt to clear it, and stared down over the sails' lip, towards the waters of the harbour. As she did, those Swords climbing after her pulled themselves over the lip. They didn't approach her, but spread themselves around the periphery of the sails with crossbows aimed.

Deferring to their master. Kali rolled as Freel's whip sliced the air, this time at a level which would have cleanly decapitated her had she remained where she was. He'd clearly given up on the idea of simply incapacitating her and lashing her to the figurehead, and that suited her just fine because, in truth, she wanted him to bring it on.

Kali allowed the roll to bring her back to her feet, wiped blood from her face, and then charged at Freel before he had chance to retract the chains for another lash.

She somersaulted again as she neared him, timing the roll so that she came out of it feet first, and with those feet slamming directly into his chest.

Freel staggered back with an involuntary exhalation as Kali impacted with him, and she took advantage of his imbalance to come upright and strike him with almost simultaneous left and right jabs to the jaw. Freel reeled before her and Kali immediately raised herself onto one leg, spinning as she did to bring the other about in a roundhouse kick that sent Freel's already battered face snapping to the side, throwing an arc of spittle to the wind. As he staggered, attempting to recover from the assault, Kali circled him, her breathing slow and heavy, almost *challenging*. Freel wiped blood from his face, smiled coldly and reined in the chain whips, reducing their length so that they might function better at close range.

This was exactly what Kali wanted, and as Freel began to lash her anew, she backed away, dodging each of his strikes as they came. The manoeuvres kept her convincingly endangered but, in reality, safe from any injury that might lessen her chances of success. There were quite a few close calls – too many, in fact – but eventually she managed to lead Freel all the way to the rear of the sails, which was exactly where she wanted him to be.

It went against everything she believed to bring the fight to a close. Her deepest desire was to finish the bastard now. But that wasn't the solution to the problem Freel had presented her.

Kali began to run, surprising Freel, angering herself, but knowing she was doing the right thing, the *only* thing she could.

She headed with grim determination down the carapace, jumping the small ridges that delineated the folded sails, following the curve in the direction of the ship's prow. Behind her, having expected a confrontation, Freel was caught off guard, and by the time he had released the coils of his whip to take in the extra distance between them, Kali was already out of the deadly chains' reach.

Freel smiled grimly, however, because this didn't matter. It was clear to him that the girl was making for the water, but it was equally clear that she was not going to make it.

The gauntlet presented by those Swords who had followed her from the deck was inescapable, their crossbows covering her from port and starboard. Freel watched as Kali began to run, but there were limits to what even Kali Hooper could do.

Before she had even made it half way to her destination a dozen quarrels had been unleashed, and while Kali did her best to dodge them, twisting and spinning gymnastically so that their deadly barbs whizzed by a hairsbreadth from her skin, at least a third of them found their target; two piercing her right thigh, one her shoulder, and another her side.

Kali staggered slightly and continued on, though the multiple impacts had slowed her, and the second wave of quarrels found their target more easily and with a greater degree of success. She cried out in pain as two quarrels slammed into her back just beneath her shoulderblades, and then another into the soft flesh at the back of the knee, bringing her down. Kali slammed down onto the carapace and began to crawl forwards, roaring with the effort and with her own frustration.

"Surrender, Miss Hooper," Jakub Freel said as the Swords' wound the tension on their crossbows for another assault. "There is no escape."

Kali stiffened momentarily and then managed to get a grip on the ridge of the last of the sails and pulled herself forward. The lip of the carapace was just ahead, below that the ship's prow and the sea. But then the sound of the crossbow's quarrels being slipped into place and locked for firing made her freeze once more. Slowly she tried to pick herself up, and though the Swords were ready to fire, Freel raised a hand to them, momentarily staying the release of their deadly projectiles.

Kali Hooper drew herself up to her full height and turned to face him. Malignant eyes stared from beneath a brow thick with blood. She was slick with it and its loss made her waver slightly where she stood, but she had enough strength to bare her teeth.

Jakub Freel stared up at Kerberos and the ever looming presence of its new companion, then down to Kali.

"It's time for a new dawn, Miss Hooper. A new era where you have no place."

"Go to the hells," Kali growled.

"No. Not I."

He dropped his hand and the Swords fired. Multiple quarrels struck Kali in the legs, arms, torso and head, their impact so powerful she was propelled from the carapace, arcing backwards over the prow and then out into the dark waters below.

Freel moved to the edge of the carapace just in time to see her crash into the sea.

Kali's body floated for a second, and then sank beneath the waves.

CHAPTER EIGHT

THE BLACK SHIP sailed at midchime that night. The torches that had been lit all along the harbourside were presumably present only to keep the crowd that had gathered there warmed against the chill sea winds, for they made little difference beneath the azure glow of Kerberos.

It was tradition that all who worked on the construction of a vessel should watch it depart on its inaugural voyage, though in truth none of them were there by choice that night, roused from their beds by the Swords and forced to attend. Why the Church should insist they assemble for the occasion none could guess, for it knew how they felt about the ship's presence in their town. To them, it was an abomination, unnatural, and, because of the many deaths that had occurred in the months it had taken to build, clearly cursed. None of the town's doctors or apothecaries could explain why the cause of death in most of those cases had been severe burning of the flesh, though some speculated it had something to do with the strange devices with whose assembly they had assisted, or even with the mysterious mineral the Faith had imported into the town and loaded aboard by the ton under conditions of utmost secrecy.

As a result, there was none of the usual cheer and acts of celebration that would normally accompany such a launch, and as the ship's ropes were cast off the people of Gransk regarded the dark hulk silently and with relieved expressions, glad that they would soon see its back. Maybe then, at last, their town might return to normal.

Kali trod water some thirty feet under the surface, her limbs moving slowly and lazily. The constant stream of bubbles from her breathing conch as she pulled quarrels from her flesh went unnoticed by those on the harbourside, though their shadows, backlit by torches and distorted by the surging of waves, appeared to be looming over her. Dammit, Kali thought. That had hurt. But the subtle gymnastics necessary to make sure the quarrels hadn't hit anything vital had achieved her aim. As far as Redigor was concerned, she was dead, and the Black Ship would sail with its hostages safe.

Down here, the sounds of the Black Ship's imminent departure were muted – a dull rumbling of engines and sporadic, almost ghostly clangs as its hull plating shifted – and the only sure way to tell the behemoth was about to sail was from the churning froth of its propellers and the slowly pulsing glow from the amberglow generators concealed beneath the ship's plimsoll line. These orange blisters, two to port and two to starboard, looking from Kali's distorted perspective like wavering suns in some alien sky, had presumably been what had made the waters boil when the ship had been launched, and with them acting as a boost to the ship's sails, she reckoned that Brundle's quoted sailing time of two months would be more like two weeks.

Kali wondered what the people of Gransk would make of the Old Race technology at play here. Doubtless they had been involved in its installation – as the ship's builders how could they not? – but none of them could have truly realised with what it was they were dealing. The Faith had doubtlessly come up with some explanation for the strange sights they had seen, perhaps each would receive a visit from one of Querilous Fitch's alumni and, following a brief but effective mind probe, simply forget everything that had happened.

Kali shifted her attention from the surface to the darker depths below her. She was pleased to note that she had positioned herself correctly as, from the shadows beneath her feet, a large and heavy shape hove into view. It trailed bubbles and silt from the harbour floor as it rose, and Kali kicked herself into position next to the thick chain to which it was attached. Brundle had remained secretive about how he was going to gain access to the Black Ship, and so had she, mainly because she hadn't worked it out at the time, but the simple expedient of hopping a lift had come to mind not long after.

The Black Ship's giant anchor, one of four that held its bulk steady, took shape as it neared the surface, and Kali grabbed at it through swirling silt as it passed. She was feeling quite pleased with herself for choosing this method, but the slight smile on her face was replaced by a look of shock as instead of touching the hard metal she expected, her hands brushed against something organic. She back-pedalled, involuntarily spitting out her breathing conch and gagging on water. The shock made her almost miss her only chance to reach the ship before it departed. Disregarding whatever it was she had touched, Kali lunged forward once more and this time felt the unyielding curves of the anchor's hooks beneath her grip. Flustered – had she imagined what had just happened? – Kali allowed herself to be carried upwards by them for a second while she stared down into the wake of the anchor's ascent and for a moment, just a moment, caught a glimpse of a silvery figure receding into the depths. She was just able to pick out its smooth features, its toothless mouth and the glowing nodules that hung from either side of its jaw – not to mention the fact that it was staring right up at her with eyes that seemed to penetrate her very soul.

Kali's heart thudded. Her unexpected companion looked just like the creature – or at least the same *kind* of creature – she had encountered beneath the collapsing ruins of Martak more than two years before.

The End Comes, came the alien voice in her head. *The Truth Awaits.*

What? Kali thought. What? But she knew she was not going to get an answer, for her strange visitor was already being absorbed into the darkness below, and a second later it was gone. The words resonated in her mind but she quickly shook them away, knowing she had only seconds before the anchor on which she rode broke the surface. Trying her best to ignore what had just happened, Kali began to scramble up the body of the anchor, getting herself into a readied position.

SOME TWENTY FEET above, on the starboard stern deck of the Black Ship, Brother Kelleher stared grimly at the press-ganged men who had been ordered straight into service to struggle with the vessel's anchor chains. He did not attempt to help as, sweating and straining, they heaved it from the water and the anchor began to rise up the sheer wall of the ship's hull. On the port side of the stern, he knew, a similar operation was underway, and similarly two more at the bow. What Brother Kelleher did not know was that, unlike his compatriots elsewhere, his men were being forced to strain just that little bit more.

Brother Kelleher nodded to the men as the anchor rose into its housing and was locked off, and a moment later they were dismissed. The initiate remained behind for a second, watching the anchor spill water and turn slowly where it rested in its housing. He contemplated the voyage ahead – how he would be venturing where no one else had been, into strange and unknown waters, and all for the glory of the Final Faith. He reflected that it was an honour to be chosen to do this, and for a second bowed his head and prayed aloud, thanking both the Anointed Lord and the Lord of All for the privilege that had been granted him.

"I'm pretty much sure that neither gives a toss," a voice said.

Brother Kelleher looked up. The anchor had turned fully turned round in its housing and, spread-eagled so that she matched its cruciform shape, a young woman hung upon it. It was difficult to make out her features through the plastered down fringe that obscured her forehead, but then she flicked the hair aside, slowly spat out a spout of water, smiled and winked. A fist swiftly followed these actions, but this Brother Kelleher didn't really see coming, and he had no chance to reflect on the fact that he had been remiss.

KALI HOPPED STEALTHILY down off the anchor, landing in a crouch over the prone body of the Faith initiative. She delivered another swift punch to his groaning form, making sure he was out cold, stripped him and then quickly dumped him overboard. Far below, Brother Kelleher crashed into the harbour waters and, his underknicks inflating like a balloon, began to bob away on his own, unexpected voyage.

Kali turned back to the deck, lit by the ship's running lights. The fact that she was still sloughing water like a naiad was a pain, but at least her dip had rid her of the stench of the creel, something for which Brundle, if they were eventually reunited, would doubtless be eternally grateful.

She slipped the brother's robe over her own bodysuit and stared about, noting that in the distance the men dismissed by the initiate were entering the bulkhead, leaving that part of the deck clear. There was no one to notice, now, that she had replaced the brother, and as far as anyone seeing her from a distance was concerned, she would be taken for him. She walked to the ship's rail to look back at the departing Gransk.

Oh gods, no, she thought.

Because from her perspective she could see what the crowd gathered there could not, namely that the guards positioned behind them were lifting the tall-staffed torches from where they had been positioned and wielding them like lances. She had her answer, now, to how the Faith intended to deal with the problems of the builders' exposure to their secretive Old Race technology, and, unless she wanted to give away her presence, she couldn't even shout out a warning.

The bastards were making it look as if this were an attack from those sea-dwellers who had raided more than a few coastal towns of late. Kali closed her eyes as the first of the people of Gransk were impaled on the flaming skewers and unceremoniously thrust into the dark waters below. She kept her eyes closed as those who turned at the cries of their friends were cut down by rapidly unsheathed swords.

Damn the Faith, she thought. Damn Makennon, damn Freel, damn them all. If this was the future of their Church, it had no place on her peninsula.

This ends. If not tonight, then one night soon. This ends.

The End Comes, she heard again. *The Truth Awaits.*

Kali took a deep breath and turned away from the scene of carnage, and it mercifully grew more distant as the ship's amberglow generators began to pick up its momentum. Soon the sounds of screams from the shore were replaced by the rush of sea winds and the constant thrum of the vessel beneath her. Kali shivered. She had to get inside, not only to rid herself of the cold but because it was there that she might begin to find some answers as to what exactly was going on on this ship. On the latter, she didn't act immediately, first finding herself a hiding place in the ship's ballast bulkheads and venturing forth occasionally to work out the pattern of the ship's watches and patrols so that when she did emerge, she could do so clandestinely.

It was two days, during which the Black Ship passed through the crackling maelstrom that was the Stormwall and she was forced to insulate herself from the electricity that danced through the ballast bulkheads, before she ventured on decks. There, she had two destinations. As it was likely that the ship's crew knew little – if anything – of Redigor's plans, one of these destinations was the elf's cabin, which she had located towards the stern of the ship. Before that, however, she had a higher priority. This involved her travelling the length of the ship to where she had previously located a set of steps leading down to the cargo hold, where she suspected the prisoners were being held.

Having donned her Faith robe once more, she made her way as far as she could along the open decks, swapping from starboard to port to avoid patrols, and then ducked through a hatch back inside. Here she stowed the robe, the heavy cloth counterproductive to stealth and because it would do little to conceal her identity in the close confines of the interior anyway, and began to negotiate the corridors.

It was like beating a maze where no other wanderers were allowed to see you, but thankfully Kali had always liked mazes. She dodged left and right, right and left, pausing at corners and then moving on, sometimes only a second behind crewmembers in whose steps she silently walked. It took half an hour during which time she hardly dared breathe, but at last she came to the steps she wanted.

She headed down into the hold, three decks below, gratified to find that her suspicions had been proven right. The entire area below decks had been converted into a makeshift prison for the many brought forcefully aboard, kept in groups in cages laid out in a chequerboard style. Guards wandered the shadowy criss-cross of spaces among them and Kali was once again forced to 'dodge the Filth' as she worked her way towards the people she wanted to see. Others – people she didn't know, just innocents who had spoken out against the Faith – rose hopefully as she slipped passed their cages, but for now there was nothing she could do to help or comfort them. Kali continued to move between the cages, inspecting their occupants, and coming at last to two adjacent cages which held her friends from the *Flagons* and Jengo Pim and his men. The fact that these were positioned the farthest back and together suggested that Redigor wanted those closest to her well incarcerated, but it also worked to Kali's advantage as it was an area the guards only glanced towards occasionally.

Inside the first cage, Red Deadnettle caught a glimpse of her face and was about to holler out when Kali put her finger to her lips, silencing him. The huge poacher nevertheless moved eagerly to the bars, Hetty Scrubb and Pete Two-Ties squeezing in beside him. At their rear, Kali could just make out Martha DeZantez tending to the stretchered Dolorosa.

"How are you?" Kali whispered, glancing sideways to keep an eye on the guards.

"Could do with a drink," Red shrugged.

"Me, too," Kali agreed.

"They could have given me a cryptosquare, to pass the time," Pete Two-Ties moaned.

Kali smiled; the man lived to complete his cryptosquares.

"Nihc," she said.

"Pardon?"

"Chin up."

"Oh, ha," Pete responded, dryly.

"Personally, I would like to rip off their balls," Hetty Scrubb hissed. The tiny herbalist was never at her best when unable to sample what she sold, and every sinew and tendon thrust prominently through her parchment skin. "Rip off their balls and ram them in their eyes."

"You'll both have what you need soon," Kali said. "I promise."

Red stared at her. Giant that he was, it was amazing how much like a child he looked. "Then you are not here to get us out?"

"Soon."

Swallowing, she checked the positions of the guards once more, ducked momentarily into shadow, and then moved across the aisle to the opposite cage.

"About time you showed up," Jengo Pim said. "We need out."

"There are what?" Kali said. "Twelve of you? Twelve thieves locked in a cage and you can't *escape*?"

"You can see that this is a rune-inscribed lock," Pim hissed.

"Even so. I really should report you to your union."

"Funny. Now are you going to find a way to get us out of here or not?"

It was only at that moment that Kali realised the reality that she had so far been denying to herself. Had denied to all of them. It was a reality she didn't particularly like.

"I... I can't."

"Can't?" Pim repeated.

"Think about it, Jengo. We're outnumbered two, maybe three, to one on a ship we don't know how to control, heading for a destination only Redigor knows the location of."

"We can handle odds like that. And unless I'm mistaken, didn't you and your people once take control of a spaceship? How hard can the Black Ship be?"

"If we take them out, we might not have enough people to run the ship."

"Then we *force* some of them to run it for us. And Redigor must have charts."

"We can't take that risk."

Pim thumped the bars, then eyed Kali carefully. "Just between you and me, these are just excuses, aren't they?" he said quietly. "You *want* Redigor to get where he's going."

Kali swallowed. She should have known it wouldn't take someone as astute as Pim long to work out the truth. "I didn't know you were all going to be here, okay? I honestly didn't. But I have to reach Trass Kathra."

"Why?"

"I don't know."

"Pits of Kerberos."

"Trust me, Pim. I think this ship needs to get where it's going, for all of our sakes."

"Even the old lady? What's her name? Dolorosa?"

Kali took in a sharp breath. "Even Dolorosa."

Pim took a second and then nodded reluctantly. "Promise me one thing. That you get us out of here before the shit hits whatever fan it's going to hit."

"Nothing's going to happen until this ship reaches Trass Kathra, I'm sure of it. And when it does, I'll have you out of there, okay?"

"Okay."

Kali hesitated, bit her lip. "See you later, Pim."

"I hope so."

Reluctantly, Kali left the prison deck and made her way back the way she had come, all the way to the stern. Her second destination, Bastian Redigor's cabin, awaited. The only problem was that Redigor didn't leave his cabin. Not then and, when Kali returned, not for the whole of that day. Nor the next. Nor the one after that. Eventually Kali concluded that, for whatever reason, the elf was going to spend the entire voyage in isolation, and resigned herself to the fact that the information she wanted would have to be sought later.

Kali didn't go back above decks for the remainder of the voyage, returning to her nest in the ballast bulkheads and spending her time foraging for discarded food, sleeping – as best she could on the violent seas – and befriending and feeding two sodden and sorry looking floprats she named Makennon and Munch. She also read through the journal Merrit Moon had given her in the World's Ridge Mountains. Kali flipping the pages eagerly, as intrigued as much by the old man's journey of discovery as the one she herself was on. The chamber from which she had rescued Moon was, according to his notes, the first of three which together formed the passage through the World's Ridge Mountains he had speculated existed. The Hall of Tales was the first, the Hall of Howling Faces the second, and the third the Hall of the Mountain... thing.

Obviously he hadn't managed to translate that last bit.

A few events distracted her during this time. The first was the ramming of an untershrak herd against the hull, sometimes so powerful she expected their triple-jawed snouts to punch through the watertight plating beside her head. The second an attack by the Great Blob itself. No one knew the exact nature or intent of this much feared aquatic denizen, though it struck Kali as being fundamentally benign – an observation based on its plaintive and almost befriending cries as it circled the Black Ship, occasionally rubbing itself up against it. Kali didn't interfere as the Faith fought the creature off – how could she? – and felt monumentally saddened when the blob's cries turned pained and then faded away into the distance.

One night – on what she calculated was the twelfth night of the voyage and in relatively calm seas – music drifted down from somewhere above, a familiar melody that reminded her of Slowhand, and for the few hours until daylight came again she felt agonisingly homesick.

At last, a burst of activity on the upper decks signalled what had to be the end of the voyage. Kali stole from her hiding place, figuring that if it was all hands on deck she should be able to go unnoticed in the crowd. Sure enough, as she emerged into natural, albeit a stormy grey, light for the first time in two weeks,

the decks were awash with so much activity that no one had time
to give her a second glance.

Kali made her way to the prow, and immediately saw why.
Couldn't miss why, in fact.

The Black Ship was heading towards a stretch of ocean that
could only be the swirlpools that Brundle had described, and
while the dwarf had intimated these obstacles were dangerous,
the word dangerous hardly seemed to do them justice.

Kali gasped. For what seemed like leagues ahead of them, and
leagues to port and starboard, sweeping away in a broad band,
the ocean was in upheaval. Great, circular eddies, hundreds of
them whirling away, crammed together and crashing together,
forming other, new manifestations of themselves, making the
waters they were about to sail into seethe and boil and explode
upward into the sky. Far higher than the Black Ship itself, these
violent eruptions of ocean seemed almost alive, made of stuff
more viscous than the seas that birthed them, somehow almost
sentient in the way they hung there before plummeting whence
they came, worsening the chaos beneath. It was like the ocean
was at war with itself, and Kali knew instantly that to enter this
battlefield would be deadly.

A shadow darkened her view. Redigor stood calmly by her side,
hands holding the rails, as if they were two friends on holiday,
enjoying the view.

"Spectacular, are they not?" the elf said.

"Personally, I prefer the banks of the Rainbow River, or the
Shifting Sands of Oweilau."

"Both beautiful, especially seen as I have seen them, awash
with the blood of battle."

"Thanks for reminding me what a fruitcake you are, Baz. You
don't seem surprised to find me alive."

"Not surprised at all. I could *feel* you infesting the bulkheads
like a filthy floprat. What is it you call such vermin these days?
Pests?"

"Then why didn't you subject me to pest control?"

"I had... other concerns."

"I can tell."

Kali studied the elf's profile as he stared impassively beyond the prow of the Black Ship. His – that was Freel's – condition had deteriorated dramatically even since they had met on the ship's gangplank, and was presumably the reason he had locked himself away inside his quarters. His long black hair was thinning and billowing about his body like a shroud, his skin flaking away, peeled from him by the sea wind and trailing behind him to be slowly scattered amidst the grey, cloudy skies like ashes from a burnt-out fire.

The man was a ghost even though he wasn't dead yet.

Not yet.

"It's over, Redigor. Give this up."

"I am touched by your concern for my health."

"I don't give a flying fark about your health, elf. It's Freel's health I'm concerned about."

Redigor's jaw tensed. "Forget your friend. He's gone."

"Not while I'm drawing breath, Mister."

"Then I shall once more have to address myself to making sure that you don't."

Kali glanced casually down over the edge of the deck, saw the white of the angry ocean rushing by the plimsoll line. There was no way she'd survive that. And even if she did, where would she go, in the middle of nowhere, here, on the other side of the world?

"Shouldn't you be ordering a full stop?"

"On the contrary. The island is my destination. I intend to reach it."

"But the ship will be torn apart."

"Yes."

Kali gasped as a particularly violent surge caused her to lose her grip and she was slammed around, her back impacting painfully with the prow. It was in that moment that she realised something that she – and Brundle, wherever the dwarf was – had missed. The only thing that mattered to Redigor was that he made landfall, and to that extent the ship was nothing more than a means to an end. It had been built the way it had to be used as an ocean-going battering ram, to get them as close to the island as it could, and if it was wrecked in the process, he didn't care.

He wasn't going home. No one on the ship was going home.

This was a voyage of the damned.

"My god, Redigor, what have you got planned?"

"Salvation," the elf said.

And with that he raised his hand, signalling those on the bridge behind him not to slow but to speed their knottage. The Black Ship ploughed ahead.

Heading straight for the swirlpools at ramming speed.

CHAPTER NINE

THE ELF TURNED suddenly away from the prow. "You must forgive me, Miss Hooper, but it is time for your friends to be released from their confines. You may help if you wish."

Kali felt the Black Ship groan beneath her. Heard the bang of exploding rivets and creak of plating from its hull as it encountered the first of the stresses that the swirlpools presented. They had only just reached their edge.

"I don't know what you've got planned but damn right I'll help," she said, following.

"Then be quick. There is no time to waste."

The two of them made their way back below decks and down to the prisoner's hold, Redigor enlisting men to help as he moved. Watching the elf dance his hand over the rune-inscribed locks of the cages, opening them, wasn't exactly what Kali had imagined when she'd promised Pim she'd get him and the others out of there, but considering the unexpected development it would have to do. Pim gave her a glance as, along with his men, he was pulled from his cage, still in chains, to join the other prisoners being ushered onto the upper decks. All Kali could do was give a shrug that said, wait and see.

Redigor opened the cage holding Red and the others from the *Flagons*, and Kali quickly moved inside to help Martha DeZantez with Dolorosa. The sour stink of infection assailed her nostrils as she bent to wrap the old woman in her blankets, and Kali had to quash a flare of fury that Redigor had provided no medication for her wounds.

Dolorosa groaned and shifted as her stretcher was lifted, and a hand slipped free. A small object trailed from loose fingers onto the floor of the cage. The old woman's prayer beads.

"Red, take her," Kali said to the poacher, and turned to retrieve the beads. When she turned back the cage was empty and Redigor was standing by its door. He closed it with a clang, his hand dancing once more over the rune-inscribed lock.

"Should have seen that one coming," Kali said.

"I believe you should have," Redigor agreed.

Kali glanced between the cages to the steps where the last of the prisoners were being taken to the upper decks. At their rear, Red Deadnettle turned and looked at her hopelessly. As he did, the entire ship rocked, almost turned onto its side despite the stability of its twin hulls, and, rather disorientatingly, began to rotate.

They were entering the swirlpools proper, and, if the sounds of the tortured hull around her were anything to go by, the swirlpools would soon be entering the ship. A second later, a bulkhead beside the steps burst and a torrent of seawater began to flood the prison deck.

"Goodbye, Miss Hooper," Redigor said.

And with that, he and the others were gone, the hatch to the upper decks shut behind them.

Kali thumped the cage bars, cursing her own stupidity, and as the floodwaters began to swirl about her ankles and then her waist, her hand searched instinctively for her breathing conch in the side pocket of her bodysuit. Feeling empty space, her mind flashed with the image of the conch dwindling into the depths of Gransk harbour, and she cursed again.

Then Kali remembered the small bag Merrit Moon had given her in the World's Ridge Mountains. A few things that might help to keep you safe, he had said, so let's see.

She dug inside, extracting first an elven memory crystal, second a small sphere that looked like one of the old man's ice-bombs and which she wasn't willing to risk finding out, and third an object that rattled and hummed in her hand but of whose purpose she had no idea at all. Fine. If she wanted to record herself being frozen in a solid block of ice while some kind of weird clockwork toy got on her tits, then Moon had provided her with the perfect tools. But if she wanted to use them to get out of here, she was bollocksed.

There was one more item. A small bag within the bag that had gone almost unnoticed in her search. She pulled it out, undid its drawstring, and then yelped in pain as a length of thin vine covered in tiny leaves wrapped itself tightly around her index finger, extracting more of itself from the bag as it did. Kali knew what this was. Tourniqueed. Back when, the elves had used it as dressing to staunch the flow of blood from wounds in battle, and it still grew to this day in the marshes of Rammora. Kali could only imagine that Moon hadn't realised it was in the bag, a forgotten piece of a first aid kit he had perhaps used in his earlier adventuring days, but ironically it was of more use than any of the other objects he had given her.

The water having risen to her neck, Kali pinched the leaves of the tourniqueed, releasing it from her finger, and wrapped it instead around one of the bars of the cage. She pinched the leaves again and the vine contracted. Many an elf had lost a limb before he or she had come to realise how to stop the vine's contractions, and left to its own devices it was strong enough to cut through anything, even metal.

It took time, though, and time was one thing Kali didn't have. The seawater was splashing about her mouth and nose now, making her gag, and when at last the tourniqueed severed the bar she had already been submerged for almost a minute. Kali quickly snatched the vine from the water and reapplied it two feet further down the bar, and as it began to cut its way through once more she hammered the bar repeatedly, knowing she'd never survive until the tourniqueed had completed its job. She lost count of the number of desperate strikes she made, but she did know that her blows were becoming weaker each time, and finally she resorted to holding onto the surrounding bars, twisting her body and booting the face of the cage. Her vision was darkening and for a second she was only vaguely aware that the bar had become weak enough and was slowly spiralling away from her. She twisted and pulled herself through the opening it had made.

Kali swam directly for the steps and the hatch above, but as she turned the wheel to open it, it stuck fast. Redigor, or one of his men, must have jammed it. Kali's eyes widened and she turned desperately, seeking another way out.

But there was none.

She pounded on the hatch, bubbles of air exploding from her, but who was she kidding? Who did she expect to come to rescue her?

Maybe the person who was now turning the wheel from the other side, opening the hatch to the equally flooded deck beyond.

Kali's mind was so starved of oxygen now that it all seemed like a dream. Maybe it *was* a dream because the person who had opened the hatch – her rescuer – wasn't a person at all. In the grey, murky waters, Kali found herself looking at the same creature she had encountered in Gransk harbour, possibly the same creature she had long ago encountered in the floodwaters of Martak. Whether it was the same or not, she didn't know, for this time the creature did not speak in her mind, but merely took hold of her floating form and pulled her after it. Familiar ship's corridors, their angles warped by the waters that filled them, segued by, and in what remained of her conscious thoughts Kali recognised that she was being taken to safety.

Thank you, she wanted to say. *Please tell me, who are you?*

But she couldn't. Finding herself lying face down on the deck above, her sodden form gasping, the creature was gone.

Kali picked herself up, but her problems were only just beginning. The stresses she'd witnessed tearing the ship apart below were far more evident above, and the ship pitched suddenly and dramatically, flinging her across the deck and almost hurling her into the sea. Except there was no sea. Clinging onto the rail, Kali looked down the precipitous drop of the hull to the part of the maelstrom in which it was caught. A section of one of the swirlpools churned right below her – or maybe above, in the constant skewing of the world it was difficult to tell – battering and lashing the ship while all the time staring back like some unblinking, giant, malevolent eye.

But the swirlpool was no eye, she knew that now. It was a mouth to the hells. A mouth that was fully capable of swallowing the ship whole. And the only reason it hadn't yet done so was that it vied with maybe a hundred others that made up the barrier around Trass Kathra.

A hundred.

And the ship was caught in the heart of them all.

As it was pulled from one to another, increasingly battered and twisted, the sound of the swirlpools' roaring hunger almost, but not quite, drowned out the sound of dull, periodic explosions and screams from along the deck.

Redigor and his people. And the hostages. It had to be. Despite her enforced delay, they must not yet have made it off the ship.

Kali began to move towards the screams. Reaching their source was not easy, however. Even as she forced herself off the rail against which she'd been thrown, the ship pitched again, and she found herself staggering back towards the hatch from which she'd emerged, slapping into it and then onto the deck as a crash of water soaked herself and the deck about her. This time, for good measure, the ship turned, too, its bow being forced around by the edge of an adjacent swirpool, and the creaks and groans of its protesting bulkheads began anew. There wasn't much time. The ship was coming apart.

The sky revolved giddily, and Kali found the only way to negotiate the wall in which the hatch sat was to allow herself to slide along it, carried by the water that flooded towards the stern. This, too, turned into a treacherous exercise as the ship dipped violently, transforming what had been a level, if unstable, deck into an acutely angled slide. Again, Kali let herself go with it, gaining speed as she skidded down, then, at the last minute, grabbed onto another passing rail before she impacted with what would have been bone-crunching finality against one of the deck stanchions.

"Woo!" she cried, feet dangling and kicking in mid-air.

She jerked herself aside as two Final Faith brothers, presumably having been engaged in some last minute business at the bow, sailed past her, robes flapping as they plummeted to their inevitable end. Their sudden departure from the ship reduced the numbers she had to deal with and she didn't feel the slightest guilt in taking pleasure from their demise. It was the silly bastards' own bloody fault for coming here in the first place.

This handy method of reducing the opposition was only momentary, however, and the ship's bow crashed back onto the water with an almighty belly-flop that jarred every rivet in the hull and loosened yet more of its plating. A sheet of seawater splashed down onto the deck and Kali was punched off the rail and found herself spiralling along, caught in a series of crashing waves and rolling banks of water. This time she could not avoid being slammed into one of the stanchions, and the wind was knocked out of her, leaving her briefly dazed. But when she recovered her orientation, she found the waters had carried her to the part of the deck from which the explosions and screams had been coming.

Kali hid behind the stanchion and stared at what she saw there.

The explosions came not, as she'd expected, from disintegrating parts of the ship, but from explosive bolts that secured the mysterious, cigar-shaped objects to the deck. As these detonated, Redigor's men were tugging the canvas sheeting from them, revealing large, dark metal objects the purpose of which Kali couldn't make out for the throng gathered about them. One thing was likely, though. From the desperation with which they worked, these things were a way off the sinking ship.

Kali's attention turned to the throng. Something was wrong here. Counting Redigor's people and the hostages – who were being forcefully jostled amongst them, still in chains – there seemed far too many potential survivors, especially as it seemed one of the cigar-shapes had been damaged during the voyage. Redigor himself was already scowling at this and, among his men, shouts of recrimination and accusations of negligence were being bandied around. This got them nowhere, of course, because it was clear that there could be only one conclusion to this realisation.

Some people would have to be left behind.

Oh Gods, Kali thought. The hostages. If it was a choice between his own men and the hostages, Redigor would surely dispose of them here.

She was about to break cover, simply take a chance and go all out to save them, when she faltered. A bright blue flash in the middle of the throng was followed by a scream, and the body of one of the Faith thudded to the deck, as a smoking and charred heap of meat. Others around him backed off, muttering fearfully, and this revealed the cause of the first flash as it happened again.

It was Redigor. Fists burning, the Pale Lord was frying his own people, any and all of them who tried to clamber onto the objects out of turn or objected to the fact that they seemed not to have a place there. For these, their desperation to escape the doomed ship overrode their fear of their leader, but it was a bad choice, a fatal choice.

What disturbed Kali the most about it was that Redigor smiled as he so casually doled out their deaths.

No, that wasn't quite true – what disturbed her most was why Redigor was favouring the hostages over his own people. If he was so intent on saving them and taking them with him, surely that suggested they had a purpose that went beyond their being hostages or simple prisoners. But what?

The ship twisted again and groaned beneath her, louder than ever before, and Kali knew it could not take the stress it was suffering for much longer. As waves crashed about her and parts of the ship's superstructure broke away to crash onto the deck, she moved closer to the desperate gathering, keeping to cover, trying to see if there was any way that she herself could find her way onto one of the mysterious objects of salvation.

There was none, however, and she could only look on as the objects revealed themselves fully. Groups of Redigor's people – the hostages scattered amongst them – were positioned beside each of the 'cigars' and, now that Kali could see more clearly, she watched as each in turn began to unfold, transforming from their original shapes into something quite different.

Kali knew immediately what she looking at – flutterbys. The deceptively charming name for elven troop carriers. Triangular shaped wings extended from the objects' sides, retractable blades from their tops, and, from the main bodies of the objects, riding platforms in the form of interlacing metal struts on which passengers were clearly meant to stand. The flutterbys fully deployed, they sat on the deck of the ship like a swarm of giant insects.

Impressive, Kali thought. They looked original, too, and she reflected that while she had never physically come across one, Bastian Redigor clearly knew where to look.

The flutterbys were filling up now, but there remained far too many people to be accommodated by them. But, as before, Redigor was ensuring that the numbers became more manageable in his own, inimitable fashion. The whole group fell into chaos as more of his own men died thrashing and screaming, and Kali thought it the ideal moment to make a dash for one of the machines to guarantee her own passage off the sinking ship.

But she paused. The balance of numbers between Redigor's people and his hostages was favouring the latter now, and for her to take a place in one of the pods meant one of the hostages would not make it, and she couldn't condemn them that way. Of everyone on board, with the possible exception of Redigor himself, she was the one most physically capable of surviving the ship going down, even if she didn't yet know how she was going to manage it.

She was sure something would pop up. It always did. But it was going to be one hells of a rough ride.

The last flutterby being boarded, now, Kali bit her lip as she watched Redigor and his personal retinue, accompanying the last of the hostages, step into position. Just as the last, a man whom she'd swear she'd last seen as one of the press-ganged, stepped onto his foothold, he turned and spotted her hiding behind her cover. For a second their eyes met and Kali wondered if he would reveal her presence to Redigor. He did nothing, however, apart from nod as if wishing her luck.

She was going to need it. As the flutterby rose from the deck, turning in a sweeping circle to head towards the island, the ship groaned beneath her as if poisoned to its core.

Suddenly the whole of the stern, where the flutterbys had been, began to break away from the hull, a rift opening from below decks that spread upwards until it began to tear the deck itself asunder. As decking warped, popped and tore under her, revealing the equally torn lower decks spilling their contents into the sea, Kali joined those few of the Faith whom Redigor had left behind alive in running towards the bow and relative safety. That they had such commonality of purpose made it all the more irksome when one of them – clearly acting above and beyond the call of duty – grabbed her and demanded to know what she was doing there. She flattened the idiot and threw him over the side.

The deck buckled as she and the others continued to run, sending a wave of wood and metal nipping at their heels, but while it caught up to and brought down a number of the Faith, Kali herself leapt for the safety of a handrail to one of the upper decks. It provided only a brief respite from the surging destruction below, however, and a few seconds after grabbing onto it, it, too, buckled and fell.

Kali cursed. The first time in her life she had been on a sinking ship and it didn't even have the decency to sink properly, which was to say slowly and languorously beneath the waves. At least then she might have had a chance to formulate some kind of plan, perhaps even grab a drink and sing a rousing song or two as the sea proceeded inexorably towards her feet. But no – the increasing stresses from the swirlpools all around were tearing the ship apart, and the screams, rather than songs, that came from all around her reflected that fact.

A scream from one Faith as the deck suddenly opened and

then closed again beneath him, cutting him in two at the waist. A scream from another as a stanchion broke from its mooring and decapitated him instantly if not cleanly. A scream from a third as the deck rail against which he hoped to gain respite broke away, plunging him into the maelstrom below.

Screams. Screams everywhere.

And then, just like that, the ship broke cleanly in two. The hull finally gave way to its stresses and parted right in front of her, bringing Kali to a skidding halt. She was suddenly surrounded, overtaken, by screaming, flailing forms as the Faith who had been following in her wake flung themselves desperately across the widening gap. One or two reached the opposite section of deck cleanly, somersaulting and continuing to run, some didn't quite make it, gaining precarious handholds and dangling desperately from struts exposed by the rent, while still others missed their mark completely and plunged into the churning mass of hull and water that waited beneath.

Kali didn't know what had made her halt in her tracks but the decision had proven to be the right one. The irony was that what they all – herself included – had thought to be the safer half of the sinking ship was not that at all. The final battering that had broken the ship's back had been caused by the confluence of two massive swirlpools challenging each other for their prize, and as Kali watched the bow of the ship was immediately taken by one, while the stern was swept away by the other. As the distance between the two halves of the ship grew, the stern section a quarter of the way around the periphery now and receding all the while, the bow was already being pulled directly into the heart of the furthest maelstrom. She could see the figures of the Faith who had made it across realising their situation and flinging themselves off the sinking ship into the water, but this was the worst thing they could have done, serving only to accelerate their deaths as their tiny forms were sucked beneath the surface in advance of the much larger wreck. Not that they would have survived that much longer, because the bow of the ship was already tipping forwards as it succumbed to the terrible forces in which it was snared, and only a few seconds later it sank beneath the waves.

Kali turned to look about her, and realised she on her own now. As the stern half of the ship listed beneath her, she was sent tumbling across the deck to its far rail, so that once again she was staring directly into the hungry sea. The list was only the result of the ship finding its natural position, however, and as it began to circle the sloping rim of the swirlpool she would, had it not been for the deafening roar of the chaotic sea, have found it almost relaxing, like being the sole passenger on some weird carousel.

But there was only one way this ride was going to end, and as the stern section spiralled gradually but inexorably ever deeper into the giant, watery crater, Kali bit her lip, deep in thought. One by one she assessed the circumstances of her situation – sinking ship, swirlpool, middle of the ocean a long, long way from home – and it didn't take her long to reach a summation of her predicament.

Farked. She was farked. All she could do was ensure that as the stern section began to sink she stayed as far from the all consuming water as she could, and when she could do that no longer... well, she was just going to have to make it up as she went along.

Round and round the wreckage went. And down and down. Its descent into oblivion more gradual but no less inevitable than that of the bow. Kali was backing up in what remaining space she had, the churning surface of the swirlpool literally lapping at her feet, when something burst through the surface of the water some hundred yards away.

It was some kind of machine that sped towards her, pumping the discoloured sea through membranes that seemed to drive its solid and barnacle covered frame forward. She didn't have the remotest idea of what it was but she did know who was sitting in what could only be the driver's seat.

Jerragrim Brundle grunted as, with the whine of some unknown engine, the strange machine slewed up onto the deck and skidded halt beside her. It still pumped out the water it had used for propulsion. Its streamlined shape was etched with dwarven runes and, though simple, its controls were far more complex than anything anyone on the peninsula could produce. Kali grinned. This was the aquatic equivalent of the mole machine she had found many months before, and she wanted one. Hells, did she want one.

"Are you gonna continue grinning like a loon or are yer gonna jump aboard?" Brundle demanded. He flicked his head toward the water. "Cos if yer haven't noticed, we don't have a lot of time."

Kali slammed her hands on her hips. "Oh, so now it's all rush. Just where the hells have you been for the past two weeks?"

"Close by, smoothskin. Close by."

The dwarf looked down.

And Kali looked at the machine. She noticed that some kind of breathing tube protruded from its control panel. There appeared to be one for a passenger, too. "Are you telling me that this thing's been attached to the hull all this time?"

"As tight as the piles up me arse."

Kali pulled a face. "How did I know you were going to say something like that? Couldn't you have just said 'limpet'?"

"Why?"

"Because... oh, never mind."

The waters began to slosh and slap over them, threatening to wash the machine off the deck. The last remains of the ship tipped dangerously as it began to be pulled down to the heart of the swirlpool.

"Are you coming, or what?" Brundle asked with some urgency.

"What do you call this thing, anyway?" Kali asked as she settled herself into the space for a second rider.

"Scuttlebarge. Now hang on."

Whatever response Kali might have had emerged only as a startled yelp as Brundle slung the scuttle barge around and, with a roar of its engine, it shot nose first into the churning sea. Kali scrabbled for the breathing tube, convinced that it was simply going to slip right beneath the waves but, as soon as it was waterborne, the membranes that pumped the water rotated in their housings so that they pointed straight down, and the machine gained its buoyancy on the surface with the force of their thrust. They didn't remain there once their job was done, however, rotating once more into a position half way between the two, and with a kick that threw Kali back in her seat the scuttlebarge began to skip across the sea.

To say that it was a bumpy ride would be an understatement. But Brundle appeared to be an expert pilot. Despite being continuously slapped and drenched by waves, more than one of which threatened to knock her overboard, forcing her to hold on tighter, Kali couldn't help but be impressed by the way the dwarf handled the scuttlebarge, playing the tumultuous surface of the sea with practiced ease, going with the flow here, using it to gain momentum there, never once hesitant as he threw the machine into each new manoeuvre.

The one thing that did come as a surprise – and caused a small lurch of shock – to Kali was that rather than piloting the strange craft to avoid any swirlpools in their path, Brundle aimed it straight for them. What appeared to be a suicidal ploy was nothing of the kind, however, as at the very last second on approaching the first of the maws, Brundle veered the scuttlebarge to starboard so that rather than heading right into the swirling water it skirted its rim, using the power of the swirlpool to carry them around the maw. Once on its other side, Brundle gunned the pumps of the craft so that they flipped over the crest of the maelstrom and then immediately flung her around so that they were carried along in the rim of another, this one swirling in the opposite direction. After successfully achieving this a couple more times, it became clear to Kali what it was he was doing – using the coriolis effect of the swirlpools to catapult the scuttlebarge between them. It could not have been the first time he had attempted such a task.

But what lay ahead of them might not prove such an easy task.

Roaring with a sound that drowned out of all its compatriots, out of all the swirlpools that surrounded Trass Kathra, this was the daddy of them all.

"You might want to use that tube now!" Brundle warned, and even as Kali fitted it tightly into her mouth, the pumps to the rear of the scuttlebarge rotated so that they were pointing upwards, forcing the machine beneath the waves. Everything was replaced by the turmoil of grey water, and all that Kali could make out was Brundle's beard, previously in danger of slapping, with all its bells, into her face, floating about her.

The reason Brundle had submerged had already become clear to Kali. Even with his expertise there was no way he could have negotiated the sheer power and violence of this swirlpool on the surface, but here, under the water, things were just that little bit calmer, even if it did still appear as a maelstrom from the hells. Brundle used the same technique he had above, riding the scuttlebarge into the outer edge of the underwater spiral and then allowing it to carry them around, to what would hopefully be calm on its other side. There was, however, something different about the swirlpool down here – caught up in the churning waters were patches of a whiter substance, still liquid but slightly more viscous than the surrounding element, which moved within it and yet not *with* it. Whatever the stuff was, it was clearly not simple seawater, and Kali noticed that Brundle put all of his effort into grimly and steadfastly avoiding it.

Dark shapes bounced around the scuttlebarge, and as the currents brought one of them smack bang into Kali's face, fleetingly revealing a horrified though quite dead visage whose lips had pulled back from its teeth, she realised they had hit a pocket of drowned men from the ship. A couple of the bodies bumped against the side of the scuttlebarge, forcing Brundle to correct his course slightly, but then, thankfully, they were through the cluster of dead. Kali couldn't help but turn to look behind her as they passed, however, and for the briefest of moments thought she saw one of the bodies caught up in the whiter substance whose nature she still knew nothing about. All she knew was that she was glad Brundle had managed to avoid it, because, as it touched the drowned Final Faith, his whole body seemed simply to drift apart.

What the hells? Kali thought.

The scuttlebarge began to rise, and Kali realised Brundle was returning it to the surface, using the last of the power of the swirlpool to throw them beyond its influence into calmer waters.

They should, now, be nearing the island, she calculated, and, sure enough, as the machine lurched above the surface, slewing water from its barnacled frame, the coastline of Trass Kathra was right ahead of her.

Oh Gods.

The island was not so much an island as a mountain in the middle of the sea, and built into its shadow and into its sides were structures so ancient and overgrown they'd come to resemble the rocks themselves. Accessed by a precipitous network of carved steps that led up from a small cove on the shoreline – what, perhaps, had once been a landing point – Kali saw strange bunkers and metal towers, many of these collapsed and bent at unnatural angles, a couple of carapaced structures that looked as if they might be some kind of warehouse, and numerous other, oddly shaped buildings whose purpose she couldn't even begin to guess at. Dominating them all, though, was the most impressive looking structure of them all. Almost at the island's highest point, on the slope of a great, thrusting clifftop, was what appeared to be a huge observatory dome.

Kali's mouth dropped open. Out here, far beyond the known world, where nothing at all should be, was the work of those whose secrets she'd spent a lifetime exploring.

An Old Race outpost.

She couldn't wait to set foot on those steps.

Disappointingly, however, Brundle wasn't piloting the scuttlebarge towards the cove but keeping an equidistant course along its coast. If they continued the way they were, they would leave the steps far behind and round the island's farthest point.

She tapped the dwarf on the shoulder, shouting above the noise of breakers on rocks.

"What the hells are you doing?"

"We're not landing here, smoothskin," Brundle responded. "Too dangerous."

Kali frowned. She looked back towards the cove and saw what her enthusiasm had denied her seeing before. The cove was filled with the grounded flutterbys from the Black Ship. And though she saw many of the guards and their prisoners snaking their way up the steps to whatever destination Redigor had in mind, others of his landing party – prisoners and guards – remained behind. A number of the guards having positioned themselves as sentries on the steps, there was no way they would get past them.

"Oh, and one more thing," Brundle shouted over his shoulder. "Yer got the name o' the place wrong. People always get it wrong. It ain't Trass Kathra, the Island of the Lost. It's Trass *Kattra*... the Island of the Four."

Kali almost fell off the scuttlebarge.

"*What*?"

Brundle smiled and turned his attention back to ploughing through the waves.

"Child of Trass Kattra," he roared, "welcome home!"

CHAPTER TEN

CHILD OF TRASS KATTRA, Welcome Home! The words reverberated in Kali's mind, begging a hundred different questions, but her attempts to gain an answer to any of them were thwarted by the choppy coastal waters they had entered. Brundle couldn't hear a thing – or chose not to hear a thing – as he gunned the scuttlebarge's engines, expertly playing the breakers, slapping and lurching the old and battered machine ever closer to land.

They rounded the end of the island, and there approached a patch of darkness at the base of a cliff. A cave. It seemed this was their destination and, considering Brundle's other words – about this being the Island of the Four, whatever *that* meant – Kali couldn't help but start to imagine what wonders it might hold.

Nothing, was the answer. Bugger all. Because as the cliff face swallowed the scuttlebarge, plunging it into shadow, there were no wondrous Old Race machines, no looming statues of ancient heroes, nothing, in fact, that suggested the island would live up to the promise of its name. Instead, as Brundle cut the engine and they drifted in, she saw a primitive jetty and walkway that was all but falling apart, lit by the few torches that hadn't been broken. Those that weren't picked out nets and seafood pots dangling from railings, spears, tridents and harpoons. There was even a pair of wellies stacked amongst them. The only signs of technology were the remains of three other scuttlebarges, in various states of disrepair, one of which bobbed by the jetty, the others lying skewed where they had been driven up against the sides of the cave for makeshift berthing.

Something splashed near her right leg as it dangled in the water and Kali looked down. She spotted a huge keep net in which scores of fish the likes of which she'd never seen swam. One, the size of a floprat, bared sharp teeth and darted at her, and she snatched her leg from the water with a yelp.

"Thrap," Brundle stated. "Vicious little sods but good wi' a shake o' sea salt."

Kali nodded, not really listening. It was still here. Too still. The acoustics of the cave were such that they blocked out the sound of the raging seas beyond, and as she continued to look about in the flickering torchlight, listening to the slow lap of waves and almost soporific drips of water from the roof, she sensed that her surroundings had been like this for literally ages; a backwater at the end of the world, never, ever changing.

"What is this place?"

"Home."

"You live here?"

"Aye. It ain't much, but it satisfies our needs..."

"*Our* needs?"

Brundle pointed down at the keepnet. "I like a piece o' thrap, lass, but not that much."

"How many of you are there, then?"

"Two."

"Two?" Kali echoed. She stared at the keepnet. "Maybe still a little greedy."

"Aye, well... yer haven't met the wife."

"Wife?"

"Brogma," Brundle said. "Wife number... blast it, ah forget

what number she is, now." He sighed, but Kali couldn't tell whether tiredly or regretfully. "Believe me, there've bin a few."

"And Brogma – she's a dwarf, too?"

"O' course she's a bloody dwarf! Are yer thinkin' ah'd marry an elf?!"

"That isn't what I meant. Don't forget from my perspective dwarves are, er... a little short on the ground. I thought maybe that in the absence of anything else she might be human?"

"Human? Pah to bloody human! There's mendin' to be done! Cleanin'! Cookin'! Forgin'! A human could no more satisfy me needs than one o' them posin' ponces, the elves!"

Equality was clearly not big with dwarves, but Kali couldn't help smiling. Of all the ways the ancient tales referred to the elves it was the first time she'd heard them called 'posin' ponces'. It almost made her feel better about Redigor's presence on the island.

The thought of the elf returned her mind to business – and the many questions she had. As the scuttlebarge bumped against the jetty and Brundle disembarked, hooking the machine's nose with a thick hemp rope he then tied off, Kali ignored his offer of a hand and hopped up under her own steam, turning to block his path with hands on her hips.

"Explanations," she demanded. "*Now.*"

"What explanation did yer have in mind?"

"Oh, let's see," Kali said. "How about that little fondling act back in Gransk? Or why you wanted to blow up the ship to stop it coming here? And hey, while we're at it, what was that thing out there in the swirlies, what the hells is this place and why's it called the Island of the Four, and – oh, oh, last but not least – *what the fark did you mean by welcome home?*"

The dwarf waited while his hair settled and the bells in his beard stopped jangling.

"Have ye done?"

"Yes!"

Brundle sighed. "I can answer some o' yer questions, lass, but not all. That tale's a long one, and it ain't mine for the tellin'."

"Then whose? Brogma?"

"No, not Brogma."

"There's someone else on the island?"

"In a manner of speaking."

"In a manner of speaking," Kali repeated, increasingly frustrated. "What is it with you, dwarf? Were you born awkward or did you take special classes?"

"Special classes. I've had a lot of time to kill."

"Funny. Take me to them, then. Whoever can tell me the *whole* story."

"You'll have yer little chat soon."

"Soon?"

Brundle smiled. "Why don't we have a little bit o' tea first?"

Kali growled in exasperation as the dwarf weaved his way past her, and, having no choice, followed. Brundle neared a rockface and, purposefully this time, jangled the bells in his beard. The sound they made was loud and distinctive. After a second, a chunk of the rock face before him, what Kali had thought was the end of the cave, rumbled aside, revealing a torch-lit passage. A waft of something cooking - powerfully fishy - came from within.

"This way, smoothskin," Brundle directed. And then shouted, "Hi, honey, I'm home!"

Kali took one last look behind her and followed Brundle, possibly more bemused than she'd ever been. She wasn't sure what she'd expected when she reached Trass Kathra - Trass Kattra, she corrected - but this certainly wasn't it. And what she expected least of all, just before they exited the passage into what lay beyond, was a set of flowery curtains that Brundle, with some embarrassment, pulled aside.

"Don't blame me," he growled. "We live with what we find."

"Live with what you fi -?" Kali half repeated, then stopped. The passage had led them into an inner cave which opened out before her, and though it was much the size of the one they had just left, there was barely an inch within it to move. The whole place was crammed with enough junk to fill a city of scrapyards, piled up against the walls, across the floor, in great piles in the corners of the chamber. At least Kali presumed they were the corners of the chamber, because as far as she could tell this rubbish might go on for ever. It was like looking at the World's Ridge Mountains made out of crap.

Despite being overwhelmed by the sheer volume of the stuff, however, she couldn't help but be drawn to specific items contained in the mounds. Because most of this stuff was old – very old – and despite it being bruised and battered she still felt a little like a child let loose in a confectionarium.

"Where the hells did you get all this?"

The dwarf shrugged. "Plenty is washed up by the storms or makes its way on the tides. Or was salvaged from the wrecks o' those daft enough to try to take on the Stormwall. When that bastard *really* packed a punch, that was."

"That's the second time you've suggested the Stormwall is less than it was."

"All ah can say, smoothskin, is that one upon a time she were magnificent. Stretched around the peninsula like a necklace o' heavenly fire, she did, from both ends o' the World's Ridge to the Sarcre Islands. Nothin' could get through it. Nothin' at all."

"You mean it was some kind of *wall*?"

"Just something that was where the mountains weren't."

"What the hells is that supposed to mean?"

"That, smoothskin, isn't me place to tell."

"How did I know you were going to say that?"

"Now, where was I? Oh, aye. That which doesn't find its way here otherwise is foraged around the coast of the mainland. Ah make trips five or six times a year with the scuttlebarge an' a sled. Generally tie 'er up in Ten Bones Bay. It was the trip before last ah learned about the buildin' o' that bloody Black Ship, an' scuttled back here as fast as ah could for me bombs..."

Kali nodded, only half listening. She was working her way through the twisting avenues created by his collection, hands caressing shapes and objects of all sizes as she went, most of them unscathed by what might have been millennia in the sea. Even though she didn't have a clue what the pieces were – especially as they were only bits of pieces, as it were – she lingered over one or two of them as she might over works of art, trying to find meaning in the precisely turned metal objects, perfectly curved and rune-inscribed plating, the sheer craftsmanship involved in their smallest parts and in every other aspect of their making. They sure as hells didn't make 'em like that anymore. Yet.

One piece she came across *was* a work of art. It was a painting of what she at first thought was herself and Brundle on the scuttlebarge, but on closer inspection realised that couldn't be the case at all. For one thing, how could it be here, now, and for another the figure she'd thought was her own was sitting in the pilot's seat, not the dwarf. The fact that the woman was also considerably older than she – more, what was the word they used, handsome? – seemed to confirm the fact. It was intriguing, though. At least until Brundle punched her on the shoulder.

"Take a left just up ahead," he instructed. "Six paces and a right, twenty left and straight on. I'll be right behind ye."

Despite the dwarf's words, he wasn't – lagging behind grumbling, tutting and occasionally striking a piece of junk with his fist, as if he'd noticed a flaw somewhere. Kali was therefore alone when, having followed his directions she emerged cautiously into what appeared to be a living area in the heart of the tunnels. It was as packed with junk as the rest of the place but one small area had been set out with chairs, a table made, it seemed, from the panelling of an elven dirigible, and a kitchen with a ferocious looking stove on which three cauldrons bubbled.

A short, squat – that was, shorter and squatter than usual – dwarf, a female of the species, stirred them one by one. Her back was to Kali and she was dressed in a pinny and flowery skirt which looked to have been cut from the same cloth as the curtain that Brundle had pulled aside.

"Hello, dear," she said, without turning. "Did you have fun blowing up your boat?"

"Er, hi..." Kali said.

The dwarf span, ladles in hands, and some fishy gloop splattered Kali's face. It was hot but she didn't move, letting it drip from her chin. The best course of action here, it seemed, was to simply stand there and smile.

"Hammers of Ovilar," the dwarf gasped. "You almost made me rust me pantaloons."

"Sorry," Kali said, cringing.

Brogma, for this was presumably she, waddled forward and prodded her in the chest. It had to be, Kali was beginning to think, a family trait.

"By the gods, who are ye, girl?"

"This," Jerragrim Brundle announced, slapping Kali in the back and almost sending her face first into a cauldron, "is Kali Hooper. You've heard of Kali Hooper, haven't yer, wife?"

"No."

"No, neither had I. But she's –" Brundle moved forward and whispered something in the female dwarf's ear. Her eyebrows rose. Very high.

"*Is she*?" she said.

Brundle nodded conspiratorially. "But where are me manners?" he declared. "Smoothskin, this is me wife, Brogma. Brogma, this is... well, bugger it, yer know the rest."

"Sit yourself down, dear," Brogma said. "You're just in time for tea."

"Look, that's very kind but I don't have time for tea. I have to help my friends and –" Kali paused, staring daggers at Brundle "– find out what's going on."

"Yes, of course, dear. As one of the Four, you must."

Kali couldn't hide her surprise. "You know about the Four?"

"Of course!" Brogma declared, ladelling up food. "Keep an *eye* on things, I do. Now, let me see – there's the shadowmage, Lucius Kane; the Sister of the Order of the Swords of Dawn, Gabriella DeZantez; the mariner, Silus Morlader; and the explorer, Marryme Moo –"

Brundle coughed. "That'll be enough now, Brogma."

"I'm sorry," Kali said. "What?"

"Keep an eye on things, I do."

"That isn't what I meant," Kali said. "*What* was that name you said? Who in the hells is Marryme Moo?"

Brundle coughed again and motioned for Kali to bend, so that he might whisper in her ear. "Brogma's gettin' on a bit," he explained. "This Marryme Moo is someone she once knew – someone much like yourself – and she's a little confused."

"She's not the only one," Kali said. She wasn't at all sure that Brundle was being truthful with her, but how could she argue? Looking at Brogma, just standing there smiling, she couldn't deny that she seemed a little, well, challenged. What to do? The obvious answer was to ask the question she hadn't yet asked, but was becoming the most important of all.

"Jerry – can I trust you?"

The dwarf looked affronted.

"It has been the Caretaker's job to wait for you since the day the Old Races died," he replied, as if that were an answer. "Now do as the lady wife asks, and sit."

Kali hesitated for a second. Two weeks of living off scraps on the Black Ship had left her starving, and she'd be of little use to anyone if she didn't eat soon. Reluctantly, she did as asked, and Brundle plopped a bowl of grey sludge in her lap. The act was the first of many which would lead to her regretting her decision.

"What is this?" Kali asked.

"Starter."

"No, I mean, *what* is this?"

"Thrap."

"Oh. I thought – I mean, from the smell – that the main course was thrap."

"It is."

"Ah. The pudding wouldn't by any chance be thrap?"

"No, smartarse. A big, juicy steak."

"Steak for pudding?"

"Okay, I lied. It's thrap."

It got worse from there. Despite the monotony of the menu, Kali devoured her food, trying to fire off questions between mouthfuls, but getting nowhere. Brundle ate like a pigrat, a series of slurps, chomps, sucks and grunts drowning out her words. His table manners were nowhere near as disturbing as Brogma's, however, who simply tipped her head back and dropped fish after fish into her gullet, like a seal. Kali almost expected her to oink and clap.

"Essential oils," Brundle said, smiling.

The meal ended at last, and Kali was about to fire off her questions once more when Brundle let out an almighty belch and excused himself for the bathroom, farting loudly as he went. Brogma, seemed to have no such need, and instead waddled to a cupboard and extracted a great tangle of what looked like wire. She slumped into an armchair and, from its side, took two large needles and began to play the wire with them, teasing, turning and pulling it up towards her. As she caught two strands, the needles began to clack, and soon the wires were being knitted together with such disturbing dexterity the act was almost a blur.

The strange thing was, Brogma didn't even look at the wires – not once. Stared straight ahead all the time. Kali frowned and eased herself from her chair, noticing for the first time a strange, silvery tint to the old woman's eyes. She waved her palm up and down in front of them and there was no reaction. Brogma, it appeared, was blind.

"Is there something I can do for you, dear?"

Kali started. "What are you, erm, knitting?"

"Brains, dear,"

"Brains?"

"Yes, dear."

"*Right*," Kali said, and backed off.

She decided that any other queries, knitting-related or not, could and should wait until Brundle returned. To pass the time – and take her mind off the noises emanating from that part of the cave into which Brundle had departed – she examined some of the odder objects she'd spotted earlier. The first was a piece of thin metal which, whichever way it was bent, returned to its original shape, which was always that of a parrot. The second, something that looked like a tuning fork but which shattered a rock when she tried it, she put quickly away. A third object appeared at first glance to be some kind of jack-in-the-box, but when Kali opened the lid it wasn't a grinning head that popped out but some strange spherical device that flew straight up and began diligently to drill a hole in the cave's roof. Kali coughed, whistled and walked away.

Her path brought her to an object that was perhaps the oddest of all. The base of a large tree trunk secured to the wall by its splayed, gnarled roots, looking like a wooden sun. The trunk had been cleanly sawn through to reveal its rings, the number of which attested to its great age. It did not seem to have been treated with the respect it was due, however, having been used as a dartboard at some point, and what was even more disturbing was the 'darts' were the feathery, desiccated remains of three small skewerbills, their tiny eyes still frozen wide with alarm from the moment of impact.

Kali turned her attention to a number of inscriptions carved into the wood. They were in a very ancient dwarven script she struggled to translate and, when she had, wondered whether she should have bothered. *Brogma 32 Gone Today, Miss Her. One Thousand Years, Candles Broke the Cake. Fish For Tea Today, Tomorrow an' the Day After. By Bollocks, I'm Bored...*

Kali was, by now, quite convinced that instead of learning something of world-shattering importance from Brundle and his missus, they were in fact inmates of some offshore institution – that this particular part of the island wasn't Trass Kathra or Trass Kattra, the island of the lost or the Four, but Trass Kuckoo, the island of the insane. She was out of there, she decided. Right now.

Kali wandered the aisles looking for an exit, and at last found a ladder leading up a shaft to, she presumed, open air. But when she reached the top, her way was blocked by a circular metal hatch. The wheel at its centre suggested that it, like everything else here, had been salvaged from some ship, but when Kali tried to turn it, it wouldn't budge. She tried again, straining, hoping to break whatever was blocking the rotation, but then noticed the entire hatch, and the rock surrounding it, was coated in some substance set as hard as nails. Nothing was blocking the hatch as such – it had been completely sealed over.

Kali slid down the ladder and negotiated more of the maze, coming upon another exit and finding it exactly the same. Then another. She felt a small stab of apprehension, wondering what exactly it was she *had* stumbled into, but then reason took over, along with no little anger, and she stormed her way back to the heart of the maze.

There, Brundle was at last returned from his toilet. Pulling up his pants unselfconsciously, he patted Brogma on the shoulder and asked, "How are the brains comin', wife?"

"Fine, dear. Just the way you like them."

"You want to tell me why all the hatches to the surface are sealed?" Kali demanded.

"I –"

"Time to spill the beans, Jerry. What the hells is going on here?"

Brundle stared at her, then nodded.

"Ah suppose ah can't avoid it for ever. This island you're standing on – or under – is, or rather was, the generation station for the Thunderflux."

"Generation station? Thunderflux? That sounds like tech speak to me. If I didn't know better, I'd say I was back at the Crucible of the Dragon God."

"In a way, you are. Trass Kattra was its sister facility. O' course, it wasn't called Trass Kattra then."

"Then what?"

"Nothin' at all. Strictly speakin', it didn't even exist."

"I think," Kali said slowly, "that you'd better start at the beginning."

"You've already been to the Crucible, so I'll spare you its history. Suffice to say it had one purpose, and this island another. Both part of the same plan."

"The Crucible was meant to launch the *Tharnak* and its k'nid payload, to destroy the deity in the heavens," Kali said, remembering what the dwelf had told her. "But it never happened. He said nothing about this place."

"He wouldn't. It was need to know. Tell me, smoothskin – have your travels ever brought you into contact with Domdruggle's Expanse?"

"Big, roaring, bearded face? Gob the size of a planet?"

Brundle laughed. "Roldofo Domdruggle. His bark always was worse than his bite."

"And you're saying he was part of this plan?"

"Not just part, smoothskin. Its architect."

Kali took a moment to collect her thoughts, particularly those involving Poul Sonpear and what he'd told her about the Expanse.

"You're losing me, shorty. The way I heard it the Expanse came about as a result of some great magical ritual. Lives were lost. Sacrifices made."

"Aye, they were. But not in the way you think."

"Then Domdruggle wasn't a wizard?"

"Oh, Roldolfo was a wizard, all right. A wizard of temporal mechanics. Of the threads. He conceived the Expanse as a plane separate from normal time. A kind of –"

"Bolt hole?" Kali finished. "Meant to be used to escape the End Time?"

Brundle smiled. "Catchin' on, smoothskin. The Expanse was meant to be a hidin' place for the entire population o' the planet while the k'nid did their work. But ah don't need to tell ya that both parts o' the plan failed..."

"But the Expanse exists," Kali said. "So what went wrong?"

"Nothin' went wrong," Brundle said, and sighed. "The Crucible project failed for its own reasons and we –"

"Something about the dragons dying, right? The lack of their magic?"

"Aye. We just ran out time."

"What do you mean?"

"We had the heavens themselves thrown at us."

"I'm sorry?"

Kali hadn't imagined that a dwarf's face could become any more gnarled, that its angry furrows could become any deeper or darker, but in this case they did.

"A rain o' fire. A rain that changed, twisted an' warped everythin'. Got inside things an' people an' turned 'em ta sludge."

Kali swallowed.

"I encountered something similar at Scholten Cathedral."

"It wouldn't be somethin' similar, lass, it would be the same thing. The Hel'ss. And that beasty out there in the swirlies is what remains of its attack. The Hel'ss Spawn."

"What?"

"They lasted as long as they could, but that bastard was determined to stop them," the dwarf said. "Roldofo and his aides stayed at their machines and atop their towers until they were reduced to ruin. The generation field started to break down, closing the expanse, until finally Domdruggle and his people had no choice but to sacrifice themselves to the void in the hope that somehow, from inside, they could keep it open long enough to allow the exodus they'd planned."

"But it collapsed completely and they became trapped," Kali said. "Alone and desperate for a way out. Ghosts of themselves."

"Aye. The Thunderflux lost focus. Dartin' an' hoppin' about it was, until it were startin' timestorms all over the planet. Those that remained were forced to cap it, workin' up there at the top o' the island while that rain continued to pour." Brundle sighed, as if lost in a distant memory. "A lot o' good people were lost that day, to the void and to the spawn."

"Jerry, I'm sorry –"

"When it was over, the Expanse was severed for ever. But in the chaos, the Thunderflux severed the Hel'ss Spawn from its parent, too. The bastard's remained here ever since, like a great blanket o' deadly snot."

"That's why your hatches are sealed," Kali realised. "The Hel'ss Spawn comes on the island, doesn't it?"

"Every now and then. As if, after all these years, it's still tryin' to sniff out those the Hel'ss itself missed. Too stupid to realise they all died a long time ago."

Kali had stopped listening a second ago. "Brundle," she asked coldly, "is this one of those times?"

The dwarf sighed. "Aye."

"Oh gods," Kali said. "The people up there."

She burst away from the dwarf and climbed back to one of the hatches, starting to hack at its seal with her gutting knife. A second later the knife was pulled from her hand and tossed back down the shaft.

"Are you some kind o' bloody loony?" Brundle demanded.

"Nope. But you've finally confirmed to me that you are."

"*Do you want to die?*"

"I'd rather die saving my friends than hiding away down here, like you!"

Brundle roared and grabbed at her, and the two of them fell from the ladder and went the way of the knife, landing in a crumpled heap. Kali was the first up, fired by incandescent rage, and grabbed the dwarf by the throat, heaved him off the floor and pinned him against the wall. His legs dangled, unkicking and unresisting.

"That's quite some strength yer have there, smoothskin," Brundle gasped. "Quite the *legacy*, eh?"

"You bastard!" Kali shouted. "That's why you've been feeding me all this crap, the fish and the potted history of this arsehole of the world! You just wanted to save your own skin!"

"No, lass, not mine," Brundle croaked, shaking his head. "Because ah'm not just the caretaker o' this island, ah'm the caretaker o' you, too."

That took some of the wind out of Kali's sails. "What do you mean?"

"That strength o' yours – or any o' yer other abilities – they aren't yer only legacy. Ah told yer there's someone here yer need ta speak to. Who's left a message for yer, if you like. An' it's vital that yer live ta hear it."

"*Why?*"

"The reason this place is called the Island o' the Four an' why ah said welcome home. So yer can save the world, o' course."

Save the world, Kali thought. How many times had she heard that phrase? How many times had she tried? She was tired of jumping onto what she thought was the last stepping stone only to find another one in front of her.

"What's this little chat going to teach me, dwarf? Where to go next?"

"No, lass. This is the end of the line."

Kali felt an icy cold envelop her, and slowly released her grip. Brundle let out a sigh of relief and slid to the floor.

"I'm not having this 'chat' until I save my friends," Kali said.

"Smoothskin," Brundle said, "that's what I've been tryin' ta tell yer. There's nothin' yer could have done ta help, either the Faith or yer friends. The moment they set foot on this island, they were already dead."

CHAPTER ELEVEN

"DEAD?" KALI REPEATED. "No, I refuse to believe they're dead."

"I'm sorry," Brundle replied. "By Ovilar, I should a' sunk that bloody boat in Gransk. At least then they'd have had a fighting chance."

"No, it's my fault."

"Yer mean for bringin' them here?" Brundle questioned. "Look, if it's any comfort, it wasn't your fault they were on the Black Ship. And if yer hadn't finished yer journey there'd soon be millions more souls followin' yer friends into the clouds. Trust me on *that* one."

Kali forced images of the Hel'ss Spawn consuming her friends from her mind, but, as she did, a thought nagged. She recalled her conversation with Redigor, when he'd *been* Redigor, a year before, in the Chapel of Screams. He'd known then what the Hel'ss was – how it had been responsible, however indirectly, for the death of his people, the last time it had come to Twilight. Though he hadn't been very forthcoming about the nature of the spaceborne entity, he'd clearly recognised the dangers it presented, and she was pretty sure he wouldn't expose himself to such danger – even if it was via its spawn – without some kind of plan. No, Redigor hadn't brought all these people all this way just to die. At least, not yet.

"Jerry, you said the Hel'ss Spawn invaded the island every now and then. Does that mean there's a way for you to know when?"

"Aye, me vertispys. Why?"

"Because I think you're wrong about what's gone on up there. I think they're alive. Take me to these vertispys."

Brundle sighed, but a glimmer of hope sparked in his eyes. He nodded and indicated Kali follow him. The pair moved towards a set of stone steps carved in the corner of the cave.

"Shall I carry on with my knitting, dear?" Brogma asked after them.

Brundle stared at her, and then at Kali, rubbing his beard thoughtfully. If there was the smallest chance that she was right...

"Aye, wife," he said. "An' it mightn't do any harm to get a bit of a move on."

Brogma nodded. And her needles clacked faster than ever before.

Kali and Brundle ascended the steps, which rose and wound through a small passage, one of many that Kali could see veering off in all directions, and she guessed that Brundle must have carved out a network of the things over the long years, granting him access to all parts of the subterrain. The passage they followed brought them to a small, round chamber in the centre of which was a device that looked, like everything else in the place, to have been built from the cannibalised parts of Brundle's wreckage. A pipe affair that dropped down out of the rock, it had a projecting, hooded eyepiece at its base and two handles made of sawn-off broomsticks jutting left and right, a means, it seemed, of rotating the pipe. The dwarf gripped the handles, leant into the eyepiece and began to turn in a slow circle. What he saw above made him mutter to himself.

"What do you see?" Kali asked.

"Boots."

"Do they still have feet in them?"

"Aye. Seems you were right, after all. I just don't understand why."

"Maybe a different vertispy'll give us a clue?"

Brundle nodded. "Come on."

The dwarf led her through passages again, to another pipe in another chamber. The angle of this vertispy offered him a view of the steps through the ancient ruins, and was much more revealing than the first. This time boots *and* their owners could be seen, enough of them to have been posted as sentries on almost every other step. Between them what Brundle estimated to be about a hundred of the prisoners from the ship were being force marched upwards. He turned the vertispy, backtracking along their route, and saw the remainder of the prisoners corralled and guarded on the small beach where the flutterbys had landed.

"They're bloody everywhere," Brundle growled. "But I'd have bet me left bollock they wouldn't have survived."

"Then that's a bollock you owe me," Kali said, then pulled a face. "On second thoughts, never mind."

Brundle frowned and was off again, this time bypassing a number of vertispys, heading for one high in his labyrinth. As he rotated the spy he muttered softly to himself before jolting to a halt, clearly having spotted something.

"Impossible," he growled. "They made it to Horizon Point."

"Horizon Point?"

"Strictly speaking, *Event* Horizon Point. But that's another story."

"It would be."

Kali determined the only way she was going to find out what was going on was to see for herself, and she shoved the dwarf out of the way. She saw the surface through a scratched and smudged lens half overgrown by vegetation. The view it offered was of the summit of the island, where, as seen from the scuttlebarge, the massive, observatory like dome was perched. She could see now that it wasn't an observatory at all, or at least had no opening to allow the projection of a cosmoscope, nor any sign of one even closed. The only detail she could make out on the convex structure was a deeply etched layer of flowing and complex runes that pulsed with raw power, and the mere sight of them made the hairs of her neck stand on end *and* sent a shiver down her spine. She guessed this was the 'cap' for the Thunderflux that Brundle had told her about.

Her attention was drawn by a flicker of activity to the right. Turning the vertispy, she saw what she guessed was Horizon Point itself, the great, thrusting clifftop she'd first seen from the scuttlebarge. Flanked by six shadowmages whose arms moved in a complex dance, presumably manipulating threads, a figure stood at the very edge of the clifftop, facing out to sea. The figure's arms were thrust out, as if trying to embrace the sky, and the flowing mane and black robes immediately identified it as Bastian Redigor.

"Do yer mind?" Jerragrim Brundle protested. "This is my bloody vertispy."

"Shush!" Kali chided him. "What the hells is he doing?"

"*I don't know.* Let me see."

"No."

"*You* are beginnin' to get on me tits."

"I get on most people's tits. Deal with it."

Brundle grumbled as the reason for Kali's dismissive response kept her glued to the spy. It was true that the dwarf obviously knew a great deal more about the Hel'ss Spawn than she did, but having heard what he'd told her about it she doubted even he'd seen it act this way. Rising from the sea far below were great patches of the viscous, milk-white substance they'd barely avoided in the swirlpools. Here, though, they had formed themselves into one semi-liquid mass that, if it resembled anything at all, looked like a jellyfish standing to attention. Any comic effect this might have engendered was, however, dispelled by the size of the thing. Towering far higher than the clifftop, and just as wide, it could have been some vast, organic cloud, and it made the silhouette of Redigor seem like that of an ant.

The Hel'ss Spawn swayed curiously, almost languorously, above him, blotting out the sky.

Its presence didn't seem to phase Redigor one bit.

The elf appeared to be trying to bargain with it.

"What's happenin'?" Brundle prompted.

Kali told him.

"Impossible. That thing's a lump o' sludge, driven by instinct alone. It doesn't bargain."

"Maybe that's how it's been all these years," Kali said. "But maybe now the Hel'ss itself is back, things are different."

"You mean he's using the spawn as some kind o' conduit ta talk wi' our friend up there? But why? What could he possibly want from it?"

"I think the more worrying question is what could he possibly *offer* it," Kali said. "Wait – something's happening."

Kali returned her full attention to the view of Horizon Point and saw that the prisoners Brundle had earlier observed on the steps had now reached the summit. They were being assembled by their guards on a patch of open ground that sloped up to the clifftop, each and every one of them staring about them in helpless confusion. Kali didn't like what she was seeing one bit, even less so when roughly a quarter of the group – Ronin Larson and Jurgen Pike among them – were separated from the others and force marched up the slope to stand behind Redigor. By the slight movements of his body, Kali could tell that the elf was once more speaking with the Hel'ss Spawn, but with his back turned she didn't have a clue what he was saying.

"Dammit," Kali snapped. "Brundle, can you get any sound on this thing?"

"Aye," Brundle said, reluctantly. "But if that is the Hel'ss Spawn up there, ah wouldn't like ta say what yer might hear."

He popped down a couple of earpieces, and Kali listened. Unfortunately, at the distance the vertispy sat, whatever there was to be heard was swept away by the wind that buffeted the promontory.

"No good," Kali said. "Can you turn it up?"

"Up? No. But ah can get closer."

"Closer?"

Kali heard the dwarf fiddling with more controls behind her back, and a second later something moved into view before the vertispy. It looked very much like an ear trumpet, and, trailing what appeared to be a hosepipe behind it, skittered towards Redigor on tiny, mechanical legs. Kali shook her head in the manner of someone who was seeing things, because as much as she applauded Brundle's inventiveness, there were some things that were just *too* weird.

The peculiar device did, though, do the trick.

"... and I bring these people before you as a foretaste of what is to come!" she heard Redigor announce. "The first of many I can bring to you in advance of your arrival. Think of it. Of the strength you'll gain. Of how much easier it will be to challenge the other!"

The other? Kali thought. Hadn't Redigor once called the Hel'ss 'the other'? If that was the case, did he now mean Kerberos? But what was he talking about – challenge?

"A whole Church – no, a whole religion!" Redigor went on. "The largest religion on this planet – the Final Faith! Hundreds of thousands of followers, all of whom once followed their Anointed Lord, but, through her, now follow me. Hundreds of thousands who have but a single mind – mine!"

Redigor's ego clearly hadn't diminished since he'd been chopped in half, Kali mused. But it wasn't the ego that was important here, was it? It was the position he was in. Now that he was, apparently, the power behind the throne of the Final Faith, it was just possible that he *could* influence the majority of the population of the peninsula, whether directly or indirectly, and through belief or through fear. The question was, why would he want to?

"They can follow you, too!" Redigor's rant continued. "Follow you, who, because of me, they believe to be the herald of your enemy! *Give* themselves to you, willingly, in the ritual they mistakenly call Ascension!"

Oh gods, Kali thought. Was that was this was about? Redigor up to his old tricks – some kind of exchange that would once again resurrect his psychopathic elven 'family', the Ur'Raney? But, no, that couldn't be, could it, because the souls of his people were with Kerberos. She'd seen them dragged back into its azure clouds kicking and screaming herself.

"And all I ask," Redigor requested, "is that I be remade as what I once was. That I walk this world in my own form once more. That I live!"

What? Kali thought. That's it? All this was about was Baz getting himself a makeover? One lousy, should-have-been-long-dead Ur'Raney pleading for the chance of a few more years of torture, incest and bloodletting? Why would an entity like the Hel'ss be interested in a bargain like that? And how – come to that – could it achieve it for him, even if it were?

Redigor's address to the Hel'ss Spawn seemed to be over for the moment, and Kali watched as the viscous behemoth swayed slightly before him, offering no sign of reaction at all. That's right, blobbo, she encouraged it, send him home with a flea in his would-be pointy ear. Of all the stupid, ridiculous...

The Hel'ss Spawn folded itself over Redigor and his shadowmages and – Kali could think of no other word for it – *licked* the group of prisoners assembled directly behind them. The lick stripped the flesh cleanly from their bones and twenty five or more skeletons stood there for a second before collapsing to the ground with a clattering sound that Kali thought she might remember forever. The last thing she saw was Redigor's shadowmage retinue gesticulating at the sky beyond the Hel'ss Spawn – where loomed the red sphere of the Hel'ss itself – and firing what she recognised as souls in its direction. Then she staggered back from the vertispy, collapsed against the cave wall and vomited.

"Oh, shite," Brundle said. "I thought it might come to this."

"It isn't what you think," Kali said, taking deep breaths. "This wasn't just the Hel'ss Spawn, it was the Hel'ss itself. It murdered them – murdered two of my friends. It's actually made a bargain with Redigor. Something about being strengthened, about a challenge, and about being able to *remake* him. Does than make sense to you?"

Brundle moved to the vertispy to see for himself. "Aye, it makes sense. All apart from *why* Redigor should want to be remade. Inta what?"

Kali laughed, a little bitterly. "Oh, I'm sorry, didn't I tell you?

Redigor isn't what he seems. You might think you're looking at Prince Jakub Tremayne Freel of the Allantian Royal Family but one year ago he was possessed by Bastian Redigor, otherwise known as the Faith's First Enemy, the Pale Lord."

Brundle started. So violently that his head thudded into the hood above the eyepiece. He pretended it hadn't happened, though, and kept his grip firmly fixed to the vertispy's handles, his eyes steadfastly on the lens.

"Ah thought that name sounded familiar," he growled. "That elf's meddlin' in things he has no business being near."

"Brundle, we have to get the rest of my people out of there, before more of them die. What can we do?"

The dwarf disengaged himself from the vertispy, flipped up its handles and thrust the pipe back up into the ceiling.

"What we can do is get that bastard off me bloody island."

"Aren't you forgetting something? Redigor has a small army up there."

"Don't you worry, lass," Brundle replied. "The Missus'll take care of everything."

"The Missus?" Kali said in disbelief as Brundle led her at some speed back through the underground warren. "The Missus? What the hells is Brogma going to do? Stab them with knitting needles? Beat them with wet thrap? Or is it more than coincidence that thrap rhymes with crap?"

"Just wait and see, lass."

"No, Jerry, no. No, no, no," Kali persisted. "I finally find myself in the place that's meant to provide me with all the answers and what have I had since I've arrived? Riddles, half-truths, hints of mysterious chats with someone who as far as I know might be a figment of your imagination. So tell me now – how exactly is Brogma going to *take care of everything*?"

At that moment they re-entered the main cave. Brogma gave them a cheery wave with her needles. Brundle waved back but continued on through the cave, leading Kali into yet another series of tunnels on its other side.

"Brundle, answer me!"

The dwarf span to face her, beard jangling, all three nostrils flaring, face redder than any face she'd seen before. She took an involuntary step back.

"Have ye no respect for yer elders? By the farting denizens of Tapoon, what's happened to patience these days?"

"Patience? I've been waiting a year to find out what the pits is going on."

Brundle snorted. "A year? A whole year? Bah! Try waiting a few millennia."

"What are you talking about?"

"Let's just say that caretakin's a full time job, eh?"

"Wait a minute, wait a minute. When you told me the caretaker had been waiting for me since the day the Old Races died, I thought you were talking generally. I mean about the *role*."

"Well, in a way ah suppose ah was..."

"But now you're telling me you're the only one who's occupied that role?"

"Aye, that's what ah'm tellin' yer. An' yer know what's the worst about it? No farkin' bastard's ever presented me wi' so much as a carriage clock."

"I –"

"Now," Brundle barked, making her jump. "Will yer let me do me farking job?"

Brundle continued his march through the tunnels, Kali dogging him every inch of the way.

"I don't believe you," she said.

"What's not to believe? Yer met Tharnak at the Crucible didn't ye? He survived. And that pointy-eared bastard upstairs. Him as well."

"That's different."

"How is it different?" Brundle growled.

Kali shrugged as she moved. "Well, Tharnak was the result of experimentation by some of the greatest minds of the Old Races, and the Pale Lord is an ancient and powerful sorcerer with all of the dark threads at his command. You – well, you're just an obnoxious, little arsehole who moans and farts a lot."

"Hmph. Why don't yer tell me what yer *really* think of me?"

"Okay," Kali said, warming to the subject, "why don't –"

She stopped as Brundle entered a large chamber carved, as far as she could tell, at the far end of the subterranean labyrinth. The reason for her sudden cessation of hostilities was that in the few seconds in which Brundle had preceded her, he'd wasted no time in tugging another embarrassingly flowery dust-shrouded curtain from before a long recess carved into the chamber wall. The way he slapped the curtain to the ground and glared at her left Kali in no doubt that he was hoping – *really* hoping – that this would shut her up.

It did the trick. Kali stared open-mouthed at the number of dark shapes, ten of them, that were standing immobile in the shadows of the recess. Squat, humanoid shapes, though forged of metal, some of them missing parts of an arm or a leg, they were all similar in one startling respect. They all wore the face of Brogma.

"Hello, my beauties," Brundle said.

The figures were so old, so neglected, that Kali was sure Brundle didn't expect a response. But then she staggered back as a slight glow lit their eyes and, as one, the figures stamped a foot onto the ground in recognition of the dwarf's greeting. A heavy and metallic crunch brought a fall of dust from the ceiling.

"What the hells is this?" Kali said, stepping back some more.

"Don't you worry," Brundle said. "There's nothing to be afraid of."

"Nothing to be afraid of?" Kali repeated.

It was all right Brundle saying that, but what she had just witnessed had brought a pang of recognition and fear she thought she would never feel again. The shape of these things, the way they were constructed, their very *aura*. The last time she had seen monsters like these they were being left to rot in the floodwaters of Martak after she had put paid to their would-be resurrectionist, Konstantin Munch.

Smaller and squatter they might be, but in every other respect it was like looking at the army of the Clockwork King.

"The Brogmas won't hurt you, lass," Brundle insisted. "Come on, come closer."

Kali hesitated, then did as bade. She studied the Brogmas'

faces – their identical faces – noting they seemed made of some flexible rubbery material. They were in varying states of decay, and if she had to hazard a guess she'd have said each of them had been stored here after being active at different times in the past.

They weren't the only Brogmas stored here either. Brundle whipped away coverings from further recesses all around. There were more Brogmas in each; in some Brogmas who had all but rotted away. Kali wasn't sure whether to be shocked, disturbed or, when she saw how tenderly Brundle looked at them, deeply saddened.

"Smoothskin, ah'd like ta present wife thirty-three," he said, gesturing at one. And then, at others in no particular order or without any favouritism, "Wife nineteen, fifty one, three..."

"Jerry," Kali interrupted. "What have you done here?"

The dwarf wiped his beard, snagging his bells so that they were pulled up silently and then flopped back with a dull tinkle.

"Made meself some company, lass, what else."

"Company?" Kali said. She hated to refer in such a manner to the constructs which the dwarf regarded with obvious affection but she could see no other way. "But these things. They remind me of a place. A place I wished I never had to go."

"M'Ar'Tak," Brundle said. "It's where ah learned mah trade."

Kali stared at him, everything falling into place even as she struggled to accept it. The sheer number of Brogmas before her, like the deceased members of a family entombed for generation after generation, back to the start of their lineage. The tree trunk whose annotations, now she came to think about it, had all been written in the same hand. But most of all, Brundle's tale about the attack of the Hel'ss Spawn on the Thunderflux. It wasn't *as if* he'd been lost in memory, he *had* been lost in memory.

"My gods, you really have been here all the time. Jerry, how can you be so old?"

Brundle pulled back his shirt and rapped a fist on his chest. There was a metallic clang. "Mechanical ticker. Doesn't last for ever but every few hundred years Brogma gives it a service."

"You worked with Belatron," Kali said, still struggling with the implications. "Belatron the Butcher, the architect of the Clockwork King."

"Aye. But don't you worry. It didn't take me long to work out what a psycho he was. Upped and left wi' me tools, wandered the world and eventually ended up here."

"But you were there when –?"

"The Ur'Raney drove the dwarves into the sea? Aye, ah was. Which is why you'll forgive me for me temper. This has become a wee bit personal."

"Jerry," Kali asked cautiously, "was there ever a wife number one? Was Brogma ever... real?"

The dwarf's eyes lowered, and when he spoke it was softly, fondly. "Aye, she was real. So many thousands o' years ago that I've lost count, she was real." The dwarf sniffed; a strange sound through three nostrils. "The old girl lasted almost seven hundred years, not a bad age fer one o' our kind, not a bad age at all. Didn't want to leave me on me own, ya see?"

"I'm sorry."

"Smoothskin, it were so long ago they could 'ave named a geological age after it. Besides, she went in her sleep. Never knew a thing. No chance ta worry about me wakin' up alone."

"That's good. Is she... buried on the island?"

"What? And let the Hel'ss Spawn have her bones? No chance. No, lass, ah took Brogma to the mainland and our clan's burial grounds 'neath what yer now call Freiport. She lies there still."

"I've never found that site," Kali said. "I'll make sure I never do."

"I thank ye."

Kali let Brundle's response hang in the air, unsure of what more, if anything, there was to say, but as it happened she was spared the problem. The mention of the Hel'ss Spawn seemed to have galvanised the dwarf back into his old self, and his mind seemed focused on his task once more.

At least she thought so.

"Wife!" he shouted. "Have yer finished that knitting yet?"

"Yes, dearest!" came the echoing reply.

"Then what are ye waitin' for? Bring it through."

"Coming, dear."

Kali said nothing, merely waited while Brogma waddled into the cave with the armful of wiring she had been working on all the while. Kali wasn't sure what to expect – an overly baggy jumper, a scarf, some baby bootees? – but it certainly wasn't the tangle of wiring that looked to her exactly the same as it had when she'd first begun. She frowned as Brundle took it and then shooed his wife away. Brogma returned to the main cave without protest. Of course she did.

"Brundle?" Kali said.

"Ah had the wife start knittin' before ah left for the mainland," he said. "Just in case ah was compromised and that bloody Black Ship got here after all. Should o' been ready but me old darlin' isn't as fast as she was."

"She isn't?" Kali asked, remembering the blur.

"Nah. Which is why ah told her to hurry up, on the slim chance that you were right. About yer know, up top."

"Jerry, what the hells are you talking about?"

"Oh, this is beautiful work," the dwarf said, ignoring her. He picked at and examined the wiring as he might fine filigree. Then he started to pull chunks of it away, opening the chest plates of each of the Brogmas as he did, and stuffing the handfuls inside. That done, he started to finger each bit of wiring individually, delicately, and, in turn, each Brogma started to exhibit further signs of life, the rotation of an arm here, the bend of a leg there, the sudden turn of a head followed by a wink in the dwarf's direction.

Kali watched as he worked.

"Jerry, I don't understand. Belatron's clockwork warriors were part organic but these aren't. They look like his army but they're not. I've never come across this kind of technology before, even at the Crucible, where they were building spaceships, for fark's sake."

"Interestin', isn't it?" Brundle said as he continued to tinker. "Scraps that washed up a long, long time ago. The remains of... well, to be honest wi' ye, ah don't know what, but ah know they had silver eyes and must 'ave walked this world long before I did. Took me centuries ta work out their ins an' outs an' what went where's but, when ah did, ah was able to build the Brogmas without the need for any poor sod's brains bein' scraped off some battlefield. Brogma – the latest Brogma, that is – is a mistress of knittin' some o' the more advanced functions together."

"More advanced functions?"

"See, when ah first built the Brogmas, they weren't just for company but designed for defence, too. Defence o' the island. Trouble was, they sat here for thousands o years wi' nothin' to defend against, an' started gettin' trigger happy. The day one o' them almost blew me brains out when all ah'd asked for was a light for me pipe was the day ah decided to strip them o' their sentry circuits." The dwarf sighed and stepped back from the Brogmas, closing their chest plates. "Well, now, here they are, restored to what they should be."

Kali stared at the Brogmas. They looked exactly the same.

"Nothing's happening."

"Battle stations, girls," Brundle said. "We've got an elven arse ta kick."

"Yes, dear," said ten Brogmas in unison.

The Brogmas stood to attention and Kali watched in amazement as their forms expanded, arms thickened and legs extended, so that each Brogma was now as tall as she was. They didn't just grow either, they sprouted – small hatches and panels sliding or flipping open on their forearms and their thighs, on their chests and in their torsos, each cavity whirring and clicking as it unleashed a weapon of some description or another, designed to operate independently or in the construct's hands. Blades, hammers, axes, small, star-like discs designed to be fired, morning stars and flails, each of Brundle's wives became in an instant a one woman arsenal. Simultaneously, they all span full circle at the waist, and as the weapons sliced the air or were beaten on their open palms with the rhythm of a war drum, their eyes flared with power.

"Oh," Kali said, numbly. "Oh, that is so cool."

"Aye," Brundle said proudly. "Now, are we goin' to take back Trass Kattra, or what?"

CHAPTER TWELVE

BRUNDLE HAD INFORMED Kali of all the exits onto the surface, and she chose the lowest, the one closest to the beach where the flutterbys had landed, from which to begin the assault on Redigor. The dwarf had left the planning to her, and the first thing she had decided was to send him in alone.

What might have seemed counter-productive folly – a lone figure emerging at the furthest point from their target – was, she'd decided, the best route to success. Because as she'd seen through the vertispys, Redigor had proven himself quite the tactician, doubtless a throwback to his days of being Lord of the Ur'Raney, where he would have led his forces into many a bloody battle. Deploying his sentries in positions perfectly calculated to offer uninterrupted and mutually supported surveillance across the island, he had the place sewn up tight. Each sentry kept an eye on not only his territory but two or more sentries, depending on their position on the rocks, at the same time. The result of this was that there was no way through them and no way other than this one to emerge onto the surface without being observed. To try to take out any one sentry elsewhere would instantly alert the others.

She could, of course, have had Brundle deploy the Brogmas to take out *more* than one sentry, but as impressive as the mobile arsenals were, they were hardly built for stealth. The last thing she wanted was for Redigor's major force – the one on Horizon Point – to be prematurely alerted to their presence as that would likely result in the execution of the prisoners, either through the sword or being fed to the Hel'ss Spawn before their time. No, they had to make it up there while Redigor was still involved in his negotiations with the parasite. Negotiations that she suspected would end not only with the sacrifice of the prisoners but those guarding them as well. It was a pity she couldn't just tell them what a bastard Redigor could be.

No, the Brogmas would have their moment, but it wasn't yet. For the time being, it was Brundle's play.

The dwarf emerged from an unsealed hatch concealed in a tangled mess of scrub grass and washed up kelp, grumbling not only because of the effort it took to shrug the detritus from the long unused exit but that Kali had chosen him for the task. It wasn't that he didn't trust her damn fool plan – in fact, it was rather good – but, all things considered, he'd rather be where she was, preparing to do what she was going to do. Now *that* was the fun part, not this floprat like scrambling up out of the ground. But she'd wanted – *really, really wanted* – to do it, and who was he to argue? He was, after all, only the caretaker, while she... well, she'd find out soon enough what she was, wouldn't she?

Apart from being a bloody annoying little girl.

Brundle sighed and quietly lowered the hatch behind him, then pulled his Cloak of Many Contours fully about his body, shoulders and head. Had any eyes been watching at that moment the cloth might have transformed from its rank and basic dingy state into the semblance of wind-blown seaweed or perhaps a chunk of driftwood that rolled in the tide. But a second later, when Brundle actually stepped out from the small lee in the seashore and into the view of actual eyes, it, and he, resembled a berobed member of the Final Faith.

The sentry standing on the shore above started slightly but Brundle simply nodded and strolled on by as if about his business, which seemed to put the man at ease. Beneath the hood of his cloak, the dwarf smiled. The first chink in Redigor's armour had just been exploited, and he suspected the sentry was more disturbed that he'd allowed what he perceived to be one of his comrades patrolling the beach to get so close without noticing, than anything else.

Brundle continued along the beach, passing the base of the path that led up into the ruins and towards the hostages that had been left behind under guard there. Nodding to the men who stood in a group watching over them – four, a number deemed sufficient not to have to be overlooked by other guards – he casually continued to their rear and then, producing the twin-bladed battleaxe he'd held under his cloak, swept the weapon around in a silent arc. Its sharpened edge cut cleanly through the necks of all four men and their heads bounced away into the tide.

"Now then," Brundle said. "Which one of you sorry looking bastards is Jengo Pim?"

Most of the prisoners watched their guards' bodies collapse onto the sand and up at the dwarf, shifting uneasily in their bonds. One, however, regarded him with steady, dark eyes and thrust himself unsteadily to his feet.

"I'm Pim."

"Well now, Mister Pim," Brundle explained as he released his chains, "your friend Miss Hooper has a message for ye…"

"She's alive?"

"Do I look like a clairvoyant?" Brundle snarled, and then realised he was still shrouded in his cloak. "Oh, sorry, maybe ah do." He shrugged the garment off and some of the prisoners gasped as for the first time in their lives they set eyes on a dwarf. A dwarf with what appeared to be a large trident stuck to his back. "Yes, she's alive, and very soon she's going to be kicking. That's where you come in…"

Brundle asked Pim's men to identify themselves and then moved to release their chains. The other prisoners he left as they were. The last thing he and Kali wanted was for a number of panicked civilians to be running around while there was a job to be done.

Brundle explained Kali's plan as he worked, and by the time the last of Pim's men was freed of his bonds, they and Pim himself knew their part in it. The leader of the Grey Brigade knelt in front of his people and gestured to each, then at the rocks above. Each man nodded, his instructions clear.

"Good luck," Brundle said, patting Pim on the back.

The group was about to move out when a figure appeared from behind the mass of one of the flutterbys. A tall, dark-haired, swarthy looking man with a peculiar x-shaped scar on his cheek, he had to be one of Redigor's men. But as Pim and his men froze, the stranger simply nodded to them. *Carry on.*

Nodding back, Pim and his men slid into the lee of the rocks, as silent as the shadows that swallowed them. Brundle, meanwhile, regarded the stranger.

"Whoever ye are," he said. "Jerragrim Brundle thanks yer. I've already enough blood ta clean from me blade."

He began to move off into the rocks himself but a question from his rear stopped him.

"Wait," the stranger said, pointing at the trident slung on the dwarf's back. "What *is* that?"

Brundle looked quite pleased to be asked.

"This, my friend is a transmitting aerial. A little something I call 'faraway control'."

"Faraway control?"

"A-ha."

The stranger frowned, none the wiser. In the rocks above, so did Pim. Why was it, he reflected that any encounter with Kali Hooper seemed to bring out the weirdest in people – or, to be honest, just the weirdest *of* people. He quickly returned his mind to the task at hand, however, for in the few seconds he and his men had been moving, they had already come close to the first of the guards on the steps. Hooper wanted he and his friends removed from their positions silently and, more importantly, simultaneously, and Pim watched as one of his men peeled off from the group, melting into the shadows behind him. More men peeled off the higher they climbed, concealing themselves directly behind the guard that Pim had allocated to them, and Pim, having reserved the highest of the guards for himself, continued on alone. The Grey Brigade's leader seemed not to exist at all as he used the patches of darkness on the rugged landscape to his advantage, darting from one to the other with the silent surety of a man who had spent a lifetime being where he was not meant to be. Without generating the merest amount of suspicion from the guards he passed between, he took his own place and waited for the rest of Kali's plan to unfold.

You'll know when to make your move, the dwarf had told him. This presumably meant that Hooper was going to give some kind of signal, but what form the signal would take he hadn't a clue.

Pim therefore waited, as still as a statue, watching the guard above him shifting slightly as he tried to make himself comfortable on his watch. All was silent other than for the crashing of the waves on the shores of the island. There was nothing to hear that was out of the ordinary, nothing to see but rocks. Then, suddenly, Pim's keen hearing picked out a slight drone coming from the sea, like the buzzing of an insect, and when he looked in its direction he made out a small dark speck, heading towards the island. The guard heard the drone, too, and began scanning the water for the source of the sound. Pim found it, his gaze suddenly locking onto the dark speck, much closer now, its droning louder, and he tensed, ready to call out a warning to his comrades in arms.

That was it.

Pim unfolded himself from his crouched position so that he was standing directly behind his victim. His preferred method of despatching him would have been a clean blade across the throat, but as his weapons – along with those of his men – had been removed on the mainland he was forced to use an unarmed though no less effective technique.

Pim slid one hand onto the side of the guard's neck and another onto the side of his forehead, locking his head in place. At various positions below him, he knew, his men would have done

exactly the same. And in the same moment that Pim snapped the
guard's head sharply to the right, so too were snapped the heads
of all of the guards lining the steps. As one they fell to the rocks
below them, their necks broken.

Pim grinned and scooped up his victim's weapons.

Miss Hooper, he thought. *You're on.*

Some quarter of a league out to sea, having swung in on an
accelerating course that had skirted the swirlpools and brought
her into a trajectory heading directly for the island, Kali watched
the distant shapes drop and gunned the scuttlebarge on which
she rode. The machine kicked beneath her, far more violently
than the last time she had ridden it thanks to the extra two
engines that Brundle had installed. The controls of the device
fought against her grip and her knuckles whitened as she
struggled to keep the scuttlebarge on course, because she knew
that the slightest deviation from her target would end in disaster.

That target loomed ever closer ahead of her; a section of hull
that had been sheared away from the Black Ship to be slammed
into the rocks of Trass Kattra, where it now rested, thrust up
against the cliffs. What Kali knew she needed to do in order not
to endanger the hostages was generate as much of an element
of surprise as possible, and to that end the section of hull suited
her needs perfectly.

She gunned the engines of the scuttlebarge until they began to
smoke and whine in protest, and the dwarven machine slapped
and bounced across the waves towards its destination.

Kali felt the scuttlebarge jerk violently and then tip sideways
as it parted company with the sea and crashed down on the
shattered section of Black Ship. Kali leaned hard in the opposite
direction to maintain equilibrium, and while the engines no
longer had anything to work against, the sheer momentum of the
scuttlebarge propelled it up the hull, aided in its passage by the
slithery accumulation of seaweed it gathered as it went. Sparks
flying where it stripped away the growth, its own metal shearing
away in chunks, the scuttlebarge reached the top of the hull and,

looking like some airborne sea monster, took off. For the briefest of moments Kali caught sight of Brundle below her, the dwarf looking up and shaking his head in some envy, and then of Pim and his men, giving her the thumbs up, and the sense that her plan was coming together was reflected in her own long and drawn out cry.

"*Ohhhhhhh yeeeeaaaaahhhhh...*"

The fact that Kali cried out so loudly was no longer a matter of concern to her, for the fact was that the 'stealth' part of her plan was over. Considering the method of her arrival onto the island, it really couldn't be anything *but* over.

Rising higher and higher into the air, above the rocks that had formed Redigor's first line of defence, the airborne scuttlebarge and its trailing fronds of seaweed came into view of the soldiers the elf had left in charge of the prisoners. As it did, they gaped upwards to a man. It was exactly the reaction that Kali had wanted, for as long as they were gaping they would not be harming those she had come to liberate, who were doing a considerable amount of gaping themselves. Kali winked as, down below, she spotted the cheering forms of Red Deadnettle and Hetty Scrubb, the latter having become so excited that she was attempting to punch the air despite her chains, the action making her repeatedly fall to the ground.

Speaking of which, as memorable as Kali's arrival had been, what went up had to come down, and in that respect she had little control over what happened next.

The scuttlebarge's nose began to dip a second after it passed over the main group of soldiers and prisoners, and Kali saw she was heading directly for a ridge from which four more soldiers overlooked the rest of the group. Two of these ceased to be a problem the moment the nose of the dwarven machine slammed into them, and they departed their duties in an explosion of blood, while the third was sent fleeing in a desperate attempt to escape the spinning chunk of metal that broke away from the hull on impact. The last of the guards was the only one to offer a challenge, standing his ground with sword drawn, ready to knock Kali from her seat, but sadly he had failed to take the scuttlebarge's continuing momentum into account. Kali yanked the controls around so that the rear end of the scuttlebarge span in a half circle, and as the soldier yelled in protest, holding his sword uselessly to block its approach, the hull slammed him off the ridge to fall screaming onto the sharp rocks below.

That particular manoeuvre brought the nose of the scuttlebarge pointing down the slope of the ridge and, taking a deep breath, Kali bucked her body to send it on its way. The machine began to slide down the slope, picking up momentum again. The juddering, bucking mass of metal with its engines whining more than ever was clearly not an object to be in the path of, and soldiers threw themselves left and right as it came, some of them not quite in time. A trail of severed, twitching limbs and screaming victims left in her wake, Kali rode the scuttlebarge across the level of the plain until it finally slewed to a halt, where she leapt out to face the remainder of the soldiers in charge of the prisoners.

They stood before her in a line, twenty or so of them with weapons drawn, sneering at what they thought was a foregone conclusion. None of them seemed eager to make the first move, however, the woman in their midst quite clearly insane. Kali played to that belief, regarding them with determined upturned eyes and a smile of invitation to come try it on. And when at last they did begin to move in on her, it was already too late, because a solid mass of metal had risen between them.

Kali smiled as the Brogmas rose on the freight elevator that Brundle, visible on a nearby rock, had activated with his faraway control. The old mechanism, he had told her, had once serviced the Thunderflux, but, since its capping, had fallen into many centuries of disuse, a situation reflected in the fact that until now it had been totally invisible, buried beneath an overgrowth of grass.

The elevator was not the only thing the faraway control activated, however, and as Brundle fiddled with it once more, the Brogmas repeated the foot stomping, weapon twirling ritual which had so impressed Kali below. 'Impressed' was not a word that could be used to describe the reactions of the soldiers for whom they now performed on the other hand, because clearly there was one thing more off-putting than a solid mass of metal between they and their target, and that was a *moving* mass of metal between they and their target. Especially one moving in their direction.

One or two of the men ran away. A few more, who might have heard barrack room tales of the rout at Martak, which only the Anointed Lord herself had survived, froze in their tracks in much the way Kali had when she'd first seen the machines. The majority, however – if only because they were perhaps more fearful of what Redigor might do to them if they did not – raised their weapons to defend themselves.

Kali admired their guts.

No, really.

The soldiers which the Brogmas proceeded to go through like a hot knife through butter were not the only ones that had to be contended with, of course, and as soon as that battle had been joined a further phalanx of Redigor's troops poured down the slope. As if that were not enough, those soldiers who had been positioned on the ridges around the slopes roared to spur themselves on and then raced at Kali and the Brogmas from two directions, closing on them in a pincer movement.

Thankfully, Kali and the Brogmas no longer had to fight alone. Having activated his machines, Brundle himself waded in with his battleaxe, and one by one, up the top of the steps, brandishing the weapons they had acquired from the sentries, came Pim and the rest of the Grey Brigade. Pim directed a couple of his people to start releasing the prisoners from their chains, and then, with his other men behind him, raced into the furore.

The battle, as all battles do, soon degenerated from an initial, full on clash to a series of smaller skirmishes fought across the slope of Horizon Point. With the aid of the Brogmas especially, the tide soon began to turn their way, though Kali herself had a couple of close calls. The first came when she was bashed on the back of the head by the hilt of a sword and went down, stunned. The soldier responsible stood above her and was about to swing down the weapon's more lethal component when help arrived from an unexpected source.

Burrowing up through the ground, having made its way to the surface at last, the small sphere that Kali had released from the jack-in-the-box, shot straight up into the air before him and, taking advantage of his momentary distraction, Kali leapt up, grabbed and twisted the soldier's swordarm, and thrust the blade into his stomach. The soldier doubled over and fell, impaling himself further, and Kali rammed the point home by booting him up the behind.

The second close call came immediately afterwards. Kali was about to salute the small sphere as it sailed away into the sky, but with her hand half in the air noticed she'd been targeted by three bowmen who had come out of nowhere. Their weapons primed, their arrows aimed directly at her heart, there was no way even she could avoid them. Then, suddenly, all three flew backwards into the air, as if they themselves had been hit in the chest by arrows, and crashed away behind a ridge into oblivion. At first Kali thought Poul Sonpear had been released from his scrambling collar and had despatched her assailants with projectiles of his own summoning, but then she saw that one of Pim's people was still trying to free him from the restraint and there was no way he could have done what she had thought.

Strange.

Kali turned, wading back into battle, and found herself joining what was effectively an advancing line consisting of Pim and his men, Brundle, the Brogmas and herself. All of the separate skirmishes were over and all that was left was a retreating line of the survivors of Redigor's forces. Those that put up any resistance were swiftly taken care of by the whirring blades or swinging flails of the Brogmas, and those that didn't – or decided there and then that they really *shouldn't* – began to stumble away in shock. Brundle raised his axe to behead one in front of him but Kali stayed his hand. They'd surrendered; let them live.

Unfortunately, Redigor had other ideas. Whether as a demonstration of his dissatisfaction with these men or of his last line of defence, each of them transformed before Kali's eyes into a cloud of dust, the result of the crackling strands of energy fired from the clifftop by the Pale Lord's shadowmages. Redigor himself stood, as he had throughout the battle, with his back to them, still engaged in whatever business he was conducting through the Hel'ss Spawn, but it was clear that a part of him was still controlling the proceedings.

Proceedings that, one way or another, were about to come to an end.

The six shadowmages stood steadfast before Kali and the advancing party. Their balled fists crackled with an energy more powerful than she had ever seen. It arced between them, across their line, forming an ever intensifying curtain of blue. It made her brain hurt.

"This could be a problem," Brundle said.

The shadowmages flipped backwards, as if hit by arrows, disappearing over the cliff.

"Or not."

"What the hells?" Kali said. She looked behind her for the source of the attack. Nothing.

"Does it matter?" Brundle growled. "We have the bastard now."

"Not we," Kali said. "He's mine."

Brundle was about to protest when he saw Kali's expression. He turned and looked at the Brogmas, who were juddering on the spot, ready to advance.

"Stand down, girls," the dwarf sighed. "Everybody stand down."

Kali nodded and began to stride up the slope to Horizon Point where Redigor remained with his back to her. The higher she rose, the worse the wind became, and as her clothing slapped against her, she was forced to shout to get his attention.

"Hey, Big Ears!"

At last, Redigor did turn, and Kali saw that her description, although facetious, hadn't been far off the mark. For what had been occupying the Pale Lord all this time was clearly the Hel'ss Spawn's – or, more accurately, the Hel'ss – response to the sacrifices it had been offered earlier. Redigor had given it a little, and it, in turn, had given a little back. Jakub Freel didn't resemble Jakub Freel as much any more. The Pale Lord Kali knew and loved was on his way back.

The process, however, was far from complete. No doubt pending genocide. But if her plan worked, it would be nipped in the bud right now.

"Is there a problem, Miss Hooper?" Redigor asked.

"Yes, there's a problem, shithead. This island's my destiny, not yours. And I'll not have you destroying my world just because you don't have the sense to know when to die."

"Brave words, Miss Hooper. But can you back them up? All by yourself?"

"Ah, well," Kali said. "There's the thing. Because I'm not all by myself, am I?"

Kali hoped that Redigor would interpret that as meaning Brundle and the others who waited impotently down the slope, but in actual fact that wasn't what she meant at all. She'd gone up against Redigor before and had only survived the encounter because of Gabriella and the Engines, and in a straight confrontation she knew she had little chance now. No, what she was gambling on was what she had learned *during* that encounter in the Chapel of Screams, when Redigor had revealed a little of the nature of the Hel'ss. If she was right, it could not only be used to her advantage but might even, however fleetingly, bring the Hel'ss onto her side.

"Look at you, Redigor – you're struggling to survive every second, rotting, being eaten from within. Face it. You're coming apart at the seams."

"I will survive long enough."

"Really? Because you know what it is that's eating you alive? It isn't the fact you don't belong in a human body, it's the fact that the body is that of a good, brave and honest man. A strong man. One who's been fighting you every step of the way."

"It's been over a year, girl. Jakub Freel is gone."

"You want to place a bet on that?"

Kali raised her gaze, addressing Redigor no longer but the Hel'ss Spawn that loomed beyond them both like a giant cowl.

"I'm willing to bet," she went on, "that there's *too much* of Jakub Freel left in this form for your bargain with this elf to ever work. I'm willing to bet that contact with it will leave you tainted, corrupted, as rotten to the core as he is. Because that's *your* destiny this time around, isn't it? Not to eradicate the Old Races but humans? And how can you do that if you help one spark of humanity to remain alive, even in a different form?"

The Hel'ss Spawn hung there, silent.

"This hybrid... this *freak* isn't part of your natural order. The elves' time has passed and we, the humans, walk this world. Humans you have returned to destroy. Isn't there, then, no other choice but to destroy this man?"

Redigor laughed softly. "That is very clever but aren't you forgetting something, Miss Hooper? If the Hel'ss takes it upon itself to destroy me, then your friend dies too. And I'm sure you wouldn't want that to happen."

Kali's brow creased. "You're right. I wouldn't. If I could help it. But I can't help it. And neither can Jakub Freel."

She paused. This was the only part of her plan that was utterly out of her hands, and it depended very much on how good a judge of character she was.

"Isn't that right, Freel?"

Redigor laughed louder. "What are you trying to do? *Talk* to him? Do you have any idea how deeply he is suppressed? How far away I have sent him?"

"I *said*," Kali reiterated. "Isn't that right, Freel?"

"Really, Miss Hooper, this is just –"

Redigor stopped. His eyes lost focus and he staggered. He snapped a look at Kali – venomous, hateful – and then as his face twisted in an attempt to prevent it, a single word was forced out from between his lips.

"Yyyyyyeeeeesssssss."

"Hello, Jakub," Kali said, smiling.

"No!" Redigor protested. Despite his vast age his voice sounded like that of a petulant child. "You will remain where you are!"

"What's the matter, elf? Is it that you just can't understand why someone might be willing to sacrifice themselves for a greater cause? You wouldn't, would you, seeing as how you buried yourself the last time this bastard came around. Buried yourself while the rest of your people died. You called yourself a Lord?

Well, let me tell you something – a Lord is as much responsible for the welfare of his people as their rule."

"O-ho no, girl," Redigor spat, barely able to stand. The wind whipped at his clothing, making cracking sounds. "I know what you're doing. Trying to distract me while your friend reasserts himself. But it won't work. I've come too far, done so much, to be halted now."

"Yeah? Well then, why don't we ask Jakub once more. Freel, tell the man. Tell him that if it stops what's happening here, you're more than willing to die."

Redigor's gaze snapped around him, as if seeking some defence from what threatened him. But there was no defence from that which came from within. He doubled over, clutching himself,,and from his mouth came words once more unbidden by himself. This time they came through gritted teeth, even more forced, and all the more determined.

"Damn. Right."

"This... will... not... happen!" Redigor screamed. He span to face the still looming cowl of the Hel'ss Spawn. "This... human has been purged. He is nothing but an echo. You cannot touch me. I am *clean*."

The Hel'ss Spawn, though, had clearly decided otherwise, and as Redigor turned, it pulled back from the clifftop as if from something horribly disfigured and diseased. Redigor opened his arms to it, pleading, and over the watery roaring of the entity Kali even heard him beg. Words she never thought she would hear from the First Enemy of the Final Faith.

Please. God.

It was too late. Severed from the process, the alterations the Hel'ss Spawn had made to Freel's body were already starting to reverse, the exotic, aquiline cut of his face, the thinning out and elongation of his limbs, the shape of his ears. And as all of these features became more human looking once more, the dark shapes that had roved his body like living tattoos returned to again consume him. Weakened, Redigor collapsed to his knees, and then onto his hands, on all fours, like a dog.

His gaze moved slowly up to meet the looming Hel'ss Spawn,

his body trembling with a mix of fear and rage.

Before him, the Hel'ss Spawn rose to its full height, and both Kali and Redigor knew what was coming next.

Redigor's whole body quaked.

"No!" he screamed. "I am Bastian Redigor of the Ur'Raney!"

Redigor's head drooped, and his back heaved in great, wracking breaths. When, a second later, he looked up again, he spoke with a different voice.

"NO! I AM JAKUB TREMAYNE FREEL, PRINCE OF ALLANTIA. I AM HUMAN!"

Kali swallowed as the Hel'ss Spawn darted down, as quick as a snake, enveloping him and lifting him from the ground in an unbreakable embrace. As Redigor/Freel thrashed helplessly in its grip, Kali saw some discolouration as it started to leech his soul, and Redigor/Freel began to scream.

It was a scream of the damned and Kali wanted so much to turn away, but couldn't. Freel had made the decision to sacrifice himself for the greater good and the least she could do was stay with him until the end. She steeled herself, therefore, as the Hel'ss Spawn continued to suck at its victim, contenting herself with the knowledge it would all be over very soon.

It was, though, taking *too long*. Longer to consume Redigor/ Freel, and in a seemingly far more agonising way, than she had witnessed with any of the Hel'ss Spawn's earlier victims.

Something was wrong.

Kali's first instinct was to rush in, unable to allow herself to condemn Freel to this, but then she forced herself to stop.

What, she thought, if something wasn't wrong?

What if something was *right*?

That had to be it, she realised. What was causing this was exactly what she'd said. She'd called Redigor a hybrid, a freak who belonged in neither the old world or the new, and when it came down to it, that was exactly what the Hel'ss Spawn was, too. The Hel'ss had left this spawn behind during its *last* assault on Twilight, when it had come for the elves and the dwarves, and that imperative had somehow remained with it. In other words, it was following the natural order of things, taking Redigor's *elven* soul before it started to consume that of Freel the human.

Gods, if that were true, Kali thought, she could save Freel. But she didn't have much time. She had to time this exactly right.

There was only one question. Time *what* exactly right?

Kali realised that she hadn't a clue how she was going to get Freel out of this but, as usual, that didn't stop her. As Freel/Redigor continued to scream, the elf's essence continuing to be absorbed, she tensed, running every kind of scenario through her mind and coming up with nothing. But again, as usual, that didn't stop her. There was a moment – a fleeting moment – where the Hel'ss Spawn seemed to pause, perhaps sated by elf and ready to begin consuming the human, and in that moment Kali roared and ran right at it.

She grabbed Freel about the waist, tore his body from the Hel'ss Spawn and, with legs pumping, took the two of them over the edge of the cliff, into the vertiginous drop towards the sea.

With the wind slapping at Kali like wet sheets of cloth, a more than little confused Freel struggled in her grip as his elven features began to fade. This was good. What was bad was that they were both plummeting towards the tempestuous sea crashing onto the rocks below. It was not an ideal situation to be in, but got instantly worse. Even as the two fell, another raging sea – the liquid form of the Hel'ss Spawn – came at them from the top of the cliff, plunging downward with the hunger and determination of a predator that had momentarily mislaid its prey. The entity roared as it came, and with both it and the sea closing on them at an ever increasing rate, it was like being trapped between two deadly, vertical jaws.

Kali wasn't sure whether to be pleased or cheesed that Jakub Freel chose this particularly troubling moment to regain some awareness, staring at her in confusion.

"Kali Hooper?"

"All right, mate?"

The Allantian craned his neck, looking down, and then up, at the pursuing Hel'ss Spawn.

"Erm, we seem to be falling to our deaths while being chased by a... well, by a –"

"Yep," Kali said. "Trying to deal with it."

"I'm presuming that, as usual, you're making this up as you go along?"

"Yep. Sorry."

"Oh, please," Freel managed, attempting to be polite but unable to disguise a slight break in his voice, "don't be, don't be..."

Kali narrowed her eyes. "I'm thinking," she said, "that we could maybe separate and dive into those rock pools down there."

"Yes," Freel answered, totally unconvinced.

"Or perhaps angle our fall so that we glide – you know."

"Perhaps."

"Or –"

"We could pray?" Freel offered.

"That's the one."

There were mere moments before the two of them impacted with the water – and rocks – at the base of Horizon Point, and they spent a couple of them staring at the Hel'ss Spawn as it accelerated beyond their own rate of descent, threatening to catch up an instant before the impact came. As a choice between horrible ways to die, it was no choice at all, and both Kali and Freel closed their eyes. With the roaring of the Hel'ss Spawn and the crashing of the waves, neither of them heard the sharp, almost insect-like *zzzzzz* that played about them for a second before being replaced by a sound something like the lashing of twine.

They did, however, feel something wrap itself tightly about both of their bodies, and then snatch them up into the air. For a few seconds neither of them had a clue what was happening but then they were swinging across the cliff face, out of the way of the Hel'ss Spawn.

They watched as, like some great waterfall that had been severed from the river that fed it, the viscous mass plunged by them with a scream that sounded distinctly elven to impact with and dissipate into the sea.

CHAPTER THIRTEEN

KALI AND FREEL hung suspended for what seemed like an age, the line that bound them tightly together creaking loudly as it swung back and forth across the cliff face like a pendulum on an overwound clock. They might have been rescued from the Hel'ss but they were not out of danger yet. Twisting and turning on the end of the line, waves crashing beneath them, both Kali and Freel had to take it in turns to kick out to avoid being smashed into projecting parts of the rock, or to prevent the line becoming dangerously snared around them. On occasion their kicks sent them into an uncontrolled spin, one or the other of them colliding with or being dragged painfully across the rough rock face, and after a few such impacts both of them were beginning to wish that they hadn't been rescued at all.

Gradually, however, the creaking softened, the swinging became less pronounced, and they came to a stop. The two of them stared at each other – in the position they were in, having little choice – and after a second the line jerked, and they felt themselves being hauled up.

They rose in fits and starts, their combined weight clearly causing whomever or whatever was doing the hauling problems. The sheer height of Horizon Point meant that they had to wait a good half hour before they found out who or what that was, and in the end they heard it before they saw it.

A deep grumbling, lots of cursing, and a slight jangling of bells.

Kali grunted as they finally reached the clifftop and she grabbed onto solid ground, being helped up by Jerragrim Brundle. He did the same for Freel and then unwound the line from about both of them. The dwarf was breathing heavily, eyes bulging and his face inflamed.

"Thanks," Kali said.

"Ye can thank me by going on a diet," Brundle countered. "Startin' with that unfeasibly well-rounded arse of yours."

"I'm sorry?"

"The one sticking out of yer troozers."

"Hey!" Kali shouted, then looked behind her. Dammit, she must have caught her bodysuit on one of the rocks. Double dammit, why was it always her arse? She *had* to get that part of the suit reinforced.

Normally she would have flattened Brundle but what he had just achieved took the wind out of her sails. "I meant it," she said, "thanks."

"Aye, well, I only did the pullin'. The man yer've got ta thank for firin' ya yer lifeline is over there."

Kali looked to where Brundle's head inclined, and noticed another figure on the clifftop for the first time, reeling the wire that had saved them into a coil. The black-garbed figure with the scar on his face was familiar to her – and yet at the same time wasn't.

"Him again?" she whispered. "I saw him in Gransk, and on the ship..."

"If yer expectin' me to know who he is, ah haven't a clue," Brundle said. "All I know is he turned a blind-eye down by the flutterbys at the moment we needed it."

Kali nodded and, bidding Freel to stay where he was, walked

over. Something about the stranger suggested that she should approach him alone. The dark-maned figure continued to patiently wind his wire but he eyed her warily from under lowered eyelids as she approached.

"I wanted to thank you," Kali said. "For what you –"

She stopped mid-phrase. The line fully wound now, the stranger was twisting himself around to place it in a quiver on his back, and as he did she caught the outline of a bow slung beside it. Partly hidden by his body before now, it was of design uniquely familiar to her. This wasn't just any longbow. There was only one longbow like it on the whole of the peninsula.

"Where did you get that?" Kali asked suspiciously.

"This?" the stranger queried. "Why do you ask?"

"Because it's called Suresight and it belongs to a friend of mine. A good friend."

"Really? Even one who deserted you?"

Kali felt surprise and a slight pull of anger, her mind flitting back to Scholten a year before. But Kali quashed the feeling, more concerned with how the stranger knew what he knew.

"I don't know what they were but I'm sure he had his reasons," she replied, tight-lipped. "What I *do* know is he wouldn't voluntarily relinquish ownership of that bow."

"He wouldn't. And he didn't."

Kali's hand lowered to her gutting knife, interpreting the words as a threat. "So I repeat – where did you get it?"

The stranger looked at her fully for the first time. A slight smile pulled at his lips and, though it was colder than she remembered, Kali recognised it instantly. But more than that it was the eyes. She *knew* those eyes.

"Slowhand?" she breathed, in disbelief.

The archer regarded her steadily, as if reluctant to admit what she evidently knew, and his smile remained as cold as when it had formed.

"Hi, Hooper," he said. "How you doin'?"

"Ohhhhh, you know," Kali said tremulously.

Her mind was spinning, not just with the impossible reappearance of her ex but his look, attitude, the fact that after vanishing from her life without so much as a by-your-leave he could be here, standing in front of her at all.

"It was you – you who killed the archers and the shadowmages. I should have guessed. Killiam, what the hells are you *doing* here?"

"Long story," the archer said, and, the line stashed, began to move away across the cliff. As he did, he nodded to Freel who, having overhead the exchange, nodded numbly back.

Kali wasn't going to have Slowhand abandon her in the same way he had in Scholten, and she trod heavily after him, grabbing him by the shoulder.

"Where do you think you're going?"

The archer span. "Why don't you tell me where I'm going?" he barked. "After all, I can't seem to make a move without you. A *successful* move, that is."

"What the hells are you talking about?"

"Like I said, long story."

"I'm listening."

"Nothing to hear."

Kali's grip tightened. Her eyes narrowed as she spoke.

"You've changed," she said. "And I don't just mean physically. Something's happened."

"*It's personal.*"

"What, and the fact that I've spent a third of my life with you, sleeping with you, saving your life and you saving mine, going through all kinds of shit together, means you don't know me well enough to tell me something personal?"

"There was a girl, okay!" Slowhand barked. "More than a girl."

"So what else is new? *And?*"

"She died."

Kali felt herself reel, but said nothing.

"She died, Kal," Slowhand repeated, after a moment. The way he spoke suggested a return to their old familiarity and the break in his voice suggested he did want to talk about it, after all. "Her name was Shay and she died because of me."

Kali stared at her ex-lover, gaze flickering, and then slowly, hesitantly, put her arms about him and pulled him to her. "Tell me," she whispered in his ear.

Slowhand did. About the carnival, about Shay, about the attack and about Fitch.

"FITCH," HE GASPED, lying there.

"Fitch," the psychic manipulator had repeated in that strange, high-pitched voice. It was as if he'd had his voicebox transplanted by that of a child's, or perhaps a bird's. "Querilous Fitch. Abandoned Fitch. Dead Fitch." He'd cocked his head to the side. "Or would have been had that master of destiny, Killiam Slowhand, had his way."

He – Slowhand – had thought back to their last meeting, a year before, in the Sardenne, when their roles had been reversed. The psychic manipulator, smashed and broken by the juggenath, had lain helpless beneath him, more so when he had rammed one of his arrows cleanly through the bastard, impaling him to the ground.

"Looking good," he'd said, trying to disguise the fact his throat was so dry.

"Flatterer." Fitch took a breath and the bladders deflated like tiny lungs. Briny liquid bubbled and popped from the tops of tubes. "Not a pretty sight, am I? Unfit for the eyes of women or children. It's really quite remarkable how much damage the body can take and yet not die. In my case, as in your's, the damage was extensive – bones shattered, internal organs crushed – and were it not for the sheer power of my will I would be one more pile of crumbling bones whose flesh had succumbed to the many dangers of the Sardenne." The psychic manipulator almost giggled. "I thank you, by the way, for the arrow you... left with me. It gave me the means to defend myself while my mind effected sufficient repairs to drag myself to safety."

"Willpower can achieve remarkable things, I'm told," Slowhand answered through gritted teeth. "You know, I once stopped – well, *dating* for a week."

"I'm not talking about willpower, you fool. If it were simple willpower, stand up!"

"*You know I can't.*"

"I can help you do so."

"How and why in the hells would you do that?"

"The abilities I began to hone in the Sardenne were, sadly, not enough to repair myself. But have since become as precise as a surgeon's tools. I can restore you to what you were."

He swallowed. "That's the how. What about the why?"

"Because I need your help. Against the Final Faith."

"Excuse me?"

"I realise how that must surprise you, but much has changed within its ranks. When at last I returned from the Sardenne, I found – how do you say – a cuckoo in the nest?"

"The biggest thing that's cuckoo in that nest is you, you sadistic bastard."

"I enjoyed my work, I do not deny it. But ceased to enjoy it when I found the whole reason for it was being subverted at the highest level."

"Subverted? By Makennon?"

"Not Makennon. The Anointed Lord no longer holds primacy over our Church. Instead, it is in the hands of one who would make a dark covenant with the Hel'ss."

Fitch told him, then, what Kali and he had, by now, learned of Redigor's duplicity, and his mind whirled as he worked out the identity of the only member of the Faith in a position to do what had been done.

"Freel?" he'd said disbelievingly.

"Your friend is no more. The wheel of destiny has turned."

"Oh, there's a wheel, now," he said with some exasperation. "Newsflash, Fitch. I turned my back on that life for this one because that whole 'destiny' thing left me with no choice."

"Look around you, archer," Fitch said matter-of-factly. "This life is ended."

His gaze moved across the Big Top, settled on the pathetically slumped body of Shay. Her eyes were staring right at him, but instead of the support and comfort they once offered, they were not seeing him at all.

"And do you know why this life has ended?" Fitch continued.

"Because of the choice you made. Because of that choice, your little sweetheart over there died. The simple truth is all our destinies are linked. Because of you she was *destined* to die..."

Whether Fitch's was deliberately provoking him or not, he'd roared. But it was the roar of a declawed beast, and all he was able to do was writhe impotently on the ground.

"... and because of you *I* was destined to live."

For a moment, he didn't realise what Fitch had meant. And then –

"The arrow," he breathed, and laughed with the sick realisation. "The arrow."

He lay there in silence, his breathing becoming shallower, until Fitch spoke again.

"Kali Hooper is once more in pursuit of the Pale Lord," he said. "Will you help her?"

"Hooper doesn't need my help. She'll survive. She always does."

"Perhaps not this time. And if she falls, someone will need to take her place."

He laughed again. "What are you trying to put over on me, Fitch? That I could step into her shoes? That in all this talk of 'the Four' someone got their sums wrong and I am, in fact, 'the fifth'? Moolshit."

Fitch smiled. "I admire your pretensions, but sadly you will always be a supporting player – one of many, whether they know it or not. No, what I attempt to suggest is that if Miss Hooper falls, *I* will need you as my eyes and ears if *I* am to defeat the Pale Lord."

"Why this sudden interest in everyone's welfare? I thought the whole point of the Filth was to coerce them into surrendering their existence to Kerberos in some kind of... rupture."

"The word is *rapture*, archer. And so it is. Not to be taken by the Hel'ss."

"The way I see it one big blob in the sky is much the same as another."

"Then you couldn't be more wrong. Kerberos is our God, our Lord of All, not the Hel'ss. It is with *his* power that the future of this world lies."

"Like I said, moolshit. Fundamentalist moolshit."

"Do you want to stay here and die? Or do you want to find out? Make a *choice*, archer. Choose your *destiny*."

He stared up at Fitch with vision that was already beginning to fade. He was dying, there was no doubt about that, so there was nothing to lose. For Shay, he might even be able to find out what wasn't letting him go. Sometimes, he guessed, being in league with the devils was better than being in league with nothing at all.

"This is all some kind of game to you, isn't it? But I'll play. What do you want me to do?"

"Stay close to Kali Hooper, for wherever she is, Bastian Redigor will be close by."

He swallowed. "Do what you have to do."

And so Fitch began. To restore him. But also to change him. It made sense when, later, he saw in a mirror a different body, a different face looking back. After all, if he was to be Fitch's eyes and ears, it wouldn't have done to be recognised by the Pale Lord.

Yes, it had made sense. But it hadn't stopped the screaming.

"IT HAD TO hurt," Kali agreed. "But not as much as... oh, gods, Liam, I'm sorry. So very, very sorry."

"I know. But, hey, at least the bad guy is dead."

Kali nodded. "That's what bothers me. What are you supposed to do now? Report to Fitch? How? Where? What exactly is it that he wants out of all this?"

"Your guess is as good as mine, better, probably," Slowhand said. "But in the meantime, I guess there are other things to think about." He pointed down the slope of Horizon Point, to where Redigor had corralled his hostages. There, among the stilled forms of the Brogmas, Jengo Pim and his men were liberating them all from their chains and, as Kali walked down, three figures emerged from the crowd. Hetty Scrubb and Pete Two-Ties were overjoyed to see her but it was Red Deadnettle who physically demonstrated how much, scooping Kali into his arms and giving her a bearhug that almost made her projectile vomit her thrap.

As it was, as she felt herself being squeezed tighter and tighter, she couldn't help letting out a prolonged fishy burp.

"Oops," she said. "Sorry."

"No me," Red said. "Me sorry."

"How you doing, Red?" Kali said as she was plonked back on the ground. "You all right? Hetty? Pete? You?"

"We have been prisoners of *kunto*, but have survived, Kalee," Hetty declared, somewhat fierily. "We are all fine."

"Apart from," Pete Two-Ties said, "'door also a woman', eight letters."

Kali nodded. Much as she loved the others, Dolorosa had been the one foremost in her mind, and she moved through the crowd to her. The old woman was on her stretcher at the heart of the group, being tended by Martha DeZantez. Gabriella's mother mopped her brow with a torn piece of skirt while Dolorosa herself stared at the sky, wincing as she did.

"How is she?" Kali asked quietly, squatting down.

"Her infection has spread," the archivist said. "In a wound this serious, she should be dead. Tough old girl."

"Eet issa nothing," Dolorosa mumbled unexpectedly. "Randy Cromwell Quaid once hadda me impaled witha his throbbing sabre."

Martha reddened and coughed embarrassedly.

"No-a, wait," Dolorosa said, only half there, "it wassa the *Robbing Sabre*."

"I'm sorry," Martha said. "She's delirious."

"No, she's not," Kali smiled, stroking Dolorosa's hair. "She used to be a pirate."

"*Did she?*" Martha said, impressed. In an effort to keep Dolorosa with them, she asked, "What was the name of your ship?"

Dolorosa sighed happily. "Eet wassa the *Fluffy Bunny*."

"That doesn't sound very... piratey."

"It was the *Run For Your Money*," Kali corrected.

"Better," Martha agreed.

Kali paused. "Has she mentioned her husband at all – Aldrededor?"

"Something about running away with a space sheep?"

"Right. That's not what it sounds like, either."

It was good to hear Aldrededor had evaded the Faith's clutches, but, wherever he and the *Tharnak* now were, she couldn't begin to guess how he must be feeling having left Dolorosa behind. Kali bit her lip. "Martha, is there anything you can do for her?"

The woman shook her head. "Keep her comfortable is all. I'm sorry, Kali."

Kali nodded, and stood. Mercifully, she had no time to reflect on her friend's mortal state, as Brundle barrelled up to her and dragged her towards the cliff.

"You should see this," he said. "Somethin's happenin'."

Kali joined the dwarf at the cliff edge, as did a number of others who'd spotted the same thing he had. Directly below was the spot where a portion of the Hel'ss Spawn with which Redigor had communicated had plummeted into the sea. It was still there, and still agitated, though not as agitated as the rest of its mass, farther out to sea. As they watched, it moved to reabsorb itself, but when it did its agitation seemed to be exacerbated, not calmed. A ripple effect headed inland and water began to crash against the cliffs in great spumes, some of it almost as high as the spot on which they all stood, catching them in its spray.

"Aw, shit," Brundle said. "Ah think there's a storm comin'."

"I'm guessing you don't mean a normal storm, right?" Slowhand queried.

The dwarf ground his teeth. "Nay, mah friend. Ah don't mean a normal storm."

"He's right," Kali said, pointing. "Take a look out there."

Everyone's gaze shifted offshore, towards the main body of the swirlpools, where the maws had begun to spin even more violently than before. Spumes had become plumes, and exploded into the air where the swirlpools clashed, and where they crashed back down again they rolled from the lips of the maelstroms in the form of huge, destructive waves. These, in turn, disrupted the swirlpools further, carrying them with them on their crest, raising them and tipping them so their normal rotation was stretched and skewed, and as a result they began to move through the waves erratically, unpredictably, more liquid tornados than the swirlpools they had been.

The deadly band that surrounded the island seemed to be going absolutely insane.

What was worse, it was heading directly for shore. Directly for them.

"You think we've pitsed it off?" Slowhand asked.

"No," Kali said, frowning. "I think something's wrong."

"Maybe Redigor stuck in its throat."

"Something more. There, where the Black Ship went down..."

There was no exact spot where the ship had sunk, of course, merely great swathes of water filled with its shattered wreckage. But wherever wreckage could be seen, so could something else. A glowing orange tint that was spreading through the swirlpools like a powerful dye.

"What is that?" Slowhand mused.

"The ship's amberglow reactors," Kali said. "They're disintegrating."

"Why would that affect the Hel'ss Spawn?"

"Gods know."

"Aye, well, we can play twenty questions later," Brundle growled. "Right now, we need to get these people underground."

Brundle was right. The deadly ring of the Hel'ss Spawn was already closing on the island and great splashes of it were pummelling its shores and cliffs, rising higher and encroaching more inland every second. A heavy and viscous orange rain started to splatter the steps and the ruins, and then the edges of Horizon Point itself, and wherever the rain fell chaos was the result. Ground fleetingly became fog-like or gaseous, or as solid as stone, flickering through all the colours of the spectrum and more before liquefying before their eyes. The shapes of boulders changed, spherical one second, square and spear-like the next, taking on the textures of glass or wood or sponge and ultimately nothing at all. Some of the upper buildings of the ruins folded and bent on their foundations, as if viewed through a funhouse mirror, as flexible as rubber one moment, fragile as paper another, before the stresses they suffered made them, too, lose their solid state and drain slowly away.

It was a mind-boggling vista, a nightmare landscape, as if the Hel'ss Spawn was trying, but failing, to find a form that it could maintain, as if this might rid it of whatever poison it seemed to have absorbed. No one wanted to imagine what would happen if it touched a human, and it galvanised them all into action.

"You two," Pim ordered two of his men, "take charge of the old woman's stretcher."

"Be gentle," Kali said. "Slowhand?"

"Already on it," the archer said.

He was moving through the crowd, ushering those too stunned to act for themselves towards the hatches to Brundle's underground warren. The dwarf himself was darting around, using his axe to unseal others, ensuring there were as many routes to safety as possible. Sonpear, Red and even Abra helped but, even so, it was a slow process, each hatch able to take only one refugee at a time, the age or health of some making it a frustratingly arduous descent.

Inevitably, there were casualties, first the stilled Brogmas – whose armour to some degree resisted the rain but smoked and sparked nonetheless, shifting out of shape until they slumped – and then the humans. The orange downpour, soaked a group of three and for a second they became one; a horrible, flailing blur of misshapen limbs, and then all that was left was the fading echo of their agonised cries. Another man stumbled as he tried to take a short cut across some rocks, and the rain caught him mid-fall, and when he hit the ground he burst like a water balloon. Yet another, a woman, stood frozen to the spot, staring at the heavens and screaming with mouth open wide, but the scream soon turned to a gurgle as her mouth erupted with her liquefied insides, coating and disintegrating her from the outside in.

Kali spotted two people towards the edge of Horizon Point, cut off from safety by a river of orange ooze. She moved to help them but found herself forcibly held back by Brundle. The two of them struggled at arm's length, the wind whipping at their hair.

"No," the dwarf shouted. "Let someone else help."

"They're going to die!"

"*Everyone*'s going to die unless you do what this island's waited for you to do."

"Which is?"

"Find out the truth. It's time for yer little chat."

"Fark it, dwarf, this *isn't* the time. Not for more of your riddles. The truth about what?"

Brundle's free arm pointed at the Hel'ss Spawn, at the Hel'ss itself, at Kerberos. "About that, and that, and that." He pulled her towards him, as if they were engaged in some strange dance, then growled in her face. "The truth about *everything*, of course."

Kali stared at him hopelessly, unable to break free, sensing somehow she *shouldn't* break free, that what Brundle insisted upon was indeed what she needed to do. Her dilemma was alleviated somewhat as Slowhand half ran, half hopped by, slapping her reassuringly on the shoulder as he headed towards the stranded pair.

"Look around ye, lass," Brundle growled. It wasn't just Horizon Point that was taking a battering from the Hel'ss Spawn but all of the island, and everywhere the disruption caused by the spawn's instability was manifesting secondary, natural effects. The island trembled, scrub and rock tumbled from its edges into the sea, and here and there sudden cracks of varying widths sundered the ground, generating clouds of dust that were starting to stifle the surface in a smoking fug. "This is lookin' to be the worst batterin' Trass Kattra's ever taken," the dwarf said. "Maybe even worse than the day the Hel'ss arrived."

"So? You said we could survive it."

"Not the problem. In case yer hadn't noticed, this entire island is riddled wi' caves, many o' me own makin' but not all. Some are safe enough but others are ancient and ain't seen shorin' for a god's age. If they go, there's a good chance the Thunderflux'll go wi' them."

Kali stared up at the huge dome, which was trembling like the rest of the island. Brundle's fears seemed justified as the glow that was emanating from its covering of runes seemed slightly diffused, as if their integrity were breaking down. One particular patch of its convex surface was already spewing a thin beam of brilliant blue light into the sky.

"What does the Thunderflux have to do with this?"

"It's where yer have to go. For yer little chat."

"It is?"

"Aye. And *now*, lass."

Kali swallowed and gazed across Horizon Point, saw the last few of the refugees vanishing through the hatches, and that Slowhand had managed to rescue those she'd intended to herself. She caught the archer's eye as he passed, supporting one in each arm, and pointed up towards the dome. Kali smiled as Slowhand – bless him – nodded in acceptance, without even knowing what was going on. Neither did she, really, but she'd missed him because of that. He didn't need to know. He was just always there.

"Fine," she said to Brundle, starting to march up the hill. "Let's go."

"Wrong way, smoothskin," the dwarf said. "The way we're headin' is down."

"Down?"

"There's no way into the Thunderflux through the cap, that's why it's a cap," Brundle said. He turned and strode urgently down the steps through the ruins, dodging the rain that continued to fall. Kali followed, instinctively but rather redundantly shielding her head with her hand, knowing all the time that if one splatter – or worse – hit it, the hand might as well not be there at all. There were a couple of close calls – Brundle cursing and ripping off a piece of his leather armour that dissolved even as it was thrown; Kali gasping as a stray spot blistered her cheek, but which her regenerative abilities seemed to keep under control – but at last they made it to cover. It was there, in the interior of a ruin whose floor had remained intact and which had steps leading down, that Brundle continued the conversation of some minutes before.

"And o' course," he said, with some hesitation, "first yer have ta go through yer trial."

Kali stopped dead. "Come again? Trial? What kind of trial?"

"Och, nothin' legal. Nothin' borin' like that. Just a trial of life and, er... death."

"Life and, er... death? Now I really am confused. You said that

I was meant to be here on this island? That I have to have this chat? But you're going to try to *kill* me before I do?"

"Smoothskin, understand," Brundle said, unusually flustered. "What yer'll hear in the Thunderflux is not for anybody's ears. Addressed to the wrong person, it could cause mass panic, and ta a person wi' the sense to understand it, grant power they shouldna have. That elf of yours is a case in point."

"Redigor's dead, Brundle. All I see is that Trass Kattra – the world – is about to fall apart, and before I can stop it you want me to jump through *hoops*."

The dwarf scratched his beard. "Ah don't recall any hoops."

"You know what I mean, dammit!"

"Ah'm sorry, smoothskin. The secrets of Trass Kattra are just too valuable. Your trial – and the trials o' the other three, had one of 'em made it here before ye – are designed so only that member of the kattra has a chance o' gettin' through."

A chance! Kali was about to yell, but then bit her tongue. What Brundle was saying was only, after all, what Merrit Moon had said years before in the *Warty Witch*. A truism she'd taken on board and used as a code throughout her life. That Twilight just wasn't ready for some things. If the Thunderflux really did contain what Brundle said – the truth about everything – could she really blame him, or blame whoever was ultimately responsible for this trial, for protecting it this way?

"I'm the one who should be sorry," Kali said. "What do I need to do?"

"Just follow me," Brundle instructed.

Kali did. Down the steps in the floor of the ruin and into a new cave system. Down into shadow. The rumbles from above quietened as they descended, becoming almost inaudible by the time they came to a cobweb shrouded arch. Beyond it she sensed a larger chamber. She swallowed. The darkness within was total.

"Tell me one thing," she said to Brundle as he ripped the thick cobweb away. "If I make it through this trial, what can I expect on the other side – in the Thunderflux?"

For once the dwarf's response was simple and to the point.

"The past, smoothskin. The past."

CHAPTER FOURTEEN

BRUNDLE MOVED INTO the chamber, taking a flint from his pocket and striking it four times. A matching number of torches flared into life with a rush of sound like a sudden squall.

As their strange, greenish light revealed their surroundings, Kali saw that each torch lit an archway carved through the chamber wall ahead. Each archway, in turn, possessed a curving lintel of gold inscribed with a large, ornate, ancient looking symbol – a different one for each arch. From left to right, Kali saw what she first took to be a snake but then realised might represent a magical thread; then a pair of hands, palms pressed tightly together as if in prayer; then a rolling crest of a wave; and finally, a clenched fist. Clenched, Kali felt, not in anger but determination, rather in the way she'd been known to clench her own.

Hanging from the lintels was the accumulation of ages, great sheets of cobweb stirring in response to sighing breezes from beyond.

"Spooky," Kali said over the flutter of the torches. "So this is the start of the Trials, huh?"

"Aye, this is the start. Each o' these arches leads to a path built to challenge the abilities of one the Four, and be traversable only by them. The first is the Path of Magic, the path of Lucius Kane. The second, the Path of Faith, the path of Gabriella DeZantez. The third, the Path of Water, the path of Silus Morlader. And the fourth, the Path –"

"The Path of Confusion, right? The Path of Kali Hooper."

Brundle gave another of his strange looks.

"The Path of Endurance," he corrected.

The chamber shook slightly, the conditions on the surface clearly worsening. A skitter of dust fell from the roof.

"There isn't much time," Brundle said.

"Okay. But if there are four paths, shouldn't all four of us be here? I mean, if this 'truth' the paths lead to is so world-shattering, shouldn't we all be here to listen?"

"The Truth awaits all four, but not all four need to hear it. The first will pass the Truth to the others... to the world."

"Four known to us, Four unknown to each other," Kali countered. "Four who will be known to all."

"Is that meant to be some kind o' weird cod philosophy?"

Well, at least Brundle was in the dark about one thing, Kali thought.

"No. You just reminded me of something a fish once told me," she said mischievously. "But if I told you, I'd have to brill you."

"Hah!" Brundle laughed, appreciating, if not the bad pun, having the tables turned. But he wasn't going to let her get away with it. "I'm glad to hear you still have your sense of humour," he said, his face looming up at hers and darkening. "You'll need it."

Kali's face, too, darkened, but not in response to his comment.

"There are only three of us, now – you know that? Gabriella... she died."

"Did she?" Brundle said.

Without another word, the dwarf moved towards the entrance to the Path of Endurance, seemingly ready to usher Kali in.

"Wasting no time, I see?" Kali said, swallowing. "Is there anything I need to do?"

"There's an antechamber beyond the arch where you can pray if you wish, or bless yourself with holy water after removing your kit and clothes. 'Course, I don't expect you –"

"O-ho-ho, back up there, shorty," Kali broke in. "Naked? You want me to do this naked?"

"The Path tests you and your abilities, not the tools at your disposal," Brundle said. "But don't worry, smoothskin, ah promise ah won't peek."

"And how am I to know you haven't got more strategically placed vertispys in there?"

Brundle sighed. "Because ah'd be letchin' over summat so thin ah could use it to clean me ruddy pipe, is why. Ah'm a dwarf, and you ain't. Yer might as well accuse me of fancyin' a worgle."

"There are some who do."

"There are?"

"Sure," Kali said. "They meet in secret. In, er, furry costumes. And they, um, have this secret handshake. Well, not a handshake exactly as worgles don't have hands but they do this kind of wobbling thing with their..."

Jerragrim Brundle's eyes narrowed suspiciously. "Yer wouldn't by any chance be tryin' to delay goin' in there, would ye?"

Kali swallowed, caught out. "Why would I do that?"

"Oh, ah don't know, but here's a stab in the dark. *Because yer might die*?"

Kali turned to face the arch. The fact was, she *was* trying to delay the start of the Trial, but not because of the danger. No, if she were honest with herself, after all her years of trying to solve the mystery of what happened to the Old Races, it was *that* she was afraid of. Finally learning the truth. Would it place more responsibility on her shoulders? Or take that responsibility away? What was she to do in either case, being at the centre of things or being out of it completely, her job done? It wasn't death but *survival* that she feared, the knowledge that whatever happened from here on in was going to change things – *change her* – for ever.

Right then, as she stared at the billowing curtain of cobweb draped from the symbol of the clenched fist, she would have given anything for Lucius Kane to be standing before his arch in her place. Let the shadowmage burden the responsibility, when she'd encountered him in Andon he'd seemed capable enough, after all. Or Silus Morlader. She didn't know the man but was aware of his supposed legacy and somehow this place – far out to sea and battered by the swirlies – seemed more appropriate to his skills. Even poor Gabriella, had she lived. Despite the doubts the Sword of Dawn had started to feel about the Church she had served all her life, surely her own admirably unshakable faith would have carried her through?

But none of them were standing here, were they? It was just her. Alone. And she could either stand here all day talking pits with the dwarf or get on with it.

"I'm ready," she said.

Brundle nodded and moved to the arch, slowly pulling away the thick cobweb. Taking a deep breath, Kali moved towards the shadows beyond.

"Smoothskin," Brundle said, placing a hand on her side as she passed, "if it's worth anythin' ah know yer can do this."

"Thanks, shorty."

"See you on the other side, eh?"

"'k."

Kali moved through the arch, and the world behind her was gone. Not gone physically but in her mind, subsumed by the feel of the chamber she found herself in.

It felt indescribably old and, despite the rumbles from above, indescribably lonely. The knowledge that this place had been created for her and her alone – that no one else had ever, *ever* set foot here and likely never would – weighed heavily on her mind. Kali examined its meagre contents; a stone trough of water and a stone bench, illuminated by what appeared to be glowing crystals in the walls, and then another cobwebbed arch which led out from the chamber opposite to the one by which she'd entered. Through there lay the Trial and whatever it had in store for her, and where in any other circumstances she would have ignored Brundle's instructions, tackled it under her own terms, here that somehow felt wrong. Here she suspected she should follow the rules to the letter.

Even if it was so farking cold.

She sighed and stripped off her bodysuit, folding it neatly and laying it on the bench. She stood over it for a second, shivering in the breeze that came from further within, allowing her naked body to acclimatise to the environment. She looked at the trough and wished that instead of blessed water it held a few gallons of thwack. That was the only spiritual aid she needed, right now, thank you very much.

Despite the temperature, she scooped up a handful of water and splashed her face and neck. She hissed but the cold liquid invigorated her and reinforced the reality of her situation. She took three deep breaths, then turned to the second arch.

She was ready.

She stepped through into the darkness.

Found the floor ceased to exist under her feet.

And fell.

Kali's yelp of surprise segued into a longer wail of alarm as she tumbled down a steep slope. Whatever she'd expected beyond the arch it wasn't to be wrong-footed from the word go, and in the seconds it took her to come to terms with her situation she repeatedly impacted hard with the walls of the passage as its curving descent bounced her down and down, left and right, deep into the bedrock of the island. Then her survival instincts kicked in and she flung out her arms in an attempt to halt her progress. For a few seconds her flesh grated against rushing rock but then the walls of the drop were no longer within her reach. Feeling only air on her palms, and then suddenly also beneath her, it didn't take much to work out the passage had ended and she was now in freefall in some kind of vertical shaft. Knowing the nature of this place, it wasn't likely there was going to be a cushion beneath her.

She flailed in the darkness, seeking a means to prevent her ending the Trial almost before it had started as a mass of shattered bones. Her hands closed on some kind of rope – ancient hemp but tarred, it felt, to preserve it – and with an organ jarring *oof* she halted her fall, bringing a shower of clattering stones and dust from far above. The respite was only momentary, however, as, while she swung there, she heard the metallic *klik-klak* of some kind of ratchet releasing itself as a result of her weight, and suddenly the rope was snaking heavily down about her and she was dropping once more. She flailed again, made contact with another rope, and the sound of another *klik-klak* made her heart thud.

Shit!

But part of her had already worked out what was going on. She leapt into dark space again, found another rope – *klik-klak* – and then another – *klik-klak* – each time falling further towards the base of the shaft, and with increasing speed. To her left and her right, throwing herself upwards and downwards amidst what she now knew to be a veritable forest of dangling deathtraps of different lengths, she moved from rope to rope all the time sensing the ever accelerating approach of whatever lay beneath her. Still shrouded in total darkness, she at last clutched a rope that seemed not to produce a response from a ratchet, and she hung there gasping, the ancient hemp creaking as she moved slowly on its end.

Klik-Klak.

Bastard!

Kali lunged, desperately, instinctively, and so violently that the next rope she grabbed onto swung wildly back and forth, crashing her against the walls of the shaft and sending her spinning in the opposite direction. This didn't exactly improve her mood but, after a few seconds one thing did.

It held. As it stilled, the rope held.

Her weight on it also seemed to activate some kind of mechanism, and to her right part of the blackness rumbled. A square of light – a doorway to another passage – appeared in the shaft's walls. As it did, it illuminated the area where she dangled. Directly beneath her Kali could now see the entire base of the shaft was rooted with spikes taller than she was, and though they were clearly as ancient as the ropes she was willing to bet they had lost none of their keenness. Kali flexed a foot, dipping the flesh off her big toe onto the tip of one of them, then snatched it away with a hiss as a bead of blood appeared.

Clichéd, she thought, but couldn't help but admire the design of the trap that could so easily have left her impaled upon the spikes. Right from the second she'd stepped through the arch, the whole thing had been a test of reaction – the kind of reaction only she, as one of the Four, would possess. That this was, she suspected, only the start of what her Trial had in store for her, brought a summation of its designer's ingenuity that consisted of just one word.

"Twat."

Despite that, Kali did now feel advantaged. She had some measure of the Trial. And if the rest of it consisted of the same perverse, impossibly difficult challenges she had just faced, it might even be fun. With a grunt of determination she began to inch her way up the rope to draw level with the doorway, then swung, let go, and landed.

The passage she was in was lit by the same growths as in the preparation chamber, but the fact that she could now see where she was going did not make Kali any less cautious. Just as well, too, as a sudden grinding of ancient gears gave her a moment's notice of the crescent shaped blades that began to scythe rapidly across the passage before her, all along its length. The *vwoop, vwoop, vwoop* of the blades was constant, and though Kali had encountered similar deathtraps in other locations, this one differed in one vital respect. The gaps between the blades were unforgiving, no wider than she was, making the old run and stop, run and stop strategy impossible, and unless she wanted to lose the bits that Brundle had fondled in the bar in Gransk, or the arse he'd commented on at Horizon Point, she'd have to use a different technique.

The sudden rumbling of a wall behind her, closing the exit from the passage and moving forward to shunt her towards the blades, forced Kali to act without thought, and she crossed her arms tightly against her chest, sucked her stomach in, and began to pirouette through the blades.

She span and span and span again, with ever increasing acceleration, feeling stupidly dizzied but forcing herself to remain upright and straight as a dye while the blades scythed within a hair's breadth of her flesh, carrying away with them long streaks of her sweat. Every spin, every quarter second, brought with it the conviction she was about to be cleaved in two but amazingly, miraculously, she sensed suddenly that she was through. There was no relief, though, for the same acute senses that had served her so well over the years warned her this wasn't quite done yet, and Kali flung herself onto her back as a final blade swept *along* the passage, between those that had stopped after her passing, and sliced a thin red line from her groin to her sternum.

Like she'd said. Twat.

So it went. Kali fought her way on, besting such classics of the athletic archaeologist's trade as the punching walls, the stomping hammers and the bubbling lava pits of doom, each challenge perversely tweaked to deliver that extra pound of her flesh. She even half expected to come up against the revolving razor rabbit, though didn't, but that was probably because she'd only encountered that once, in the dark, and in truth had been very drunk at the time.

She at last emerged onto a narrow rock bridge spanning a vertiginous void and, before she proceeded, collapsed to her knees to take a breather. But the breather didn't last for long. Her first thought as the bridge beneath her began to rumble was that they were rolling out that old chestnut, the giant boulder, but then the ceiling began to rain debris and she realised she must be somewhere near the surface, where the death throes of the Hel'ss Spawn were continuing. Cracks started to appear in the bridge before her, and Kali picked herself up and ran, heading for the safety of another cave mouth with the symbol of her Path at its end. But before she could reach it a fall of rocks blocked her way through. Her Path of Endurance, it seemed, was at an end.

Or was it? As dust settled after the tremor, leaving the bridge intact if skewed, Kali looked into the void the bridge crossed and found it not to be a void at all.

The design of the Trials was cleverer than she'd thought, not in terms of the challenges they offered but the fact they also seemed to intersect each other, for below and, indeed, above her, she could make out cave entrances with the symbols of the Paths of Magic, Faith and Water – the latter a pool in the floor rather than an entrance – inscribed in their frames. Staging points, like this one of her own.

The solution was obvious. She could no longer continue on her own Path so would have to choose another. But which?

No choice, really. It seemed fitting that she took the one she felt closest to.

Gabriella's Path.

Not that it was easy jumping tracks. With a series of grunts, Kali threw herself from the bridge and managed, precariously, to gain a hand and foothold on the cavern wall. From there she began to inch her way upward, almost losing her grip more than once, but at last found herself in a position just below the lip of the entrance inscribed with the symbol of the praying hands. She flipped herself upwards, ready to journey in, when it occurred to her that the direction she was facing was back the way she had come.

She turned and found that the way ahead lay through a similarly inscribed portal – but one that was at least two hundred yards away on the other side of the cavern. There was no bridge that connected them like her own.

How in the hells was she meant to get across? How in the hells had Gabriella been meant to get across? Was there in fact a bridge there like one of those she'd heard about, built in such a way it disguised itself against its background? Or was it one made of perfectly carved crystal, refraction free, that would only reveal itself when sprinkled with dust?

Kali almost kicked herself. It could be neither of those, of course, because if it were, how could she have flipped herself upwards? All she would have ended up doing was flattening her arse on rock.

What, then? A bridge that revealed itself stage by stage with every footstep you took? A bridge controlled by some mechanism handily concealed in a nearby room full of monsters? Dammit, there were just too many kinds of bridge.

Including one she'd forgotten.

This was the Path of Faith, right?

What if this was a bridge of Faith? Had Gabriella been here, would all that would have been required of her be a *belief* that the bridge was there? A bridge that was provided by her God?

There is a bridge, there is a bridge, there is a bridge, Kali thought as she closed her eyes tight and took a tentative step forward. She must have been doing something right because she didn't tip into the cavern below. Another step. *There is a bridge, there is a bridge, there is a bridge.* Another, then another, then another. Oh, this was a piece of pits, she thought, and began to run. *Bridge, bridge, bridge, bridge, bridge.* All right! It was really quite astounding how you got religion when you needed it.

Oops. Impious thought.

Kali suddenly felt air beneath her feet. Well, not beneath so much as rushing by. Her eyes snapped open and saw that, luckily, she had almost made it to the other side. She roared and flailed forward, grabbing onto a vine that dangled from the opposite entrance, and pulled herself up. She rested for a second. Close call, smartarse.

Kali strode through the entrance into the next stage of Gabriella's Trial – and straight into an inferno. The passage ahead was blocked by fire burning with a heat so searing she wondered if it was meant to represent the Hells. The religious hells, that was, not the bastard in the skies – the place where Gabriella and her fellow devotees preached you went when you'd been a naughty boy or girl. Another test of her faith, then? A demonstration that as a Sister of the Order of the Swords of Dawn she could walk through the hells unscathed? Maybe. But the Trials were tests of the person *and* their abilities, so what if this was meant to challenge Gabriella's magical resistance? What if this was a magical fire that Gabriella might be able to saunter through but would roast anyone else alive?

Kali reached out a hand and pulled it back with a hiss, her palm reddened and blistered. Okay, it felt like real fire but that didn't prove anything. Maybe all she needed to do was concentrate like she had on the bridge – or, considering her surroundings, maybe a little bit more. Kali closed her eyes and put out her hand once more. The heat of the fire began to lessen. And when it had lessened enough, she began to walk forward. Flames enveloped her but she continued on unharmed.

She'd been right the first time. She had to admit that Gabriella's Trial was a bit of a breeze compared to her own.

Kali was halfway along the passage when she began to smoke. Began to hurt. And however much she concentrated the pain wouldn't go away.

Oh gods, she realised. This wasn't a test of Gabriella's faith *or* her magic resistance. It was a test of both.

Kali ran. Ran faster than she ever had in her life, the flames licking at her, blistering her, turning patches of her skin an agonisingly raw red. She burst forth onto another bridge but it too was lined with fire. There was nowhere to go but down.

Kali threw herself off the bridge without a clue what was below, and landed hard, on rock. She patted herself down, wincing, and saw that once again she was in some kind of juncture between Paths. Looking around, guided once more by the symbols carved into the rock, she saw that the only other Path accessible from this point, and again only with difficulty, was Lucius Kane's.

Kali picked herself up and made her way across the rocky hinterland. The entrance to whatever stage of Kane's trial she would face lay some eight metres away, on the other side of a precipitous and apparently bottomless ravine. She backed up, taking deep, preparatory breaths, then raced forward with arms and legs pumping and leapt over the unwelcoming depths.

Her roar of determination echoing throughout the subterrain, she made the leap with a foot to spare, but landed hard, and the pain of the sharp rock on her bare soles made her somersault forward not once but three times. The last of these gymnastics took her onto Kane's symbol-inscribed path, and even before she could right herself she spotted three coruscating, variously coloured orbs in a triangular formation heading directly for her, and fast, along the narrow passage beyond. Kali squealed, rose and span, intending to retreat while the orbs shot by, but an invisible wall now blocked her in, and she span back, mind racing. The orbs had resolved themselves into balls of blue crackling energy, hissing ice and – oh great – more fire. Kane's trial was wasting no time and she guessed this was a test of his reactions, his ability to swap between threads at speed, finding the right ones to counter the different elemental threats, diffusing, destroying or repelling them before they hit.

Yep, that made sense. For him. But what the flying fark was *she* supposed to do?

Fly. It was all she could do. Fly through the lethal looking orbs as they came, launching herself through the small gap in the heart of their formation. This she did, feeling like some kind of circus act, turning almost three hundred and sixty degrees as she kept her body streamlined. But she was a human thread passing through a needle's eye, and some contact was unavoidable. Kali took the pain from grazing the fire orb almost as a matter of course – how could it be any worse than Gabriella's inferno? – but she gasped in pain as the ice orb grazed a hip and ribs, the temperature contrast on her reddened skin agonising enough, but not quite as agonising as then having that same skin instantly frozen and stripped away. A streak of raw flesh now running half the length of her right hand side, the last thing she needed was contact with the last of the orbs, but this was unavoidable, too. The blue, crackling energy sent her entire body into spasm in what remained of her flight, and Kali hit the ground clumsily, twitching and coated in sweat, small darts of lightning dancing over her before discharging into the air.

She watched the orbs hit the invisible wall and disappear. Her eyes narrowed.

She hated this farking place. It had actually made her pee.

Kali forced herself up on trembling arms and wearily began to limp further down the passage. She remained on guard for more lightning, thunder, acid rain or whatever was going to be thrown at her next, but in actual fact she reached a chamber that was in stark contrast to any she had encountered before. That wasn't to say it wasn't equally dangerous, of course, even though all it seemed to contain was a door.

That was it. A door. A door standing all by itself in the centre of the chamber. A door that you could walk all the way around. And in the centre of the door, a lock. But what was the point of a lock if all you had to do to get through the door was move to its other side?

Kali frowned. The sheer fact that she was looking at a locked door seemed to indicate this was a test of Kane's thieving skills rather than his magical legacy, but that wasn't necessarily so. If this path had the same duality of purpose as Gabriella's it could be either.

No, she realised suddenly, it couldn't. Or at least she didn't think so. Because if it were a test of thieving skills and it was Kane who was attempting this trial, if he'd reached the island before her, then he, too, would be doing it naked, and what was he supposed to pick the lock with, his – well, she didn't need to picture it, did she? She wasn't denying the shadowmage might have hidden talents but she doubted that was one of them, so this had to be a kind of a hybrid test – a thief's challenge that needed to be solved by magic. If that *was* the case, then she could...

No, again. Who was she kidding? Either way she was bollocksed.

Frustrated, Kali kicked the door.

And then found out what would have happened if Kane had failed this test.

The rapid *shnik! shnik! shnik!* was a dead giveaway, and she would have been dead had she not encountered similar traps on more than one occasion. She berated herself for not having noticed the myriad circular holes that punctured the walls of the chamber, even though they had become filled and disguised by the dust of ages, and once more leapt into the air.

What was it to be, she wondered? The tree, the stag or the teapot? In the end, she found herself in an unidentifiable and vaguely sillier position than any of them, suspended where she'd leapt between the hundred or so pointed bars that had erupted from the walls, roof and floor horizontally, vertically and diagonally, ramming themselves into the opposing areas of the chamber in a series of thuds and explosions of dust. Kali hung there immobile, her neck trapped between an intersection of bars so tightly she felt it had been removed and mounted, her left arm bent back and behind her at the elbow, her right thrust straight down under her, toes almost but not quite touching the ground. Her torso and right leg, meanwhile, were twisted at such an angle she could easily see all the way down the livid scar on her right hand side. She reflected she hadn't done badly considering what the chamber had thrown at her, but the bar that had skewered her left thigh, punching all the way through by the bone and impaling her on the latticework, elicited a long and weary groan. Kali waited, watching the drips of blood from her leg puddle on the chamber floor, then, as she'd hoped, the trap reset itself. With the dull rumble of some hidden mechanism, the bars slowly retreated to their housings, and, bit by bit, Kali was released from her confinement, slithering downwards from bar to bar.

The one that had punctured her thigh, the dust it had gathered grating on her inner flesh, hurt like the hells as it came out, and she gritted her teeth, finally thudding to the floor with a gasp.

That was it. Sod the world. She wanted to go home. Now.

There was no going back, though, was there? Only forward. And in that respect, the trial was offering Kali the first break she'd had. This trap, like all the others, was multilayered, and though she had failed the door test – as Kane conceivably *could* have – the trap itself was as much of a test of skills as the door had been. Whatever magical wheeze the shadowmage might have used to avoid a change of career to a pin cushion – some spell like skin of steel, spongeflesh or size of a worgle, whatever he called the bloody things – survival satisfied the test's conditions as much as success.

The locked door was gone. Transformed into a shimmering portal.

Kali sighed, picked herself up and, leg slick with blood, limped through.

Another bridge.

That'll do, Kali thought. She'd had more than enough of the Trial of Lucius Kane.

She dropped down into what she thought was going to be

another hinterland, hoping to find a cave inscribed with the symbol of Endurance. But all there was was a dark and uninviting pool of water in the rock floor.

Guess who? she thought.

The memory of what had happened on the sinking Black Ship still fresh in her mind, it was the very last thing she wanted to do, but Kali inhaled one slow, very deep breath and then dived beneath the surface into the Trial of Silus Morlader.

CHAPTER FIFTEEN

IT WAS LIKE swimming through soup. Cold, leftover and half-rotten soup filled with every unwanted ingredient that could ever be imagined. As Kali propelled herself down with determined strokes, still moving painfully slowly against the swell – the murk around her offered up great patches of silt from the cave floor, wooden flotsam that bobbed and bumped against her, detritus that had accumulated over the ages, and finally, but by no means the least, lengthy, cloying strands of seaweed and other marine vegetation that slithered over and clung to her body and, on occasion, her face, making her want to release her air and gag.

These were not the only obstacles she faced. The crystalline formations that lit the rest of the Trials were far less abundant here, worn away for the most part by the roiling water and eroding effects of its contents, and the further Kali swam from the entrance the darker the waters became. The darkness itself was not the danger, of course – with no idea of what form these submarine caves took, or even of which direction she was meant to be heading, she was blind in more ways than one, and her hands scraped repeatedly and painfully against boulders, sharp growths of coral, and rock walls. Kali began to trail blood, and at one point another length of the seaweed wrapped itself around one of her legs, sliding down to entangle her ankle. Repulsed, Kali kicked herself away so violently that she span in the water, her head cracking an unseen boulder so hard she saw stars.

Disorientated, having involuntarily released a quantity of her air, Kali scrabbled back to what she thought was an upright position. But the disturbed water had become thick with silt, and there wasn't even the faintest patch of light, and for all she knew she could have been attempting to swim downwards or sideways.

The first stirrings of panic set in as all Kali could feel, whichever way she stroked her hands, was rock, and she turned again and again, this way and that, but finding no hope for her predicament. She twisted herself around once more. This time her hands dug into the base of the cave, scooping up fistfuls of sand and shells and, as she cast them away as if they were contaminated, another flare of panic came. She found the rock wall – *a* rock wall – once more, and groped her way along it, hoping that this time she had chosen the right direction in which to kick off.

She had, finding a bend with her fingertips which she pulled herself around, but as she began to thrust herself forward once more the stark reality of her situation was already starting to hit home. It had been all right telling herself that she could negotiate the path designed for Silus, that her abilities would get her through, but the fact was if this path was meant to be as much of a challenge for him as her own had proven to her, then, despite the fact she was already faltering, she would only have, as it were, dipped her toes in the water.

The realisation brought with it a desperate burst of energy, and Kali propelled herself through the water as fast as she felt it safe to do so, ignoring the bumps and scrapes to her arms and hips that had earlier given her cause to tackle the liquid path more cautiously. One pain that she couldn't ignore, however, was the one growing in her breast, a searing heat of constrained, exhausted breath that was beginning to feel more and more as if someone were scraping the blade of a knife up and down her trachea. The pain made her want to cough and, more dangerously, swallow reflexively, and, as she did, her mouth opened slightly, expelling some of what was left of her air in a cloud of bubbles and allowing the taste of the mire through which she swam inside her. Kali swallowed it, for there was nothing else she could do, and knew it was only a matter of time before her lungs would involuntarily start to fill with more of the tainted liquid. There was nothing else for it. She swam on, determined but ultimately not built for that which she had been forced to endure, and then felt her stomach, her chest, her entire torso begin to spasm, fighting against her to draw in the great, gulping breath that she didn't want to take.

More bubbles exploded from her mouth and struggling, slowing to a stop, Kali hung there and then gradually began to incline vertically upwards, her limbs floating. She flailed in the water, bucking, resisting, knowing her fate was inevitable. She could hear her own resistant moans inside her head, magnified because she was unable to release them, whimpering and animalistic. Her eyes widened in desperation, even now seeking a way out of this deathtrap, but seeing nothing but the mire that was sure to become her watery grave.

Then suddenly, waveringly, *there*. Kali wasn't sure whether she was actually seeing it or whether it was the result of the increasing, spotted flaring of her vision, but above her seemed to be light. She began swimming upwards, brushing gleefully welcome, upwardly sloping rock as she did, and then unexpectedly burst the surface with a single, long gulping inhalation of breath. The breath caught on the muck that had settled within her and immediately she vomited up the dire water she had swallowed.

Taking another gulping breath, hacking and spitting, Kali looked around. There wasn't much to see. Illuminated by a small collection of crystals, a small, hollow niche surrounded her, not quite big enough for her to fully stretch out her arms. At first she thought it might have been some kind of rest area for Silus – a staging post on his trial, maybe – but she then realised he would have no need of such respite. Studying the rock, she realised it was a natural formation, the result of erosion into which the swirling waters below must periodically rise, trying to find an alternate exit from the labyrinth through which they flowed.

Kali forgot what such a feature was called but, in actual fact, didn't give a toss. She was just grateful it was there. Had she been able to reach it, she would have kissed the rock above. Shagged it, if the rock had been in the mood. This tiny pocket of air could prove to be her salvation. It could even prove the means by which she might survive Silus's trial after all. Using it as a base, a central point, she could reconnoitre the labyrinth that lay ahead, gauge distances, directions, each time returning here for vital oxygen. And each time, hopefully, having managed to map the trial a little further. This was nowhere near a guarantee, of course – who but its builders knew how far the trial extended – but it was a *start*.

Kali wasted no time, filling her lungs, dipping her head back beneath the water and power-stroking down. Less panicked now, with a brain filled with thoughts rather than adrenalin, she twisted, eel-like, around a bend in the cave she could now discern. The bend led to a narrow flue that dropped vertically and she twisted again, doggy-paddling herself into position to descend it. The flue dropped about a hundred yards and, at its base, she found a number of passages radiating off a small chamber. Kali decided to explore them clockwise, and swam into the first, finding, after about ten yards, a dead end. She retraced her path and was about to tackle the second passage when she started to feel the familiar burning sensation in her midriff. Time to return and refuel, as it were.

Done, Kali tried the second passage, and then the third – dead ends again – though the second proceeded so far in that she thought it was leading somewhere, and only just made it back to the airhole. On her return trip, the fourth passage proved to be the one she wanted and, after a winding route, she shot with surprising speed into another chamber, one much larger than the last. Again, though, she had reached the limit of her explorations, and twisted herself around in the water to return from whence she came. But there was a problem. Her accelerated arrival into the chamber had been the result of the strong current generated in the passage she'd used, and returning to the passage, swimming against the current, wasn't possible. Kali struggled, her arms pumping and legs kicking, but she made no headway at all, and, ever weakening, found herself spat back into the heart of the chamber, where she was tossed and rolled helplessly.

Panic flared within her once more as she felt more currents tugging at her and, using what little strength she had left simply to remain stable, realised she was in the middle of a maelstrom. The chamber, like the one above, offered a variety of exits, but in this case many, many more, riddling it like Gargassian cheese, and from each and into each water poured under such pressure that attempting to fight or resist its flow was a lost cause. Not that she had time to fight or to resist as her breath was almost gone now, the searing pain in her chest urging her to take one breath, just one breath...

An involuntary burst of bubbles escaping her mouth, Kali's mind raced as fast as the currents clashed with each other around her. Like the rest of the aquatic labyrinth this chamber had clearly been designed as a challenge for Silus, but surely not simply to confuse and to trap him here, because for a man with no need of breath, what would be the point? He could take all the time in the world to negotiate his way through. If not a trap, then, what? Some kind of gauntlet? A test of his endurance and skills? If that was the case, what skills, other than the ability to breathe under water, did Silus Morlader possess?

Think, woman, think! He was a mariner, right? He had lived all his life with the sea. The fact that his legacy had endowed him with the preternatural ability to survive in a submarine environment could, in a way, almost be considered a bonus. But there was little doubt that his abilities, even when latent, must have drawn him to the sea, because that, after all, was his destiny, as much as it had been her destiny to spend her life burrowing beneath the ground. Silus Morlader and the seas of Twilight were complementary forces. They were one with him, and he was one with them.

One.

That was the answer. You didn't fight that which made you whole. You didn't struggle. And the purpose of running a gauntlet was to prove it presented no danger to you, that you accepted its dangers and were comfortable with them. Yes, that had to be it.

Unless she wanted to die here, decomposing until her flesh became one with these waters, her bones battered on the chamber's rock walls until they, too, were silt, it was her only chance.

Kali relaxed her body, closed her eyes, and allowed herself to drift into the strongest of the currents. She forced herself to remain relaxed as it snatched her away, ignoring the presence of the rocks that projected all around her, trusting, as Silus would have done, the tumultuous ebb and flow of the chamber's currents, allowing them, with only the slightest instinctive changes in her posture, to deliver her where she was meant to be.

Her body was carried through the waters of the chamber, bending and twisting, supple and slithery as a snake, and, while occasionally she felt looming masses of rock flashing at her or within inches of her side, or her whole body buffeted as one current crossed another, she did not resist and simply went with the flow. Even the now agonising tightness of her chest seemed to dull as she proceeded, accepting the inevitability of her underwater journey, which could now only end one of two ways, neither of which she had any say in at all.

On through the waters she continued, until at last the current transported her into one of the many passages that led off the gauntlet, which Kali was only aware of because of an increased darkness about her. Down, then sideways, then up she travelled, the slight shifts in her posture occasionally misjudged, her body scraping the passage walls but unharmed, the rock worn to an organic smoothness by the force of the water that travelled through it. But the darkness around her wasn't the only darkness, now, her body finally succumbing to lack of oxygen, and heavy shadows began to close in on her mind. As unconsciousness loomed, insidiously, like slipping into a dream, any attempt at manoeuvring was forgotten and, less Kali Hooper now than piece of living flotsam, her body began to drift in the current, bouncing and then slamming with increasing force off the passage walls as it was carried seemingly forever onward.

And as it did, her mouth yawned opened, and water began to enter her lungs.

Kali's eyes snapped open. The cold shock of the liquid inside her brought her back from the brink of oblivion, extinguishing the fire within her breast but not welcome for doing so, and with a loud blub she expelled it back from whence it came. The urge to inhale again was immediate, and she almost did, but, angry now – angry that she had almost allowed herself to die, angry that these Trials conspired to kill her when she was so close to the truth – she decided that she wasn't dead yet.

No way. No farking way.

Kali forgot everything except reaching the end of the Trial. Her body already black and blue from the battering it had taken against the walls, she cared little what further damage it took, because this was do or die. Instead of allowing the current to simply carry her along, she began to kick, punch and throw herself off the walls, rolling, flexing and punching herself ever forward, like a sentient bullet trying to find the end of the barrel of a gun. Her progress was lost in a welter of bubbles, thrashed water and flailing limbs as on and on she went, but, so long as she felt the current still pushing her from behind, she was going to be all right.

She had to be...

... she was going to be all right...

... going to be...

... going to...

... going...

A sudden, deafening roaring filled Kali's ears, she felt air on her face, and she heaved in a gasping breath so deep that for a moment she felt that her upper half was going to implode.

The roaring resolved itself into the sound of thunderously rushing water through which, feeling it smash into her back from above, she was falling. Kali looked down and saw that far below her, almost obscured by a billowing cloud of white spray, the water was pouring into the base of another cylindrical flue, but this one much broader – and, of course, unsubmerged – as those earlier. The fact that it *was* unsubmerged gave her a sense that she was at last close to the end of Silus's Trial, but it wasn't quite yet time to rejoice, for if she didn't do something about her uncontrolled plummet the impact into the waters below would snap her into pieces.

Kali twisted and flexed until she was pointing headfirst at the water, her body straight and her arms outstretched beside her. As she cut through the waterfall, wind that had never been more welcome whipped at her. Then, a few seconds before she disappeared into the cloud of spray, she inclined her arms beneath her, as straight as the rest of her, waiting for her fingertips to slice neatly into the waiting water.

Kali plunged into the foaming mass that filled the base of the flue, feeling its swirling, roiling presence strangely warm and all over her skin like a reaffirmation of life, and then she burst the surface with the cry that she had been wanting to vent the moment she had been able to breathe again.

"*Yeeeeeeeee-haaaaaaaaahhh!*"

She'd done it, she'd survived the Trial, and not her Trial but Silus's Trial. The cry she'd emitted, even though it was inaudible above the sound of the waterfall, segued into laughter as Kali looked up and splashed her face. Gods, she was good. Yes, Kali Hooper was *good*. She'd *proven* herself to be one of the Four.

Kali's laughter faded as she began to turn involuntarily in the waters that surrounded her, and then she frowned as, amidst great disturbance on its surface, the water began to rise, taking her with it. Within a second of the phenomenon occurring she had risen twenty feet within the vertical flue, spinning dizzyingly all the time, and all that she could see above her were its revolving walls becoming submerged ever and ever faster. What the hells was this? What was happening now?

But if Kali had learned anything during this Trial it was to let things simply take their course – not that she really had any choice – and as she rose she studied the flue's sides, trying to gauge, to prepare for what was to come. There seemed to be some kind of opening on what was momentarily the left, and another opposite, slightly higher, on the right. The purpose of both were unknown. Pits of Kerberos, she thought, if she was going to be dumped into either of these, this whole process beginning again, she'd save the Trial the trouble and quaff the waters down like thwack. Enough was enough.

As it turned out, however, the whole process was not going to begin again, because as Kali rose to the level of the first opening she saw that the rising water was already beginning to spill into it, flowing down a short, sloped channel then cascading away as a waterfall like the one through which she'd been dumped here. She turned in the water and saw that the opposite opening had a set of ancient stone steps leading down, bridging the gap between the two. So that was it, she thought, the flue wasn't a flue but a means to bring whoever had survived the earlier journey into it to this point, the whole thing acting as a kind of giant cistern and the water that cascaded away recycled, no doubt, through another labyrinthine series of passages so that the process would repeat over and over again.

She felt the tug of the new waterfall drawing her towards the first opening but kicked against it, and a second later drew herself onto the steps that the second proffered. Water dripping from her, hair plastered to her head, she ascended them slowly, to an arch that awaited her at their top.

Kali stepped through the arch and gasped.

She had entered the most massive cavern of the underground labyrinth yet, what had to be *the* most massive cavern, as it seemed to fill the entire centre of the island, a hollow core beneath a rock roof whose inverted topography matched what she knew to be the landscape above. It wasn't the above that drew Kali's gaze, however, but what was ahead of her, and below. She was standing at the beginning of a narrow rock bridge, one of four that entered the cavern from each point of the compass, the other three what could only be the ends of the Paths of Magic, Faith and Survival. She might have reached this place by the wrong route but it didn't matter, because they converged here.

Each bridge spanned the cavern across a raging body of water, and as she looked down Kali could make out various caves that she presumed opened into the sea. This was doubtless the same water which supplied Silus' Path, the one she had just negotiated, and now she would have to negotiate it again, this time from above. This wasn't a path she was looking forward to any more than Silus's, because the water, thrust by violent tides and slapped by the walls of the cavern – and doubtless made all the more tumultuous by what she had seen happening to the Hel'ss Spawn – frequently crashed above the height of the bridges, momentarily drowning them with such force that if she timed her crossing badly she'd be instantly washed away.

But cross the bridge she must. Because at its far end, in the exact centre of the cavern and towards which the other three bridges also led, was what she presumed was her ultimate destination. A huge column of intertwined, multicoloured lightning that shot powerful whips of energy throughout the cavern and towards its roof, dancing and dissipating where they struck its walls with a force Kali could hear and feel even this far below. This had to be the phenomenon that Brundle had mentioned to her.

The Thunderflux.

Whatever the Thunderflux was.

Kali swallowed. It wasn't so much because the phenomenon looked as though it might be capable of incinerating her at the merest touch, but because, if what Brundle said was true, that inside it the truth lay. *The* truth. The truth she had been searching for for years. The fate of the Old Races. The secret of who she was. The destiny of mankind.

All she had to do was reach it, and the answers would be hers.

Kali's heart thudded as she stepped onto the bridge, immediately backtracking as a wave crashed down directly in front of her, swamping the narrow thoroughfare and leaving behind a detritus of seaweed that dangled from the stone like vines. Kali took another step forward, feeling some of the aquatic matter crunch beneath her bare feet and some, its surface suckered, adhere to her soles like glue. She kicked it away and continued on, watching the ebb and flow of the waters beneath her every step of the way. A wave crashed directly under the bridge and a heavy spray buffeted her on both sides, and then she ducked, clinging onto the rock, as the bridge was swamped in a backwash. Kali was knocked onto her side, almost slithering off the bridge on the slime that coated it, but managed to hook a foot in some of the seaweed on its opposite edge, preventing her fall. She heaved herself onto her hands and knees again, most of her body coated now in a green marine goo, and uttered a small curse as she stared ahead and saw there was perhaps still two thirds of the bridge to go. She would not be stopped now, though, and decided to use the bridge to her advantage rather than treat it as an obstacle.

Kali waited where she was, hanging on for dear life, as three more waves crashed about her, and then, having worked out a rough pattern to the water's movements, raised herself into a sprint position and flung herself forward. The slime caused her to lose her footing almost immediately, of course, and she managed only three pounding steps, but that was exactly what she wanted, and she allowed herself to fall forward, crashing back onto the slime and allowing it to do what slime did best. Grimacing as her body became coated in an ever accumulating layer of green sludge, pulling a wrapping of seaweed with her, Kali slid along the bridge until she came within yards of the Thunderflux.

And didn't stop.

Shit. *Shit, shit, shit.*

Kali felt the surface of the Thunderflux prickling her bare flesh, *warming* it, as she neared, and having no desire to enter it until she had a far better idea of what she was dealing with she fought madly to bring herself to a halt. Her desperate scrabbling and slapping at anything and everything that might halt her progress turned her in a slow circle as she slithered closer and closer, as if she were coming to the end of some carnival ride, but she came to a stop at last, mere inches away from the crackling column.

The waves were not striking this close to the Thunderflux, but Kali still rose hesitantly, unsure whether one of the whips of energy might catch her and fry her where she stood. Other than the prickling, warming effect of the column itself, however, they seemed harmless enough, one even passing directly through her, leaving her with little more than a slight sense of disorientation.

Slowly, Kali stretched out her arm, her palm touching the column's surface, and she felt a thrill she'd struggle to describe. The closest she came brought a smile, as she remembered a phrase from a year before, the speaker of which was no longer with us.

All tremblous in the underknicks.

The phrase – and the feeling – reassured her. There was nothing to be afraid of here, surely? After all, what would be the point of having her – of having any of the kattra – go through the Trial only to have them zapped into oblivion when they completed it?

This thing had waited a long, long, long, long time. It wasn't going to hurt her.

Kali took a breath and was about to step into the Thunderflux when she stopped dead. There was something she'd forgotten. The bridge on which she was standing was not her bridge. And if the truth was protected from those who were not meant to hear it by the Trials, who was to say she wouldn't be committing some grave error by entering the way Silus was meant to enter? Should she somehow try to make her way to her own bridge?

Kali didn't know whether her hesitation was valid or not, and as she weighed up its pros and cons – not least the seeming impossibility of reaching her own bridge from where she now stood – she failed to notice what was happening below the bridge, in the still tumultuous waters behind her.

Through one of the sea caves that fed the cavern, a slick of orange goo had mingled with the waters within, and as Kali continued to stare at the surface of the Thunderflux, the slick moved closer to her. Thicker and more soup-like than the liquid through which it flowed with a clear intent, the first thing that Kali knew of its presence was when it exploded from the waters to loom above her.

Kali span, but it was too late. In much the same way as it had earlier on Horizon Point, the Hel'ss Spawn darted at her and slapped her off her feet and the bridge. With a yelp, Kali found herself falling into the waters below, her heart almost seizing when the cold struck her. Momentarily numbed, she struggled to come to terms with what had just happened, and when she did, despite being underwater, roared in fury. Thanks to the Hel'ss Spawn she was going to have to do this whole damned thing again!

Fury, however, was not nearly a powerful enough word to describe the emotion that overtook her a few seconds later. For as Kali kicked her way to the surface the orange slick enveloped her like the caress of a rough lover, and as it did she felt a fundamental difference between what had attacked her earlier and what was attacking her now.

The Hel'ss Spawn had meant to do her harm, of course it had, but in a sense it had been impersonal, the attack of an entity which cared not at all for the individuality of its victim. This, though, was different, and she sensed something - a presence - almost immediately. There was, as far as she was aware, only one dirty old bastard who'd try to cop a feel in this way.

"Redigor," she growled. "You just don't know when to farking give up, do you?"

There was no answer, of course. How could there be? Redigor's body had gone and all that was left of him now was the same non-corporeal parasite that had been hitching a lift inside Jakub Freel. It seemed he'd gone up in the world - literally - having presumably infested the Hel'ss Spawn as it had plunged with his soul off Horizon Point, and she reflected that only the Pale Lord could be arrogant enough to try and possess a god. Or at least the agent of a god.

Kali had to admit, though, that he was making a pretty good job of it. The Hel'ss Spawn, under Redigor's control, seemed determined that she was not going to win, dragging her back under the water and flinging her about until her breath, hastily snatched as she went under, was forcefully expelled by the battering she was taking. Thankfully, Redigor provided her with an opportunity to replenish her lungs as she was hauled from beneath the waves and flung violently towards the distant walls of the cavern. Here Kali's lungs exploded again, this time as the impact winded and dazed her, and she tumbled from the wall onto a rock below, where she rolled weakly back into the raging sea. Undulating, constantly shifting shape, the Hel'ss Spawn came at her again, enveloping her and then plunging to the bottom of the submerged cavern, dragging her along the rough sand there until her flesh was rubbed raw and bleeding. Then, lifted through a cloud of her own diffusing blood, Redigor returned her to the surface and high up into the air.

Kali dangled in the entity's strange grip like a marionette whose strings had been severed, glowering, despite her pummelled state, at the viscous form before her. For one fleeting second she was transported back to the observatory at Scholten because the Hel'ss Spawn rearranged itself into a semblance of Redigor's features and returned her gaze, smiling coldly.

She knew then that she was only suffering the first act of Redigor's perverse game. The battering he was giving her was not meant to kill her, only soften her up. Redigor wanted her utterly helpless, broken not just physically but mentally, so that she could do nothing when he eventually rammed the Hel'ss Spawn's hungry tendrils inside her, ripping away her very soul.

Well, she'd felt Redigor's touch before, when he'd tried to drain her of her essence in the Chapel of Screams, and she'd be damned if she was going to let it happen again. If Redigor wanted to knock the fight out of her, she'd show him just how much fight she had left.

Kali began to kick and pummel in the Hel'ss Spawn's grip, only for it to fling her through the air towards the cavern's unforgiving rock walls again. The undulating form followed immediately, ready to snatch her up again, but this time she was ready.

As she flew through the air, Kali grabbed onto one of the lengthy strands of seaweed that dangled from each of the bridges, and swiftly swung herself around so that she smashed back into – and through – the viscous entity that Redigor controlled. As she'd guessed, the manoeuvre was so unexpected that even the Hel'ss Spawn had difficulty adjusting, and part of the shape-shifting entity collapsed, unable to reform itself in time to stop her. Redigor's avatar did so a second later, of course, but by then it was too late, Kali having used the seaweed in the manner of a vine and swung herself to a point where she let go, flailing through the air towards the hanging detritus of the cavern's adjacent bridge.

Swinging from marine vine to marine vine, Kali built up a momentum that enabled her to use them all as ropes to evade Redigor, and changing her course frequently and unexpectedly the entity found itself being stretched to the limits of its shape-shifting abilities, breaking apart, as it pursued her about the cavern. Exactly where this was leading, Kali wasn't sure, but she suspected that the orange taint from the amberglow that had caused so much disturbance to the Hel'ss on the surface – the same glow that infused it here – was damaging it somehow, and hopefully it was a chink in its armour that she could exploit.

All she had to do was keep moving. Survive long enough to find out.

What Kali hadn't taken into account was that in some way Redigor himself seemed aware that his alien host was damaged, and rather than be cowed by the fact that the Hel'ss Spawn was breaking apart in its crazed pursuit of her, he pushed the entity to double its efforts to succeed. Kali was guessing but it seemed to her that Redigor *didn't care* that the Hel'ss Spawn might be destroyed, that this was no longer about his survival, or his insane plan being resurrected, but just between he and her. It was revenge Redigor craved. Petty revenge.

This was personal.

There would be no stopping a madman, Kali realised. This coupled with the fact that even she couldn't keep this up for ever, that she was rapidly tiring from the exertion involved, led, inevitably to a moment where Redigor's avatar gained the upper hand.

It was an appropriate phrase, for as Kali made a minor error that caused her to miss a leap between seaweed strands, forcing her to swing for it a second time, what remained of the mass of the Hel'ss Spawn exploded from the water and clenched her in what resembled a giant fist. Kali struggled and slithered within it but the fist held her fast, and she roared in frustration as Redigor's features appeared fleetingly in the viscous matter once more.

The bastard was smiling. He had everything that he wanted.

All that remained was for him to deliver the finishing blow.

Kali swallowed repeatedly, tensed in anticipation, remembering how Redigor had invaded her in the Chapel of Screams, tried to strip away her soul, and would have succeeded had it not been for the intervention of Gabriella DeZantez. It had been the worst pain she had ever felt, agonising beyond words. But this, this was going to be different.

It was going to be one hells of a lot worse.

Kali flung back her head and roared in pain as the Hel'ss Spawn coated her body and began to insinuate itself into her flesh through every orifice, every pore. She watched horrified as it travelled beneath her skin, seeking out muscle, tendon, sinew and bone, every vital organ, and she began to buck and groan as each part of her began slowly to be reworked from the inside. It couldn't be happening but it was, it was, and as her vision pulsed with blood pumped wrongly through her body, in great, warm washes where it should not have been, she saw that her flesh had already begun to dissolve, her arms and legs shrinking, deforming into shapeless, liquid things, her stomach collapsing and her flesh running from her in streams, like candlewax.

She would be nothing soon, and her universe consisted of one endless, deafening scream.

Then, suddenly, as one small part of her recognised the Hel'ss Spawn had worked its way up, was spreading now over her thumping heart, ready to take that, too, she felt another kind of pain. No, not pain, but the kind of red-hot, nagging insistence in her chest she had felt when almost drowned. This feeling was different, though, not the result of a desperate need to draw air from without, but the need of something to be released from *within*.

Images flashed unbidden into her mind. The moment at the Crucible when Tharnak had told her she shared a legacy with him. Brundle, placing his hand on her in the tavern in Gransk, the gasp he had uttered thereon. Herself, standing in front of a mirror in the *Flagons* that one dark night she had told no one about.

The night that she had become aware of the thing she believed made her what she was.

The night that she had seen the thread within her *glow*.

Oh Gods, Kali thought, as it began to glow again, brighter than ever before. What was this? What the hells was this? And then the pain of what the Hel'ss Spawn was doing to her was forgotten as her spine arched so acutely it seemed to snap in two, and she screamed with an agony she thought could get no worse as something broke from within her and the cavern exploded with light.

Kali felt herself falling, released from the grip of the Hel'ss Spawn, remade miraculously whole. Instinctively, unthinking, she grabbed onto a strand of seaweed and swung there breathlessly as before her the Hel'ss Spawn roared. She had no idea what she had done but suddenly the entity – Redigor's screaming face within it – was retreating from her and flinging itself about the cavern as though infected with some deadly toxin. Against rock after rock and wall after wall it crashed, each time breaking itself apart into smaller and smaller segments, and then, when there was little of it left, what remained of it collapsed into the waters and, bobbing on the waves, began to drift lifelessly away.

Kali hung where she was, gasping, unable to believe what had happened, waiting for the Hel'ss Spawn, for Redigor, to rear up once more. But after five full minutes had passed, it, and he, did not.

The Hel'ss Spawn was gone.

Bastian Redigor was gone.

Slowly, Kali lifted herself hand over hand up the seaweed strand and then collapsed onto the bridge above. She lay there on her back for a few seconds, her palm caressing her chest, feeling the place the light had come from. It was back within her now, that she could feel, but, despite what it appeared to have done, it was of no comfort.

Gods, what was it? What was *she*?

Was this a part of the Truth?

Kali stood and stared ahead of her. The lightning column that was the Thunderflux waited no more than ten yards along the bridge on which she stood, and somehow she knew that this was the right bridge, *her* bridge, and that whether by accident or design of fate she'd been delivered to the right place. Whatever lay within was the end of the Path of Endurance, the end of the path of Kali Hooper.

Her destiny.

Kali took a breath and strode inside the Thunderflux. She found herself rising and then stopping inside a domed chamber, and she guessed she was inside the Thunderflux cap. The same energies that had danced in the column danced here, too, all around her, beating at the walls, but they did her no harm.

The only shock she felt was when a face appeared before her.

A woman.

An elf.

CHAPTER SIXTEEN

"HELLO, KALI," THE elf said. She spoke slowly and her words trembled in the air, as if they were the most delicate things in the world. "As I speak, I am separated from you by many thousands of years, and the civilisations I represent are about to end. They shall be gone from this world soon – taken by the entity you will already have encountered. The elves and the dwarfs and all of their grand achievements will be no more. But we leave behind us the seeds of a new race – the human race – whose origins lie in the depths of the oceans of this world, and not, like us, in the skies above... or on other worlds, far beyond your skies." The elf paused. "I expect you have many questions. Please feel free to ask anything you wish."

"I, er, don't suppose you have a towel?"

The elf smiled. "No, I don't have a towel."

"Right. Sorry about that. I guess I'm a little nervous. How about who are you? And how can we be speaking like this?"

"My name is Zharn. And I am able to speak to you because I

am trapped in a moment of time. A moment created when the Thunderflux was capped, that links the Trass Kattra that is now with the Trass Kattra that was then."

"You're here on Trass Kattra. In the past?"

"Not just the past, Kali. The End Time. Even as I speak, the darkness is upon us, and were it not for this moment, I would already be dead."

Kali swallowed. "Who are you, Zharn?"

"One who tried to help save our world. One of four."

"Four?" Kali repeated. "You mean like the *Four* four?"

"Yes, that is what I mean. I was of the kattra of this time. And it was I who was chosen to come to the Thunderflux to relate the tale you need to hear."

"Okay," Kali said cautiously. "I don't seem to have anything else on at the moment."

"We share a singular heritage, Kali – and a singular foe. One that will be difficult to explain because its history is ages in the making. But it must be explained if you are to succeed in what you must do. It is a tale of growing knowledge, of constant adversity, and, until now, of failure. Steady yourself, for we are about to begin."

What? Kali thought. But then the dome in which she stood was suddenly a dome no more. Its walls vanished and she found herself adrift in a void, floating, and somehow knew she was in the centre of the strange expanse she had seen when she had risen above Twilight in the *Tharnak*. This 'space' was as immense as it had been then, her confines utterly gone, and she felt that if she began to travel in any direction, she might never reach its limits.

There was only one difference: where within this void she had then been able to see Kerberos and Twilight's distant sun, marred slightly by the body she now knew to be the Hel'ss, here there was nothing. Nothing in the void. Nothing at all.

"My gods," Kali breathed.

"In the beginning," said Zharn, "there was night. Worlds without light. Rocks without life."

Kali found herself stunned, backpaddling as she might in water to keep afloat, as a number of blindingly bright spheres appeared out of nowhere in the space all around her.

"And then, the gods came."

The spheres hung about Kali at various distances – unimaginable distances – illuminating the void and the lifeless worlds she could now see scattered throughout it. Each was also far more than a sphere, Kali sensed, because from them all she could feel the same strange and powerful sentience emanating.

"They came to this desolate corner of the universe," Zharn continued. "To this dead space. They were the Pantheon."

Kali swallowed. "The Pantheon?"

"Twelve entities – creatures, powers, gods – call them what you will. Kerberos, the Hel'ss, Faranoon, Chazra-Nay, Rehastt, along with eight others whose names we might never know, for they are long gone."

"Wait. Are you telling me one of these spheres is Kerberos?"

"As Kerberos was, when it was young. Like the Hel'ss, it shone brightly, then. It had feasted well before it came – as had the Hel'ss, as had the others."

"Feasted?"

She gasped and began to drift through the expanse before her – or was it that the expanse drifted about her? – she wasn't sure. She found herself directly above the surface of one of the spheres as it rotated beneath her, massive and filling her vision completely. But it was what filled the sphere that drew Kali's attention – a swirling sea – no, ocean, entire *world* – of writhing forms that resembled Bastian Redigor's Pillar of Souls. But there was a difference – where then she had seen only human forms, the dead of Twilight, here she was looking at what could only be the dead of other worlds, a multitude of strange forms that both awed and disturbed her at the same time. Octopoid things and serpents that were leagues long, pyramidal creatures and creatures of jagged contours, gaseous entities, distinct from that in which they were trapped, and dark, flowing shapes, like liquid shadow. There was nothing familiar about them, and Kali realised she was looking at the souls of another universe.

"Gorged is perhaps a better word," Zharn said. "Gorged until there was nothing left in their old domain. And so they came, came in search of new life, so that they might feast again."

Kali looked at the planets around her. "But these are dead worlds."

"All worlds are dead," Zharn said. "Until their gods come."

Kali watched as each of the spheres – each of the Pantheon – began to move to one of the worlds and take up position above it, hanging there as Kerberos hung above Twilight. Though she could somehow see them all, she knew that billions upon billions of miles must separate them.

For as she continued to watch, the spheres that were the Pantheon infused their individual dead worlds with life, life that from her heavenly vantage point she could see begin to spread across the worlds as their respective civilisations grew. What kind of lifeforms thrived beneath her she didn't know, but thousands upon thousands of years of their history must have passed before her eyes, and when it had, the process that each of the Pantheon had begun was, it seemed, done.

Each sphere had lost its brilliance now, each of the Pantheon became a different hue, and as Kali observed a barely distinguishable thread connecting each sphere to its planet below, a thread which pulsed upwards constantly, she knew from what that hue had grown.

The fact that she was witnessing each member of the Pantheon feeding on its planet's souls was somehow forgotten as her eyes were drawn to the sphere with a familiar azure hue.

To the planet from which it fed.

"Oh gods. Is that Twilight?"

"No, Kali. It is not. For there begins the next part of this tale.

"I don't understand."

Zharn paused. "This is what the Pantheon were, and had they remained so, these worlds, these civilisations, would have enjoyed millennia of existence before their gods moved on. With this there was nothing wrong, for that was the nature of things."

"Something changed?"

"The Pantheon changed. They were ancient beings when they came here, and now they were more ancient still, and some of them chose their worlds unwisely and fed less well than others. Across the vastness of space some began to sense their more successful brethren, became jealous of their conquests, and instead of moving onto neutral worlds the weaker among them began to follow in the wake of the stronger. For a while they were allowed to bask in the essence of those they followed but the worlds available to the Pantheon were becoming fewer, too, their resources scarcer, so that, gradually, the Pantheon were drawn into conflict with each other. They began to draw souls not only from the planets they had created but from each other. They began to consume themselves..."

Kali watched as one of the Pantheon – she didn't know which – hung above a world whose surface glittered with the light of campfires, signifying life, if a primitive form. Then she became aware of another of its kind encroaching on its space from afar. The second of the Pantheon gradually began to move towards the first.

"What am I seeing?" Kali said. "Is this the Hel'ss and Kerberos?"

"No, Kali. You are seeing the merging of Faranoon and Chazra-Nay. Witness, Kali. Witness the end."

It might not have been the Hel'ss and Kerberos that Kali was observing, but the similarity to what was happening above Twilight right at that moment was clear. As the Hel'ss was nearing Kerberos, so too was Faranoon nearing Chazra-Nay. But in this case drawing close enough to touch. As Kali watched wide eyed, the edges of the massive, gaseous spheres came into contact and then, slowly, Faranoon began to eclipse Chazra-Nay. Chazra-Nay did not disappear, however, remaining visible inside the other, like a nucleus within a cell. At least for a while. Then, at first in pockets and then in great spreading clouds, the atmospheres of both bodies became increasingly disturbed, as if each raged with unimaginably large storms – but if they were storms, they were storms of souls, the meeting and conflict of the life force of each of the so-called deities. Seething and roiling ever more tumultuously, the surfaces of the spheres changed hue and composition again and again, sometimes so rapidly that they appeared to pulsate in anger, and it was apparent that a great battle was being raged. Kali had no idea of the length of time that passed during this struggle but in the end Faranoon emerged the victor.

The way that victory came would have made Kali stagger, had she something solid on which to do so. Because though Chazra-Nay vanished inside Faranoon, the size of Faranoon suddenly doubled, and as it did its hue changed and it enveloped the atmosphere of the world below.

"This," Kali gasped, "I've seen this. With Pim in Domdruggle's Expanse. Kerberos was bigger, darker, more threatening. This is the End Time, isn't it! This is the darkness!"

"Wait, Kali," Zharn countered.

Faranoon was now enveloping the alien world like some giant membrane. Hanging there in space for what seemed an eternity, it seemed to be passing on a message to the cosmos. This world is mine. And then, from the surface of the alien world to the surface of Faranoon, countless strands of light began flow. Kali knew instantly what they were – souls – the souls of every living creature on the world being consumed all at once by the deity. She knew now why the elves and the dwarves had vanished so quickly from Twilight, seemingly unable to prevent their fate, because it took only a matter of minutes before the strands of light were fully absorbed into its biosphere and the world below was emptied of life. All across the surface of the world, the campfires went out.

"That is the darkness," Zharn said.

Kali was momentarily speechless.

"How many worlds have the Pantheon destroyed like this?"

"Those it took to reduce their ranks. Faranoon was consumed by another as little as five thousand years later. Rehastt took two worlds before it was itself consumed by the Hel'ss. Ten worlds in all lost to their conflict until only two of the Pantheon – Kerberos and the Hel'ss – remained."

Kali hated to sound flippant about what she'd witnessed but it seemed relevant.

"Kerberos didn't seem to get the munchies."

Once more she was on the move, zooming through space

towards the azure sphere and the world she had mistaken for Twilight. It was her longest journey yet.

"No. Kerberos was the most distant of the Pantheon, here, on the very edge of this space. It had found a world whose own god it had subsumed and which satisfied its needs. Because of this and of the great distance between itself and its brethren, it took no further part in the affairs of the Pantheon."

"But Kerberos is above Twilight now, right? So something must have happened."

"The third part of our tale. Of the many races the Pantheon created, this was one of the few that developed the capacity for travel in space, and with it the means to escape Kerberos' domination of their world. A band of refugees managed to leave the planet in search of a new home. What they did not know was that Kerberos, angered by their audacity, would decide to follow them. But what Kerberos, in turn, did not know, was that its passage across the vast void would bring it close to the realm of the Hel'ss."

Kali watched as the great azure orb that was Kerberos moved across space. There, perhaps billions of miles distant but close enough, it briefly eclipsed another orb, purple in colour, which also began to move. Very, very slowly, it began to close the gap between them.

"The hunter," said Zharn, "became the hunted."

The distance between the spheres was so great, Kali realised, that thousands of years could conceivably pass before the Hel'ss caught up with its prey, but this was nothing to the two deities, and she knew from experience that the end of the pursuit was inevitable.

She found herself following Kerberos through space, then floating around its axis, where she gasped. Below her hung Twilight. At least she thought it was Twilight. Because there was something about it that was *wrong.*

"The refugees from the dead world eventually led Kerberos to this world, your world," Zharn explained, "where they mysteriously vanished. Despite this, Kerberos had no choice but to remain, for the journey here had left it weak."

"Twilight looks different," Kali said. "But I can't work out why."

"Yes, Twilight is different. Because there was a fundamental difference between this world and any other that Kerberos had seeded."

Kali began to swoop down into Twilight's atmosphere, at first soaring high above the clouds and then punching through them. She flew above an unfamiliar landscape, across which figures raced. No, not raced – pursued each other. She stared as the predatory creatures – strange, green-skinned hulks and short, vicious, rat-like things – then engaged in battle.

"Oh gods," she said. "Twilight was already populated."

"Indeed it was. But Kerberos was angry that the fugitives he had pursued across space had once more escaped him, and he was also desperate. For the first time since arriving in this universe, Kerberos chose to transform an inhabited world."

"Transform?"

"First it sent its dragons, creatures who appeared to magically create life but who, in fact, were assessing the make-up of the world, ready for disassembly. And when they had done their job, it sent the Great Flood to cleanse the world. The creatures who called it home – those your myths call orcs and goblins – were swept from their lands in the flood and became assimilated in the endless waters. A few survived – somehow – but they no longer belonged on this world."

"This 'assimilation' – it was what was happening in the swirlies? I mean the swirlpools off the island?"

"Yes. The creation – or uncreation – of life."

Kali cringed. "I never thought I'd feel sorry for an orc or goblin."

"Their fate was perhaps merciful considering what happened next. Others eventually would come to live in the great ocean – the Chadassa, the Calma – but the landmasses which the orcs and goblins called home were about to be changed for ever."

"By what?"

"By the more powerful form of the dragons. By the dra'gohn."

Kali sailed back into the skies until she was facing Kerberos. Shadows seemed to be building within its gaseous mass and, then, after a second, burst from the entity's depths. Kali recoiled as these cloud-like things resolved themselves into creatures that were all too familiar. Somehow translucent and more ghostly here, perhaps, but the last time she had seen one of the same it had carried her to the edge of a space before disintegrating before her eyes.

One single dra'gohn that was no more.

But this time, there were hundreds of them.

"The dra'gohn were sent to your world, as they are to every one of the Pantheon's worlds, when the time is right. Spawned in the core of Kerberos, these creatures would make the land on which its people would grow, and on which they would live. The dra'gohn were beings that channelled the very stuff of the universe, of creation, and they were magnificent."

Kali swallowed as her perspective changed once more and she found herself back on the flooded world, standing on the summit of a mountain that appeared to be the only piece of land anywhere. Except it wasn't land, because the mountain was made of glass. Then one of the dra'gohn flew directly at her. The massive creature filled her vision, its wings blotting out the sky, and then she was somehow scooped up and found herself riding on its back. The glass mountain was left far behind her and they flew above an endless expanse of water that spread from horizon to horizon. The sky darkened about her as other dra'gohn joined the one on which she rode, until they were once more present about her in their hundreds, and as one they began to angle down towards the sea.

And then, they made the land.

Kali found herself gasping for breath, so overwhelmed was she by what she saw. The mouth of each dra'gohn opened wide and each *breathed*, massive jets of red and yellow that intertwined and together looked like roaring fire. But this was not fire – this, as Zharn had said, was the stuff of creation itself. The dra'gohn were breathing threads.

Below her, where the ocean had been, a strip of land began to form, the water evaporating, transforming, solidifying gradually into a desert landscape, as the dra'gohn flew above. Kali twisted on her mount's back and gasped again, for behind her a great ridge of rock rolled in the dra'gohn's wake, a crease in that which was being made, nothing less than a mountain range separating the land that was fully formed from that still being breathed.

The dra'gohn ceased breathing and turned, swooping back over the mountain range. Here, they peeled away from each other, some heading to the east, others to the west, and began to breathe again. The somewhat featureless land that they had created on their first pass began to be shaped more now, the weaving patterns of the dra'gohn in the sky creating the shape of a coastline, of river inlets, lakes and valleys and gorges and hills, and when at last they stopped breathing once more, Kali found herself looking not at a strip of land anymore but a landmass that was whole and complete.

A landmass that was as familiar to her as the back of her hand.

The peninsula.

The location of all her adventures.

Home.

"My gods," Kali said. "It's all there. The World's Ridge Mountains, the Sardenne, Vos, Pontaine. All there."

"Except of course," Zharn pointed out, "they were not yet known by these names. For as yet there was no one to name them."

"The Old Races," Kali said. "But that means that Kerberos *was* their god, because it created them!"

"In a way, I suppose. But Kerberos's motives were not those of a god, they were those of survival. Knowing how little time it had – relatively speaking, of course – before the Hel'ss reached Twilight, it made the decision that the battle for survival between itself and the Hel'ss could no longer continue as it had. They were the last of their kind and one of them needed to gain the advantage. To this end, it determined to create not one but two races to inhabit its new domain, gifting each with the potential to be more than just mere fodder but to actively assist it in the fight against its old enemy."

"The elves and the dwarves," Kali said.

"The elves and the dwarves."

"But that doesn't make sense. If Kerberos wanted their help, why create two races that were at each other's throats for millennia? It was only in their third age that they found any kind of peace at all."

"You are wrong," Zharn went on. "Of course the two races fought, but that was exactly why they had been created so. To be diametrically opposed. The el'v, meaning, in the ancient language of the Pantheon 'of the mind', and the dwarves, a corruption of dou'arv, hammer and anvil, 'of the body'. It was only by throwing mind and body into conflict that Kerberos believed they would, eventually, reach their full potential. I suspect it is the same story on a thousand worlds, far beyond the Pantheon. That many of the indigenous races' greatest achievements come about – can *only* come about – as a result of war."

Kali stared at a peninsula overrun with soaring towers and factories, fortifications and battlefields.

"The whole of the peninsula was a forge," she realised.

"A forge for the dwarves, perhaps, a laboratory for the elves. The distinction is immaterial. Each managed, in their own way, to create horrifying weapons of destruction. And the souls of the hundreds of thousands of each race who fell before them across the long years served only to strengthen Kerberos."

"So wouldn't it have served Kerberos better if it had created lifeforms with potential for nothing other than destruction? Some kind of a... warworld to supply it with victims for evermore?"

"Even millions of souls would have been insufficient for Kerberos' needs, so weakened was it. What it needed to recover was the constant ebb and flow of *billions* of souls. The population, in other words, of a full and thriving planet."

"But," Kali said, "all there is is the peninsula. It would never support that many people. Are you telling me that there are lands beyond the World's Ridge Mountains – beyond the Stormwall – beyond the seas?"

"On the contrary. I am telling you there are not."

"I'm sorry. I don't understand."

"Each time one of the Pantheon grants life to a world, it begins, as you have seen, with the creation of a small section of land – in your case, what you call the peninsula, what is to you, in effect, Twilight. This land serves its purpose until the demands upon it begin to exceed its capability, at which time it must expand."

"The deity having drawn strength from what it's already created," Kali gathered.

"You are perceptive."

"So," Kali asked, "the dra'gohn return?"

"Yes, the dra'gohn return," Zharn said. As she spoke Kali's viewpoint changed yet again, and she found herself so far above her world that she looked down on the peninsula as she might a representation of it on a map. Its coastline was fully visible from end to end, all but featureless at this height, looking almost unreal. Then she became aware of massive shapes that momentarily blocked her vision – the dra'gohn swooping once more from the heart of Kerberos – and when she looked again, these shapes were clearly delineated above the peninsula, heading as one to where a small ripple in the map indicated the presence of the World's Ridge Mountains. Kali gasped as the heavenly forms flew majestically above the towering range and once more began to breathe their red and yellow threads, and, as they did, land began to form *beyond* that which she knew to be the edge of the world.

And as it formed, as she'd seen in her earlier flight, the World's Ridge moved with it.

"Wait," Kali said. "There's something wron –"

For the first time since their conversation had begun, however, Zharn did not pause in what she was showing to her, as it if were something she *had* to witness. It didn't matter because, anyway, Kali's question trailed off into silence. How could it not? She was, after all, seeing something she would likely never see again.

Far below her, as the land grew, the flights of the dra'gohn diverged once more, banking gracefully out to all points of the compass, and where they went, they continued to breathe. Kali's heart thumped until it felt fit to burst as she watched a vast continent begin to take shape, spreading for thousands and thousands of leagues in every direction, rich with forest and lakes, prairie and desert, rolling hills and mountain ranges that, this time, remained where they were created. A coastline that would take her lifetimes to explore weaved, darted and thrust itself out into the surrounding sea, but even as a multitude of small and large islands began to dot its waters offshore, the growth of the land did not stop, continuing on out of view, far, far beyond the curve of the world.

It *was* a world. A whole, new world.

Kali could hardly breathe. Her eyes ran with tears.

And then the world was gone.

"You had a question," Zharn prompted gently.

Kali swallowed, gathering her wits before she spoke.

"It's what I meant when I said something's wrong. I understand now what the World's Ridge Mountains are. They're a *barrier*, aren't they? A barrier meant to prevent exploration. To prevent people leaving their world before they – before the rest of the world – was ready. Before Kerberos *wanted* them to leave."

"As, along the coast, was the great elemental barrier – the phenomenon that you call the Stormwall – designed to prevent exploration of the seas. Such exploration would have been, after all, a voyage that would never end..."

Kali suddenly felt very heavy, the weight of 'the truth' beginning to hit her.

"But something happened to the Stormwall, didn't it?" she said. "Just like something happened to the World's Ridge Mountains."

Zharn smiled. It was the smile of someone who knew she had chosen her audience well.

"Why do you say that, Kali?"

"Because the World's Ridge Mountains never *moved*."

Zharn drew in a trembling breath, and the void in which Kali hung seemed to tremble too.

"It is true," the elf said, after a second. "What you have just seen was what *would* have been, were it not for the unimaginable tragedy that occurred. Something that broke the cycle of Kerberos, damaging the deity so badly that it might never be restored."

"What?" Kali said.

"The death of the dra'gohn."

CHAPTER SEVENTEEN

"Oh gods," Kali said. She did, of course, know that the dra'gohn were gone, but she had never learned the circumstances of their demise – or realised they had such an important link to Kerberos or Twilight itself. "How did it happen?"

"The time came when the civilisations of the elves and the dwarves were at their peak, thriving in every sense," Zharn said. As she spoke, the chamber flared to life again and this time Kali found herself with a far more intimate perspective of the peninsula, swooping down across the land, passing over – and sometimes between – the buildings of towering cities of both elven and dwarven origin, witnessing the wonders that filled them. From the technology on view – steam-powered but nonetheless impressive dwarven engineering; the more organic path that the elves favoured – she guessed that in time she was somewhere very near the end of the second or at the start of the third age of the Old Races, the time where, at last, the two had begun to work together. But it seemed Zharn had been almost understating the facts when she'd said they'd thrived in every sense of the word. Their populations growing with the prosperity that peace between them had brought, both races had spread across the peninsula until there was little of it left, taking with them their phantasmagorical devices, their clockwork chariots and their flying machines, the remains of many of which she had come across in her travels. Kali even recognised the genesis of many of the sites she had explored as ancient ruins: Robor's Skyway, the Avenue of the Fallen, and on the coast the bay-encompassing Amphibitheatre of Rossox, where now lay Vosburg but where once the Calmamandra had come to play.

It was clearly time for the Old Races to expand, for the land to grow. But as Zharn had already intimated, there was nowhere for them to go.

"Tell me," Kali said.

Zharn nodded. "Whether it was by accident or design there was an... encounter between the Old Races and one of the dra'gohn," she said. "The encounter ended with the death of the dra'gohn, its form torn asunder by the weapons and powers that its opponents wielded."

"The death of one dra'gohn caused the collapse of Kerberos's plan?"

"Not one, no. It is what happened *after* its death that was to lead to the collapse. Many flocked to the site of the encounter, wishing for whatever reason to observe the remains of the heavenly form, and it was one of these visitors who eventually noticed something very strange. Where the essence – blood or threads, think of it as you will – of the dra'gohn had seeped into the ground, the rock below changed, infused with some kind of energy that made it pulse as if alive."

"This rock," Kali asked hesitantly. "It wouldn't by any chance have been orange?"

"I see you are once more ahead of me, Kali."

"Amberglow," Kali said, swallowing.

"Amberglow. What was to become the power source for most of the elven and dwarven machines that followed. The element that sparked the Old Races final era of magical technology."

"Are you trying to tell me –"

"Its discovery," Zharn spoke over her, "led to the wholesale slaughter of the dra'gohn. The extinction of the very creatures that were needed to save them. Even as the dra'gohn returned to breathe the land, the elves and the dwarves were waiting for them with their airships, with their mages, their ballistas and their cannon emplacements atop the highest peaks."

"I can't believe it. How could they be capable of such greatness and yet so stupid?"

"They were not to know how integral to their future the dra'gohn were. How could they? Besides, if you were handed the power of the Pantheon – the threads, the power of the gods – are you sure you would be able to resist?"

"Of course I –"

Kali stopped. Would she? Would she really? How much had she enjoyed being at the controls of the scuttlebarge? The dwarven mole? Carried into the skies and beyond by the *Tharnak*? Even wielding something as simple as a crackstaff? None of these things would have been possible without amberglow.

It was a question she might never answer, and certainly not now, for the images resumed. This time she witnessed the effects on the land the end of the dra'gohn had wrought. Their slaughter, Zharn explained, sent ripples through the threads that became tsunamis of change, and Kali saw the peninsula they had created reforming once again, this time in turmoil. Great cracks appeared in the land, into which many of the Old Races' achievements tumbled, to be lost forever. Earthquakes felled building after building and shattered roads and trade routes. A huge rolling ridge of land – similar to the World's Ridge but here rolling free and uncontrolled – came to rest in the heart of what would become Vos, the upheaval leaving behind it what were now the Drakengrat Mountains. Most dramatically of all, the coast of the peninsula to the west and to the north began to break apart as a result of the stresses elsewhere, and Kali gasped as she witnessed huge chunks of land shearing away into the sea. She was awed by the sight for what she was watching was the formation of the Sarcre Islands and of the home of Jakub Freel, Allantia itself.

"The Stormwall," she said. "This is what destroyed the Stormwall."

"Yes," Zharn confirmed. "Following the Great Upheaval all that remained of the barrier was that which now separates the Sarcre Islands from the mainland, and a much weakened zone of meteorological disturbance along other parts of the coast."

"Much weakened?" Kali reflected. "Pits of Kerberos."

"This, then, was the last time the dra'gohn had any influence on the future of our lands. What remained was to become the stage on which would be played out the final act of the Old Races."

"The darkness," Kali said.

Zharn nodded. "It was three thousand years, measured in the Old Race's calendar, before the Hel'ss reached this world, and in that time the elves and the dwarves became masters of the magical technology their wholesale slaughter had brought them. But in mastering it, they forgot the roots from which the amberglow had come. The threads that the dra'gohn had breathed were but one segment of the Circle of Magic – sometimes called the Circle of Power – with which Kerberos had imbued this world and on which its survival depended. Had the dra'gohn threads – the dragon magic – remained in the Circle, Kerberos might just have had the strength to fight the Hel'ss, but without them the entity was the weakest it had ever been."

"Kerberos's experiment to defend itself against the Hel'ss had succeeded," Kali said. "But because of the folly of its creations, one vital component was missing."

"Yes. The ship and its k'nid were ready to be launched at the Hel'ss, while here, on Twilight, Domdruggle's Expanse was ready to be used as a sanctuary by our people during the chaos that might ensue. But the ship was found lacking. Without the armour of the Circle of Power it would have carried with it, it could not penetrate the Hel'ss defences, and was never launched. And without the Circle of Power defending Twilight, the Hel'ss was able to launch its attack on Trass Kattra."

"By the ship, I take it you mean the *Tharnak*," Kali queried. "Strange, flying thing?"

"The guardian's name," Zharn said, and smiled.

"If only they'd waited. They'd have developed another means of power."

"That is the tragedy of it. Soon afterwards, the darkness came."

"Now, that's what I don't understand," Kali queried. "If the darkness *did* come, if the Hel'ss merged with Kerberos and fought that battle you showed me, why didn't Kerberos die like Chazra-Nay, Faranoon or the others? Why wasn't it consumed?"

"You might equally ask why Kerberos did not consume the Hel'ss. Both entities had travelled so far that they were equally weakened – starved of souls – and what should have been the final, decisive confrontation between them ended in stalemate. The struggle for supremacy lasted a thousand years and more but neither the Hel'ss nor Kerberos emerged victorious, in fact they emerged as far from victorious as they could possibly be, wounded, scarred and almost dead. Kerberos became the shadow of itself that looms above your world to this day while the Hel'ss retreated to deep space, regaining, through the long ages, what strength it could. The strength it knew it would need to one day return."

"And now, here it is," Kali said ominously.

"Yes. Returned for an unprecedented second confrontation – the first time in the history of the Pantheon that this has occurred. And because of it, the Four have the best chance to end their war that we have ever had."

"Okay, here's the other thing. Who the hells are 'the Four'?"

"The last survivors of a world Kerberos drained long ago. A world before this universe but with a race not dissimilar to your own. Four individuals who came to perceive the true nature of their god and who voluntarily surrendered their souls to it. Souls which, through their mental discipline, were able to insinuate themselves into Kerberos's Cycle, to be reincarnated once on each planet it seeded. Souls that might eventually find a means to rebel against the Pantheon and end their devouring of worlds."

"Which is why you're where you are now? Or why you involved yourself in what was going on? To help the Old Races destroy the Hel'ss."

"The Hel'ss, and then Kerberos."

"Hold it right there," Kali said. "You said the Four were reincarnated *once* on each planet Kerberos seeded. And you also said you were one of *your* Four. But this is the same planet, so where did we – Morlader, Kane, DeZantez and me – come from?"

"The past. Now. My now, that is."

"Whoa, whoa, whoa. Are you saying that your souls are *our* souls?"

"I am."

"How is that possible? I mean, how is... oh, fark."

"It must be difficult for you to understand, but I will try to explain. When the End Time came, or at least when it was near, the four of us knew that it would be our end time, too. If we were returned to Kerberos, or taken by the Hel'ss, then we would either be trapped within a dying entity above a dying world or within an entity adrift in the cosmos, possibly for the remainder of time. We were faced with a situation where the kattra might never return. Before either could take us, therefore, we assigned our souls to a different place..."

Kali let out an involuntary laugh of disbelief. "You said 'no' to the gods?"

"In essence. In practice, we found a way to bind part of our souls to the threads – to *particular* threads – that would one day release them where and when we wished. For thousands upon thousands of years they remained hidden and dormant, drifting within the weave, waiting for the faint tremors in the Circle of Power that would signal the return of the Hel'ss. And then, they would be born again. The souls themselves were not enough, however, for being part souls, they carried with them no memory of what they were or the threat they faced, which is why this message awaited you today. We had, of course to ensure that you all survived long enough for one of you to receive the message, and to that end we granted the abilities which each of you possess."

"My – our – powers came through the threads?"

"No. With the exception of Silus Morlader – whose apparent abilities are the result of a tragic encounter and whose true legacy is not what you think – that was not possible. Physical abilities needed to be transferred physically, and so we instilled them – dormant once more – into bloodlines that paralleled the threads."

"Pits of Kerberos," Kali said. "Those bloodlines began with the humans you experimented on at the Crucible, didn't they? The yassan, the others. The ones – the *other* four – who were being prepared for the ship?"

"Themselves the children of the Chadassa and the Calma, some of whose dying kin, following a great disaster that struck them, crawled onto the land where they were adopted – *adapted* – by the Old Races, who pitied them. This magnanimous act was the best thing they could have done, for in creating the humans, they gave Twilight a second chance."

"But is it a second chance? I mean the very fact we're having this chat only confirms what you've already said. That every attempt by the kattra to stop the Pantheon has ended in failure. Why should this time be any different?"

"Because of what is happening. For the first time in our endless struggle the Four that were and the Four that are can work together. With the knowledge I have given you – with what you have already discovered and found – the Four can become *eight*. With that, we have a fighting chance."

Kali frowned. Despite everything Zharn had said, she'd gone through too much and been surprised so many times to accept her words hands down. She needed more.

"Who were you?" she asked. "You and your Four?"

Zharn paused, but when she answered her response was accompanied by a faint smile. "I was no one of consequence, like the others. And yet bound by my legacy, as you are by yours. As for the other three, Rollin Dumarest was a dwarf, but unlike so many of his race a gentle, kind and loving man. Tremayin Fireflak, an elf like myself, prone, as befitted her name, to combustible temperament and absolute disregard for authority of any kind. And last, but far from least, Traynor Boom, a dwarf again, whose contribution to our cause were the blades of his two-handed battleaxe, Bloody Banshee. Its eloquent use bought the Drakengrat facility additional time, though regrettably not enough to save it."

"He died there?"

"Alongside Tremayin, fighting to protect the ship even as the darkness enveloped them."

Kali warmed to Zharn, despite the sadness she related. The fact that they were both talking of similar experiences made her feel a kinship with the elf, even though she and Zharn had never met. A kinship with her and the other three that was beginning to make her believe everything she'd been told.

"And Rollin Dumarest? What happened to him?"

"Rollin? Lost with Rodolfo Domdruggle, somewhere in the Expanse."

There it was again – that common experience – and Kali's mind whirled. Were it not for the fact that she, Lucius Kane and Silus Morlader were still alive, Zharn could have been speaking of them. And of Gabriella before she'd sacrificed herself. The similarities between the present and the past continued to be staggering.

"I'm sorry," Kali said.

"Don't be. Though their sacrifices are fresh in my mind, in a sense it all happened a long time ago," Zharn responded. "As I imagine is the case with yourself, I did not know my companions well, for that is the nature of our legacy. But they are sadly missed."

What did it for Kali was the question she asked next.

"If we each have one of your souls, which of you am I?"

"Can't you guess?"

"Combustible temperament?" Kali said. "Absolute disregard for authority of any kind?"

"Hello, Tremayin."

Kali put a hand to her mouth, holding back a sob. It took a moment for her to recover, and when she did she *believed* Zharn. But a couple of problems remained.

"When I came here you called me Kali," she said. "How did you know my name?"

"Because you told me."

"No, I didn't."

"If you say so," Zharn said slowly. "There are some questions that I can't answer."

"Okay, then, here's another one. You said that our abilities were sent by a bloodline, but as far as I know I don't have one. I wasn't born to any family. I was found, as a baby, in a dome."

"And," Zharn sighed, "there are some things that you can't yet know."

"*Why?*"

"Because they haven't yet happened."

"I haven't come this far to hear more riddles! Tell me, dammit!"

Zharn considered for a moment.

"Then first tell me – would it benefit you to know that you are dead?"

For the first time since her ordeal had began, Kali felt freezing cold. "What?"

The way Zharn couched her response could have sounded threatening, pitying, even sad. But it didn't. It actually sounded rather amused.

"Poor Kali Hooper. The girl who never was."

Kali's anger was diffused in a swirl of confusion. "Zharn, I don't understand."

"I know. But you have to trust me. Trust yourself. Now is not the time to speak of this."

Kali remained silent for more than a minute, torn by what she'd heard. She couldn't deny that in coming this far to learn about the Old Races, she'd wanted to learn about herself also – *expected* to – and Zharn's words hadn't just sent her back to square one, they'd knocked her completely off the game board. The fact was, though, she now accepted what she'd been told, and as a result felt the time would come when she *would* discover her origin. With whomever it was that would finally give her the answer.

In the meantime there was the small matter of saving the world. Again. She might as well get on with it.

"What," Kali said at last, "do I need to do?"

"Many things, and none will be easy. Your first task will be to unite the Four, and when you are together, unite what lies within you all."

"What lies within us –?" Kali began, and then suddenly her mind flashed back to the final encounter with Redigor in the cavern below. What had exploded from within. Somehow now she knew why it had had such an effect on Redigor and on what had remained of the Hel'ss Spawn.

"That was dra'gohn magic? What's missing from the Circle?"

"Yes. A sliver of it was implanted within each of your bloodlines."

"But how? I thought it was all gone?"

"There are some things –"

"That I can't yet know?"

"I'm sorry. But you will come to understand."

"Yeah, right. So, okay, unite what lies within us all. How do we do that?"

"There is an artefact – an enchanted rod of my own manufacture known as the Guardian Starlight – that was hidden in the Anclas Territories and is currently sought by Lucius Kane. Find this rod and it will provide you with the means."

"Me? All this magical gubbins sounds more like a job for Lucius himself."

Zharn smiled. "It will not be necessary for you to use 'magical gubbins'. The Guardian Starlight itself knows what it must do. But it is Lucius Kane who will wield the rod when the Guardian Starlight is complete, for only he has that power."

"Fair enough. Unite Lucius, Silus and Gabriella. But isn't there one small flaw in your plan?"

"There is?"

"Gabriella DeZantez is dead."

"Need I repeat that so, child, are you."

"*Riiigghhtt*," Kali said hesitantly. "So we've united and powered up this rod – what next?"

"You must travel beyond the World's Ridge Mountains and there use the rod to restore the Circle of Power."

"Whoa, stop. *Beyond* the World's Ridge Mountains? But I thought there was nothing there?"

"It is true that your journey will end beyond the mountains. But also begin. Be patient, Kali, and you will see."

Kali's mind flashed back to her rescue of Merrit Moon. And to the journal she'd read.

"At least I think I know a way through. Or a start. A place called the Hall of Tales?"

"Indeed."

Kali frowned. "The old man finding it is a bit convenient, don't you think?"

"Convenient, or destined?"

"O-ho, no, don't you start that. Don't you dare start that."

The dome rumbled and parts of the energies that surrounded Kali and Zharn started to diffuse. The dome wall reappeared and Kali saw cracks appearing throughout its structure. As Brundle had warned, the cap was beginning to fall apart.

"I think," said Zharn, "that our moment in time is almost over."

"Problem our end," Kali replied. "We're taking a bit of flak at the moment."

"Kali," Zharn said, her image starting to flicker, "Listen to me. You have the means to finish this once and for all, but I cannot tell you how because I do not know. But you have time to ask me one more question that might help you, and I will answer it as best I can."

Kali could think of a hundred, but her brain was so busy that she couldn't pin down one. Finally, she asked something that, despite sticking in her mind, she immediately thought may not have been relevant at all.

"Have you ever heard of someone called Marryme Moo?"

"The name" said Zharn, "is Marryme Moon."

And then the dome exploded.

CHAPTER EIGHTEEN

IT WAS OVER.

Kali found herself standing suddenly in what remained of the
Thunderflux cap, wind whistling through the shattered structure,
less dome now than a ring of jagged projections. The Thunderflux
was gone, diffused, and with it the link to the past that had existed
for uncountable centuries. She was alone, and any more questions
she might have, she'd have to answer herself. Including the most
personal ones of all.

Poor Kali Hooper, the girl who never was. And *the name is
Marryme Moon.*

Kali shivered, exposed in more ways than one. She was therefore
grateful when behind her a crunch of boots on debris signalled the
arrival of Slowhand. She didn't even need to turn to know it was
him, merely sensed his comforting presence, and murmured her
thanks when the archer slipped his shirt over her naked body,
helping when her aching arms struggled with the sleeves.

Now she did turn, looking up at him. Slowhand's shirt draped her like a tent, hanging below her knees, but it still couldn't fully disguise the bruises and burns, the patches of crusted muck and weed, and here and there the spots of blood that were already seeping through the thick cloth.

"Fark, Hooper," Slowhand said. "What happened to you?"

"Long story," Kali replied, numbly. "Old story."

"Want to share it?"

"Not yet."

Kali cocked her head. It had only just occurred to her that, other than the whistling of the wind, the island was silent. No more tremors, no more screams.

"The Hel'ss Spawn is gone," Slowhand said. "Come see."

He took Kali by the hand and led her out of the ruin. They walked slowly up the slope to the clifftop that was Horizon Point. The bodies – what had been left of the bodies – of the Faith and their own people were gone, the landscape normal once more, and the only signs of the struggles that had taken place were the half-melted remains of the Brogmas, standing there slumped and still on the bleak promontory. Maybe one day, Kali thought, someone like herself would come to the island and see these things, wonder at their meaning and the role they had played in its history.

If there *was* a one day.

She took a breath. At least, as Slowhand had said, one small part of the battle was done. Gazing out to sea, she saw that the waters around the island were smooth, that the dra'gohn magic that had burst from her in the cavern far below had indeed delivered the killing blow to the alien entity and the bastard who'd possessed it. In a way, it had been the Hel'ss and Kerberos who'd fought the battle – their essences clashing in a preliminary skirmish – and for now, at least, Kerberos had won.

Kali took no comfort in the fact. Though the sea looked quite beautiful, coloured by the remains of the amberglow engines, as if lit by the rays of a glowing sunset, she knew now what she was really looking at. And all she could see was a series of majestic, spectral forms swooping above a slowly diffusing bloodstain that, when it was gone, would once again make Twilight an emptier place.

"Do you know what they did, Liam?" she said quietly. "Do you know what they did to the dra'gohn?"

The archer stepped up beside her, surprised to see tears on Kali's cheeks. She seemed only half aware of his presence, staring out to sea, haunted somehow, and he noted her fingering her breastbone, as if contemplating something a long way, or a long time, away.

"Do you want to tell me?"

Kali did, and Slowhand pulled her to him as she related the tale, and when it was over he found all he could do was hold her, because there was nothing to say.

"We're all that's left now," Kali said eventually. "The Four."

"So what happens now?"

"We get the dra'gohn magic out of us and where it's meant to be. One way or another, we end the wars of the Pantheon once and for all."

Slowhand moved her to arms' length, lips forming a small smile. "You never do anything *small*, do you?"

Kali laughed. "Well, the first thing we have to do is get off this farking island."

"Being sorted as we speak. The others are below."

"Then what are we waiting for?"

The two of them wound their way down the steps through the ruins, back to the beach where Redigor and his forces had landed. The place was a hive of activity, Sonpear and Pim and his men tinkering under Brundle's supervision on the flutterbys, while Hetty, Pete Two-Ties and Martha DeZantez were helping the rest of their people, who had taken refuge underground, out from the access hatches, assembling them back on the surface. Kali bit her lip, looking in vain for the stretcher carrying Dolorosa, and fearing the worst when it didn't appear. But as it happened, she shouldn't have been looking for a stretcher at all.

"You arra the mess," a voice criticised at the same time a bony finger prodded her in the shoulder. "We cannot take-a you anywhere."

Kali span. "Dolorosa?"

The old woman loomed in her face, eyes narrowed, though there was a hint of humour in them. "Who elsa you theenk speaka thees way?"

"But how?" Kali said. Her gaze was drawn to Dolorosa's wound, now nothing more than a patch of dried blood on her torn clothing with a hint of strange, gold stitching on her skin.

"If there's one thing yer can say for me wife, it's that she knows her 'erbs," Brundle said from where he lay under a flutterby, bashing it with a spanner. He rose, wiping his hands with a rag. "That an' a bit o' the old knitting, eh?"

"Clack-clack," Dolorosa said.

Kali smiled, patted the old woman on the shoulder, and moved towards Brundle.

"I wanted to thank you."

"Me? It's Brogma yer shou –"

"That isn't what I meant," Kali interrupted. And punched the dwarf hard in the face.

Brundle crashed onto his backside, hand over nose. Three streams of blood ran between his fingers.

"Owww! Wod de fark wad dad for?"

"The Trials," Kali said. "You did design them, didn't you?"

"Aye, well," Brundle said, but was spared further defence when Kali offered him a hand up.

"Forget it," she said. "They kept me on my toes, and I've a feeling I'm going to need to be kept on my toes."

The dwarf, like Slowhand and Dolorosa before him, looked her battered and bloody body up and down. "Looks like yer made a bit of a worgle's arse of it, to me."

"Hey! There were complications, all right?"

The dwarf's expression turned to one of surprising concern, knowing full well what the complications must have been. "If ah had a badge yer could have one. Bu ah don't. Good to see yer made it, smoothskin."

"Me, too. So what's happening?"

Brundle pointed at the flutterbys.

"It's taken a bit o' tinkerin', but these beasties should get most o' yer people home."

"That's a long way. I thought they were short range flyers?"

"They are. Which is why I've had to cannibalise some ta handle the journey. It'll take a week or so an' ah can't guarantee they'll make it intact through the Stormwall, but they should come down within' range o' the peninsula's shipping."

Kali nodded. "Good enough. But if you've stripped them down, there won't be enough room for everybody, surely?"

"No," Brundle said, and hesitated. "But with those lost on both sides, fewer'll have ta remain behind than yer think. Ah reckon five or six volunteers."

"My hand's up."

"Ah don't think so, lass. Yer know by now where yer should be."

"And I know where these people should be," Kali said, looking at the freed prisoners. "I'll get there, Brundle, don't you worry. Meantime, like I said – my hand's up."

"Fair enough," the dwarf conceded. "An' ah don't think yer'll havta look far for the rest."

Kali jumped, suddenly aware of the forms of Slowhand, Dolorosa, Sonpear, Pim and Freel beside her. She studied the Allantian, glad to have him back with her, but aware also that his efforts to help since he'd been freed of Redigor had left him exhausted. His experience wasn't something recovered from easily. "Jakub," she said, calling him by his given name for the first time, "please, go with the others. We might need your strength when we get home."

The Allantian faltered, then nodded, tromping wearily towards those who had been assembled to leave. Slowhand slapped his back as he departed.

"So the rest of us swim?" he asked Brundle. "Or do you have another plan?"

"Me scuttlebarge, o' course," Brundle said. He made an obvious point of staring at Kali's behind and then added, "She'll be a little low in the water, but we'll make it."

"Hey!" Kali protested.

"Hey yerself," the dwarf replied. "Now let's get these people on the move."

Brundle moved among the flutterbys, starting up their engines, and the beach was filled with the sound of their insect-like drones. The choice of pilots was left to Kali, and she chose those whose determination she knew would get them home – Martha, Hetty, Abra and Freel himself among them. Civilians were led to the flutterbys in small groups, settled in, and then with a series of complex hand gestures that Kali was sure were more to do with showing off than actually necessary, Brundle walked from machine to machine, signalling each pilot that they were ready for take off.

"Good luck to all of you," Martha DeZantez said.

"You, too," Kali replied.

"See you at home, Kalee!"

"The gods be with you, girly, lady, madam, missus-woman."

One by one, their noses dipping slightly, the flutterbys rose from the beach and headed out to sea. They skimmed the waves at first but then began to rise until they were silhouetted against the coming sunset, which was already starting to paint the waters. A few minutes later they were dots, and then they were gone.

"They'll be fine," Slowhand said, sensing Kali's concern.

"I hope so."

Kali studied the archer. He hadn't turned as he'd spoken, but continued to stare out to sea. No, Kali thought, not out to sea but across it, doubtless seeing the distant shoreline of the peninsula in his mind's eye. A peninsula that had one less thing to offer him when he returned.

"What about you? Will you be fine?"

Slowhand straightened, drawing in a deep breath through his nose.

"I guess I've finally realised what my destiny is."

"Which is?"

"Today, to have been right there on that clifftop, where I could save your life," Slowhand said. "And tomorrow... tomorrow, well, somewhere else where the shit hits the fan."

Kali smiled. "I'll try not to keep you too busy."

The archer turned at last. "So then – it's business as usual."

"Not quite usual," Kali said, regarding Slowhand's altered appearance disapprovingly. If he intended to remain by her side, there'd have to be changes. "Poul, can you do something about this?"

The mage approached, circling Slowhand and inspecting his features with darting, close cocks of the head that made the archer scowl and pull warily away.

"I think so," Sonpear said. "Presuming Mister Slowhand doesn't want me to rebreak *all* of his bones, returning his physiognomy to what it was should require only a minor incantation."

"Then would you please do it?" Kali asked.

"Hey, hey!" Slowhand objected. "I'm here too, remember. Do I get a say in this?"

"Not really," Brundle interjected. "Unless, that is, you actually *want* to spend the rest of your life looking like an orc's knob found its way into yer mammy's panties."

"*Listen, shortarse...*"

"Slowhand, shut up!" Kali said. "I mean, what's the problem here?"

"The problem? The fact that it farking *hurts* is the problem."

"Don't be such a baby."

"You weren't *there*, Hooper. I'm telling you, those few minutes I spent on the Big Top floor felt like an eternity and... ow," Slowhand concluded. "OW. OWW!"

Sonpear smiled, his hands already weaving the threads, and as he did the coarser elements of Slowhand's features began to dwindle, reforming themselves into the more familiar lines he had once possessed. Kali nodded approvingly as she witnessed the return of the lantern jaw, the cute, concave nose, the mouth whose edges splayed laughter lines, though they had clearly been challenged of late. Even his hair returned to its natural colour and length, which the archer wasted no time tossing manfully in the wind.

"What about the scar?" Kali said, frowning at the 'x'. "The scar's still there."

"It is?" Slowhand responded, running his hand over his cheek.

"It shouldn't be," Sonpear said slowly. "But it won't seem to go away."

"Dammit!" Slowhand cursed.

Kali stroked and then playfully slapped Slowhand's cheek. "Never mind, pretty boy. I've had worse scars and it kind of suits you in a an ugly kind of way."

"Oh, it's all right for you," Slowhand protested. "Your scars recover because of that... regeneration thing you have going on..."

"Why," Sonpear mused, "won't it go away?"

"What?" Slowhand said.

Something flared in their midst, and the archer let out a cry far surpassing those when Sonpear had begun his work. Maybe even surpassing those when Fitch had begun his work. It was only after a few seconds that Kali realised the flare had come *from* him.

Slowhand dropped to his knees, groaning in pain, hand clutching his scar. Kali bent to help but faltered. She hesitated because between the cracks of Slowhand's fingers, light was leaking. A light that was starting to grow so bright it was shining through his flesh.

Rays of it began to punch between his fingers.

"What the hells?" Kali said. "Sonpear?"

"Mister Slowhand," he said cautiously. "I want you to remove your hand. And I want you to do it very, very slowly."

Slowhand nodded, but clearly had difficulty. His teeth clenched, the rumble of what would become a roar filtering through them, his hand seemed adhered to his flesh, pulling glue like strands of light with it. Then at last it broke away, revealing what lay beneath.

The 'x' shaped scar was pulsing a brilliant white.

"What... the... fark... is... happening?" Slowhand rumbled.

"Haven't a clue," Kali said honestly.

Dolorosa worked her way through the group about the kneeling archer, saw the scar and drew in a sharp intake of breath. Her eyes narrowed suspiciously.

"This looka familiar," she said. "A horribly familiar..."

"Familiar?"

"Yessa," Dolorosa insisted. "Do you notta see?"

Kali realised she had been paying far too much attention to the glow than to the detail of the scar, and as she studied it saw that around the weal of raised flesh, another tracery of light was slowly appearing. Having started beneath the scar it was working its way up left and right, like a burning fuse on Slowhand's flesh, enclosing the 'x' in a perfect circle. Then, as its two paths joined, it flared as brightly as the rest of the scar.

"Did I notta tell you, Kali Hooper? That's –"

"Oh gods," Kali finished. "The symbol of the Final Faith."

"The what?" Slowhand said. "The *what*?"

Kali stared at the crossed circle, burning now as brightly as a white-hot furnace. Then she felt Sonpear's hand on her shoulder, easing her away.

"There's nothing that can be done," he said. "Stand back. Everybody stand back."

"Stand back?" Slowhand repeated, panicked. "What – *am I going to explode*?"

"Not quite."

"Not quite?" The archer responded, having become quite high-pitched. "What the fark do you mean, *not quite*?"

He doubled over once more, wanting but resisting the need to slap his hand back over the pulsating scar. For the crossed circle of the Faith lifted *away* from his skin, becoming something quite independent of him, floating in the air. Gasping in both shock and relief, Slowhand scrambled back as the glowing emblem began to grow, its diameter widening.

It stopped then burst into flame. The four arms of the 'x' burned away into the surrounding circle. And in the space that was left, the face of Querilous Fitch appeared. He smiled like some visiting deity, but a smile did not sit easily on the psychic manipulator's emaciated features and the last thing anything felt was that their visitor was here to do good.

"Fitch," Slowhand said, "what the hells is going on?"

"Ah, the archer," Fitch said. "I should like to thank you for acting on my behalf. Through you, I have been able to witness the emergence of that I have waited so long to see."

"What the hells are you talking about?"

"Your scar was a spell called a Roving Eye," Sonpear determined. "Not to be confused with an Eye of the Lord, it is a magical thing. An observer – a conduit, if you like – between here and the mainland. Or wherever it is Fitch currently lurks."

"Poul Sonpear," Fitch said. "It has been a long time since last we met."

"You two know each other?" Kali asked.

"Once upon a time, Querilous was a student of mine. I'm sorry to say I taught him many things he should never have known. Including the Roving Eye."

"Teachings long since surpassed, Poul. But I thank you for the human perspective on the power of the threads."

"What do you mean, human perspective?" Kali asked, suspiciously.

Fitch smiled. "Of all the things you should have learned from Slowhand, Redigor and your own recent discoveries about yourself, it is that few things are what they seem," the psychic manipulator said. Then his features began to change, seemingly to melt, his flesh becoming waxier, greyer and moister as it did. This unexpected physiognomy took on a number of new features, including a lipless mouth, enlarged eyes, and a pair of glowing, bulbous nodules that hung from the side of his head, swaying slightly, as if caught in a gentle stream.

Kali's mind whirled. A flashback of a face from long ago, in the floodwaters of Martak. Of a shadowy shape in Gransk harbour. And of a fleetingly sighted rescuer on the other side of a sealed hatch on the Black Ship.

"You," she said. "All the time."

"Me," Querilous Fitch responded. "All the time."

"Er, you want to tell me what's going on?" Slowhand prompted Kali. Like most people on the peninsula, he had never seen such a creature before.

"Fitch is one of them. A fish."

Slowhand paused.

"The slippery bastard."

"Was it you at Scholten, too?" Kali asked Fitch. "My liberator from the Deep Cells?"

"Of course. I could hardly leave you at the mercy of the elf, now, could I?"

"Somehow I never pictured you as my knight in shining armour."

Fitch smiled, though in his new form it was less of a smile and more the slow, crescent shaped gaping of a freshly slashed throat.

"I had no interest in protecting you, girl. Only that which you carry."

"The dra'gohn magic?" Kali gasped.

"Do you realise how long I have waited for you to manifest its power? To even realise you possessed such power?"

"Sorry to keep you waiting. I suppose you want it?"

"Of course."

"Well, guess what – you're not having it."

"We'll see about that, won't we?"

Fitch's face began to move towards Kali, and in doing so the whole of his form physically followed it through the Roving Eye. Slowhand noticed that it was no longer in the strange wheelchair he had seen but walking independently – if walking was the word. The psychic manipulator still retained the semblance of human legs but seemed to glide rather than walk towards them, slime trailing behind him, making his approach all the more threatening. The archer and everyone else backed away. Only Sonpear made any kind of move, his hands weaving what may have been the beginnings of a spell, but none of them would find out which because a second later the mage from the Three Towers was dead. Very, very dead. Fitch simply raised his hand and Sonpear was struck all over his body by what seemed like a hundred invisible sledgehammers, each of them pummelling him so hard his robes billowed beneath the impact, disregarded the flesh beneath, and shrouded the mage in explosive puffs of dust from his own, obliterated bones. Sonpear jerked and spasmed and then the floppy remains of what he had been fell onto the beach on what remained of his face.

Kali refused to be weakened by what had happened. She wouldn't let Fitch see that.

"Why, you bastard? What do you want from the magic?"

"What do you think I want? Its power! With it, all can be made as it should be. A world of water. One vast ocean in which my kind can flourish undisturbed, can thrive."

Kali laughed out loud. "You want to play god? Use the power of the Pantheon to remake Twilight?"

"Why not? Without the interference of the Four, the last of the Pantheon will destroy each other, consume themselves, and in the process you landwalkers will be gone."

"I'm sorry to disappoint you but the Four might have something to say about that. Or at least one of them."

"Which," Fitch said, "is that?"

His hand moved again and, behind him, the still fiery circle of the Final Faith started to unravel until it became an open-ended strand of fire, like a glowing whip. It flexed and snapped in the air and then straightened, less whip than spear, one end pointed directly at Kali. She swallowed, knowing, somehow, that she had only a second left.

"What I don't understand," she said, "is why the Faith? Why involve yourself with them?"

Fitch smiled. "Where better to hide yourself than amongst the blind?"

The spear of fire shot forward, straight into Kali's chest and out through her back, and then twisted in the air to return to Fitch. It penetrated him in the same way it had her but, this time, did not re-emerge. The psychic manipulator – the fish – took a deep, satisfied breath.

"At last," he said.

Kali slumped to the beach as heavily as Sonpear had, landing in an almost foetal position. Unlike Sonpear, she still lived, though it hardly seemed so. What Fitch had done – stripped her of the dra'gohn magic – had hurt more than when Redigor had tried to take her soul in the Chapel of Screams, but there was a worse pain. An emptiness. Everything she had fought for – the true nature of which she had only just discovered – had been taken from her the moment it mattered most. And the worst of it was, it had left her too weak to do anything about it.

Kali's foetal position tightened, her knees rising, her fists clenching, her head dipping into her chest.

"What," Dolorosa shouted, "have you done to my girl?"

The piratess moved towards Fitch but Slowhand grabbed her and held her back.

"Don't," he warned. "He's too dangerous."

"Dangerous, but leaving." Fitch said. "It's been a long, long time since I have been able to delegate my more unsavoury tasks. I miss that."

Slowhand glared at him. "And what exactly are you delegating?"

"Your deaths, of course."

A sneer formed on Slowhand's lips, but faded as Querilous Fitch began to retreat from him. Because the psychic manipulator – the *fishman* – glided once more, this time backwards down the beach, towards and then into the sea.

Staring at them all the time, Querilous Fitch receded beneath the waves, the water lapping about his waist, his chest, his head, until he was gone. And as he disappeared, in his place, other figures waded by him from the depths, at least twenty of them, sloughing dark water and seaweed from their muscular forms as they came. Forms green of skin and scaled, and even without their talons, armed to their very sharp teeth.

"I think," Jengo Pim said, "that we should get the hells out of here."

"I'm open to suggestions," Slowhand responded.

"Back up the steps. We can make a stand on the cliff."

Slowhand nodded and pulled Kali's slumped form to its feet, supporting her as they began the climb. Pim, Brundle and Dolorosa brought up the rear. The old woman hissed at the fishmen as they crossed the beach in pursuit.

The climb seemed to take forever, and night closed in, but there seemed to be more than shadows in the rocks and ancient ruins around them. Hisses and sibilant rattles punctuated the darkness, and shapes flitted here and there, preternaturally fast, leaving a peculiar dampness in the air. Every member of the party cast uneasy glances as they rose higher and higher, but it was down to Brundle, as they at last reached Horizon Point, to voice what they all feared.

"They're everywhere, yer know," the dwarf said. "There must be hundreds of 'em."

It was true. As Slowhand, Pim and the others formed themselves into a defensive huddle on the highest point of the island, those that Querilous Fitch had sent from the sea to be their executioners emerged from all points of the compass, up the steps, from behind rocks, out of the shattered remains of the Thunderflux's cap, and over the lip of the cliff behind them.

All of them swarming onto Trass Kattra in search of their prey.

"It's over," Kali said, lying weak in his arms.

Slowhand started at her words.

"That doesn't sound like the Kali Hooper I know."

"That's because I'm not the Kali Hooper you know. Not any more."

"The dra'gohn magic," the archer said. "We'll get it back. Finish the job."

Kali stared over his shoulder to where the blood red orb that was the Hel'ss hung in the sky. It was almost touching Kerberos, now. She shook her head. "Too late. Just like last time, too late."

"Not if I have anything to do with it," Slowhand said.

"Make that *we*," Brundle rumbled.

"I'd go with that," agreed Jengo Pim.

Dolorosa nodded. "We will make sure these feesh havva their cheeps."

Slowhand lowered Kali's head to the ground. "I have to leave you now. Just for a while."

"What the hells are you doing? This is suicide."

Slowhand grinned. "Hey, I'm your sidekick, aren't I?"

He rose, pulling Suresight from his back and notching an arrow, the tension of it creaking in the night. Beside him, Brundle unslung his battleaxe from its scabbard with a *sching* and hefted it before him. Pim drew a short sword and Dolorosa twin daggers, slashing the air with their blades.

Slowhand stared at the surrounding circle of fishmen, jaw clenching as it began to close in.

"Bring it on," he said.

THE END

Mike Wild is much older than he has a right to be, considering the kebabs, the booze and the fags. Maybe it's because he still thinks he's 15. Apart from dabbling occasionally in publishing and editing, he's been a freelance writer for ever, clawing his way up to his current dizzy heights by way of work as diverse as *Doctor Who*, *Masters of the Universe*, *Starblazer*, *'Allo 'Allo!* and – erm – *My Little Pony*. Counting one *Teen Romance*, one *ABC Warriors* and two *Caballistics Inc*, *Engines of the Apocalypse* is his seventh novel. However, only his beloved wife and tuna-scoffing cat give him the recognition he deserves.

TWILIGHT of KERBEROS

Now read the first chapter of the penultimate novel in the series

The WRATH of KERBEROS

JONATHAN OLIVER

ISBN: 978-1-907992-35-3
US ISBN: 978-1-907992-36-0

COMING: JANUARY 2012

£7.99/$9.99

WWW.ABADDONBOOKS.COM

CHAPTER ONE

WHEN THE FIRST boot crashed against the door, Stanwick Tassiter dropped the candle. The flame caught the folios he had been reading and the scholar was caught between the horror of whoever was battering down his door and the sight of his precious scriptures burning. A blade appeared through a rent in the wood of the door as he battered at the pages. The fire extinguished, he looked up and was dismayed to the see the design on the weapon. He now knew exactly who had come for him and he wasn't all that surprised. The texts he had been pouring over were high on the Final Faith's list of prohibited works. Stanwick had thought himself well guarded. Was it possible that Tremayne and Finch had given him away? They had always been amongst the most weak-willed of his acolytes.

Whatever, Stanwick had known the risks when he had taken up his studies, and so he had made sure to create copies of his most important tomes. These the Faith would never find.

The door finally gave way and four heavily-armoured members

of the Order of the Swords of Dawn burst into the subterranean archive. One of them sped across the room and pushed a sword to his throat, while another forced his arms so far up his back that he let out a high-pitched squeal.

The commander – Stanwick could tell her rank from the intricate designs on her breastplate – riffled through the charred pages on the desk and grunted with satisfaction.

"These will make a fine addition to the archive of forbidden literature at Scholten cathedral. Thank you for your help in taking such dangerous works out of circulation, Stanwick."

Stanwick sat stoically, not responding to the woman's sarcastic tone. He knew what awaited him now. He would spend a short amount of time in the depths of Scholten, at Katherine Makennon's pleasure, before being sent to the gibbet. There would be no trial. Makennon probably wouldn't even be aware of his passing.

"You know, it would save us all a lot of time if you just spilled my blood right here. You could say I resisted arrest. It would be so much easier, in the long run."

"I don't think so," the commander said. "Brother Sequilious was quite adamant that he wanted you all taken alive."

A hood was thrown over Stanwick's head and he was hustled from the room. He fell twice on the steps up to the surface – once so badly that he sprained his ankle – and by the time he was bundled through a narrow door and onto a bench, his leg was singing with pain. He bit back tears, not wanting the Swords to witness his grief, but he couldn't help a sob escaping his lips.

"Stanwick? Stanwick Tassiter?" a voice said, close by. A hand fumbled into his. "Yes, it's Stanwick all right. I'd recognize those soft academic's hands anywhere."

It was Alex, the blind weaver who lived not far from Stanwick.

"Alex, what are you doing here?"

He knew full well that the weaver regularly paid his dues at the local church. He couldn't begin to imagine how the old man had come to the attention of the Swords.

"It sounds like the whole of Westbay is being rounded up." Alex said.

The room lurched and there was the sound of wheels rumbling over cobbles. Stanwick realised then that he was surrounded by people whimpering and praying. He recognized many of the voices amongst the multitude, all people he knew would never consider going against the Faith. Why had Makennon ordered this mass abduction?

The carriage travelled for about ten minutes before coming to a halt. Stanwick could now hear the sound of waves pounding against rocks and, just below that, voices raised in song.

The doors of the carriage were opened and Stanwick was herded out, along with the rest of the villagers. Alex still held his hand, until it was batted away by the flat of a blade. Chains were looped around Stanwick's wrists and he could feel the same being secured at his ankles.

To shouted commands and a sharp tug on the chains, a slow shuffle began up a steep and uneven path. A strong, icy wind blasted against Stanwick's left-hand side, and he sensed a sheer drop just a short distance from the path. A gust tore the hood from his head and he could see, stretching away before him, a line of hooded figures; all chained together and all heading towards the mouth of a cave. Below them the sea thundered against the sides of the sheer cliffs. All along the line, men and women, wearing the ceremonial tabards of the Order of the Swords of Dawn, ushered their captives on. Stanwick was appalled to see the priest from Westbay's own small church amongst them. Despite his misguided beliefs, he had never struck Stanwick as a particularly cruel or duplicitous man. As he passed, the priest refused to meet his eyes.

"Henry, please tell me what's going on." Stanwick pleaded.

"I'm sorry, Stanwick. Really I am."

Stanwick, however, was soon out of sight of the priest and the shadow of the cave mouth fell over him.

The singing was louder now and Stanwick was taken aback when he realised that the words were elvish. Why were the Final Faith using a song of that ancient race? More importantly, what were they using it for? As soon as he entered the cavern, however, Stanwick could tell that this was no ordinary song. He could taste the magic in the air – burnt cinnamon and wet stone – and when he saw the choir, he gasped.

Twenty-five pale young boys sang with the voices of angels. From the pitch of their song, he could tell that they had been emasculated. Their flesh was heavily scarified and tattooed. The designs on their bodies seemed to dance to the ethereal cadences, and Stanwick felt a deep nausea as the illustrations held his gaze.

A knife jabbed into his side soon snapped him out of his reverie.

"Move along. You're holding up the line."

Stanwick looked at the blood beading his trews. He left a trail of red dots as he followed the rest of the captives.

The choir stood on a natural balcony cut into the chamber wall and a slope lead down past it into the main body of the cave itself. The roof of the cavern was far above their heads and at the far side was a brilliant blue lake, its water slowly undulating to the distant sound of waves. Stanwick looked around him as the hoods were pulled off the prisoners. The frightened faces that greeted his tugged at his heart, and the stench of fear – even in this vast space – was stiflingly close. It wasn't just the men and women of Westbay the Faith had taken, there were children here too. A makeshift corral had even been constructed, to house the village's modest collection of livestock.

Behind them all the choir's song rose in volume as the torches surrounding the lake were lit.

A man stood in front of the line of torches. He was tall and thin, emaciated even. His skin was smooth and pale, his head hairless, and as he disrobed Stanwick saw that the rest of his body was much the same. He passed his garments to a young man, who knelt briefly to receive a blessing before hurrying away with his bundle.

A priest – Stanwick saw that it was Henry – came forward and placed an unsteady hand on the thin man's head as he knelt for his own benediction. Stanwick saw by Henry's gestures that he was also performing the ceremony of absolution. He wondered what sin this member of the Final Faith had committed that he sought forgiveness. Maybe, he considered with a start, he was seeking forgiveness for a sin that he was about to commit.

The ritual over, the priest withdrew and, at a gesture from the gaunt, naked man, the choir fell silent. The only sounds now were the whimpering of the prisoners and the lapping of the lake against the shore. A cadre of priests moved through the crowd, flicking a pungent oil from silver sprinklers.

Stanwick's stomach clenched as he recognised the smell.

It took him back to his mother's deathbed – more than twenty years earlier – and the look of terror in her eyes as a priest had anointed her with the oil to ease her soul's passage to Kerberos. Stanwick's mother had never been a believer, but his father was, and it had been he who'd insisted she take the last rites. The ceremony had done little to relieve her terror though, as her had life slipped away and she stared into oblivion.

Stanwick knew something of his mother's fear now and he pulled at the chains that bound him, but there was no give in the links.

They were all going to die.

BROTHER SEQUILIOUS STOOD, staring at the chained villagers gathered before him as he prepared the spell.

"What have we ever done to you?" someone in the crowd shouted. "What has the Faith got against Westbay?"

The fact was that the Final Faith had nothing against Westbay, but this coastal settlement was small enough that the disappearance of its populous could easily be covered up. Bandits would be blamed, or maybe the Chadassa.

Brother Sequilious closed his eyes. Behind him a last small wave lapped at the shore of the lake, before the water became unnaturally still. Sweat began to bead his forehead as he envisioned the wheel of dark energy that he turned with his gestures. The temperature in the cavern dropped and flames erupted from his open palms and raced across his body, though he was not burned. Instead, the fire seemed to tease his flesh. With a stifled groan he came; where his semen jetted onto the stone of the cavern floor it hissed and spat.

The cries coming from the prisoners were louder now, but nothing could break the concentration Brother Sequilious wielded. The words that he spoke had been memorised from a fragment of Chadassa manuscript – the recovery of which had made this sorcery possible. He had never before used the magic of the sub-aquatic race and, as the last of the glottal syllables died away, he braced himself for a backlash of arcane energy. Instead, he felt a thrumming of power deep within and his hands blazed with an intense, pure light. If he held onto this power for too long Brother Sequilious knew that it would consume him, and so he unleashed the tide of living fire over the huddled villagers.

They burned so fiercely that they were reduced to little more than bundles of blackened sticks within seconds; yet still they stood, held aloft by the terrible magic that filled the chamber. The intensity of the passing of so many souls strengthened the spell, and Brother Sequilious began to weave the strands of the final enchantment together.

Turning his back on the devastation, the sorcerer stared into the calm waters of the lake, channelling the energy that surrounded him into its depths. At the same time he envisioned the *Llothriall* – the vastly treasured ship that Katherine Makennon had tasked him to retrieve.

A cool wind blew against his face and he could hear the crash and hiss of rolling surf. At first, just the merest sketch of a ship was visible above the lake, picked out in pale silver lines. If Brother Sequilious squinted, he could just make out the prow, rearing above him as though it were cresting the swell of a wave. But then it was gone and, as the wind dropped, the sorcerer desperately clutched for the contact he had briefly made.

There it was again.

The sound of the sea was suddenly, shockingly loud and Brother Sequilious stepped back as mountainous waves rose up all around him. He mustn't loose his focus though, else the *Llothriall* would be permanently lost.

He stood in two locations at once – one below the ground, one above the waves, far from here – and, as the last of the villagers burned out behind him, he tried to bring these worlds together.

With a terrific bang the sorcerer was flung onto his back as a wall of ice-cold water crashed over him. There was the burn of salt at the back of his throat and he floundered on the cavern floor for a moment, before he realised that he was not drowning.

As he got to his feet an octopus dropped to the ground, its tentacles uncoiling from his thigh. All around him fish littered the floor, mouths gaping as they drowned. There was a strange smell in the air. A smell that made the sorcerer's balls shrivel in fear; the smell of magic gone wrong.

Brother Sequilious turned to the lake, to see just how wrong.

He had retrieved the *Llothriall*, though only half of it. The broken section of vessel sat a while on the water, before beginning to keel over. He got a brief glimpse into the interior of the ruined ship as the lake flooded in. Cabins had been sheared in half, spilling shattered furniture and broken cargo. Brother Sequilious thought that he saw a body hit the water as the ship sank.

Soon, only a curve of the bow was visible. In despair, he began to wade into the lake, desperate to salvage anything from his disastrous summoning attempt. But as the cold water rose above his thighs, he knew that it was useless. Brother Sequilious had lost Katherine Makennon her greatest prize.

For information on this and other titles, visit www.
abaddonbooks.com